Killing the Dead

Paul Ferguson

2QT Limited (Publishing)

This First Edition published 2011 by
2QT Limited (Publishing)
Dalton Lane, Burton In Kendal
Cumbria LA6 1NJ

Cover Design by Hilary Pitt
Cover Images supplied by iStockPhoto.com

Printed and bound in the UK

The author has his own website: www.pferguson.co.uk

A CIP catalogue record for this book is available
from the British Library
ISBN 978-1-908098-24-5

To Bernie, Casey and Jordan for your love,
patience and endless support
and to Larry and the guys in BTE
for your help.

DAY ONE

CHAPTER ONE

It was a couple of minutes past five in the morning when Joe Tubbs leaned forward on his couch with a video remote control in his hand and pushed the fast forward button forcing the images on his TV monitor to flicker violently. A short time later his thumb crashed down on the play key at the precise moment his face appeared on the screen. He'd done this before. A huge smile appeared on his face as he watched himself swagger across the room to a plump blonde dressed in tennis whites.

"Do you come here often?" asked Joe.

"I come wherever I can," whispered the woman in a husky drawl.

Critics wrote that this was TV soap at its worst, bad script and bad acting, but Joe loved it. He mouthed every line that came out of the speakers and moved sympathetically with his on screen character. It was Joe's last appearance in front of the camera. The soap was a "turkey" and had been taken off the air after a few nights. Joe's performance was so wooden that he became a laughing stock in an industry that doesn't forget. Joe didn't see it that way, he was convinced that he looked and sounded great and took what some saw as a misguided belief to the front door of every studio and agent in L.A. Rejection followed rejection. Castings dried up and the phone no longer rang, but Joe refused to give in. He wanted the show business life and he wanted it bad. Perhaps if he had gone quietly he would have been given a second chance somewhere down the line. But Joe didn't do quiet. With every door that slammed in his face he became more aggressive and threatening. He yelled at studio receptionists through closed doors and left obscene messages on answer phones and it wasn't long before he was blacklisted by most of the studios in Hollywood. When it came down to it, he couldn't get a part as a stiff in a morgue.

Joe switched off the television and gulped down what was left of his beer. He thought for a moment about hitting a line of coke that snaked across the table, but instead he headed off to the fridge to get another cold one. His house was a mess. The kitchen work surface was littered with empty beer bottles, takeaway pizza boxes and KFC buckets while cigarette butts floated aimlessly among the dirty dishes piled high in the sink. In the center of the room, a single white plastic three-legged chair lay crippled on top of a Los Angeles Department of Parks and Recreation picnic table. The chair was there when he moved in and he had no plans to redecorate.

With a fresh Bud in his hand, Joe zigzagged carefully past sticky beer stained patches of linoleum and then stopped to gaze down at a piece of paper that he had rolled into a ball and tossed on the floor. In a mocking voice, he whined:

"You've missed your last four appointments, you're not taking my calls, are you taking your pills? Please call me... fuck you Dr Frankenstein, no more mind games."

Joe kicked the paper ball across the room then threw himself down on the couch and laughed as a small cloud of dust exploded around him. Overlooked by a precariously hung poster of Jimi Hendrix, Joe scooped a pile of papers up off the floor, put his feet on the coffee table and began to read aloud.

"*A Ride on the Main Line*; a film script by Joe Tubbs."

From the outset, he knew that was a lie, for the script was actually written by his mother Alice, a singer in a folk rock group, who died of a drug overdose when he was just fifteen. When she joined company with the likes of Hendrix, Joplin and Morrison she left Joe a couple of bucks, a six string guitar, the poster on the wall and some beer stained pages of drug induced ramblings of life on the road.

"Drugs take you down a road to nowhere," she once told Joe, "but at least it's a scenic route."

He didn't know his father and he suspected his mother hadn't known him either. The son of the ultimate rock chic knew life was never going to be easy.

A detour into the more cerebral side of the entertainment business didn't mean that he'd given up on acting; he was just determined to crack the film industry one way or another. Secretly he thought that plagiarizing his mother's script would be a back door to stardom. That was a big mistake and somewhere beneath the layers of bravado, he was aware that Hollywood was an unforgiving town and few people get a second chance. His time as an actor taught him that. Although Joe refused to change a single word, he corrected the spelling mistakes and added his name as the author. Initially he struggled. It wasn't an easy decision for him to say he wrote the script, but he justified it by telling himself it was a tribute to his mother.

"I'm doing this for mom," he would say, *"that's what she would have wanted."*

It was stupid to put his name to something he hadn't written and deep down inside he knew it. Feeling like he was on the rebound from a broken marriage and desperate to get back in the game, he grabbed the first thing that came along and the first thing to come along was an incoherent dreary mess that should never have been shown to the big hitters in Hollywood. If Joe was to get anything out of this, however, it was a desire to write. From the moment he found his mother's papers hidden away in an old guitar case, he began forming ideas of his own. The more he worked at it the easier it became. Being creative agreed with him; it gave him a buzz and for the first time in a long time he felt good about himself.

CHAPTER TWO

Eight hours later and a couple of miles down the road the entire Hollywood police force gathered at Pinecrest Cemetery to say goodbye to one of their own. Mike Turner, a bachelor in his early thirties, had been a detective with the force for less than a month when he was shot dead following the routine stop and search of a man driving a car with a broken tail light.

Mike's partner, Dan Scott, a seasoned police veteran, was asked to say a few words at the graveside at the very last moment when it was discovered that no one else in the force knew anything about Mike. Dan hated public speaking and found the whole thing very awkward. Not only was he a man of few words, but he also knew very little about Mike. They'd only worked together for a few weeks and had little in common. Mike liked rap, working out and eating salads whereas Dan was into the Beatles, spent most of his time in bars and ate fast food a couple of times a day.

Dan stood next to the grave holding a small piece of paper given to him by his Captain, Jerry Esposito. He hadn't read what Esposito had written until he started to speak.

"Mike was a brave cop... he was dedicated and had a wonderful future. He was too young to die. We'll miss him."

Dan paused nervously and then flipped the paper over, hoping there would be more, but that was it; the page was blank. He felt embarrassed and regretted ever agreeing to do this. Gritting his teeth and glaring into the Captain's eyes, he eventually bowed his head and stepped away from the graveside while at the same time Father Daley moved forward to say a final few words. But before he could speak a slim attractive brunette in her thirties walked through the crowd and said loudly, "Mike was my brother." There were looks of surprise all around.

She continued, "He was extremely caring and generous and had a heart the size of the moon. He loved his family and we loved him more than anything. His only ambition throughout his short life was to be the best cop he could be. He was brave, that's true, but he was also impetuous and a little crazy. Perhaps if he had been a little less crazy, we wouldn't be standing over him now. I'll miss him and I'm sure if you knew him like I did, you'd miss him too."

A final short prayer from Father Daley completed the ceremony and the coffin was lowered slowly into the ground. As the crowd dispersed, Dan approached Mike's sister.

"I'm Dan Scott, Mike's partner."

"Hi, I'm Leigh," she replied shaking his hand.

"Sorry for your loss," said Dan.

"God I hate that expression," she said, "it sounds like I just lost a puppy."

She must have realized just how bad that sounded and she quickly tried to make amends.

"I'm sorry, that was stupid of me. You see I'm just like my brother."

Acknowledging her apology with a discreet nod, Dan turned with Leigh and walked towards the parking lot, passing Esposito and a local TV crew on the way.

Neither spoke until they got to Dan's car and then Leigh broke the silence.

"No offense, but why didn't the guy with all the medals give Mike's eulogy... he seems to be the one in charge?"

"No cameras at the graveside."

"What?"

"Some time ago the Department placed a ban on the press getting up close and personal whenever a police officer is buried because they have a way of turning a funeral into a circus. And since Esposito won't waste his breath unless the media is present... I got the job... Can I give you a lift to the police station? A few of the guys are having a drink to say goodbye to Mike... you can pick up his things while you're there."

"Sure," said Leigh obviously trying to come to terms with Esposito's shallowness.

As Dan drove out of the cemetery and headed west on the Parkway, Leigh looked around the car and ran her fingers over the seat.

"Is this where Mike was sitting?"

"No, he was driving."

"What happened?"

The detective opened his mouth to speak, but was interrupted long before any sound came out.

"I mean what actually happened?"

Dan looked puzzled. What was she implying?

"We stopped a car with a broken tail light, checked the plates... drew a blank. Mike approached the driver who was alone. He asked him to turn the engine off and get out of the car. The guy turned off the engine, but when he opened the door he started shooting."

"Then what happened?"

"He tried to start his car, but couldn't. It must have been flooded. As I approached from the other side, he fired a round at me and missed and I shot him."

"Why did you stop a car with a broken tail light, you're not a traffic cop?"

"Well," replied Dan who was reluctant to answer.

"Well... " said Leigh waiting anxiously.

"Mike insisted we stop the guy. He was in a bad mood about something and wanted to let off some steam. I know I should have pulled rank and said no, but it seemed harmless at the time."

"Why didn't the guy just roll down the window and shoot. Why did he open the door first?"

Dan was impressed yet a little annoyed with the line of questioning.

"Are you a cop?" he asked

"No, I'm an investigative reporter."

Shaking his head and rolling his eyes, he mumbled, "Great, a fucking journalist." He wasn't a fan. Sensationalizing stories and spreading fear in the community to sell newspapers didn't sit well with him. Experience had taught him two things; if they couldn't get a quote they made one up and they never let the truth get in the way of a good story.

"What did you say?"

Ignoring her question, he preferred to explain why the guy opened the door to shoot Mike, "It turns out he borrowed his brother's car without him knowing. The window didn't work and I can only assume that he didn't want to shoot through the glass because his brother would have spotted the bullet hole when he returned the car."

"Considerate," said Leigh, "who was he? Was he wanted?"

"He was nobody... until now."

For a long long time nothing was said, then Leigh mumbled quietly, "This stinks, something's not right."

CHAPTER THREE

Joe jumped into his rusty red '65 Chevy pickup truck and drove four miles to a small newspaper store next to the mall. Along the way, he jammed in a Jimi Hendrix cassette, cranked up the volume to max and joined in when the sixties legend began singing, "Hey Joe, where you goin' with that gun in your hand?"

There was something about the lyrics in this song that made him feel important. It was as if Jimi was talking directly to him. And the thought of going into town with a gun was cool.

Waiting for the Xerox to churn out ten copies of his script soon got the better of Joe and his low boredom threshold kicked in. He felt like a pin ball bouncing from one side of the store to the other as he struggled to pass the time. Stepping outside, he pulled a ready made joint from his back pocket and blew smoke rings into the air. Suddenly, he was no longer wired. Smoke a joint, pop a pill, snort a line was his answer for everything, and most of the time it worked.

As he leaned against the tailgate of his truck, a man with long hair and a scruffy beard walked passed on the sidewalk. He'd seen the guy before, but never this close up. He was filthy. Resting on his shoulder was a sign that read, *I got Jesus, what have you got*? Joe looked down at his joint and just smiled.

A few minutes later he was back inside the store calmly watching the photocopier as it spat out hundreds of A4 sized pages. When the machine finally stopped, a young girl working behind the counter picked up the last remaining script, bound it together and read the title page,

"*A Ride on the Main Line*, a film script by Joe Tubbs."

Joe's face lit up. It sounded so right.

"Is this you?" asked the girl as she held up the script.

"Yeah, that's me," he said hesitantly.

"Wow."

She was only a spotty faced teenager, who hadn't read the script, yet he didn't care. Hearing that three-letter word gave him an incredible lift. He wanted to stick around, talk more about himself and be adored, but a new customer in the store quickly took his place. As the young girl's attention shifted, Joe gritted his teeth and reluctantly stepped aside.

Out on the sidewalk, he placed six of the scripts in large stamped envelopes addressed to Hollywood's top agents and film companies, gave them a kiss for luck and dropped them into a mail box. Four were kept in the truck to hand out at work. After months of sitting around waiting for the phone to ring, he was finally getting his shit together. It felt good, but it wasn't always like that.

Living with a rock 'n' roll mom wasn't ideal, but being placed in a foster home the day she died was even worse. They tried to recycle him and it didn't work. After a lifetime of being on the road and sleeping in vans and shit hotels, it wasn't easy adjusting to a normal existence with daily doses of high school and regular Sunday morning church sermons. Feeling frightened and alone, he ran away and had been on his own ever since, bouncing from one mindless job to another. He wasn't stupid or lazy; he just couldn't find a job he liked. The only thing he ever wanted was show business, but until now it had eluded him. Watching his mother perform on stage night after night really ticked all the boxes, even if she was playing toilets.

Joe wasn't proud or work shy. He would do anything to earn a buck to pay the rent and keep himself in beer and drugs between his small and infrequent acting roles. In the past his employment was a means to an end; however, his latest job, working as a valet car-parking attendant at Tata's Restaurant, was more calculated. Although he felt that parking cars was something a monkey could do, his job choice was a shrewd one. Tata's was where the moneymen and the decision makers in the film business hung out and where big deals were brokered and dreams of stardom could be made or shattered. Where else could he rub shoulders with Hollywood's elite? He certainly wouldn't get an appointment to meet with these guys and experience taught him that they didn't return phone calls. He thought it would be perfect.

Under strict instructions from management to hide his truck from Tata's paying customers, Joe tucked his vehicle next to a tree immediately behind the building. With a rolled up script sticking out of his back pocket he sauntered towards the front door and the valet parking station.

"You're five minutes late, Tubbs, get your ass out here or I'll keep all the tips," joked Gomez, a twenty nine year old Mexican.

"Gomez, you wet back," replied Joe. "Where's my cell, I'm gonna call immigration?"

Laughing like a couple of kids, they greeted each other with a high five followed by a routine dapping of fists. This ritual of insults and tribal handshakes started almost as soon as they began working together just six weeks ago and was unique to them. Anyone else who called Gomez a 'wet back' would be severely punished. Coming from similar backgrounds they understood where the other was going. They weren't friends and they didn't socialize; they were a team of two and covered each others asses when they were late or doing something they shouldn't be doing in someone's car.

"What you handing out today?" asked Gomez with laughter in his voice.

Joe smiled and looked around before he spoke.

"Got a script for them today... this could be it... my big break."

Gomez didn't appear surprised. He'd seen it all before. Pictures, show reels, résumés, Joe had them all and wasn't afraid to press them into the hands of those who might be able to help his struggling career. He lacked subtlety and couldn't care less that Tata's was a restaurant and not a place to promote Joe Tubbs. He just didn't give a damn and jumped on every opportunity, believing, "if you don't ask, you don't get".

———————————————————

It was lunch-time and people were starting to arrive at the restaurant. Gomez had just taken the keys from the owner of a new silver Mercedes S Class when Joe spotted the car.

"Mr Levy, Mr Levy," he yelled.

Levy, the owner of a successful indie film company turned and looked at Joe, who shoved his rolled up script into Levy's hand.

"Can you have a look at this and get back to me? I think you'll like it. It's got your name written all over it," said Joe arrogantly.

Levy didn't appear impressed; he snatched the script from Joe without saying a word and entered the restaurant.

"Man, you gotta slow down," said a bewildered Gomez. "Be cool! These dudes are big time, they don't like to be told what to do."

Joe just shrugged his shoulders and thought, *fuck it,* then went to his truck and grabbed another script.

CHAPTER FOUR

Making small talk with a room full of strangers just a few minutes after burying her brother wasn't easy, but Leigh went through the motions and exchanged pleasantries with detectives Moose Andolina and John Heinz before wandering around the office on her own. She saw Dan had been watching her, he knew what she wanted.

"It's over there," he said, pointing to a desk in the corner.

"Where are his things?"

A pregnant woman carrying a small empty cardboard box interrupted, "They're in his desk. I thought you'd want to sort things out yourself. I'm afraid he didn't have much... Hi, I'm Alexis – secretary, coffee maker, agony aunt and surrogate mother to a room full of grown up, yet often immature, detectives."

"When are you due?" queried Leigh.

"Any day," replied Alexis.

"What are you still doing here?"

"Good question. There's no one to take my place. We've been let down by employment agencies and just can't seem to find anyone to cover for me while I'm away."

At that moment, Captain Esposito entered the room, walked over to Leigh and introduced himself. He asked her if she would stay around for a couple of days to help sort out Mike's affairs.

"Sorry for your loss," he added.

Dan grimaced and looked away in anticipation of a smart-ass response from Leigh, but she said nothing.

"I also want to apologize for not contacting you after the shooting, but your brother's next of kin details weren't in his file when it arrived."

Leigh acknowledged the mix up, but Dan was curious.

"How did you know Mike was dead if we didn't contact you?"

Leigh took a step towards Dan and whispered in his ear, "I'm one of those 'fucking journalists'… investigating is what I do."

Rummaging through Mike's desk was painful. But a picture of her brother spraying her with a garden hose in front of their house brought a fragile smile to her face. She remembered that moment like it was yesterday. Those were happy times. He had just passed the police exams and didn't have a care in the world. In amongst a pile of receipts, wallet, cell phone, keys and badge lay a picture of her mother and father celebrating their 30th anniversary. This time there was no delicate smile; instead she lowered her head and fought hard to hold back the tears. Suddenly her sadness turned to embarrassment.

"What's this doing here?" she mumbled, as she picked up a framed picture and quickly placed it face down in the bottom of the drawer.

As people drifted slowly back to work, Leigh sat on the edge of Mike's desk and watched life return to normal. The sounds of tapping keyboards, ringing phones and even laughter gradually broke the temporary silence, becoming louder and louder as time passed. *That's it,* she thought, *life goes on.* It was harsh, but true. Life does go on and there are no exceptions, especially for those working in Homicide. There were leads to follow and criminals to catch. No matter who dies, the wheels keep turning.

Dan was reminded of this when he returned to his desk and found a massive pile of files teetering over the side.

Although he agreed to take Leigh to Mike's apartment, he quickly realized he had business of his own to look after.

Moving like a man with a handful of thumbs, the detective showed why he shouldn't be left alone with more than one piece of paper at a time. Within seconds, important documents tumbled from case files and scattered indiscriminately across the floor and under his chair. More at home on the street than behind a desk, Dan was an old fashioned cop who didn't like filling in forms. As far as he was concerned, paper work was something that rookies do and that's the way he always played it. All of a sudden though, his rookie was dead and papers were stacking up. Looking on from the sidelines in amusement, Leigh offered a helping hand.

"Let me do that; you make coffee," she said with her tongue firmly in her cheek.

A hush fell over the room. No one had ever told Dan to 'make coffee'. He may have been a gentleman, but he'd seen it and done it and didn't like being told what to do. The next few seconds were tense as everyone waited to see how he would respond. With both palms facing up, he weighed the situation. Pretending that his right hand held coffee and his left, paper work, he balanced the two until coffee came out a clear winner.

"No contest," he said with a huge smile as he headed across the room.

Soon Leigh had organized Dan's desk and put his files in chronological order with the most recent cases on top. She'd even stuck in a couple of notes reminding him to make calls. When Dan returned with her coffee, she said politely, "no thanks I had one earlier."

CHAPTER FIVE

"Do you think that guy, al–Megrahi, was really responsible for the Lockerbie bombing back in '88?" asked Leigh as she and Dan drove through town.

"What?"

"You know – the Libyan guy they put in jail in Scotland; do you think he did it?"

Dan looked totally confused by this random conversation, but stayed with it to be polite, "I guess so; he was convicted wasn't he?"

"I think it was the Iranians. They wanted revenge because the US shot down one of their passenger planes earlier that year."

Dan didn't have a clue where this conversation was going and didn't really care. He was just happy to have arrived at the apartment and to be getting out of the car.

Mike's place was located on the top floor of a two-story building that stood alone on a small plot of land.

"I didn't picture it like this," said Leigh. "Mike told me he stumbled across the place by accident when he got lost looking for somewhere to stay nearby. He went in to Kim's Hardware for directions and came out an hour later the proud owner of this place."

As Leigh looked up at the outside wooden stairs leading to the front door, Dan was aware that she might want to be alone.

"Should I wait in the car?"

"No, come on, I'll be OK."

Leigh started to climb the stairs and then stopped. Looking at Mike's key ring she went back down to the parking lot, placed a key in the lock of a thirty-year-old white Volkswagen Beetle and opened the door.

"Looks like Mike found a car that was almost as old as he was."

Their first glimpse of the apartment took their breath away. Speechless and with eyes bulging, they scanned the huge open plan room in front of them. To the real estate agent, this was a place with "potential" and ideal for the DIY enthusiast, but to them it was a bomb site. Floorboards and walls were missing leaving beams exposed and gaping holes everywhere. Electric wires dangled dangerously from openings in the ceiling and water pipes ended in mid flow.

"How could he live like this?" asked Dan.

"My brother loved a challenge, but this is ridiculous."

Leigh knew instantly she was going nowhere. Her plan to drop into L.A., bury Mike, sell his apartment and fly back to her uncomplicated small town life wasn't going to happen. Mike's affairs were not as straightforward as she had originally thought. There would be an inquiry into his death, compensation issues because he had been killed on duty and of course there was the small matter of the apartment. What would she do with the apartment? She could leave it for someone else to deal with, but she wasn't like that. She wanted to be involved, that's the least she could do for him.

As she stepped warily across the room like a soldier crossing a minefield, she found her way into the bedroom.

"Well at least he had somewhere to sleep," she said, staring at an unmade bed.

"And there's water in the bathroom," yelled Dan from across the hall, "but there's no electricity," he added as he flipped the light switch. A moment later the lights flickered on and off and on and off.

"Just what I need," said Leigh sarcastically.

While Leigh continued to dodge the debris, Dan made his way out of the room and down the steps. A few minutes later he came back carrying a plastic bag.

"Mr Kim offers his condolences and said you could have these with his compliments," he said, emptying a flashlight, a box of candles and some matches on to the kitchen table.

"You didn't happen to show him your badge or mention anything about building inspectors, did you?"

"You're so suspicious," laughed Dan sensing she was defrosting slowly.

Maybe it was because she'd just buried her brother or perhaps she wasn't good at socializing that made him think she was a pain in the ass, but Leigh was starting to relax and he liked what he saw. Aside from the obvious good looks and great body, she seemed intelligent and had a sense of humor. But as far as he was concerned, the jury was still out on that crap about the Lockerbie bomber.

————————————————

It was time to get back to work. When Leigh insisted on staying in the apartment instead of going to a hotel, Dan gave her his card and wrote his cell number on the back.

"Call me anytime," he said.

"Anytime?"

"Yeah," said Dan.

"I don't want anyone to think I'm a pain in the ass."

"OK, never call me during the last five minutes of a Lakers game."

"That's not what I meant," said Leigh.

It took a moment, but then Dan realized what she was getting at, "There is no anyone," he muttered, "just me. No wife, no girlfriend, no dog and no cat. I don't even have room in my life for a goldfish. Just me – me – me and as I've been told before... there lies the problem."

CHAPTER SIX

Joe was coming to the end of his shift at Tata's. He'd handed out three scripts in eight hours and was feeling good. One script went to Ben Levy an independent filmmaker, another to an actor whose name he couldn't remember and the third to the snooty PA of the CEO at Stardust Films.

There was just one car left on the lot and Gomez offered to stick around until the owner came out, so Joe made his way to the rear of the restaurant and stopped to talk to a couple of the waiters who were having a smoke at the back door. He looked inside the kitchen and watched as two Mexican cleaners worked their magic on a greasy oven.

Shit job, he thought to himself. *They come all this way and risk jail for what – a few meagre bucks and the prospect of sleeping ten to a room.* Just then a third waiter appeared at the door.

"Hey, you're Joe Tubbs, aren't you?" he asked.

Joe nodded.

"Then these must be yours," he said as he handed Joe a couple of his scripts. "I think there's a third one in the garbage," he added with a smirk on his face.

Joe was angry and couldn't hide it. He kicked over a garbage can and swore at the waiter.

"What the fuck are you swearing at me for?" screamed the waiter.

"You think you're so smart," snarled Joe, "but one day you'll be waiting on my table, kissing my ass!"

Humiliated beyond belief, Joe climbed into his truck, slammed his fist on the steering wheel, spun his tires on the gravel and sped quickly away. He was still fuming when he pulled up outside PJ's bar a couple of miles down the road. This was his home away from home and the place he headed for when the walls started closing in around him. He knew everyone here and felt safe. It was a strange thing to say, but he'd been coming here since he was a baby. His mother had brought him here when she was singing on the small stage in the corner and he was right beside her fifteen years later when her life ended upstairs on a soiled mattress. Joe knew the place like the back of his hand. In three decades, it hadn't changed a bit. Like most bars the walls of dark slatted wood were spotted with neon beer signs and pictures of bands that had performed through the years. Over the bar, a bumper sticker proclaimed, 'In God we trust, everyone else pays cash' and license plates from every state in the Union hung crudely around a huge mirror while an over-sized cash register, built during the California Gold Rush, rested proudly next to the bottles of hard liquor.

Groucho, the barman, watched as Joe lowered his six-foot frame slowly onto a stool without acknowledging him or the cold beer he'd placed on the bar. Not a word was spoken. But when the contents of the bottle finally disappeared and a signal went up for a refill, Groucho seized the opportunity.

"You got a face like a smacked ass, what's up?" he said fiddling with the large clump of hair under his nose.

"Same old shit," said Joe. "Those arrogant bastards have stuck the knife in again."

Joe didn't need to explain any further because Groucho knew him better than anyone. He was aware of his obsession with the film industry and his resolute desire to be famous. He was there when Joe, a young boy, sat at the bar idolizing his mother as she milked every last hoop and holler from the predominantly male audiences that came to see her. He watched as Joe failed when he tried desperately to emulate her mediocre success by becoming an actor. Now he was there again, watching and listening as Joe suffered for his dream.

"You'll make it…you just have to stick with it," Groucho encouraged.

"Why do they treat me like shit?"

"Are you still seeing Dr Frank?"

Joe shook his head.

"Why not?"

"She thinks I'm crazy."

"She's concerned that's all."

"She wants to unscrew the top of my fucking head and climb inside. Stop sending her money. I'm not going anymore."

"You always feel better after you see her."

"I don't know why I let you talk me into that shit. Do you think I'm crazy?"

"No, I don't, but... "

Joe didn't wait to hear his old friend's answer. He just shrugged his shoulders and moved down the bar to where a couple of young girls were seated.

"Can I buy you ladies a drink?" he asked. "My latest script has just been picked up by Fox and I'm celebrating."

Groucho shook his head and smiled as he reached into the cooler for a couple of cold beers.

He's right, he thought, *it is the same old shit.*

DAY THREE

CHAPTER SEVEN

Moose wasn't a morning person. Most days he didn't speak until ten and if he couldn't get hold of a double espresso he could stay quiet all day. It was unusual then to hear him so vocal so early.

"Dan," yelled Moose as his boss walked into the office, "who actually shot Reagan, John Hinckley or one of the Secret Service guys on the roof of the Washington Hilton?"

"Wasn't it John Wilkes Booth?" joked Dan.

"No, that was the guy who shot Lincoln," replied Moose.

Dan smiled, looked around the room and saw Leigh standing next to Alexis' desk.

"I should have known," said Dan. "Good morning Miss Conspiracy!"

Leigh ignored his jibe and lowered herself onto Alexis' chair.

"I got a call from a girl in Personnel last night. Did you arrange this?"

"Hey, we needed someone to take over from Alexis while she's having her baby and you need something to do while you're hanging around in L.A. Besides, Esposito had no hesitation pushing it through quickly. I think it had something to do with finally having some eye candy in the office."

"Thanks, I can use the money. I just had a coffee and muffin for breakfast and it was double what I pay back home."

"I would avoid lunch then if I were you," quipped Dan.

CHAPTER EIGHT

Delusional and prone to exaggeration was how Joe's high school teachers described him fifteen years ago and those personality shortcomings were still very much a part of him now. After just one all night writing session, he was convinced that he had stumbled on an idea for a film script that would make him a star.

This is it, he thought, *the key to that elusive Hollywood door that has slammed in my face so many times.* For a moment he stopped what he was doing, smiled, closed his eyes and rested his head on the back of the couch. He could see it all, the contract negotiations with Warner Bros, meeting the stars at the finest restaurants and collecting his Oscar for best film script from Julia Roberts. Lost in his own little world, he drifted away peacefully until his head snapped forward like he'd been hit from behind by a baseball bat. The time for dreaming was over. He had to get his thoughts down while they were still fresh in his mind, but he needed some help. Bending across the coffee table, he snorted a line that had been skillfully placed on the VCR case of Costner's JFK and then once again began pounding the keys on his laptop. The more he wrote the more he enjoyed it. He soon discovered that making a right click on a word took him to synonyms, which introduced him to a vocabulary he'd never known. He was like a child on an adventure and everything he looked at was a source. Television, videos, the phone book and the Internet all filled his weary head with ideas. It was starting to come together, but at what price?

In the end, the combination of drugs, booze and no sleep proved too much for him and he passed out on the couch, beer oozing down his chest from a bottle that didn't make it to the table. For hours he was comatose until the sound of rustling paper stirred his senses and he slowly got to his feet. Peeking through the curtains, Joe watched as the mailman retreated to the street leaving a large envelope tucked into the mail box. Joe recognized it immediately as one of the scripts he had sent to PJ Franz, a top writer's agent. Written across the envelope in large red letters was, *"RETURN THIS SHIT TO SENDER."* Joe rubbed his eyes in disbelief. He was devastated. Running back into the house, he removed a floorboard from inside his bedroom closet and pulled out a bag of blow.

"Bastards," he yelled as his Amex card cut out a couple of fat lines on the coffee table.

"Bastards, fucking bastards," he shouted as he rolled up a five dollar bill and placed it to his nostril.

Then, as the white powder made its way up his nose and exploded into his brain he fell back on to the floor, giggling like a child.

"Someone up there is pissing on me," he slurred as he stared up at a damp spot on the ceiling.

It was several hours later when Joe awoke on the living room floor with a stiff neck and a dry mouth. He felt like shit! With eyes barely able to focus, he grabbed a tray of ice cubes from the freezer compartment in his fridge, smashed it against the counter and emptied the cubes into a bucket before filling the bucket with cold water. He took off his shirt, tied back his long brown hair and slowly lowered his face beneath the floating ice cubes.

Jesus Christ its cold, he thought as he jerked himself upright and frantically rubbed his head. "Brain freeze", he screamed.

Paul Newman carried out this stunt in two movies, *The Sting* and *Slap Shot*, and Joe thought it must be a good way to sober up. He was just beginning to realize that maybe Newman didn't use real ice cubes.

CHAPTER NINE

Leigh was working late at the Station when Dan returned from a long day spent testifying in court. He was tired and fed up. As much as he loved his job, there were two things he could do without, paperwork and talking to lawyers. Catching the bad guys and putting them behind bars was all he wanted to do. To him, everything else was bullshit. If he was completing a pink form in triplicate or answering questions as to why he shot someone who had just shot at him, then he wasn't doing what he was paid to do.

"Coffee?" said Leigh.

"No thanks, I had one earlier," he said with a wry smile.

"Touché, can I buy you a real drink then?"

"Great idea, just give me a minute to get organized," he said.

"You are organized; I did everything while you were in court."

Dan inspected his desk then took a step back. "You keep this up and we won't want you to leave."

Leigh smiled. "Now that there's nothing to do, how about that drink?"

"Sure," he said, returning her smile.

"Have you got rustic?" asked Leigh. "I'm feeling homesick."

"I've got the perfect place, let's go."

At the same time as Dan was struggling to get through traffic, Joe was struggling to get through the day. Still smarting from comments made by PJ Franz and desperate for something other than little blue pills to lift his spirits, Joe rang Mega Pics, one of the film companies that had his script. It was getting late, but he thought he'd give it a shot anyway. To his surprise a girl with a squeaky voice answered, told him to wait and then placed the phone down on the desk, leaving the line open. Joe could hear everything.

"A guy on the phone wants to know if you've read, '*A Ride on the Main Line?*'" asked the girl.

"Read it, I wouldn't wipe my ass with it. This is the same guy who threatened to beat the crap out of me for not inviting him to an audition. He's crazy, tell him to fuck off."

The girl picked up the phone, but the line was dead. Joe had already dropped to the floor and curled up in a ball with his arms wrapped around his knees and his face buried between his legs. There was no swearing this time and no tears, just a gentle rocking motion back and forth, back and forth.

CHAPTER TEN

"Rustic enough?" asked Dan as they walked through PJ's front door.

"Just like home," said Leigh. "Is this where you hang out?"

"No, but I spent a lot of time here in a previous life."

As Groucho placed their drinks on the bar, Leigh wandered off alone to have a look at an old jukebox standing against the wall. It was a classic Wurlitzer with records spinning at 45 rpm and multicolored fluids bubbling along tubes that arced over the top of the machine.

"This is fantastic," she said.

"Most old things are," laughed Dan.

"I do have a problem with the music though."

"What, no hillbilly?" Dan was trying his best, but he wasn't getting a reaction.

"The first song is 'California Girls' by the Beach Boys."

"Good song," said Dan.

"The second is 'Hotel California' by the Eagles."

"Another excellent tune."

"And the third is 'California Dreamin' by the Mamas and Papas."

"And your point is?"

"Do I really have to say it?"

"Please do," said Dan teasingly.

Leigh threw her arms up as if to surrender and walked back to the bar. "There is a world outside of California, you know."

Groucho had been listening to their conversation while stacking glasses behind the bar and was desperate to get involved. "Aside from thinking we're the only place on the planet that matters," he injected, "there is another explanation why we have so many songs on there about California."

"Enlighten me," said Leigh sarcastically.

"A few months ago we had a competition with our sister bar in New York to see how many songs mentioning our states we could put on our jukeboxes. Most of the records were removed after a while, but a few of the big ones are still there. The visitors from out of state like it."

Leigh sipped her beer and then asked, "I don't know why I'm bothering to ask this, but who won?"

"Nobody, they stopped making vinyl singles years ago so the whole thing was pointless. But we now have a CD full of songs about California if you'd like to hear it?"

Leigh could see that Groucho was fooling around and wasn't expecting an answer, but she still shook her head politely just in case.

Up until now the conversation had been easy and light-hearted with some bad jokes, a bit of sarcasm and lots of laughs. Things got serious though when Dan asked about her family.

"There is no one else," she said lowering her head to hide the sadness in her eyes. "My parents were killed by a hit and run driver a few months ago while on holiday in Tijuana."

"I'm sorry," whispered Dan.

Leigh continued, "I was hoping my investigative skills would someday help find whoever killed them. Mike was hoping to help make the arrest."

"Any luck?"

"Not yet, the police move very slowly down there."

"Is that why Mike came to L.A.?"

"Yeah, he packed in his job back home after spending time in Tijuana. I think he was tired of the small town mentality, but I also think he wanted to keep his eye on things across the border."

"He didn't say anything to me."

"He wouldn't, he kept things like that close to his chest… can we change the subject now… what about you?"

Although Dan was better at listening than talking, he sensed that Leigh was at the point of emotional overspill so he opened up for the first time in a long time.

"I've been a cop all my life… and just like Mike; it's all I ever wanted to be… unfortunately it was all consuming."

"Unfortunately?"

"Yeah, for ten years I thought I was happily married and then all of a sudden she was gone. I think it took about forty eight hours before I noticed she wasn't there anymore. It was then I realized what she went through."

"It usually takes two to —"

"She was dying of cancer and I didn't even know it until her mother called the day she passed away."

"Oh shit," was all Leigh could say.

"She chose to die at her mother's house rather than be with me."

Leigh didn't know what else to say, so she blurted out the first thing that came into her head.

"Do you have children?"

"Not that I know of."

This was painful and Dan didn't want to do it anymore. Sitting with his back to the bar and slowly nursing a beer, his mind wandered to a special time in his life as he gazed at the stage in the corner of the room. A long time later, his thoughts were interrupted.

"A penny for your thoughts," said Leigh.

Startled first and then embarrassingly aware that he'd been caught daydreaming, Dan quickly tried to kick start the conversation.

"What's with all the conspiracy stuff?"

"I've always been interested in things like that and I guess that's partly why I do what I do. I take nothing for granted. My father was a great advocate of that old axiom: believe nothing of what you hear and only half of what you see."

At that moment Groucho tapped Dan on the shoulder and asked, "Can I get you guys another drink?"

"No thanks," said Dan, "it's time to go."

As they moved away from the bar, Groucho stared at Dan for a moment and then asked, "Do I know you?"

"No, I don't think so," said Dan as he got off his stool and headed towards the door.

"Mmmm, I'm sure I know you from somewhere."

CHAPTER ELEVEN

Joe was impatient. He wanted everything and he wanted it now. It was in complete contrast to his mother's way of thinking that hard work would pay off in the end. Busting her ass in no name towns before faceless crowds was suppose to be her ticket to stardom, but instead it left her penniless and dead and he didn't sign up for that. Advice and criticism fell on deaf ears as he refused to hone his skills as an actor and now it was happening all over again as he attempted to become a writer overnight. Having put together the first draft of his new script, he knew he should have done what every other writer does and returned to page one for the first of many rewrites, but not Joe. Instead, he printed off a copy, rolled it up, placed it in his back pocket and headed off to work. That was it. Job done!

Twenty minutes later when Joe drove into Tata's parking lot, Gomez and Pete Savage, the manager, stood talking at the front door. Out of the corner of his eye, he saw Savage lift his arm, extend his finger and point to the rear of the building.

"I know, I know," shouted Joe irritated by the gesture.

Knowing where to park his "bucket of rust", as Savage liked to call it, was one thing, but even more important was not pissing off his boss by parading in front of him with a script or photograph dangling out of his pocket. Joe was lucky, Savage put up with a lot of his shit because he was trustworthy and did what he was paid to do, but his patience was wearing thin. Even Gomez, who not long ago was fighting for his life in the slums of Mexico City, was aware that his friend was running out of warnings.

"What are you doing today Joe, a book signing?" laughed

Savage.

"No sir, just good old fashioned car parking," replied Joe.

"That would be a nice change," the manager replied sarcastically before disappearing into the restaurant.

"I think he likes you," said Gomez surprisingly.

"He loves me," said Joe with confidence.

"Get away."

"No really."

"How come man? You're a major fuck up."

"The other night I caught him in the back seat of his car with Carol, the new waitress... He was slammin' her like there was no tomorrow. I promised him I wouldn't tell Mrs S and even swore on my mother's life."

"But your mother's dead," said Gomez.

A wry smile appeared on Joe's face.

Just then a black Cadillac Escalade ESV stopped at the valet parking space in front of the restaurant and a tall thin man in his sixties with unfashionable shoulder length gray hair and a gold tooth in the front of his mouth got out and tossed his keys to Gomez. The Mexican lowered himself on to the soft black leather seat like he was sinking slowly into a hot bubble bath and said in an exaggerated accent, "Dees is beeger dan my house."

"Who's that?" asked Joe.

"You don't know?" questioned Gomez.

"Why the fuck would I ask if I knew?" snapped Joe.

"That's Phil Weinberg, aka *The Sultan of Sleaze*. Makes porn flicks, but the word is that he would film his own mother dying if he thought somebody would buy it."

Suddenly Joe became very animated, almost to the point of jumping up and down. He snatched the keys to the Escalade from Gomez and raced over to his pickup. Reaching through the window on the passenger side he scooped up the script on the seat.

"Tubbs," yelled Savage.

Joe was startled. He hurriedly placed the papers back through the window, but in doing so the top page fell to the ground and floated beneath his truck.

"Yeah," yelled Joe.

"Move the yellow Lamborghini next to the front door."

"Why?"

"Mr Horowitz has a meeting here in ten and wants to impress."

"Dickhead," whispered Joe.

"Another thing," the manager added in a loud voice.

"What?"

"Can you work Thursday, I'm down a man?"

"Sure, no problem, anything else?"

"That's all for now."

Joe waited until Savage went back into the restaurant then collected his script off the front seat and hurried to the Escalade. The lone piece of paper remained on the ground under his pickup. With eyes scanning 360 degrees, he opened the back door of the vehicle and found a battered old silver metal briefcase lying on the back seat. Surprised yet delighted to find it wasn't locked, he quickly slipped his script beneath a folded newspaper and a pile of documents before placing his hands together in front of his chest. With eyes closed he spoke slowly and softly.

"Kissing those babies didn't work last time so maybe a word with the Man upstairs will help."

A long hesitation with head bowed followed an even lengthier session of throat clearing before Joe started to pray.

"Dear Lord, please smile on this one for me... you know I don't ask for much, in fact I've never asked for anything... I just need a goddamn break. Thank you... oh by the way... I call my new script... *"Killing the Dead."*

Two hours later, Weinberg left the restaurant, drove to LAX and flew to New York.

DAY FOUR

CHAPTER TWELVE

In the distance, giant headlight beams crept slowly over the hill and grew ever closer as Leigh stood motionless in the middle of a tarmac strip. As tiny beads of sweat rolled down her face, a voice inside her head told her to run. Violently twisting her torso, she threw her body into the darkness and raced inside a narrow steam filled tunnel. The harder she pumped her arms and legs the heavier they became and the more difficult it was to move forward. Soaking wet, physically drained and unable to see the way ahead, she stopped, waited and listened. The sound of her thumping heart and air gushing in and out of her mouth were all that she could hear. Even the distant lights had vanished. With outstretched arms, she touched the warm metal walls of the giant tube, aware that with every step she had taken down the tunnel, the narrower it had become. In fact, the tunnel was so narrow, she felt confident the car would no longer be able to follow her. Relieved that her nightmare was over, she wiped her cheek with the back of her hand and tried to continue walking. But something wasn't right. The tarmac had melted in the heat and her feet were stuck like glue. No matter how hard she tugged and pulled, they wouldn't budge. Then, not far away, the deafening roar of a car engine drove a wedge through the midnight calm while the giant headlight beams returned to haunt her. The nightmare was back. Powerless to move, Leigh faced the oncoming vehicle as it ripped quickly through the gears, hitting top speed in a matter of seconds.

This is crazy, she thought, *the tunnel isn't wide enough.*

Shielding her eyes to block out the blinding light, she tensed her muscles, braced herself for impact then waited and waited, but nothing happened and nothing could happen, because for the third night running she'd suffered the nightmare simulation of her parent's cruel and untimely death.

Disorientated and still trembling, Leigh turned on the lamp next to the bed and looked at her watch. It was 5:47 a.m., too early to go to work and too late to go back to sleep. She hated the night-time, believing that the darkness was to be shared with a lover, family or friends. Even sleeping alone was doable as long as someone you care for was within earshot. For a brief moment she smiled as she drifted back to her childhood when bedtime was fun and when each night the entire family played out that famous final scene from the Waltons. *Goodnight John Boy, goodnight Jim Bob,* and on and on they went until one by one they gently fell asleep.

Feeling sorry for herself wasn't something she did on a regular basis and she was annoyed that it was happening now. With Mike and her parents gone she knew she had to be strong.

"Come on, get your act together," she growled as she threw on Mike's bathrobe.

The reflection in the mirror of a little girl wearing her big brother's clothes brought yet another smile to her face and suddenly she realized it wasn't all bad, she still had fond memories and she still had a sense of humor. And boy was she going to need both to tackle the job of getting Mike's apartment ready to show to a real estate agent.

Minor repairs were not a problem. She could swing a hammer with the best of them, but it was all things electric that frightened her most. Since moving in, the lights, TV and anything else with a plug developed a mind of its own, switching off and on like a neon sign with a short circuit. When jiggling wires and swearing didn't work she promised herself she would call an electrician, but L.A. was expensive, money was tight and there were bigger priorities, like eating.

Wide awake and with too much time on her hands, Leigh rolled up her oversized sleeves and got down to making the place more habitable. Her first instinct was to tear down a plastic ivy plant that was wrapped around an eight-inch square wooden floor to ceiling support beam one third of the way across the room. Ripping the 'Made in Taiwan' piece of greenery off the pole, she grinned and whispered, "Mike, you were so tacky."

Quickly moving on, she began laying down floorboards over the many gaps dotted across the apartment.

Meanwhile, on the opposite side of the country, Weinberg strutted into the Sheraton on 7th Avenue feeling confident, almost cocky and why shouldn't he? Back in L.A. he was the "man", the "go to" guy if you wanted your flicks bluer than blue or stranger than strange. Everything was possible, nothing was taboo. Midgets, animals, butt slammin' circus clowns, S&M housewives and good old fashioned daisy chains made up a film catalogue large enough to give an old man with erectile dysfunction wood for a week. For decades his little studio dominated the West Coast x-rated market, but things were changing and money was tight. It was time he introduced himself to the Empire state. This was a business trip that he hoped would help balance the books and put a smile back on his accountant's face. Times were hard in the Golden State and maybe his expectations of scooping up a cool million in New York were over the top, but he believed he could do it and belief is what got him this far.

Tossing his briefcase on to the bed, he headed straight for the mini bar and cracked open a bottle of scotch.

Not bad for a Jewish boy from the Lower East Side, he thought as he took in the surroundings of his palatial top floor suite.

Then, without even brushing his teeth or changing his shirt, he rode the elevator to the lobby, stepped outside, jumped in a cab and said, "Take me somewhere sleazy."

DAY FIVE

CHAPTER THIRTEEN

Joe sat cross-legged on the couch and stared at the floor. He was at a very low point in his life with each new day bringing another hammer blow to his confidence. Even when his mother had died and he'd been dragged kicking and screaming into a foster home he'd managed to pull himself out of that disturbingly dark place. But things were different now. His downward spiral had nothing to do with death or the law; it was more about being the victim. With each rejection he dipped closer to the point of no return and without family or close friends he reached out for drugs. He refused to accept that using his mother's script was a bad idea or the script itself was a pile of crap. He couldn't understand why it was rejected and he couldn't get his head around the ridicule and wickedness that came from the industry he loved.

Too many bridges had been burned and there was nowhere else to go, Weinberg was his last hope. He sat patiently waiting for a call from the King of Porn, but his phone remained silent.

It had been less than forty eight hours since he slipped *Killing the Dead* into a briefcase on the back seat of Weinberg's car and every minute felt like a lifetime. He'd heard nothing and was going crazy. As far as he was concerned, no news was bad news and he had to find out what was going on. He knew that unknown writers would be lucky to have their scripts read at all, never mind in less than two days. But it was the same old thing all over again. His impatience got the better of him and when he found Weinberg's number on line, he gave his studio a call. A woman with an Eastern European accent answered the phone and tried to explain that Weinberg was unavailable.

They're doing it to me again, he thought. *The bastards are ignoring me.*

"Has he read my script?" shouted Joe.

"What is it called?" she replied trying to be helpful.

"Killing the Dead."

The woman left Joe hanging on while she looked through a bundle of scripts in a filing cabinet. A couple of minutes later she returned to the phone.

"Sorry, we have no script called *Thrilling in Bed,*" said the woman in broken English.

Joe grimaced and wanted to climb inside the phone to get to her.

"You stupid bitch, I said, *Killing the Dead.*"

Again she put the phone down and searched through the scripts.

"We have no script by this name," came her reply after a short delay.

"You goddamn Commie, it must be there… I gave it to him two days ago."

The woman hung up!

Joe was stunned and sat motionless as anger ripped through his body. Then, with head bowed, he took a deep breath and slowly got to his feet while the fingers on his right hand clung tightly to the neck of his beer bottle. Raising his right arm and leaning back like a pitcher winding up for a 3 and 2 delivery, he threw the bottle across the room and watched poker faced as it smashed against the wall and shattered into a million pieces. Just when he thought he couldn't fall any further, the ground beneath his feet opened up.

CHAPTER FOURTEEN

Weinberg was born in the Big Apple, but hadn't been back for more than thirty years. He didn't like it much. It was too big and too noisy and there were days when you didn't see the sun. He missed California and the laid back life and he missed doing business with people he knew. New Yorkers were hard to please; make it faster, slower, longer, and shorter; nothing he showed them was good enough. He was beginning to wonder why he had made the trip East in the first place. Then he remembered; L.A. was no longer in love with him.

Back in his hotel room, Weinberg revisited the mini bar and poured a miniature bottle of scotch over a solitary piece of ice. He sifted through his briefcase and pulled out *Killing the Dead*.

Where did this come from? he thought as he quickly scanned the document.

There was no covering letter or page with the author's personal details, just the script with the title, *Killing the Dead*, on top of page one. He tossed the papers on the floor and walked into the bathroom. A knock on the door cut his visit short.

"Yeah," he grunted, as he opened the door to his room.

A tall leggy brunette wearing a long black leather overcoat leaned against the doorway. Twenty years ago she would have been starring in films for guys like him. Today, she's working the streets. The porn and motion picture industries have at least one thing in common. If you're female and your looks go south then you're out, washed up, finished! Years of abuse and messing with nature haven't helped her and no amount of Botox could save her now, he thought.

She purred, "Lonnie sent me," and slowly opened her coat to reveal that the only thing she was wearing was a tacky silver pendant that read 'Welcome to New York'.

Lonnie and Weinberg went to school together in The City and had stayed in touch over the years. Whereas Weinberg knew from an early age that he wanted to make films, Lonnie just knew he wanted to make money. He drifted from dealing drugs to pimping and the years spent in detention on Rikers Island and other correctional facilities had not changed him one bit. He was still chasing the fast buck.

Weinberg studied her closely and thought *she's an old dog; do I really wanna do this*? Then without further hesitation he stepped aside and watched as she unfastened the pendant and threw it in his direction. "Catch," she squealed.

"I hope it's the only thing I'm going to catch tonight," he said dryly.

CHAPTER FIFTEEN

PJ's was heaving with customers three deep at the bar. The dance floor was packed as The Edge, a four-piece rock band, whipped up the crowd with every cover they played. The music was melodic and uncomplicated, the words easy to remember.

"Play some Hendrix," cried Joe, from his stool at the bar.

"Who pulled your chain?" laughed Groucho as he propped himself up on the cooler.

"Nobody plays Hendrix," mumbled Joe, while knocking back another beer.

"The Edge want people to dance not slit their wrists," joked Groucho.

Joe smiled. He and Groucho had been having this conversation for years. It always ended with the same line and somehow it always made Joe smile. Groucho was a "chart" man. He was happiest when the bands playing at PJ's were knocking off stuff that everybody knew and could sing along with. People dance to happy upbeat songs. When they dance, they get hot; when they get hot they buy drinks. It was a simple formula that had been working since the days of the "Speakeasy".

"So what's next Joe?" asked Groucho.

Joe shook his head as he peeled the label off his beer.

"I don't know I'm clean out of ideas… I guess parking cars is what I was born to do."

"It's a shame you can't do what The Edge has just done," said Groucho as he continued to serve customers.

"What's that?" replied Joe with a sudden renewed interest.

"They tried for years, but couldn't get a record deal. Then they made their own record and started selling it at gigs and on-line. Next thing you know a small independent label heard the song, liked it and signed them up. I know that you can't go out and make a movie, but if you could somehow get your story out there in a different format then hey, who knows?"

While Joe sat thinking about his friend's remarks, Groucho moved along the bar with a damp cloth. Looking directly at a handful of college kids and trying desperately to keep a straight face, he shouted. "Look at this mess," he said glancing down at a puddle of beer, "you're nothing but a bunch of pigs."

A roar of laughter came from the opposite side of the bar followed by a predictable "oink oink" sound, but Groucho had the last laugh when he zapped them with a quick blast of soda water from the pressurised hose.

Joe was still running things over in his mind and was completely oblivious to what was going on around him. Suddenly, a girl's voice interrupted his train of thought.

"Hi, I'm Marion."

Joe nodded and raised his bottle, but didn't turn around.

"I've been watching you from over there," she said, as she pointed to a table in the corner where her two girlfriends were seated.

Joe continued to stare blankly at the liquor bottles lined up beneath the mirror.

"Can I buy you a drink?" she asked while staring at the back of Joe's head.

Joe put his beer on the bar and lowered his head into his hands, "Are you stalking me, woman?" he said rudely.

Marion was momentarily knocked back by Joe's outburst. "No, I just thought you looked lonely and might want some company. Sorry, I obviously misread the situation."

Then as she turned to go, Joe spun around on his stool and grabbed her arm.

"I'll have a Bud, if the offer still stands?"

Marion looked hesitant for a moment and then gestured towards the bar.

"Two Buds please... on my tab... You know, sometimes

two heads are better than one... everybody needs a sounding board, look what happened to McCartney after Lennon left."

Joe was annoyed with himself for being such an asshole. He still didn't know why he did things like that even after years of counselling. She was nice. She was plain, but not unattractive and definitely not fat. Joe didn't do fat. He particularly liked her name. Coincidentally it was a name that played a part in his script.

"How many beers do I have to buy you before you actually say something?" teased Marion.

Joe spent his whole life building a wall around his heart to stop people like Marion getting to him. If someone got close he built the wall higher. If that didn't work he ran away. He'd never received love and didn't know how to give it. His idea of a relationship was a one night stand. So what was going on here? A woman he'd known for less than a minute was trying to walk through the goddamn front door of his fortress and what was he doing about it? Nothing?

"My name is Joe."

"Well that's a start," laughed Marion. "Are you single, married, divorced or gay?"

"Single," said Joe, a little upset that he could be mistaken for a homosexual.

"Me too," said Marion. "What do you do?"

"What is this, twenty questions?"

"Sorry, do you want me to shut up?"

Joe didn't respond, instead he sat staring at the label on his beer. This was the moment he had dreamed of. It was a scenario that passed through his mind a million times and each time he would respond to "what do you do", by puffing out his chest, throwing his shoulders back and proudly announcing that he was an actor or a script writer and that his most recent work was the latest Hollywood blockbuster. Maybe it was the beer or maybe he was just too tired to bullshit.

"I park cars," he replied.

Marion was quick to respond even though her tongue was firmly in her cheek, "Are they nice cars?"

Joe smiled and added, "I'm a writer too, but I'm struggling."

Marion looked at him as if to say, *and?*

"I can't get anyone to read my scripts."

"I would estimate that you are in a line of at least ten thousand similar souls," joked Marion. "Anyway, don't you have to sleep with someone to get ahead in Hollywood?"

"I wish it was that easy."

"So what's the problem?"

"I've pissed off some VIPs." Joe paused, then added, "Lots of VIPs"

Marion took a mouthful of beer and then told Joe a story about a friend of hers in college. The girl was a cheerleader who had written a play. Those in the drama department considered her to be a "bimbo" because of her chosen extra curricular activity and wouldn't even look at what she'd written. To get their attention she crashed one the department's late night meetings, locked the door and stuffed the key down the front of her blouse. She promised to unlock the door once they'd listened to her play.

"What happened?" asked Joe expectantly.

"The group sat and listened for about forty five minutes while she read her story aloud."

"Did they like it?"

"No, it was absolute crap," laughed Marion, "but they liked her voice and the way she read her lines so much that the professor asked her to join the drama group."

"And your point is?" questioned Joe somewhat disappointed.

"Desperate times need desperate measures... Make them stand up and take notice of you and don't worry about what anybody thinks. If she hadn't done what she did then she never would have known that her play wasn't any good or that she had a great voice for the theater. Remember, put yourself out there... Hey, my friends are leaving; I'm out of here... next time."

"Sure," said Joe, "thanks for the beer."

As soon as Marion left the bar, Groucho started teasing Joe about his new girlfriend, but Joe didn't take the bait. His mind was elsewhere. Then, after a long silence he blurted, "I know what I'm going to do."

"Whatever it is, old buddy, I'll be behind you all the way," replied Groucho, trying hard to be supportive.

"Somehow I don't think so," mumbled Joe. "I'm on my own with this one."

_____

Joe was alone when he left the bar about midnight. With "Hendrix" blasting on his stereo, he drove into the city and parked down a dark side street, turned off his engine and waited in silence. It wasn't long before the familiar sight of a thin dishevelled man with a beard and shoulder length hair walked by his truck. His ragged floor length overcoat dragged along the road as a cardboard poster rested on his shoulder. It was that guy again. When Joe opened the door the man spun around and looked deep into his eyes and said, "I am the light of the world; he that follows me shall not walk in darkness, but shall have light of life."

The man motioned with his hands as if to bless Joe then turned away and moved towards the canal. Keeping a safe distance, Joe followed and watched as he curled up on a makeshift bed next to the water under a bridge.

Perfect, thought Joe, *fucking weird, but perfect.*

DAY SIX

CHAPTER SIXTEEN

Like a kid in a candy store, Leigh didn't know where to look first. With Dan at the wheel they headed west through Hollywood on Santa Monica Boulevard, cruising slowly into Beverley Hills and over Rodeo Drive. It was all too much to take in. The street names were as familiar to her as those in the one horse town where she lived and the sights were straight out of every movie and TV show she had ever seen. Snapping pictures with her cell phone, she squealed with delight as they crept by the homes of the rich and famous until suddenly her three by two inch screen picked up an image that sent a chill through her body. The 1986 tan Chevy Monte Carlo in front of them was the same car Mike stopped on the day he was shot.

And the damn taillight is still broken, she thought.

Bouncing in her seat, too excited to talk, Leigh pointed to the car with a quivering finger until Dan finally spotted it too. Seeing the Monte Carlo brought back terrible memories of the past, but that's exactly where they were, in the past. What concerned Dan most was how Leigh knew about the car, "How did you know?" queried Dan.

"I read the file," she replied quickly.

Shaking his head in disbelief, Dan was seconds away from losing his temper before realizing that her position at the station gave her the opportunity to look at anything from parking fines to top-secret undercover investigations. Leigh's predecessor, Alex, never read a file of any kind and couldn't have cared less about what was down on paper. Even when she typed statements, the words never made it past her finger-tips. She had other priorities like sorting out everyone's personal problems.

Not wanting to get involved, Dan made a signal to turn right, but Leigh begged him to keep going.

"Please," she said, "let's see what he does."

"I didn't go with my instincts last time and look what happened."

"That wasn't your fault and besides, we're not going to stop him we're just going to follow him."

Dan gazed into her eyes for the shortest of moments. He didn't stand a chance.

"Great, I get one day off a week and what do I do, play cops and robbers?" he said sarcastically.

The tan Chevy meandered through the back streets, made a U turn and headed south on The Freeway then back north before turning off at Venice Beach.

"Either this guy has no sense of direction or he's trying to make sure he's not being followed," said Dan.

"This is so exciting!" Leigh whispered.

For Dan it wasn't exciting; it was routine and just another day at the office. This is what he did all day, every day.

Turning his head to the right, he stared at her as she fixed her eyes on the car in front. He could tell she was thinking something bad was about to happen and he was reluctant to rain on her parade so just for the hell of it, he decided to throw a little fuel on the fire

"It looks like something's going down," he muttered softly while trying not to laugh. "Could be a drug deal, a drive by shooting or maybe the guy's going to hold up a liquor store?"

A wry smile came across his lips as he switched lanes and let a small red Toyota slot in between him and the Chevy. A couple of minutes later the Monte Carlo pulled into a parking space a block from the beach and Dan slipped into a gap one hundred and fifty feet behind him. They sat and waited in the unmarked cop car as a mountain of a man wearing a short sleeved shirt covered in pink sombreros with huge sweat stains under the armpits slowly and painfully extracted himself from the front seat of his car.

"Who is he?" asked Leigh.

"Sergio's brother, Ricardo."

"Are you going to arrest him?" she asked excitedly.

"What for, wearing a loud shirt?"

Ricardo started walking towards Dan's car. Speaking through clenched teeth while slowly sliding down the back of her seat Leigh started to panic. "He's coming this way... what should we do? ... Dan, he's getting closer."

Still trying not to laugh, Dan waited for a moment and then turned to her and said, "Let's do what they do in the movies when this happens."

Before she had time to respond, Dan wrapped his arms around her neck, pressed his lips firmly against hers and held the kiss until Ricardo had passed the car and was out of sight.

"I don't think he saw us," said Dan with a straight face as he relaxed back into his seat.

Leigh was speechless. She sat open-mouthed staring out the window like a teenager having just experienced her first kiss. Of course this wasn't her first kiss, she'd had many boyfriends, but this was definitely the first time she'd been kissed by a man nearly twice her age, and she liked it. It could have been like kissing her dad, but it wasn't. Dan had a few issues, but he was a good-looking man with a nice body and boy could he kiss. How could she not like it?

So many things were going through her mind as she sat staring out the window. *Was that a real kiss or just a tactical police maneuver? If it was real, does this mean we are... no, don't be silly*, she thought, *it's a California thing... Even guys kiss each other in this state.*

Leigh was still analyzing that kiss when Dan tapped on the roof of the car, "Come on let's go, we don't want to lose him."

Regaining her composure, she got out of the car and followed Dan to the end of the street just in time to see Ricardo enter Jodi Maroni's Beach Hut. Five minutes later she watched as he emerged holding a king size sausage sandwich smothered in onions and peppers with a large Diet Coke to wash it down. When he pulled a rolled up newspaper out of his back pocket and sat at a weathered wooden picnic table on the concrete boardwalk next to the beach, it was a sign that they were in for the long haul. Drifting casually onto the sand, Leigh pointed to the ocean and pretended to make small talk.

This was the first time she had been to the coast and the first time that she heard the sound of those magnificent Californian waves crashing on the shore. It should have been breathtaking and maybe even romantic, but it wasn't because she had other things on her mind. The brother of Mike's killer was just a few feet away and he was making her stomach churn. She couldn't ignore him any longer. Turning away from Dan's side, she marched towards the fat Mexican. With arms pumping and blood rushing through her veins she got within ten feet of him before he looked up from his newspaper and said, "I'm sorry for your loss."

She hadn't expected that. Not only did he know who she was but it genuinely seemed like he meant what he said. He took the wind right out of her sails. She was standing at the plate without a bat. Then Dan came along, grabbed her by the arm and quickly shuffled her down the boardwalk,

"How does he know who I am?"

"He was at Mike's funeral," said Dan.

"Why?"

"Wouldn't you want to see the face of the man who killed your brother?"

CHAPTER SEVENTEEN

With his laptop straddling his thighs, Joe locked onto Google and typed in a load of words including birth and death certificates, government agencies and "vital statistics" and soon found what he was looking for. Now it was time to check things out.

Dressed in an old pair of faded jeans, T-shirt and cowboy boots he made his way along the side of the house, closing the outside doors that led down to the basement. There was no need to lock the house because his drugs and the two beers left in the fridge were the only things worth stealing. He was confident his blow was stashed in a safe place, and everything else belonged to the landlord, so it wasn't really his problem. Shutting the cellar door was simply to stop the cat from somewhere down the road getting into the house. The last time he left the door open it tracked black dust from the coal bunker right through to his bedroom before leaping on to his face in the middle of the night. The cat was unceremoniously drop kicked through an open window, but it hasn't stopped it from returning.

It was almost noon when Joe pulled into the parking lot in front of the Bureau of Vital Statistics. Looking to the left of the building he noticed that it was connected to the police station.

Christ, I guess I won't be breaking into this place, he thought.

Joe had never even broken into a sweat let alone a government building, but this whole writing thing was starting to take hold of him. As he strolled into the entrance hall wearing shades and a baseball hat, like some undercover sleuth in a "B" movie, he instantly joined the end of a long line of people leading up to a large black woman sitting behind a counter. She spoke into a microphone attached to a flexi-cable while documents were pushed through a small opening at the bottom of a bullet-proof glass window. At the side of the hall was a door for staff to access the secure area behind the glass. It had a coded entry device and a CCTV camera scanned the area from overhead. As Joe leaned against the wall by the door, pondering his next move, a man from UPS walked to the front of the line and tapped on the window. A tall thin girl working behind the counter opened the door and signed for a handful of packages. Joe took advantage of the moment to look inside and spotted a short unattractive woman in her fifties sitting in an open plan work-station.

"Yes," he whispered to himself through gritted teeth, "yes, yes, yes!"

Joe left the building, picked up a copy of his script from his truck and then sat on a bench on the opposite side of the road. Shortly after one o'clock the same frumpy woman with scraped back gray hair tied in a pony-tail, came out of the building and walked down the street to a small coffee shop. Joe was right behind her. She ordered a sandwich and a cold drink and sat at an outside table for two. With more and more people entering the shop and all the outside tables full, Joe quickly grabbed a cold drink and rushed to where the woman was seated.

"Can I join you?" he said with his hand already pulling back the vacant chair, "I hate being inside on a day like this."

The woman seemed unable to speak with her mouth full of food and just nodded. Joe placed his drink on the table and removed the rolled up papers from his back pocket allowing them to unravel in front of her. The words, *A Ride on the Main Line*, a script by Joe Tubbs, jumped off the top page and immediately caught her attention. Her eyes lit up as she swallowed hard.

"I don't mean to be nosy, but are you in the film business?" she asked excitedly.

"Yeah," he replied casually. "I write scripts. This is an old one that I'm making some changes to before we shoot next week."

"That's so cool," she enthused.

"Are you interested in the movies?" asked Joe, having just seen that her work-station was covered in more movie junk than most souvenir stores in Hollywood.

"Am I?" she laughed. "I'm the world's biggest fan... you should see where I work, it's wall to wall Hollywood."

"No kidding," said Joe. I'd love to see it, where do you work?"

"Across the street at the Bureau of Vital Statistics."

Looking over at the building, Joe commented, "And what do you do there?"

"I look after a team that inputs personal data into our system...you know, dates of birth, death etc."

Joe couldn't help notice that she was staring at his left hand.

"I see you're single like me," she said.

"Huh?"

"No ring."

"Oh yeah, just haven't found the right girl I guess. Hollywood's full of phoneys and retreads... I'm more of a family man."

The woman pulled her shoulders back and ran her fingers gently through her hair as Joe continued, "How come you're not attached... I'd have thought guys would be breaking down your door."

A large smile appeared on her face. "Can we do this again?"

"I'd love to and hey, maybe I can get some movie stuff for you. Would you like that?"

"That would be awesome; you're very kind," she said as she looked into his eyes while reaching across the table to touch his hand.

Inside, Joe was dying a million deaths. *What is she doing?* he thought, *she's old enough to be my mother!*

He wanted to pull his hand away and wipe it on his shirt, but he knew if he did he would ruin everything. He flashed back to the days when he was a boy and his mother's girl friends would smother him with big wet kisses and then laugh when he tried to rub off the bright red lipstick from his cheeks. He stayed calm as she gently caressed the back of his hand with her index finger.

"I've got to go," she said in a seductive tone, "but here's my number, call me."

The woman wrote down her number on his script and then walked away.

"What's your name?" shouted Joe as she crossed the street.

"Mary Lou," she giggled, "like in the song."

Despite his lack of years Joe knew that the song she was referring to was Ricky Nelson's 1960's hit 'Hello Mary Lou'. It was a piece of cake for a guy who grew up listening to bar room jukeboxes and could name the artist, song title and the record label for most songs before the singer had even reached the chorus.

How sad, he thought. *She lives in a fantasy world, uses words like "cool" and "awesome" and hits on men half her age. And her only claim to anything exciting is a name that comes from a fifty year old song title.*

For a moment he actually felt sorry for her. Above all, he knew he was lucky to find her. Now if only he could get to her computer he'd be able to join up all the dots in his new story and take things to the next level. Instead of just another made up piece of fiction it would involve real people with real emotions. Everyone would play a part.

Although he had only just said goodbye to Mary Lou, he wanted to keep things moving so he immediately headed over to Tata's. It didn't feel right being there when he wasn't working and it didn't look right either. If Savage saw him he'd think he was doing a little self-promotion so he had to be quick. On the wall in the reception hung several photos of famous people including a signed picture from Harrison Ford.

Would this be enough? he thought.

Joe was aware that he may have to make the ultimate sacrifice and was prepared to do it, but felt that all other possibilities should be exhausted first. Standing at the entrance next to Gomez, he engaged in mindless chatter until the girl on reception escorted a couple to a table on the far side of the room. This was his moment. Without any hesitation and with Gomez in mid sentence, he darted through the door, ripped the framed photo off the wall and returned to the young Mexican's side with his prize neatly hidden beneath his T-shirt. Gomez was cool. He acted like nothing happened and as far as he was concerned, nothing did.

An autographed picture of a major Hollywood star should have been enough to get someone as desperate as Mary Lou into bed never mind a few minutes on her computer, but Joe wasn't taking any chances. On his way home he stopped at a jeweler and asked them to make an engraving on his Ronson lighter. It was a classic, the old silver one that somehow found its way into his pocket after a night of heavy drinking at PJ's.

It was the end of a long hot day and when Joe got home he found himself racing towards planet earth at a thousand miles an hour. With minutes to spare before what he knew would be a spectacular crash landing, he had a couple of blue pills washed down with a cold beer and they quickly put him right back where he was happiest. It was a familiar routine that set him up nicely for the night ahead.

Munching on a slice of pizza straight out of the fridge, he sat back with his laptop and for the first time read his new script line by line. It was like Swiss cheese, full of holes, but with Mary Lou's help he knew he could turn it round. And that was a problem. So much depended on her that it was beginning to worry him. He preferred to fly solo. The more he thought about it the more he questioned what he was doing.

What if she tells me to fuck off? Why should she let me use her computer? It's serious shit. It's not like I'll be tapping into the Pentagon, but it is personal and confidential stuff about people's lives. We could go to jail. Jesus, screwing her may be the least of my worries. I may have to marry her to get the information.

Joe laughed out loud and looked into the eyes of his mother posing with her guitar in a photo on the wall and said, "It wouldn't be the first time someone in this family gave their body for art, would it?"

CHAPTER EIGHTEEN

A clicking noise at the door woke Weinberg in the middle of the night. The hooker had left the building. Jumping out of bed, he flicked on the light and quickly made his way to his briefcase on the far side of the room. He was relieved to find that it was still there and still locked, but he didn't totally relax until it was open and his wallet was safely in his hands. Weinberg trusted no one, especially prostitutes. And he didn't care whom they worked for, even if it was his oldest friend. He also checked the closet to make sure she hadn't taken any of his clothes.

Many years ago after a drunken orgy in an L.A. hotel room, two pros stripped him of everything he had including his underwear. He laughs about it now when he tells the story, but at the time he was so mad he put a contract out on them. Fortunately for everyone concerned he didn't have to go through with it. Within twenty-four hours the girls returned his possessions including the money he paid for their services. One advantage of being in the porn business is that there are lots of crazy people around who will do anything or at least threaten to do anything, as long as the price is right.

Wide awake, naked and seriously hung over, Weinberg stood staring at his reflection in the mirror on the bathroom wall. It wasn't a pretty sight. Tousled hair covered the lines on his craggy pale face, but his tired stooped body lay totally exposed along with the ribbed Trojan still clinging to his manhood. A smug look appeared on his face as he removed the latex sheath and washed himself in the sink.

"Rabbi Leibovitz," he said proudly, "you did one helluva job."

A moment later he was back in bed with his thumb pressing heavily on the TV remote and for the next couple of minutes mindlessly surfed the hundreds of available channels.

What a load of shit, he thought. *Why do I have to watch stuff made before even I was born just because it's the middle of the goddamn night?*

Tossing the remote on to the bed, Weinberg picked up the stack of papers Joe had left in his briefcase. He started to read and then the phone rang.

"Hi mum, yes I'm awake. It's about 3:30, no... in the morning. How are you feeling? That's good. No, not tonight, but I should be home soon. Is the nurse with you? Good. Don't forget to take your pills. I love you. Bye."

DAY SEVEN

CHAPTER NINETEEN

"Hello… Mary Lou," sang a voice at the other end of the line.

I don't fucking believe it, thought Joe as he rolled his eyes. *She answers the goddamn phone like she's singing that stupid song.*

Joe quickly composed himself knowing that sucking up to her was crucial.

"Hi, it's Joe, the script writer... we met yesterday at the café."

"Hi Joe, I was hoping you'd call."

"I've been thinking about you and have something for you. Can we meet?"

"What is it?"

"Wait and see."

"Oooh I like a mystery, OK, same place… one o'clock?"

"See you then."

Mary Lou signed off with the word "cool" and Joe reacted immediately by sticking his finger down his throat to fake a gagging motion. Arranging to meet her was always going to be the easy part. Convincing her to let him loose on her computer was the real test. He knew he was putting his acting skills on the line but he was confident he could pull it off.

With time to kill, Joe headed to the outskirts of town and

paid a visit to motel alley where rooms were more likely to be rented by the hour than by the night. It was a strip with no frills and no questions asked, a place for truckers to catch forty winks and hookers to ply their trade. By claiming he was getting married and needed accommodation for his twenty guests, he was given the red carpet treatment and allowed to inspect the rooms. It wasn't easy to find exactly what he wanted because the name of the motel was just as important as the layout of the room, but he eventually saw the perfect fit.

Walking back to the motel office with the manager, Joe stopped outside the screen door claiming he wanted to call his fiancée to give her the good news. Alone on the porch, he clocked the motel phone number from a small sign on the wall and tapped it into his cell. Seconds later the phone in the back office behind the reception began to ring drawing the manager to it. Seizing the moment, Joe rushed through the screen door, leaned over the wooden counter and grabbed the last key from the rack on the wall. The rack swung violently from side to side and Joe was forced to lean over the counter again to steady it. When the manger returned, Joe was gone.

The drive back into town was a strange one. Joe was excited because things were starting to fall into place, yet he was nervous and edgy, confident and insecure. So much depended on a meeting with a woman he didn't like. He tried telling himself that it was no big deal, but deep down inside he knew that was bullshit. This was the first and the only thing he had ever written. *Who knows, it could be his last.* He felt it was good and desperately wanted everyone to know about it.

_____

Mary Lou was already waiting at the table when Joe arrived. She'd combed out her pony-tail, applied some lipstick and was looking more like a woman on a mission than a public servant having lunch. An unscheduled stop to pick up a few pills made Joe a couple of minutes late, but she didn't seem to mind nor did she seem to notice that he was as high as a kite and struggling to act normal. It was like being a teenager again and coming home drunk for the first time. You think you're standing still when you're swaying and you think you're making sense when you're talking shit. Your parents know immediately, but Joe wasn't sure about Mary Lou. She was so happy to have a man at her table that she probably didn't notice, and if she did, she didn't care. He took a deep breath and presented her with the photo of Harrison Ford. She was ecstatic and leaned across the table and kissed him on the cheek.

Joe saw an opening. "I was wondering if you could help me?"

"What is it?" she said, staring at the autographed picture

"Fox are all over me like a rash and are threatening to cancel my contract if I don't meet the deadline for my latest movie script."

"How can I help?" asked Mary Lou.

Joe took another deep breath and went on, "My story is based on real people and how their lives change because of who they are. I need to make it factually correct and to do this I need information that I can't get on the Internet."

An ugly silence followed as Mary Lou looked him square in the face. He could tell she was disappointed. She lowered her head and placed the picture on the table. He thought she was going to get up and leave.

"This was all planned, wasn't it?" she asked.

Joe was flying at ten thousand feet and quickly needed to get his brain into a better state. He remembered Groucho's philosophy that an apology would always diffuse an argument. This wasn't quite an argument, but it soon could be and besides he couldn't think of anything else.

"I'm sorry," he blurted. "I was wrong to do this, please forget that I even asked." Joe put his hand into his pocket and pulled out the silver Ronson lighter.

"Here," he said. "You can have this too."

Mary Lou took the lighter that was engraved with the

initials HF on the side. Her eyes lit up.

"Is this really his lighter?"

"Of course it is," said Joe with a straight face.

"Awesome, this is so awesome, Harrison Ford's lighter." Mary Lou looked at Joe for a moment. Suddenly she sounded very serious, "Do you know that there are people who would kill for the type of information you want?"

Joe nodded.

Mary Lou clutched the lighter in one hand and slowly caressed Harrison Ford's photo with the other, "Would you be able to get me something from Tom Cruise?" she asked.

Joe's smile stretched from ear to ear. He knew he was in.

"I'll meet you at six o'clock sharp. Go to the fire door half way down the right side of the building," Mary Lou said nervously.

"Thanks," said Joe. "You won't regret this."

"I hope not."

Milking it to the very end, Joe stood up like a gentleman and waved to Mary Lou who was now on the other side of the street. Once she was out of sight, he clutched his fist and punched the air smugly.

"Hey, you Hollywood assholes, how about that for a performance?"

———————————

Things may have been heading in the right direction for Joe, but Weinberg wasn't so lucky. In fact, his day started out badly and quickly got worse. Locked in a cramped smoke filled studio in Lower Manhattan, he was surrounded by guys he didn't know saying things he didn't like.

"Phil, have you got something with more of an edge to it? Mr Weinberg, is this all you have today?"

He was pissed off. Not only did he have a sore ass from sitting on a metal fold up chair for twelve hours, he also realized he'd got it completely wrong. After years as the number one sleaze king in L.A. he incorrectly assumed that he would just walk in and take over New York. Maybe he was too comfortable in the sunshine. Had he become complacent? Whatever the reason, he had to fix it, because he was fast running out of people to see.

CHAPTER TWENTY

Joe parked his truck down the street from the Bureau of Vital Statistics and walked around the block to approach the fire door from the rear. Having seen a security camera in the entrance hall, he assumed that the outside of the building would be covered in them, but he was wrong. There wasn't a camera in sight.

It was a couple of minutes to six when he arrived at the door and tugged on the handle; it was locked. A couple of minutes later he made another unsuccessful attempt to open the door.

"Where the hell is she?" he muttered through gritted teeth.

He started to panic and paced incessantly. Then, with his back to the door, he slammed the heel of his right boot into the base of the fortified fire exit and shuddered as the sound reverberated off the adjacent concrete walls like an exploding bomb. At that same moment, Mary Lou opened the door and glared menacingly into his eyes. With chin jutting forward, veins on her neck punching through the skin and eyes just about bulging out of their sockets, she looked nothing like the sweet, sallow, mid fifties woman he'd met a few hours earlier. If looks could kill, he'd be suffering a long slow painful death.

"What the hell are you doing?" yelled Mary Lou. "If your dumb ass move had been ten seconds earlier you would have been face to face with my boss instead of me. Are you trying to get me fired?"

Joe was almost knocked over by her outburst, but he knew she was right. With head bowed like a schoolboy being ticked off by his teacher, he braced himself as her rant continued.

"Why couldn't you just wait? I said I was going to be there

at six and I was. Never mind losing my job... we could have been arrested."

Mary Lou took a deep breath and waited for Joe to respond, but he'd already said sorry earlier in the day and didn't want to do it again. "Sorry" was for special occasions like when the shit is about hit the fan and you haven't got time to duck. "Sorry" made Joe feel as if he'd surrendered and that wasn't something he did very often. Eventually the extended silence got to him so he said the first thing that came into his head.

"There are no cameras," he mumbled while staring at the floor.

"Government cutbacks," replied a less tense Mary Lou as she led him down a dimly lit hallway.

The interior was typical of most local government buildings. Pale green paint, similar to that found in public restrooms and swimming pools, covered the walls while cold marble floors ensured that the occupants didn't get too comfortable standing around in the hall. There was a stiffness, a business like atmosphere that spread throughout the core of the building, until that is, he stumbled upon Mary Lou's work-station.

Here was a shrine to Hollywood and almost every male hunk that had ever made it on to the screen. Huge brightly colored film posters adorned the wall behind her chair while on the front of her desk hung pictures of stars spanning over half a century. Bogart, Hudson, Curtis, Redford, Newman, Stallone and many, many more were strategically situated along her sight line. Harrison Ford's picture and lighter had been given pride of place next to her computer. There wasn't a picture of a female star in sight.

With one hand on a CD and the other on Joe's shoulder she issued instructions like she would to a child. Using words of mostly one syllable, she spoke slowly and directly at Joe.

"If anyone asks, you work for JMS and you're here to install this program in my computer... OK?"

She spoke to him like he was a retard and he knew why, but didn't care. He just nodded and sat down at the computer while Mary Lou stood behind him, leaned over his right shoulder and logged on. Long after she'd finished she remained hunched over, pressing her breasts into his body Once again Joe bit the bullet. The "come on" looks, the touches and the innocent giggles were now more acceptable to him than when they first met. He had no choice, but to put up with it and in a strange way he enjoyed it. Knowing that she wanted him gave him power. He liked power.

"You have twenty five minutes," said Mary Lou as she left the room to get a coffee.

"Why?" yelled Joe as he stared at the screen.

"Cleaners."

Joe couldn't believe the amount of detailed information available to him at the touch of a key. It was heaven and the Holy Grail all wrapped into one for anybody into identity theft and it was a nightmare and an accident waiting to happen for those civil liberty groups that say our government holds too much personal information. It was all there at his fingertips. There wasn't anything he couldn't find. Addresses, previous addresses, marriage and divorce details, dates of birth, maiden names, names changed in the County court and even details of gender changes flashed before his eyes. In the time available, Joe printed off as much information as he could.

"You have to go," said Mary Lou with a sense of urgency in her voice, "Did you get what you wanted?"

"Just about," said Joe grabbing his jacket from the back of the chair. "Any chance I can come back?"

"It'll have to be the same time tomorrow night. After that I'm all out of late shifts for a while."

"Perfect," said Joe as he made his way to the fire exit, "see you then."

As Joe pushed down on the hand-rail Mary Lou squeezed between him and the door before he could open it. She placed her arms around his neck and pulled his head down until it rested against hers and with mouth wide open her tongue shot forward and darted between his lips. Joe was trapped and there was nothing he could do.

"I want you," she whispered.

Hearing the clattering noise of cleaner's buckets in the

background; she released her grip and stepped to one side. "See you tomorrow, honey."

Joe forced a smile then walked quickly back to his truck. Supporting himself on the door handle he hunched over and began coughing and spitting violently like a cat trying to dislodge a fur ball from its throat. Tears flowed from his eyes and the sleeve of his jacket became drenched in saliva as he tried in vain to wipe away every last remnant of that kiss.

"Honey," he growled. "I'm not your goddamn honey."

DAY EIGHT

CHAPTER TWENTY-ONE

Leigh stared blankly across the room while rolling a pen between her thumb and forefinger. She felt like her brain was shrivelling up inside her head.

"If I don't use it, I'll lose it," she mumbled as she looked down at the stack of papers labeled filing. A few days in the secretarial pool and already she was feeling twitchy. She needed a challenge. Performing mindless tasks while chained to a desk was how she started and coming full circle wasn't in her game plan. With the buzz and excitement of real life detective work just a few feet away, she wanted out. She knew that being an investigative journalist and having a brother who was a cop didn't entitle her to hang out with L.A.'s finest. She didn't expect to hit the streets and kick ass. She wasn't a cop and didn't pretend to be one; she just wanted to think like one.

But it should have been obvious when she first walked through the door on the day of the funeral that this was a "Gentleman's Club". There wasn't a female detective in sight. A couple of pretty young girls work as "gophers" and Alex was there to massage the male ego when bruised, but that was it.

And if there were to be a President of this Club it would have to be John Heinz. And if there was one guy who made Leigh's toes curl, it would also have to be Heinz. An ex-marine with a tour of duty in *Operation Desert Storm* he was the epitome of the male chauvinist. His chiselled features, his "high and tight" haircut, tattooed forearms and immaculately shined shoes were signs that he was "clear and present danger" for any woman who got in his way.

"How many men does it take to open a beer?" asked Heinz when Leigh entered the office. "None," he said without waiting for an answer, "it should be open when she brings it to him."

That would have been enough to send most women running for cover, but not Leigh. She had the tools to mix it up with the best of them. She wasn't Lara Croft, but she could handle most weapons, drive large off road vehicles and drink just about any man under the table so she wasn't about to be intimidated by Heinz.

Focusing her attention on the first mundane task of the day, Leigh collected a stack of case files and headed towards a large gray multi drawer cabinet on the far side of the room. On the way, she bumped into Moose.

"How's it going?" he asked with a smile that stretched the width of his face.

"I'm good, and you?"

Moose nodded as his six foot three and two hundred and forty pound frame towered over her. She was glad he'd broken the ice. She'd been watching him for a couple of days; there was something about him she liked. She didn't know if he was just shy or didn't have anything to say, although she heard through the grapevine he had a habit of spewing out endless reams of trivia collected from years of watching TV shows like *Jeopardy*. Despite his size he wasn't threatening, in fact just the opposite. And she loved the story the girls told about his mother, a French Canadian, who called him "my little mouse" because, as a baby, he nibbled his food while holding it with both hands. Apparently, "Mouse" quickly became"Moose" because she spoke with a heavy accent. Leigh said nothing as she stared at him, but she wasn't convinced that this was how the nickname came about. The word in the office was that no one ever messed with him. He carried a gun, but never took it out of the holster. He didn't need to.

––––––––––––––––––––

There may have been an interesting mix of people around her, but Leigh was still bored. With a job description that included such mundane tasks as typing, filing and answering the phone, she knew that it would only be a matter of time before she quit or put a gun to her head. She not only needed a challenge, but she needed it now and she knew exactly where to look. Having already scanned the Sergio Ramos file on her first day at work, it was an obvious place to start. And the more she read the more she realized that so many things about this case didn't make sense.

To begin with, Ramos wasn't on the run or carrying drugs so why did he shoot a cop who just wanted to talk to him about a broken tail-light? Who or what was he afraid of? The records show he held a "Green Card", so he wouldn't have worried even if Mike had been from Immigration.

She felt angry and frustrated too when she saw the words "CASE CLOSED" stamped in capital letters across the cover of the file. It would have been so easy for her to put the file back in the cupboard and let "sleeping dogs lie", but she believed that Mike deserved better. She knew that he would have done the same for her.

Who was this Mexican that took her brother's life? She had to know but if she were to do anything she would have to do it alone. This was Dan's case and any intrusion would be as good as saying he messed up, got it wrong. Besides she thought, *who was going to join forces with someone nicknamed, Miss Conspiracy?*

CHAPTER TWENTY-TWO

It had taken several hours and more than a couple of beers for Joe to justify swapping spit with Mary Lou, but he finally did it and it was so simple. He was an actor and the role he played involved making out with a woman old enough to be his mom. It wasn't prostitution; it was part of the script. And now that he was armed with more personal ammunition than he could ever believe possible, he set about trying to bring that script to life. With a bottle between his legs and his Hendrix tape crackling through his fragile speakers, he drove his pickup deep into the city knowing that things would be more complicated than when he first started putting this idea together. He understood that fiction is made up, imaginary, and anything is possible. If he wanted to say there's a train wreck then he'd say it and the audience would believe him. But what he was planning to do was real with real people, real emotions and real consequences. He wasn't just saying it, he was about to do it. Planning and timing were essential. It had to be right because this was going to be a train wreck that would affect at lot of people and one *they* would tell their grandchildren about.

With a page full of names and locations to research, Joe crisscrossed the city stopping for long periods at a time with engine off and lights out. It was exciting and for a while he felt like Gene Hackman in the *French Connection*. Watching, listening, spying, ducking and diving and then running like hell for cover when he got too close. Even though he couldn't think straight and it was impossible to make notes because his hands were shaking, he wondered why he'd never thought of doing this before. He was shit scared and he loved it. His heart was beating at a hundred miles an hour and his mind wasn't far behind, but he wouldn't trade it for anything. It was unbelievable and the titles hadn't even started to roll.

Running on empty with the sun coming up and traffic building, Joe decided to call it quits for the night and head home. On the way, he pulled into a twenty-four hour gun shop to buy a rifle, but was told that it would take a minimum of ten days for Federal and State checks to clear him. Tired and hungry and unwilling to take no for an answer, he argued he was an American citizen and had the right to bear arms, but was told that checks were made to ensure that guns were not sold to felons or anyone with mental illness.

"Do I look like a criminal or a goddamn lunatic?" yelled Joe to the man behind the counter.

It was a rhetorical question and Joe wasn't expecting an answer, but he got one.

"Take a look in a mirror, asshole. That should answer your question."

Joe clenched his fists and glared directly at the guy who just called him an asshole.

"Don't even think about it," said a deep voice from behind a tinted glass window.

Joe couldn't see who owned the voice, but it didn't matter. He didn't like the odds. After slamming the door on the way out, he climbed into his truck and started to pull out of the yard then quickly pressed on the brakes and glanced in the mirror. The guy was right. He looked like shit. Unshaven with bloodshot eyes and circles so dark and large that he could have easily been mistaken for a member of Kiss.

An hour later Joe had showered and shaved and was sitting on his couch in his underwear eating coco puffs from the box. The milk in the fridge was given a wide berth because it was turning into cheese. Two slices of bread laced with green mould occupied the bottom shelf along with a six-pack of Bud. He couldn't remember the last time he went to the supermarket to buy anything other than beer.

With the toe of his right foot he pushed a tape into his VCR and then pressed fast forward on the remote. The picture came to an abrupt halt when it got to a TV commercial starring Marty King, "King of the Road." A well-dressed black man standing in front of a sea of used cars announced, "Hi, I'm Marty King."

Joe stopped the tape and like a child watching an English pantomime, shouted, "Oh no you're not."

He laughed as he rewound the tape and played it again.

"Hi, I'm Marty King."

Again, Joe shouted at the man on the screen, "Oh no you're fucking not!" It was a private joke that was soon about to become very, very public.

CHAPTER TWENTY-THREE

Gomez was standing next to a brand new white Bentley Continental GT when Joe pulled into Tata's parking lot.

"What do you think, should I buy this one?" yelled the young Mexican as Joe got out of his truck.

Gomez came from a poor family and loved to pretend that he could buy the cars that he parked and Joe always went along with the gag.

"I don't know," said Joe shaking his head, "I think it makes you look like a pimp."

"Really?" questioned Gomez moving to his right. "How about this?" pointing to a black Mercedes SL.

Joe deliberated for a moment. "Mmmm no, that one makes you look like a drug dealer."

Gomez then ran across the lot and stood next to Joe's pickup.

"What about this beauty?" he shouted with a big smile on his face.

"No, that one's not for you either," said Joe, "unless of course you want to look like a farmer taking his chickens to market."

Joe's remark brought an abrupt and awkward end to the joke. It was the first time that Gomez had heard Joe say anything negative about himself. Usually he was cocky and confident with a "go for it" attitude. Was this a sign? Was Joe letting Gomez get close to him or was he trying to get closer to Gomez?

As they walked towards the vehicle drop off and collection point Gomez was asked about growing up in Mexico and his new life in California. Joe's questions were personal and caring and surprised the hell out of the man from south of the border.

Who was this guy? he thought. For the first time ever Joe was taking an interest in someone other than himself. They talked for about fifteen minutes and not once did they mention drugs or getting laid. It was a refreshing change for Gomez who lived in a neighborhood where violence, drugs and prostitution were in his face 24/7.

Their conversation was put on hold while Joe parked an immaculately restored deep blue 1963 Corvette, the one with the split rear window. He looked it over inside and out and ran his hand gently along the body-line.

"They don't make 'em like this anymore," he yelled across the lot. "It's all about luxury and comfort and nothing to do with the thrill of the ride."

Then as Joe walked back to where his friend was standing and without even blinking an eye he asked, "Do you know anyone who can get me a semi automatic rifle?"

Wow! Gomez hadn't seen that coming. For a moment he was stunned, but then he realized that Joe had been building up to this all along. Their conversation had just been foreplay.

"You piss me off man," shouted Gomez. "Why the fuck didn't you just come out and ask me instead of filling my head with that caring, sharing crap?"

Joe hung his head and said nothing. The Mexican couldn't tell whether he was acting or genuinely didn't know what to say. After a long pause Joe finally asked, "Well, yes or no?"

It didn't take long for him to make a decision. Gomez wasn't a guy who held a grudge especially when there was money to be made.

"I know a guy who can sell you a tank if you want one... you do know that you can buy a rifle a whole lot cheaper in a gun shop?"

"I need it now," said Joe, avoiding his stare.

"Hunting?" asked Gomez

"Yeah, something like that."

Gomez walked away from the front of the restaurant and made a call on his cell phone and was back before Joe knew he had left. "He'll be here in an hour," Gomez said.

"I don't fucking believe it," laughed Joe, "you got a guy on speed dial who sells guns?"

"Hey man, with the touch of a button I can get you just about anything you want. Don't you just love technology?"

"Where were you when I needed someone to read my script?" asked Joe.

While Joe paced anxiously around the outside of the restaurant waiting for his gun-runner to show, Leigh sat patiently at her desk and set out her investigation strategy. It was simple: find out more about Sergio Ramos. To do this she would either have to talk to his brother or talk to US Customs and Immigration Services. Thirty minutes into her call with the country's immigration service Leigh had lost the will to live and was kicking herself for not making the journey to the fat man's house. Number punching took forever and when she finally got to speak to a human, she was passed from one department to another. Time and time again she heard the same impersonal message.

Your call is important to us, please hold.

She couldn't take anymore. She hung up.

Leigh may have been temporarily stalled, but Joe's day continued to roll as a black Maybach Landaulet slinked on to the lot and then shot to the rear of the restaurant before backing in next to Joe's pickup. A moment later a second Mercedes stopped just inside the entrance.

"He's here," said Gomez, tapping Joe on the shoulder.

"Who are they?" enquired Joe pointing to a couple of large men in a Merc at the entrance.

"Back up."

As Joe and Gomez approached the car a large black body guard the size of a small house got out from behind the wheel.

"You Gomez?" he asked.

Gomez nodded obediently. The bodyguard then rapped his knuckle on the window of the car and out stepped a skinny little white man in a gray suit looking more like an accountant than a gunrunner. He popped the trunk and showed off a selection of handguns and rifles.

"It's for him," said Gomez pointing to his friend.

Joe introduced himself and reached out as if to shake the skinny man's hand, but was completely blanked with the man preferring to concentrate on what was in the trunk.

"Take your pick," he said, "they all come with an 'out of sight' guarantee."

Joe couldn't believe this was going down right before his eyes. It was surreal. Rifles, shotguns, handguns and even a sub machine gun filled the trunk of the big Mercedes. He was desperate to pull one out, lock it into his shoulder, look down the barrel through the sight and pull the trigger, but that wasn't going to happen, not here anyway. He was having so much fun. A few hours ago he was on a stakeout, climbing fences and peeping into houses through cracks in curtains. Now he was standing shoulder to shoulder with a genuine bad guy.

"Hurry up," said the man in the gray suit, "you're not in fucking Wal-Mart now."

Anxious not to piss the guy off, Joe pointed to the rifle on the top of the pile. "I'll take that one."

"Semi automatic, good choice... that'll be fifteen hundred bucks."

Joe swallowed hard. He had the money, but wasn't expecting to pay that much. The guy at the gun shop was going to charge less than half that amount, but there was a catch, a ten day wait and the name Joe Tubbs written all over the gun.

Fuck it, he thought as he pulled out a wad of money and handed over fifteen Ben Franklins.

"Got some ammo?" asked Joe, trying to be cool and fully expecting them to be included in the price of the rifle.

A small cardboard box was slipped discreetly into his hand. "Two hundred bucks," said the guy without moving his lips, "and don't forget to pick up the spent cartridges ... it's against the law to litter."

Joe took a breath. He knew he was being taken for a ride, but there was nothing he could do about it. He had come too far to turn back now. Squeezing the rifle tightly in his hand his mind wandered. Hendrix was talking and this time he was talking only to him. *Hey Joe where you goin' with that gun in your hand?* Joe smiled and slipped the rifle under his jacket in the cab of his truck. When he looked around everyone except Gomez was gone.

———————————————

It was now five forty-five p.m. Joe should have been at work until eight p.m., but he had arranged to see Mary Lou in fifteen minutes.

"Cover for me," he yelled as he drove quickly past the front of the restaurant.

"No problem, catch you later," shouted Gomez.

CHAPTER TWENTY-FOUR

It seemed like a good idea at the time, but now Leigh wasn't so sure. Sitting huddled in her Beetle outside Ramos' house; she carefully scanned the neighborhood before even thinking about stepping out on to the street. Just ahead of her was a gang of teenage boys playing "king of the castle" on a refrigerator that had been dumped on the corner. Twenty feet to the rear of her car stood two middle aged black men. They didn't speak. They didn't have to. *What the hell are you doing here* was written all over their faces?

Over to her right, Ricardo's Monte Carlo was parked diagonally across the lawn blocking the path that led to his front door. His house was desperate for a little TLC and DIY. Peeling paint, missing roof tiles, broken windows and a screen door with a hole so big you could walk through it gave the impression the house was derelict. Overflowing garbage cans on the lawn told a different story. This was a far cry from small town Montana where every house was well presented and the tiniest piece of litter was often collected before it hit the ground. Leigh was curious yet afraid.

As she sat alone thinking about her next move the front door of her car swung open. Falling to the right she raised her left arm for protection. A huge body in a garish shirt stood by the open door. Leigh recognized the sweat-stained armpits; it was Ricardo Ramos.

"If they want to take your car they'll take it," said Ricardo, glancing at the kids on the corner. "They don't care if you're in it or not. A local myth says they can even steal a set of hubcaps at speeds up to thirty miles per hour, but I've never seen it. Would you like to come in?"

Leigh glared at the offer of a helping hand. *This is surreal,* she thought. *It's not right.* Most normal people would have been out of there in a heartbeat, but she wanted to get to the truth and Ricardo Ramos was possibly her only hope.

Placing two fingers to his lips, the Mexican let go a short high-pitched whistle that quickly caught the attention of the kids on the corner. The boy on top of the fridge looked over at him and nodded, "Don't worry they'll look after of your car," he told her.

Leigh threw her bag over her right shoulder and placed her hand in the bag as she walked towards the house.

"I don't suppose you've been in California long enough to have a license for a firearm, so I can only assume that your right hand is holding either a knife or a can of CS gas," stated Ricardo. "Relax I'm not going to hurt you. You didn't kill Sergio, he killed himself."

Leigh entered the house with her hand still tucked inside her bag.

CHAPTER TWENTY-FIVE

Joe was late. An accident on the road to the Bureau left traffic at a standstill. When he eventually arrived there was no time to drive around the block and park behind Mary Lou's office so he pulled into a visitor bay in front of the police station. Running first along the front of the station and then the Bureau, he made a left turn down the path leading to the fire exit where he stopped and waited. Barely thirty seconds passed before he glanced at his watch. Another thirty seconds and another time check. Pacing up and down, he suddenly caught a glimpse of his boot mark still clearly visible on the base of the door and knew that he had to calm down. But it wasn't that easy. It was 6:10 and time was running out. The cleaners would be there soon. Finally, Mary Lou came to the door.

Looking at Joe, she said in a patronizing tone, "You've been a good boy, haven't you?"

At first he wasn't sure what she meant so he just smiled.

"Thanks for not kicking down the door. I just got rid of Rambo, our head of security. Christ, if he knew what we were doing he'd shoot us both."

A chill ran through Joe's body. Mary Lou's reference to getting shot reminded him that his rifle was in the truck and his truck was parked in front of a building full of cops. There was nothing he could do. He didn't have time to go back to get it and even if he did, there was nowhere else to hide it.

"Great," he said sarcastically as if replying to Mary Lou's comment. Once inside, Joe ran to Mary Lou's work-station, hurriedly lowered himself onto her dark blue, hard as a rock, swivel chair and immediately began to pound on her keyboard. Mary Lou quietly circled the desk.

"What's up?" said Joe keeping his eyes on the screen.

"I was wondering if we could go for a drink tonight."

"That would be great, but not tonight. I need a couple more days to finish the script. Once I get this thing off to Warner Brothers, I'll be clear."

Mary Lou went quiet. She glared at Joe. Although he wasn't looking at her he sensed that something was wrong. He could feel her eyes burning into the back of his head.

"Now what's up?" he asked, rolling his eyes.

"Are you jerking me around?"

"Huh," said Joe completely shocked by her change of attitude.

"You told me Fox, the script was for Fox."

Joe kept his eyes focused on the screen and carried on typing as if nothing was wrong. *Shit,* he thought to himself. *How did she remember that? Fucking women, they got memories like elephants.*

"You're right, the script is for Fox," said Joe with conviction, "but I have another one I'm working on for Warner's. This whole goddamn thing has been so stressful... and when I get stressed, I get confused."

Joe held his breath. Had he done enough or would she reach over, press the "off" button and tell him to go?

The answer came quickly. Mary Lou fell for it hook, line and sinker. "Poor baby," she whispered as she began massaging his shoulders. "I know a great way of getting rid of all that stress."

"Sounds good to me," replied Joe, like he'd been asked if he wanted fried eggs for breakfast. "Just let me finish."

Mary Lou gave up. She knew she couldn't compete with what he was doing so she left him alone. As soon as she walked out of the room, Joe clenched his fist and punched the air to celebrate another convincing performance.

"And they said I couldn't act."

It was now 6:30 p.m. and Joe had finished what he had come to do, but instead of trying to find Mary Lou to say goodbye, he deliberately set off in the opposite direction. She was no longer needed and besides he was tired of her immature references to sex. He'd used her just like she was going to use him. He didn't feel guilty. He didn't feel anything. It was strange. It was like she never existed.

For the next couple of minutes Joe wandered around the building just because he could. He didn't have a clue where he was going and soon found himself in a hallway leading to a door with a sign that read "Authorized Personnel Only". Then, as he turned to retrace his steps, he heard voices in the corridor. He was trapped. His mind flashed back to when he was a small boy crawling through a tiny opening in a fence to get away from a gang of older boys who were trying to steal his candies. Once through the hole he felt safe and even took time to tease the kids on the other side of the fence. His self-satisfaction soon turned to fear when a deep rumbling growl from a German shepherd dog the size of a horse broke the silence of his safe haven. Joe's little legs quickly carried him to a nearby shed and as he slammed the door it caught the tip of the dog's nose. An ear shattering yelp sent shivers down Joe's back. He sensed the dog was now even more annoyed than before. Peeping through a crack in the wood he came eye to eye with the beast while in the distance he could see a gate and freedom.

Having accepted that this could be a long tedious stand off, he sat on the floor with his back pressing tightly against the door and munched quietly on Life Savers and Tootsie Rolls. Then, out of nowhere came a stroke of genius. Opening the door to just over finger width, he flicked a Life Saver on to the lawn. The dog turned and was on it in a flash. With the door open even wider, he threw another Life Saver into the air and again the dog pounced. He liked what he saw. It was now or never. Stepping outside the shed, he tossed a handful of Life Savers in the opposite direction to the gate. The German shepherd reacted as expected and Joe ran to safety.

Two lessons should have been learned from this experience.

Sometimes when you jump out of the frying pan you end up in the fire and sometimes you have to make big sacrifices to save your ass.

As the voices in the corridor got closer Joe was ready to dive into the unknown just like he did all those years ago and once again he wasn't worried about who or what was on the other side. His philosophy was simple. Take care of the first problem and deal with the next one as and when it comes along. Would there be sacrifices? Only time would tell.

With shoulders back and chin lifted he strolled confidently through the door into an open plan room filled with cluttered desks, used coffee cups and ringing phones. Turning 360 degrees, he couldn't believe his luck; the place was deserted. He felt smug until he discovered that he had stumbled through a connecting door that led to Homicide. Running away crossed his mind, but he couldn't; it was too exciting to leave. The whole thing was giving him a rush and there wasn't a drug in sight. Strolling casually around the desks he stopped to peer into drawers and sift through papers. It was like he had all the time in the world. When he arrived at Leigh's desk he looked through two drawers until he turned over a framed High School photo that prompted him to scream, "thank you God, thank you, thank you, thank you."

Joe's journey into the unknown had just produced a gem. He was happy. Now it was time to go. As he made his way along the wall towards the exit, he reached out to push the swinging door just as Dan came into the room. The detective's hand landed squarely on Joe's chest

"What are doing here?" asked Dan in a stern voice.

"Working, what do you think?" replied Joe arrogantly.

"Where, smart-ass?"

"In the Bureau, installing this program," said Joe pulling a disc out of his back pocket.

"So how did you end up here?"

"I got lost; it's a fucking maze in there."

Whoever he was, Dan didn't like him. He was cocky, aggressive and had a look deep inside his eyes that put him right on the edge. Just as the detective was about to delve a little deeper his phone in the office rang. With no one around to answer it, Dan reluctantly pulled his hand back from Joe's chest and stepped aside. Both men studied each other closely before going their separate ways.

When Joe made it safely outside he took a deep breath and chuckled. "Joe Tubbs has finally left the building."

Reaching into the pocket of his jeans he pulled out his keys and the notes he'd printed off Mary Lou's computer. During the short walk to his truck he studied the paper and quietly mocked, "Thanks Mary Lou, this stuff is awesome." Inserting his key into the lock, he opened the door and then quickly slammed it shut again when he saw a uniformed officer coming towards him.

"Do you own that pickup?" asked the cop.

Shit, thought Joe.

As the cop came closer, Joe thought for a brief moment about going for his gun, but decided against it and then he considered running away, but where would he go? His mouth was dry as he began to speak.

"Yeah, you wanna buy it?"

"No," laughed the cop, "but my brother-in-law has got one just like it and is having trouble getting a replacement tailgate."

With color slowly returning to Joe's cheeks, he deliberately moved towards the rear of the truck to keep the cop from poking his nose inside the cab.

"Got a pen?" asked Joe

The cop handed over his pen and Joe scribbled down a number, "If this guy doesn't have it then he'll know someone who does."

"Thanks," said the cop, "appreciate it."

Joe waited until the cop was back inside the station before he opened the door to his truck. He shook his head, looked down at the partially covered rifle and said, "I need a drink."

Upstairs, Dan hung up the phone and went to the window overlooking the parking lot just as Joe turned onto the street. He got a good look at the truck, but couldn't see the plates. The pickup disappeared down the road.

"What were you really doing here, smartass?" he mumbled.

CHAPTER TWENTY-SIX

Leigh couldn't believe her eyes. Ricardo's bungalow was spotless. The wooden floors were highly polished and the coffee table was clean with no sign of coffee cup or beer bottle rings and the sofa nicely covered with Mexican throw rugs.

How could this be? she thought. *The man's a slob and the outside of his house is a pigsty.*

"Can I get you something to drink?" asked Ricardo.

"No thanks."

"Do you mind if I have a beer, it's been a long day?"

"It's your house," Leigh snapped.

As he disappeared into the kitchen, Leigh spotted a letter on the coffee table. She picked it up and turned it over. It was addressed to Ricardo with a return address from Mrs A. Ramos in Tijuana.

"I guess you're wondering how I keep this place so clean?" said Ricardo walking back into the living room.

Leigh was starting to wonder if this guy was psychic. He seemed to know what she was thinking. "It had crossed my mind," she said

"Mexican cleaners are cheap," he laughed, "some of the women will even work for nothing if you give their husbands a job. I do it all the time at the car wash. Maybe you should get one for your place above the hardware."

Leigh was shocked. "How do you know where I live?" she asked angrily.

"Don't panic, I'm not a stalker. I followed Dan, the detective friend of yours, when he drove you home after the funeral."

"Why?"

"To kill him," said Ricardo nonchalantly.

Leigh thought he was just joking and waited for his

expression to change, but it didn't. "You're serious," she said.

"The gun was loaded; the safety was off."

"Why didn't you go through with it?"

"It wasn't right, shooting a cop...you gotta be crazy to do that."

"Like your brother?" she asked.

"Sergio mixed with the wrong people. He was always going to die a violent death."

"Why did he shoot Mike?"

"I don't know," said Ricardo, "I wish I did."

She didn't believe him. Sensing he knew more than he was prepared to say she tried to make eye contact, but he refused to look at her.

"I gotta go back to work," said Ricardo abruptly

"Thanks for your time," said Leigh.

"Sorry, I couldn't help."

At the front door she turned her head and looked into the room, "Do you ever go back to Tijuana to see your parents?" she asked.

Ricardo glanced over at the envelope on the coffee table and smiled knowingly. "My father's dead... and no, I haven't been back to see my mother for about six months."

"You should see her more often; you never know when you're going to lose her." Leigh smiled thinly at the look on the Mexican's face. He wasn't sure how to take that. Was she just being caring or was it a threat?

When she got back to the street Leigh was grinning from ear to ear as she opened the door to her Beetle. It wasn't conclusive, it wouldn't stand up in court nor would it convince Dan that there was anything more to investigate, but she had finally found something to link her killer to her brother. Tijuana! Her parents had been killed there, Mike had gone there to bring back their bodies and Sergio Ramos and his family lived there.

As soon as Leigh was gone, Ramos called his mother, "Hi Momma, are you well? Good... Miguel from the garage is coming in the morning to take the car away. I know it's only a year old... don't worry I'll handle it. I'm sending you an airline ticket. We'll talk later... love you, bye."

CHAPTER TWENTY-SEVEN

When Joe got home he wrapped the rifle in an old blanket and hid it next to the coalbunker in the basement. Upstairs in the living room, plans were being made for an all-nighter. Lines of "nose powder" stretched across the table, the fridge was packed with Bud and family packs of pretzels and lightly salted potato chips were thrown on the couch. One by one the lights on his stereo came to life. The turntable rotated in a clockwise direction as Joe's favorite Hendrix album, *Are you Experienced*, was taken from the rack on the floor, wiped with a small clean cloth and placed gently on the spinning disc. Joe believed in vinyl. He loved the sound. The imperfections, the crackling and the feeling that you are there with the band were what made it so special. He felt the same about AM radio. CDs and FM were going in the wrong direction. Everything was too perfect, too clean. There was no edge. The sound had become "airbrushed" just like the faces of those models you see on the front of fashion magazines.

It was just after eight o'clock when Joe slouched onto the sofa and placed his fingers on the keys to his laptop. It had been a crazy day. He had bought a gun, stolen confidential information and bluffed his way out of a couple of sticky situations with the cops. Now it was time to put the finishing touches to his story.

Weinberg was still trying to make a buck from his disastrous week in New York. He was tired, fed up and planning to go home. His movie catalogue had failed to excite in every sense of the word. He would have had more luck selling tanning machines to a skin cancer ward.

Lonnie, his old school buddy and full time pimp, had arranged for them to have lunch at Katz's Delicatessen on the Lower East Side. This is where Meg Ryan faked an orgasm in *Harry met Sally*. Weinberg knew it well. Not only was he partial to films with orgasms, but he was also a big fan of the pastrami on rye and secretly yearned for his photo to be placed on the wall of fame alongside those of the presidents, rock legends and movie stars who had eaten there.

Lonnie wasn't aware that Weinberg was having a bad week and Weinberg wasn't about to tell him. He didn't exactly lie, but Weinberg did mention *"future projects"* and *"things in the pipeline"* when asked, "How's it going?"

Standing next to each other, the two men looked comical. Weinberg was tall and thin with long unkempt hair. A monobrow gave his pointed facial features a sinister look. Lonnie was short and overweight with a round "full moon" face. His hair looked like it had been styled by a monk and he had the breath of a dozen camels.

"Phil, I'm gonna cut to the chase," said Lonnie as he worked his way through a plate of liverwurst. "I invited you here because I wanted to see you again, but also because I wanna do business with you. Well, that ain't exactly true..." He added reluctantly, "My wife wants me to go straight and you're the only guy I know who isn't a crook."

Weinberg didn't know what to say. This was fantastic news even if Lonnie's reasons for wanting to go into business with him were less than flattering. He couldn't believe it. He thought about checking the date on his BlackBerry to see if it was April 1st, but that wasn't necessary. He knew Lonnie better than anybody and could tell from the look on his face that his old buddy was serious. Weinberg reacted calmly although inside he felt like dancing on the table.

"Is your dick big enough to be in one of my movies?" he joked.

"I've seen the girls in your movies and my left leg wouldn't be big enough never mind my dick," replied Lonnie, "Look,

I don't wanna be a star... I wanna back you but not with that porn shit... I want to make a real film, you know with action and suspense... Can you do it?"

Weinberg was so desperate he would have said yes to a remake of Mary Poppins.

"No problem, but it's gonna cost," he said.

"I got the money, don't worry. We just have to be a bit creative about the source," said Lonnie quietly.

"I'll start looking at scripts," said Weinberg. "This is great; it'll be just like the old days."

"Shit, I hope not," laughed Lonnie. "I spent most of the old days in jail."

CHAPTER TWENTY-EIGHT

After three hours of staring at the ceiling, Leigh turned on the light, propped her pillow up against the headboard and grabbed a pencil off the bedside table. She'd had enough. The meeting with Ramos was still spinning round and round in her head and wasn't about to go away. Something had to be done. She needed to see things in black and white. With a newspaper on her lap she started to doodle in the margin next to her unsuccessful attempt at completing a crossword puzzle earlier in the evening.

Tijuana was the key and the center of her diagram. At twelve o'clock she drew a line that ended with "Mom & Dad". At four o'clock she drew another line leading to 'Mike'. A third line at eight o'clock finished with "Sergio Ramos". A line was then drawn from "Mike" to "Mom & Dad" and another from "Mike" to "Ramos" to show that they had been in contact with each other. The left hand side of the triangle was open. There was no line between "Ramos" and "Mom & Dad".

Suddenly, things were more black than white. The power failed for the second time that night.

"Mike, my darling brother, what the hell were you thinking when you bought this place?"

She knew there was nothing she could do to kick-start the power. Banging walls, pulling wires and swearing at anything with a plug just didn't work. The electricity would flow again in its own sweet time.

What the hell am I doing here? she thought as she sat helpless in the dark.

Ten minutes later everything returned to normal. The refrigerator motor hummed from the far side of the kitchen while the small electric clock next to her bed began to tick. It was 2 a.m., give or take a few minutes for power outages. Leigh got out of bed still clutching the newspaper and went into the kitchen to make herself a coffee. She paced up and down avoiding the gaps in the floor, while the water came to a boil. Over and over she repeated, "Mike, my parents and Ramos spent time in Tijuana. Mike pulled Ramos over because of a broken taillight, but did Mike know Ramos before he stopped him? Ramos shot Mike, which everyone says was a random act, but did Ramos know Mike before he killed him?"

Leigh stared at the sketch she'd made on the newspaper. If she could draw a line between her parents and Ramos it would close the triangle. It would show that her parents had been in contact with Ramos and it would mean that coincidence was no longer an option.

It wasn't going to be easy though because everyone in the triangle was dead. But she knew from experience that even the dead have a story to tell. Making her way back into the bedroom she opened the closet door and pulled out the cardboard box filled with Mike's personal effects. Next to the box was a plastic folder containing his private papers. It was hard enough living in his apartment with his clothes hanging on the rails and the scent from his aftershave still lingering in the bathroom. The last thing she wanted to do was delve into his private life, but it had to be done even if it was like reading someone else's diary.

Leigh placed Mike's papers carefully on the bed. She grabbed the pillow, stuffed it under her head and tucked her feet beneath the blanket. It was going to be a long night.

CHAPTER TWENTY-NINE

Joe needed a break. He'd been hunched over his laptop for so long that his back was killing him and his neck wasn't much better. A loud cracking noise echoed around the room when he tilted his head to the left.

That was scary, he thought, *it's time to get my ass out of here.*

Massaging the back of his neck with one hand and collecting his keys with the other, he calmly headed for his pickup. PJ's was calling. Officially the place closed at 3 a.m., but he knew if he could get through the door, he could stay until Groucho kicked him out. They had a history of marathon drinking sessions and it wasn't unusual for them to be still going at it long after *Good Morning America* had signed off.

Joe smiled as he pulled up outside the front door with a couple of minutes to spare. The doors closed, the lights dimmed and Groucho placed a Bud on the bar without even being asked. A large straight scotch stood inches from Grouch's hand.

"You look like shit, have you been shovelling that white stuff up your nose again?"

Joe didn't respond. Groucho could see that he was mentally and physically whacked, so he quickly backed off.

"You should have been here earlier," said Groucho, "that girl was asking for you."

"Which one?" asked Joe with a smirk.

Grouch laughed and called him a big head, but it was true. When Joe wasn't strung out on booze or chemicals he could have his pick of most of the girls in PJ's. He was tall and thin with rugged good looks, but if you were chasing smooth, he wasn't your man. Wearing jeans, T-shirt and cowboy boots and a couldn't-care-less attitude he played women like a gambler played the wheel. If his number came up then fine, but if it didn't, so what!

"The fat one with the moustache," came Groucho's deadpan reply.

Joe smiled, but didn't take the bait. His face lit up though when the big guy handed over a note with a cell number and a message that read, *Call me, Marion.* Letting her go home the other night without first writing down her number was a huge mistake and he was angry with himself for not getting his priorities right. This, however, was fantastic news and changed everything.

As usual Groucho was quick to bust his chops, "Could it be that Mr Cool has finally met someone he wants to be with for more than one night?"

Joe was careful with his response.

"I don't know about that, but I can promise you one thing, it'll be one hell of a night."

DAY NINE

CHAPTER THIRTY

The California sun blasted through Leigh's bedroom window waking her long before the alarm was set to go off.

"Buy curtains for bedroom window," she mumbled as she rolled over to look at the clock that was no longer working.

"Find an electrician," she growled pulling the blanket over her head.

This wasn't how she had pictured life on the west coast. The brochures, movies and TV programs made it look so easy, so carefree, but Leigh hadn't felt so stressed in years. Things were much simpler where she came from. She had curtains and non-stop electricity and there were no holes in her floors even in the barn. Her car had seat belts, shock absorbers and electric windows, unlike the relic from the days of flower power that Mike left her.

Things can only get better, she thought. *I just wish it would happen sooner rather than later.*

Wide awake, she threw back the covers and with it scattered Mike's papers all over the bedroom.

"Oh no!" she screamed.

Searching through Mike's bank statements, bills, and personal letters during the night had been tiring and a waste of time. She checked, rechecked and cross-checked everything, but found nothing. It was disappointing and she was beginning to wonder if this whole thing was just a figment of her imagination. Although her nickname, "Miss Conspiracy" was given in jest, Leigh resented it big time as it implied that there was no substance to her theories. However, with absolutely zero to go on she was beginning to wonder if maybe her nickname was more appropriate than she could ever have imagined.

Think outside the box, she said to herself with a wry smile as she recalled her father's words. "Think outside the box," she said again, aloud this time.

Barely had the words cleared her lips when she yelled, "No way dad, this time you're wrong – think inside the box."

Racing back to the closet, she dragged the box of Mike's personal effects into the bedroom and pulled out his cell phone.

"Shit," she mumbled as she stared at a black screen.

Fumbling in the box, she found his phone charger and plugged it in a socket next to her bed. Almost immediately, the screen lit up. There were four calls with a Mexican area code, three outgoing and one incoming. Leigh immediately rang the number of the incoming call because she figured the person who made it probably had something to say to Mike. Who knows, maybe the caller would have something to say to her. After about a dozen rings a man sounding like he just got out of bed answered the phone in Spanish.

"Good morning, do you speak English?" shouted Leigh in a slow deliberate tone.

"Yeah," came an understandable but accented reply.

"What is your name?" she asked in a loud voice.

"Vejar."

"My name is—"

Mr Vejar interrupted her before she could finish. "Lady, I am Mexican, not deaf; please stop shouting."

Leigh realized what she had been doing and giggled. *Why do we yell when we speak to foreigners?* she thought.

"Sorry, my name is Leigh Turner… you knew my brother Mike?" she said.

"We talked on the phone."

"Did you know he's dead?" she asked.

Vejar didn't speak.

"I need to know what you talked about," she insisted.

Vejar remained silent.

"Please."

A long pause followed before the Mexican began to speak.

"He was trying to find out who ran over his parents... I got his number from a guy at a local cantina."

"Did you see it happen?"

"No."

"Why did you call him?"

"The day your parents were run down a man brought a car into the body shop where I work. The front right hand side of the car was smashed in. It was strange, it was a nice day yet the car was wet... it had just been washed."

"What's wrong with that?"

"No one ever washes a car before it goes to a body shop. That's like cleaning your house before the maid gets there."

"Who owned the car?"

"Sergio Ramos."

Now it was Leigh's turn to be quiet. It was like a weight had been lifted off her shoulders, a feeling of relief washed over her. Was that it? Could it be that Ramos and her parents were linked after all and that the third side of the triangle was now complete? Maybe Sergio didn't know her parents; he just ran them over.

"Did you know Ramos was also dead?" she asked.

"Yes... and maybe if I had said nothing, they'd both still be alive."

"Did you tell the police about the car?" asked Leigh.

"You don't do that down here."

"Did you know Mike was a cop?"

"No, I read about it in the paper. Sergio's death was big news in Tijuana."

"Would you have helped my brother if you knew he was a cop?"

"Good talking to you," said Vejar and he hung up the phone.

CHAPTER THIRTY-ONE

Groucho opened the front door to PJ's and playfully pushed Joe out onto the step. The morning sunshine took them both by surprise and they quickly shielded their eyes.

"Get some sleep," said Groucho. "Marion will never let you into her pants looking like that."

Walking with his head down, Joe raised his right hand to acknowledge the remark, but was too drunk to reply. He staggered to his truck and with great difficulty placed himself behind the wheel, but when he fumbled for his keys, he came up empty. Then out of nowhere he saw Groucho dangling a set from his finger.

"You're in worse shape than I thought. Put your head down and get some sleep and I'll be back at noon with your keys."

Looking through bleary eyes, Joe nodded and then asked, "Why do you waste your time drinking with me... are things at home that bad?"

Groucho just closed the door to the pickup and walked away.

Like an obedient child, Joe leaned across the seat and placed his head on his outstretched arm and with eyes closed stayed perfectly still until he was sure that Groucho had gone. After a couple of failed attempts, he finally managed to place himself upright and tumble out of the truck onto the dirt-covered parking lot. From there, he crawled to the front wheel arch, slipped his hand above the tire and peeled off a magnetic case containing an ignition key. Once back in the cab, he removed the cap from a large bottle of water used to refill his radiator and poured it over his head. Rubbing his face and scrapping back his hair with both hands he muttered softly to himself. "I can't spend time sleeping... I got things to do, places to go and a script to follow."

Joe rolled down the window, turned on the ignition and eased his way slowly into the rush hour traffic. It was more by luck than judgement that he made it home without killing himself or anyone else. He was stinking drunk and threw up the moment he placed his head over the toilet bowl.

"Now that's what I call timing," he said while moving across the bathroom floor on his hands and knees.

Lowering his shoulder to the floor, Joe performed an ungainly forward roll on to his back then attempted to take off his jeans, but his fingers didn't belong to him anymore. The harder he tried the more frustrated and tired he became until he finally gave up and crawled into the shower, boots and all. Sitting in the corner with his knees pulled up against his chest and his head back, he opened his mouth, closed his eyes and let the warm water crash over him. It felt good and it wasn't long before he was asleep.

Even in a sober state, Joe couldn't have known that somewhere in New York his script was lying open on an unmade bed. If he had known, there would have been hope instead of despair and possibly acceptance instead of rejection. Weinberg wasn't entirely to blame. He tried on more than one occasion to read the script, but there were always phone calls, meetings and hookers to distract him. This time it was a call from a writer he had found through a friend of a friend of Lonnie's. With a meeting set up for two days time, Weinberg was now able to book his flight and start thinking about going home. L.A. had hundreds of writers, but he agreed to this meeting to keep Lonnie happy and to keep the project fresh. He trusted his old friend, but a lifetime in the film business taught him there was no such thing as a sure thing. Finding the right script was a priority and Weinberg knew that he was going to struggle with this assignment. He had never seen a real movie script in his life.

Boy meets girl, boy screws girl, was his idea of the perfect story line.

CHAPTER THIRTY-TWO

Homicide was buzzing with excitement and packed with cops from every department when Leigh walked through the door. It was like the Dodgers had just won the World Series. She watched in disbelief as grown men hugged each other and threw out high fives to anyone and everyone. It took a moment to find out what all the fuss was about, but it soon transpired that during the night Dan had responded to a call for help from a uniformed officer who was on the scene of a robbery at an all night convenience store. Two gunmen were still inside the store when he arrived. The manager, an elderly Indian gentleman, had already been shot dead.

According to the cop on duty, the gunmen were hiding behind a six-foot high display of Campbell's soup tins in the back left hand corner. When asked to wait for back up, Dan had replied that he was the back up and crept through the front door and quietly moved along the aisle on the opposite side of the store. Stopping half way down the aisle, he'd placed his gun on the shelf and signalled to the officer standing outside to join him. On the count of three they began throwing bottles of wine and beer against the wall above where the gunmen were hiding and it wasn't long before they were drenched and covered in pieces of broken glass. Dan grabbed his gun while the officer ripped open bags of flour and tossed them over the shelves into the corner of the room. A large circular security mirror located above the men allowed the detective to monitor the fugitive's movements. Their predicament was dangerous yet comical and the two armed men could no longer bear to stand in the corner and do nothing. Soaking wet and covered in white flour they moved slowly in opposite directions. Dan gave a signal to the patrolman to throw a bottle ten feet to the right of the spot where the men had been hiding and as the bottle smashed against the wall one of the gunmen had become temporarily distracted. Dan seized the moment, stepped into the aisle and shot him in the chest. The second gunman had been more successful and somehow managed to get behind the uniformed officer and placed a gun to his head. The gunman yelled for Dan to drop his weapon or he'd shoot the cop, but Dan ignored him and continued to move cautiously down the middle aisle. Looking back at the security mirror he'd seen that he was directly opposite the gunman and his hostage in the far aisle. Quietly and calmly Dan rested the barrel of his gun on the shelf between cereal boxes and waited. A moment later the gunman's head appeared in the line of fire and the siege was over. Two of Hollywood's most persistent armed robbers had been taken off the streets.

Despite their many differences, it was clear to Leigh that the players in this station were a team. They celebrated together and they mourned together. She felt alone on the sidelines, not part of the squad, not even on the bench.

CHAPTER THIRTY-THREE

The water from Joe's shower suddenly turned from a warm soporific flow to an ice-cold blast that jabbed like needles into his flesh. Waking in a panic, dazed and confused, he rolled out of the shower and onto the bathroom floor.

Why do I do it, he thought as he struggled to get to his feet.

Stripping off his clothes, he took a drink from the water in his boot before emptying what was left into the sink. He dried himself off, combed his hair and put on a pair of chinos and a clean shirt. This was a big day and first impressions were important.

Down in the kitchen Joe brushed crumbs from an old wooden chopping board on to the floor. A handful of barbiturates were scattered over the food stained block of timber and each pill was delicately split in half. The extracted powder was then poured into a small Tylenol container and pushed into his pocket. Two large blue pills popped into Joe's mouth as he picked up his key and walked out the door.

Traffic was heavy, but Joe didn't mind. He was scared and hung-over and needed time to get his shit together.

Hi, Mrs. Delaney, my name is Joe, my father was a dentist, No... no, Hi, Mrs. Delaney my father studied dentistry with your husband; over and over he rehearsed the lines in his head until suddenly he'd had enough.

"Fuck it... It'll be alright... Where's Jimi?"

Without taking his eyes off the road, he plucked his favorite Hendrix tape from a pile of cassettes deep in the glove compartment, pushed it into a small opening below the dash and cranked the volume to max. The effortless guitar solo led smoothly into a haunting vocal beginning, *Hey Joe where you going with that gun in your hand,* but instead of singing along to the lyrics as he had done so many times before, Joe made a sinister change and sang, "Hey Joe, where you going with those pills in your hand?" A short burst of nervous laughter followed as he tossed the Tylenol container in the air and drove across town.

The tree-lined street where Joe parked his truck was quiet. The area was typical of middle class America. Each house mirrored the next. A manicured lawn stretched from the sidewalk to the steps leading up to the front door while the ubiquitous 4 x 4 stood tall in front of the two-car garage.

Joe didn't feel well. He was sweating and had difficulty clearing his throat as he walked along Anna Avenue. Heavy legs made the journey of fifty yards feel like five hundred. House number 154 was now just a few feet ahead.

You can still turn back, he thought to himself as he walked nervously up the path to the front door. *Nothing has happened, you can walk away.*

Joe was still an arm's length from the door bell when a small frail woman with gray hair opened the solid dark oak door until the chain lock would allow it to go no further.

Shit, he thought, she'd caught him off guard.

"Mrs Delaney, Mrs Marilyn Delaney?"

"Yes," said the old lady through the narrow gap.

"Hi, my name is Joe Tubbs, my dad Vic wanted me to say hi to your husband Maurice. I gather they studied dentistry together at the University of California."

"Maurice isn't here right now, can you come back later?"

Of course he knew that Maurice wasn't there, but this wasn't how she was supposed to react. In his script things went smoothly, there were no hiccups and definitely no one saying, "Can you come back later?"

Joe had to think fast. The pills had kicked in, but his mind was still lagging behind his heartbeat. "Sure no problem, but do you mind if I call a taxi? The guy who brought me here wouldn't wait – I think he was at the end of his shift or something."

The old lady glanced along the street and then stared hard at Joe through her wire framed glasses. The longer she looked at him the more his face hurt from his exaggerated smile. Trying to act like the boy next door was not something he could do easily and it didn't help that he was standing there with a pony tail, blood shot eyes and beer breath that could fell a tree. Suddenly the door slammed in his face and Joe became angry and confused.

The bitch, how could she do that? She didn't even say goodbye.

"Mrs Delaney, can I use your phone?" begged Joe.

Several seconds passed before the door opened wide.

"Sorry to take so long," said Mrs Delaney rubbing her hands, "arthritis you know, it makes the simplest of tasks so difficult at times."

"My mother had it bad, so I know what you're going through," said Joe without the slightest hint of remorse for such a barefaced lie.

A quick and discreet examination of the living room revealed numerous happy family photos on the walls, side table and mantelpiece. But like so many elderly people, the Delaney's had given up on life the day the kids left home. Time had stood still at 154 Anna Avenue and this was clearly reflected in the way she dressed and the interior décor of her home.

"Can I get a glass of water; it's very hot out there?" asked Joe.

"Of course," she said.

The kitchen was just a few short steps away and like the living room it was a throwback in time, black-and-white checkered linoleum, curling up at the edges, covered the floor. A small gray Formica table with seating for two stood against a cold white wall. In most homes the kitchen is the hub, the center of family life. It's where plans for the day are discussed over morning coffee and large glasses of red wine are consumed during preparation for the evening meal. There were no such signs of life here. Everything had a place and everything was in its place. Even the cut-down sunflowers drooping in a pale blue Charles and Diana teapot were unable to breathe life into this dying room.

Mrs Delaney handed Joe a glass of water then returned to

the living room and waited beside the phone. Hanging back in the kitchen, Joe took the deadly powder from the Tylenol case in his pocket and hurriedly emptied it into the glass.

"Do you have the number for the cab company?" she asked.

"No, I don't," said Joe making his way into the living room.

"No problem, I'll find one."

"Put the phone down," said Joe.

"What did you say?"

Joe stepped forward and pushed the glass to her lips. "I said put the phone down and drink this."

Mrs Delaney put the phone down on the table and pointed towards the front door. "Get out of my house young man, Maurice will be home any minute."

"Your husband's drilling teeth until five o'clock; I booked the last appointment of the day to make sure he didn't come home early."

"Who are you?"

"Right now I'm no one, but soon everyone will know my name. Now drink!"

"And if I don't?" she said defiantly.

Joe bent over, pulled a long sharp knife out of his left boot and waved it in front of her face. "I'll cut your throat and when your husband gets home... I'll kill him too... but if you cooperate, he'll be fine."

For a moment Joe was confused as his words echoed around his head. He wasn't sure who said what. He had never spoken like that before, but it came so effortlessly and felt so natural. After a lifetime of bottling up his feelings the cork had finally popped. At last, he felt free. *This is the real Joe*, he thought.

"You're sick!" she cried.

"You know that's what Doc Frank said, but it took her two years to make the diagnosis. I should have come to you first."

Mrs Delaney shook violently when Joe's blade pressed gently against her cheek and offered only token resistance when he grabbed a clump of her hair and pulled her head back. With her mouth wide open his poisonous concoction flowed unhindered passed her lips.

"Please, don't do this, Maurice needs me," she cried as she was taken to the bedroom and placed on the bed. "I have some money and this ring," she said holding her left hand in front of his face.

"I'm not a thief," growled Joe.

"Then why are you doing this?"

"It's not my fault; your name came up on the computer. If you wanna blame anyone, blame your parents."

Tears streamed down her face. She looked completely bewildered and appeared even smaller and more vulnerable than she did when she answered the door. With heavy eyes and slurred speech it wasn't long before she couldn't support the weight of her own body. Her bony withered fingers curled into her hands as she doubled over clutching her stomach. Despite the adrenalin rush and the high he was experiencing from the uppers he swallowed earlier, Joe took care to place her head lightly on the pillow and lift her legs gently on to the bed. As he removed her glasses with a tissue from his pocket and placed them on the bedside table a violent cough followed a stream of mucus and then she was still.

Joe stared impassively at the lifeless form in front of him. There was no regret, no joy, nothing. Casually he wiped his fingerprints from the glass. When he was sure she was dead he took off her shoes and put them beside the bed. Her blouse and skirt were removed and carefully folded and placed on the chair in the corner along with her underwear. Joe didn't look at her naked body. That was not why he was there. A cursory check of the house was all that was needed because the only thing he had touched was the glass and he had already wiped it clean. It was time to go, but he stood motionless in the middle of the room. Something was bugging him. Something wasn't right. He retraced his steps through the kitchen, living room and back into the bedroom. His mind was racing and his senses were working overtime.

"Come on, come on, think," he said angrily. A moment later it came to him.

"Yes," he cried as he hurried towards the bedside table, picked up the dead woman's hand and placed her fingers around the glass so her fingerprints were there for all to see.

"That was close," he whispered.

Pulling his shirtsleeve down to cover his hand, Joe squeezed the doorknob and opened the front door just enough so that he could survey the street. It was safe to leave. The short walk back to the truck was uneventful. He had twenty minutes to pick up a sandwich and get to work.

CHAPTER THIRTY-FOUR

"Do you do this hero thing often?" asked Leigh playfully as she perched on the edge of Dan's desk.

It wasn't a question that Dan was about to answer now or at anytime even if it was said in jest. He was a modest guy doing a job he loved and putting his life on the line was part of what he did. It was no big deal.

The office was no longer buzzing with activity. Gone were the uniformed officers, cleaners, secretaries and just about everyone else working in the building that had come to shake Dan's hand and pat him on the back. It was flattering, but he hated being in the spotlight even more than he hated the dreaded paperwork that he was now expected to do.

"Let me do this," said Leigh, scooping up the file that had been lying unopened since he sat down ten minutes ago.

"Thanks, I'll make coffee," joked Dan.

"A beer would be better," whispered Leigh so that no one else could hear.

"You're on," said Dan with a big smile.

Leigh wasn't sure whether Dan was smiling because he was happy to be off loading the paper work or happy to be going out with her. Deep inside she was hoping it was the latter.

On the far side of the room Heinz had been engaged in a long drawn out conversation. When he finally hung up the phone he yelled across the office to Dan, "Some old lady over on Anna Avenue has topped herself – should I check it out?"

A look of disgust fell across Dan's face. He saw Heinz as a strong reliable cop, but his personality shortcomings made it difficult to like him. Too many years in the trenches had cost him dearly. Social niceties had been replaced by a crassness that sometimes defied belief. A reluctant nod from Dan and Heinz was on his way. But before leaving the office he turned to Leigh and asked her if she wanted to come with him. She didn't even get the chance to reply when he shouted, "Pick up a vest and a shotgun and I'll meet you at the car."

Laughter filled the room and even Leigh found herself smiling at macho man's remark.

"Jerk," yelled Leigh as Heinz disappeared down the stairs.

"You'll have to do better than that, if you want to survive around here," said Dan.

CHAPTER THIRTY-FIVE

"Hey man what's wrong with you today?" asked Gomez. "You look like shit."

Joe peered into the wing mirror of a new red Mustang parked next to the entrance of the restaurant. The color had drained from his face.

"Rough night," he murmured.

"Every night is a rough night, you gotta start takin' care of yourself or one day you're gonna wake up dead," said Gomez.

"Whatever."

Joe wasn't in the mood for talking; besides he had nothing to say. His mind was fixed on the pathetic image of Mrs Delaney shrivelling up like a dead flower, the sparkle fading from her eyes and the last pitiful breath seeping over the saliva on her lips. Then, out of nowhere, a smug grin came over his face as he gazed across the lot.

That was so easy, he thought.

"Hey a smile, what's that all about?" asked Gomez as he jumped into a shiny new BMW 5 Series.

"Things are looking up."

"You getting laid?"

"Much better than that."

"What?"

"You'll see."

"Whatever it is I hope you keep doing it coz it's nice to finally see a smile on that ugly face of yours."

As Gomez drove the BMW away, Joe snatched the keys to a silver Mercedes S-Class from the Valet rack, turned the engine over and flipped through at least a dozen radio stations.

"Nothing," he yelled and smashed his fist down on the dashboard, "not even a fucking whisper. Fuck them and the big cars they ride in on, I'll give them something to report!"

CHAPTER THIRTY-SIX

Heinz was already convinced that this was a suicide. From the moment he left the station, until he pulled up behind the black and white outside 154, the telephone conversation with Mr Delaney played over and over in his mind.

"Were there any signs of forced entry?"

"No."

"Were there any signs that she had been attacked – any bruises or wounds that you can see?"

"No."

"Was anything taken... money, jewelry, TV?"

"No."

"Do you know of anyone who would want to harm your wife?"

"No."

A uniformed officer and a couple of guys from forensics were already on the scene when Heinz walked into the living room. Mr Delaney was sitting on the couch with his head in his hands. When Heinz introduced himself saying he was there to investigate his wife's suicide Delaney went crazy insisting that she wouldn't do such a thing.

"She didn't leave a note, she would have left me a note... she wouldn't have gone without saying goodbye," sobbed the old man, but it made no difference to Heinz.

"About half of all suicide victims don't leave a note," he said abruptly. As far as he was concerned the case was closed.

CHAPTER THIRTY-SEVEN

By the time Joe pulled up outside his house it was 11 p.m., but the day was far from over. There was still a lot to do. Dragging two large planks of wood from the shed in the back yard, he placed them carefully on the ground in the shape of a cross. Three long nails were then driven into the spot where the boards intersected. Sliding the heavy structure back onto the truck, he tied an old shirt around the end of the plank that stuck out beyond the tailgate and then went into the house. After watching the news channel for about twenty minutes he shook his head in disgust.

"Give it time Mrs Delaney, they don't wanna know you now, but they will, they will."

A day spent shifting cars back and forth had a sobering affect on Joe. His head was clear and his body no longer ached. He hated it and needed strength to do what he was about to do. Another line, a couple of pills and a beer took Joe to a different level. He knew what happened at the Delaney house was nothing compared to what was going down tonight. He had to be ready.

Down in the cellar, Joe picked up a pair of wire cutters and some string. A dirty torn work sheet that had been covering an old black and white television set was wrapped around the planks of wood just before he drove towards the city. Looking at his watch he realized that the night was still young so he took a detour to PJ's.

There was a smile on Grouch's face as Joe entered the bar, but it quickly turned to anger.

"You idiot," yelled Goucho handing him his keys to the truck, "where were you, I was worried?"

"Sorry," said Joe like a son to his father, "I should have

called."

Unexpectedly, a tirade of foul language directed everyone's attention to the dance floor where a couple of guys were standing toe to toe, but they weren't dancing. With chests puffed up like a pair of peacocks, it was obvious what was about to happen. Despite being overweight and closing in on his fifties, Groucho leaped over the bar clearing all but one of the bottles of beer in front of him. Smashing down on to the floor he clutched his chest in agony. A look of concern came over Joe as he helped his friend to a stool. Insisting that he was OK, Groucho tried to get back on his feet and over to the dance floor.

"Let me do this," said Joe confidently as he reached over the bar for Groucho's handgun.

"Jesus Joe, what's got into you?" said Groucho quietly, "put it back."

With his shirt pulled out and the gun pushed down the front of his jeans Joe ignored Groucho's pleas and walked casually over to the dance floor and stood inches away from the troublemakers.

"Hey," he yelled lifting his shirt just enough to reveal the handle of the gun. Nothing more was needed and nothing more was said. The men went in opposite directions and dancers returned to the floor.

"A bit over the top, but thanks for your help," said Groucho.

"How you feeling?" asked Joe.

"I'm good; it was just a little heartburn," Groucho replied unconvincingly.

"You gotta take more care what you put into your body," commented Joe without a hint of sarcasm.

"Priceless, that's priceless!" murmured Groucho returning to his rightful place behind the bar. "And it looks like the hero is about to be rewarded."

Spinning on his heels Joe came face to face with Marion. She looked good.

"So you're a writer and a fighter?" she said.

"I've been meaning to call you," blurted Joe.

"Yea, yea, that's what they all say."

"No, I mean it, let's go out some night."

"How about tonight?" asked Marion, pressing her body against his.

"I'm busy tonight," replied Joe awkwardly.

"You're busy at midnight... Yeah right! What's her name?"

"No seriously, I've got something to do, but I'll call you."

"Sure you will," said Marion returning to her table with head bowed.

"Boy, you blew that," said Groucho.

Without saying a word, Joe shrugged his shoulders, collected his keys off the bar and walked quickly to his truck. It was a fifteen minute drive to the canal giving Joe time to forget about what he just turned down and think about his next move. Talking out loud he assured himself that everything would be fine.

'This is serious shit. OK , this morning was serious, but fuck me... this is right off the Richter scale. Keep to the script and it'll be fine, just keep to the script."

Jimi was thrown back in the slot and once again Joe was in full voice as he sang, "Hey Joe where you going with that cross in your truck, I said, hey Joe where you going with that cross in your truck." This time there was no nervous laughter.

Canal Street was next on the right, but instead of turning, Joe slowed down to a crawl and went straight ahead. Glancing along the narrow passage he saw that it was free of cars and people. Under normal conditions he wouldn't have thought twice about making a U-turn in front of oncoming traffic, but tonight was different. The last thing he needed was to be pulled over by the cops while he had a giant cross in the back of his truck. Even Joe may have had trouble bullshitting his way out of that one. Keeping to the script, he drove around the block until he was back on the main road.

Entering Canal Street, Joe turned off his lights, put his gear stick in neutral and coasted gently down the cobbled alley that led to the water. Two blocks away the red light district was business as usual. Sleazy bars pumped out loud music and hookers of all shapes, sizes and ethnic origins strutted their stuff while their pimps spied from the shadows. You either had to be stupid or very horny to go there. On Canal Street life was non-existent, but it was just as dangerous. A row of derelict warehouses leading up to and along the water provided a barrier between the districts and a haven for anything illegal. This dark, damp and deserted no man's land was surrounded by high fences, barbed wire and threatening signs for trespassers, yet people still died there.

Pressing gently on his door handle, Joe pushed open the door and placed his feet quietly on the ground. Walking on tiptoes he reached the iron railing that overlooked the water and a concrete platform that housed the bridge supports. Tucked in along the wall was a solitary figure sleeping under a plastic sheet. His full beard and shoulder length hair were clearly visible. Beside him lay a cardboard poster with the message "Jesus Loves You" written in a child like scribble. Joe smiled and returned to the truck. There were still a few things to do. Standing on the back of his pickup he used his cutters to snip off a section of barbed wire that ran high above the fence alongside the building. Back in the cab, he cut the string into three pieces each of which was looped and held together with a slipknot. Finally, two eight-inch strips of tape were ripped from the roll and stuck to his shirt. It was time.

The sheet covering the cross was removed and tossed onto the front seat. Slowly and quietly Joe lifted the wooden structure on to his shoulder and walked towards the stone stairs that led to the small concrete platform beneath the bridge. It was heavy and difficult to carry. One slip and he would be in the water. Gradually he eased his way down the stairs taking one step at a time until he reached the platform. The cross was then lowered next to the plastic sheet where the man lay oblivious to what was happening and the string loops were carefully hooked over the ends of the wooden beams. Joe locked his hand on to the cold steel hammer-head and eased it from inside his belt. One by one the nails were painstakingly removed from his pocket and placed nearby.

As he crept towards the Jesus look-alike a strong acrid smell of urine drove him back. He began to retch and was forced to turn away.

Not only does this guy sleep in his goddamn clothes, he pisses in them too, thought Joe.

Looking out over the water he wiped his eyes, took a large intake of air and then held his breath. Quickly he turned and knelt next to the man's head. A strip of duct tape was plastered over the man's mouth with a second piece stuck over his eyes to disorientate him. Reaching under his armpits he dragged him onto the cross and then immediately spun around and sat on his chest with both knees pinning the man's arms to the cross. Moaning sounds emanated from beneath the tape. The man was awake, he was angry and he was trying to kick his way out of this terrifying dilemma, but Joe was too heavy and too strong. Looping the string around the man's right arm, Joe pulled the knot so tight that it created a deep crease in his wrist. The same procedure followed for the man's left arm. Joe then grabbed the hammer in his right hand and placed one of the six-inch nails in the middle of the man's palm. Unaware of what was about to happen, the man kept his palm open. Joe seized the opportunity to smash the hammer on to the nail driving it through his flesh and crunching bones and into the wood. The man's head rocked from side to side while a muffled scream that seemed to last forever came from under the gag. A second blow of the hammer slammed the nail even deeper into the cross and sent a stream of blood flowing onto the concrete.

For a moment the man was still. Perhaps he was in shock. Realizing that he could no longer hold his breath, Joe hurried to get the job done. Picking up a second nail he tried to stick it into the left palm, but this time the fist was clenched. Withdrawing the nail, he licked it with his lips and then slid it between third and fourth fingers of the clenched hand until it rested firmly. Two crushing blows powered the spike about two inches into the wood. Having nailed both hands to the cross, Joe rotated his body to fasten the third piece of string over his feet. There was no need to hurry. The fight was over. The kicking and wriggling had stopped and the moaning was all but inaudible. With the man's legs crossed it took a further eleven massive strikes to put the final nail through the flesh and bones of the right foot and into the main support. Joe was exhausted. He rolled away until he was able to dip his hand into the water and wipe it over his face. Slowly his breathing returned to normal.

Glancing down into the canal he saw the reflection of a man he didn't know. He looked over his shoulder, but there was no one there. Another quick look into the canal confirmed his worst fears. The reflection in the water was his.

He got back to his feet, shaped the barbed wire into a crown of thorns and placed it on the man's head. The knife tucked in his boot was used to cut away the Jesus freak's shirt leaving him naked above the waist.

Using every bit of strength he had left in his body, he lifted the cross and leaned it against the bridge stanchion. After a few seconds, the tape over the man's eyes was ripped from his face taking with it the hairs from his eyebrows and eyelashes. At first there was no movement. The man appeared to be dead until his eyelids flickered and his eyes rolled involuntarily in their sockets.

A second large clump of hair was pulled from his beard when the final piece of tape was yanked from his mouth. A stream of saliva dribbled slowly over his bottom lip. As the flow of blood from his wounds turned to a trickle Joe could see that death would not be imminent and there was even a chance if he was left like this his victim could survive. Surviving was not an option. Without the slightest bit of hesitation, Joe plunged the razor sharp blade of his knife firmly into the man's side forcing blood to gush from his body like water from a leaky hosepipe. The end came quickly.

Crucifixion may be bizarrely artistic, but there wasn't time to stand around and admire his work or think about what he had done. Joe had to get out of there. Two blocks away people were partying and there was always the chance of a spill over into Canal Street. The only way out was back the way he had come. Reversing slowly in the dead of night with lights off, Joe stopped a few feet from the main road. He watched and waited until it was quiet and then made his move and headed to PJ's. It was the second time in twenty-four hours that he'd got away with murder.

DAY TEN

CHAPTER THIRTY-EIGHT

The morning madness hadn't really started yet as Leigh drove at a leisurely pace through town to the police station. On the way she decided that she would come clean with Dan about her investigation into Mike's death. She expected him to be angry and was prepared to be ticked off, even fired, but that didn't matter. What did matter was that she wanted to be up-front with him as she would expect him to be with her. She also needed his help.

As she arrived at the station, Dan, Heinz and Moose were moving quickly through the front door.

"What's the rush?" she asked. "Is there a two for one sale at Dunkin' Donuts?"

"Cute," replied Dan with a smile.

"If you had a radio in that piece of junk you'd know," added Heinz before pulling out of the parking lot and into traffic.

A moment later, Leigh walked into the office and found everyone gathered around the television. She couldn't believe her eyes. A man, naked to the waist, had been nailed to a cross and left to die.

Only in California, she thought.

––––––––––––––––––––

Canal Street was a media circus. It all kicked off when a passerby spotted the crucifixion and, instead of calling the police, sent a phone video to Channel 7 News. Within minutes the pictures had traveled around the world.

"Anything for a buck," said Dan bitterly.

The crime scene was a forensic nightmare. It looked like Times Square on New Year's Eve.

"Get these bloodsuckers out of here," yelled Dan to a couple of uniformed cops.

Eventually the crowd of sightseers and photographers was pushed back along the street to the main road, but a flotilla of small boats still lingered a few feet away in the canal while a blue and red striped TV News helicopter hovered overhead. Cameras with oversized lenses were everywhere.

Finally, the forensics team arrived and within a few minutes a tent was erected around the body. An air of calm and respectability returned to the scene. Dan, Heinz and Moose stood quietly as they stared at the man on the cross. Heinz was the first to speak.

"Poor bastard...I saw some bad shit in Iraq, but this is in a league of its own."

For the ex-soldier to be affected like this was a departure from his normal gung ho, kill or be killed approach to life. Dan and Moose were touched by Heinz's sentiments until he spoiled it all by adding, "This is the worst case of suicide I've ever seen."

It was an old joke and it was still funny, but nobody laughed. How could they?

CHAPTER THIRTY-NINE

Shuffling out of the bedroom in his underwear and a T-shirt, Joe picked up the remote, turned on the TV and headed for the kitchen to make a strong black coffee. A stained mug with a large chip on the lip edge was perched in the middle of a pile of dirty dishes in the sink. A closer investigation revealed a thick flooring of mould on the bottom of the mug.

"Neil Young was right," said Joe as he poured in a heaping spoonful of instant coffee before adding boiling water. "A man needs a maid."

As he slumped onto the sofa he had no idea the effect his actions were having around the world, but he was about to find out. ABC, NBC, CNN and all the local news stations ran the crucifixion as their lead story. The recession, Afghanistan, Iraq and even a piece about Madonna and her latest toy boy were relegated to minor news items. Watching in amazement, Joe sat and listened to the various theories about the killing.

"This was the work of the Muslims," said a woman venomously as she clutched a small cross with both hands.

A local priest provided a different viewpoint. "We must now ask ourselves, who was this poor wretch spreading the word of our Lord? Was he sent from above? Was this the work of the devil?"

Joe laughed and yelled at the TV, "Jesus Christ, whatever you folks are on, I want some."

He couldn't believe the crap that was coming out of their mouths. It was like they were high. It hadn't occurred to him that nailing a man to a cross would be analyzed and dissected and that every man, woman and child, sane or insane would have an opinion. This was good. No, this was better than good, it was fantastic and Joe jumped up and down to celebrate before turning the volume to zero, closing his eyes and resting his head against the back of the sofa. Running his hands through his hair he said softly, "Shit, what have I done? The old lady was a mother and a wife and that guy on Canal Street was someone's son."

For a moment there was silence. Then Joe gradually climbed to his feet, threw his head back and stretched his arms open wide and began to laugh.

News of the macabre killing made it to New York City in a nano second. When the story broke in the Big Apple, Weinberg was reading the New York Times and enjoying blueberry pancakes with maple syrup in the hotel coffee shop. A sharp intake of breath from a woman seated at the next table drew his eyes away from the paper and on to a large plasma screen where the images left nothing to the imagination. Like most televisions in bars and restaurants the sound was turned off so he shouted to a waitress to turn up the volume, but like most waitresses in bars and restaurants she ignored him. The sight of a man hanging on a cross underneath a bridge had triggered something in Weinberg's mind but, aside from the obvious place, he couldn't remember where this image came from. Leaving his table, he stood below the wall mounted TV set hoping to see a landmark that he recognized. It wasn't long before the camera from an overhead chopper panned the area to reveal the L.A. skyline.

"Son of a bitch," said Weinberg as he threw a twenty-dollar bill onto the table and ran out of the coffee shop, through the lobby and into the elevator. Now he remembered. Back in his room he emptied the contents of his briefcase on to the bed, but it wasn't there.

"Come on," he yelled impatiently.

He searched the wardrobe and checked the drawers of the desk before falling to his hands and knees to look under the bed.

"There you are," he said as he pulled out a bundle of papers.

Sitting on the carpet with knees bent and his back to the side of the bed, he began reading the script that he had found in his case. The opening chapters talked about the frustrations of a guy trying to make it in the film business and how the humiliation of rejection leads him down a path he never wanted to go. Every detail surrounding the death of Marilyn Delaney and the gruesome facts of the crucifixion of a Jesus freak on Canal Street were included in the opening chapters.

Weinberg stopped reading for a moment and turned the TV on to CNN. With a sober look on her face and a serious tone in her voice, the morning anchorwoman relayed the grisly facts of the killing exactly as they were written on the pages in Weinberg's hand.

Son of a bitch, he thought, *this can't be a coincidence.*

Weinberg knew there was one way to find out, so he called his office in L.A. and got his girl to get him Mrs Delaney's number. As the phone rang in California, Weinberg was experiencing mixed emotions; part of him was hoping that this frail little old lady was still alive while another part of him was thinking, *This is too good to be true… what a great film it would make.*

When a somber male voice answered the phone Weinberg instinctively knew that she was dead, but he went through the motions to be sure.

"Hello, can I speak to Marilyn Delaney please?"

"That's not possible, she passed away."

"I'm sorry for your loss. When did this happen?"

"Yesterday… Who is this?"

Weinberg hung up the phone and immediately booked a flight back to L.A.

CHAPTER FORTY

"I don't believe it," screamed Heinz as he slammed his note pad onto his desk. "A guy gets nailed to a cross in the middle of L.A. and nobody sees a damn thing. How can that happen?"

"That was a rhetorical question, wasn't it?" asked Dan with a smile.

Heinz had been questioning people on the streets in the canal area since daybreak and was about to go back for a second time to interview the weirdos that come out after dark. No one expected him to be handed anything on a plate. Most people hanging out in that neighborhood were doing something they shouldn't be doing so it wasn't going to be easy to get people to talk.

"Any luck?" asked Leigh innocently as she entered the room.

Heinz, who was not in a good mood, was about to trash her when Dan jumped in quickly before the ex-marine could open his mouth, "Nothing so far, but we're looking through the files for anyone with a religious hate crime background."

"I don't think it was religiously motivated," said Leigh without thinking.

"Why?" Dan asked.

"This oughta be good," quipped Heinz.

Suddenly Leigh was in the spotlight. Glancing around the room she could see that everyone had stopped working to hear what she had to say. Heinz was grinning like a cat about to pounce on a wounded mouse.

Me and my big mouth, she thought.

"I don't think it's linked to religion because this guy was nothing to do with the church. He was a wannabe, a crazy pretending to be Jesus. If someone hates religion so much then why not kill the real thing? Go for the Pope or at least a priest?"

It was a valid argument and for a moment Heinz was silenced.

"So who should we be looking for?" asked Dan.

"I don't know," admitted Leigh.

"Well that helps," said Heinz in a mocking tone, "at least we know who NOT to look for."

Nevertheless, Dan was impressed. Thinking outside the box was not something his team did very often. It was good to have a fresh opinion, a different point of view.

"I still owe you a beer," whispered Dan. "Are you free tonight?"

Leigh smiled acceptingly and returned to sorting a stack of files on her desk, but her mind was on other things.

CHAPTER FORTY-ONE

Growing up as an only child to a single mother playing in a rock band wasn't all bad. An endless stream of male visitors meant that it was inconvenient for Joe's mother, Alice, to have him around while she entertained. The solution was simple. Have your lovers buy the kid presents that could only be used outside. BB guns, slingshots, kites and boomerangs littered Joe's bedroom. It didn't take long for him to realize that a knock on the door during daylight hours equalled something new to play with. The BB gun was his favorite and was stashed in a closet at PJ's while he was on the run from his foster home. He was grateful to Groucho for keeping it safe. Holding the gun in his hands again felt good and brought back a truck-load of memories although some weren't very nice. Being shuffled outside and hearing the door lock behind him while standing in the pouring rain wasn't one of his fondest recollections.

"We have to take care of some grown up business," his mother would shout through the window, "it'll only take a minute."

The minutes always turned into hours and the daylight into darkness. On one occasion Joe was left outside all night while his mother lay unconscious on the floor following a drug filled afternoon. The next morning she apologized and that was the end of it.

"Shit happens," she would say, "get over it."

Standing at one end of the basement of his house Joe loaded his BB gun and fired into a circle drawn on an old mattress at the far end of the room. Although he hadn't touched the gun in years he was still a good shot.

"And now for the real thing," he said picking up the rifle

he had bought from the man in the parking lot. "I just hope it doesn't blow up in my face."

Joe loaded the gun, took aim and squeezed the trigger. A massive explosion echoed off the basement walls while a serious kick slammed the rifle butt into his shoulder.

It was an incredibly powerful experience with the shot blowing an enormous hole in the mattress and thrusting feathers high into the air. The target was only a few feet away and it wasn't moving; nevertheless, Joe felt good about hitting it dead center. As always, his impulsiveness got the better of him. No more practice shots were needed.

With the rifle slung over his shoulder he marched upstairs like a little boy playing soldier. At the top of the stairs he relaxed, raised his arms and looked down the sights of his rifle and said with a sinister smile, "Ready or not, here I come."

CHAPTER FORTY-TWO

Since the Beatles invaded America in the 60s Hollywood has had a love affair with everything British. The town just can't get enough of Brit music, fashion, film, double decker buses and that lovely soft accent. Dan was a Beatle fan and a fan of most things from England except the pub. A two-week holiday in London, shortly after he joined the force, filled him with enough bad food and warm beer to put him off eating and drinking for life. When he got a text from Leigh to meet him at The Royal Oak, a two hundred year old English pub from Cheshire now relocated to the center of Hollywood, he broke into a cold sweat.

"I'm sorry to inflict this place on you," she laughed after hearing about Dan's experience. "What do you expect from a tourist?"

Despite his many doubts Dan agreed to go inside. He wouldn't go near the food, but the beer was cold and the non-stop sounds of the Fab Four on the jukebox put him in a mellow mood after a stressful day.

Like most couples getting to know each other, the conversation centered mainly on what they had in common and right now that was work. The bizarre murder down by the canal was the hot topic, but Leigh was desperate to tell Dan about her Ramos investigation, even if it upset him. She just didn't know how to bring it up. An awkward pause gave them the opportunity to sip their drinks and scan the décor that surrounded them. Bartenders dressed in tweed pulled pints with wooden handles, while tall patrons ducked to avoid hitting the huge oak beams that ran across the low ceiling. Tiny oil lamps hung on brick walls and a magnificent stone fireplace, complete with bellows and coal bucket that would not have been out of place in a Dickens novel, stood idle at the end of the room.

The jukebox fired up another Beatle's tune and Leigh seized the opportunity. With the opening word 'Help' blasting out of the speakers, she jumped in with both feet, "That's appropriate."

"What's up," asked Dan, sensing something was bothering her.

Nervously she began to tell Dan about the uneasiness she felt after Mike's murder, how the whole thing didn't make sense and why she decided to follow her gut instincts despite what others may think. When she told him about her visit to Ricardo's house and the letter she spotted from Tijuana, a look of utter disbelief came over his face. She knew what was coming so before he could mutter a word she spoke faster and louder, describing the Tijuana link between Mike, Ramos and her parents and then concluded with the revelation that Sergio's car had been in an accident the day her parents were killed.

"I think Sergio killed my parents and that's why he shot Mike when he stopped him."

There was a long silence while Dan gathered his thoughts. With her hands clutched together on her lap, she sat anxiously waiting for him to speak. He was a man and like most men he had an ego. The question is, did her investigation dent his ego or would he be cool and accept what she did was good police work.

"Are you sure you're not a cop?" asked Dan repeating the question he asked shortly after they first met, "because if you're not, you should be... that wasn't bad."

A large smile came over Leigh's face until Dan carried on speaking. His tone was now forceful, but concerned, "I don't believe you went to his house alone, what were you thinking? His brother was a cop killer!"

He wanted to say *you're impetuous, just like your brother,* but stopped after the first word. It would have been unforgivable and he knew it. Then after a long pause, Dan added, "Promise me you won't do anything like this again."

Feeling like a scolded child, but at the same time sensing that he cared, she nodded in agreement.

"Let me make some calls and we'll see if we can get to the bottom of this. Now let's get out of here and go somewhere they serve good old American food," suggested Dan, already rising from his seat.

Stepping away from the table Leigh accidently brushed against Dan. Tiny goose bumps appeared on her arms and the color in her cheeks intensified. She felt stupid, like she did as a teenager at the Ark High School prom. Back then her seventeen-year old date was cool and gorgeous and she just couldn't cope.

"I look like a tomato," she had said to her best friend as she stood at the washroom sink splashing cold water on her face.

Several years on and she was once again reliving that teenage nightmare. Dan was cool and still pretty gorgeous and she was having difficulty coping.

CHAPTER FORTY-THREE

JFK was chaos as usual. Long twisting lines jutted out from the check-in desks and bags lay strewn across the floor. Screaming children ran amok while their parents tried unsuccessfully to restrict their movements to a few square feet and muffled airline announcements only added to the stress. A feeling of smugness came over Weinberg as he strutted passed the hordes of Economy Class passengers to the First Class desk where check-in was fast and painless. Within minutes he was sitting in a large soft armchair in the First Class Lounge sipping a glass of cold champagne. It wasn't always like this.

Heading west from New York to seek his fortune in L.A., Weinberg was forced to walk and hitchhike across America after his face was punched in and his life savings of five hundred dollars were ripped from him by a couple of thugs a block from the New York Port Authority Bus Terminal. It would have been so easy to turn around and go home, but Weinberg knew what he wanted and was prepared to do whatever he had to do to get it. With a large hole where his front tooth once stood, he swore that the replacement would be made of gold. For over two years he had no fixed address. Home was often the passenger seat of an eighteen-wheel truck steaming along the interstate or a piece of grass in a field somewhere that looked like Kansas or Oklahoma. He washed dishes and he washed cars. He shovelled snow and he shovelled shit and he did some things that he still refused to talk about.

His first job in the film business was cleaning up after the porn stars had finished performing. He was treated like something you find on the bottom of your shoe, but he watched and learned and paid his dues like every other young hopeful did back then. Eventually he progressed from the lowest of the low to the top of the tree. The timely death of the old man who ran the show, coupled with his family's hatred of pornography and Weinberg's ruthless business tactics, enabled the young Jew from New York to walk into a ready made deal. His mentor had once said, *"As long as there are perverts, voyeurs or exhibitionists this film company will survive"*.

What no one could see coming were the new breed of competitors who work out of toilets in places like the Philippines or on a shoestring in the US employing illegal immigrants. Everybody was taking a slice of the action and Weinberg knew that it was only a matter of time before he would be squeezed out. He had to diversify or die.

While fellow passengers slept during the overnight flight, Weinberg absorbed the contents of the script. He loved the story even if it was a bit patchy and didn't have an ending, but couldn't understand why anyone would go to so much trouble and not leave a contact name and number. There were so many unanswered questions. Who wrote it and why was it given to him? Was he the only one with a copy? And if not, has it been handed to the police? Would the author of the script be prepared to make a deal after all that had happened?

With feet up and a glass of chilled Chablis in his hand he began fantasizing about who would fill the lead roles. He chuckled out loud as he reeled off Hollywood's elite including *"Harrelson, Depp, Zellweger, and Kidman"*. After a disastrous week in the Big Apple, things were starting to go his way. Weinberg had been handed financial backing and a knockout script. All he had to do was find the author.

DAY ELEVEN

CHAPTER FORTY-FOUR

Joe didn't get many visitors. He kept to himself. Before people can come to your house you have to tell them where you live and that was not something he did very often. His mother was just the opposite, with a trail of lovers and dealers regularly beating a path to her door. So when he heard the sound of someone knocking, he automatically thought the worst and picked up his rifle.

"Yeah," he shouted.

"Is Mr Tubbs here?" asked the caller.

Through a crack in the curtain he saw a short balding man wearing a pair of bad taste Bermuda shorts and a golf shirt. From a different vantage point, he scanned the full length of the street and recognized every car. The guy, who was holding a large brown envelope, didn't look like a cop so Joe relaxed, put the rifle away, and opened the door.

"Hi," said the man on the doorstep, "I live a couple of streets away and this letter was delivered to me, but I think it's yours. Sorry, I've had it for a few days, I've been busy."

Joe's eyes lit up and his heart rate increased when he spotted a large logo with an old-fashioned movie projector and the words West Coast Films emblazoned across the upper left hand corner of the envelope. He snatched it out of the man's hand and closed the door.

"Thanks," he yelled in an excited voice, long after the door had slammed.

Standing in the middle of the room he stared at the

envelope like a kid staring at a present under a Christmas tree. He was smiling and energized with anticipation when just a moment ago he feared the worst and held a loaded gun in his hand. Carefully he opened the large brown envelope and read the letter aloud.

"Dear Mr Tubbs, thank you for sending us your script, 'A Ride on the Main Line.'

Our normal practice is to either accept or reject scripts and only correspond with those who we wish to engage in further discussions. In the case of your script, however, it was so bad that we decided to pass it to our junior script editor for training purposes."

Joe stopped reading and lowered his head. He could hear the sound of his teeth grinding together. "Bastards," he shouted as he continued reading the letter.

"Spelling and grammatical mistakes have been highlighted in red and places where the story lacks cohesion or just doesn't make sense are in yellow. Constructive comments have also been added. I hope this will be of benefit to you should you ever consider script-writing again. Yours truly, Fred Esche, Senior VP."

Joe was stunned. Each page was a sea of red and yellow. There was barely a word untouched. Comments like *"boring"*, *"even more boring"*, *"this doesn't make sense"*, and *"so predictable"*, were crammed in to the margins and between the lines. On the bottom corner of the last page a mark of zero out of ten was written in pencil. Joe thought that this was probably meant to be a joke for West Coast eyes only, but someone forgot to rub it out before the letter was sent.

"Why?" screamed Joe. "If they didn't like it why not throw it in the garbage? Why do this shit?"

It didn't take long before Joe got his answer. Written in bold blue letters at the bottom of the page was the line, *"West Coast Films is a subsidiary of Fat Cat Promotions."*

Joe nodded knowingly and mumbled, "Payback time."

About a year ago he had auditioned at Fat Cat for a part in a TV commercial and went ballistic when he was told he couldn't act and should consider another profession. Joe threatened everyone in the building, including the old lady mopping the floor and had to be physically escorted off the premises. This was a humiliation twice over. He was still paying the price for his past and now he was getting dumped on for something he didn't write. What was really strange is that he took it personally, as if he had written it.

"I'll show them," said Joe, "give me a couple more days... they ain't seen nothin' yet."

CHAPTER FORTY-FIVE

It was just after midnight when Dan and Leigh parked themselves in a booth at PJ's for a nightcap. The evening was going well. The conversation had moved on from office anecdotes to likes and dislikes and finally to stories about their ex's. Leigh did most of the talking, which is normal for a journalist while Dan, a typical cop, felt that anything he might say could be taken down and used against him. Surprisingly, her nonstop chatter only once touched on a conspiracy theory and that was Neil Armstrong's moon landing in '69. Was it all just a sham filmed in a studio outside Vegas or did the astronauts really go to the moon? Leigh didn't have any strong views on this one, but still tried to get a reaction from Dan. She got it wrong and had the sense to drop it when she saw the look of disbelief on his face. He was a patriot through and through and this was a step too far.

On the opposite side of the room, a girl in her early twenties dressed in a short denim skirt, brown leather boots and a yellow T-shirt stood beneath a single blue spotlight. Her fingers glided over the strings of her acoustic guitar as she moved closer to the microphone. At first the song she was playing was unrecognizable, but then a mystic sounding voice, similar to that of Stevie Nicks, began belting out *Dreams* and the place went wild. Leigh was in mid sentence when Dan broke his concentration and stared across the room at the bleached blond performer. For the moment he was lost and nothing Leigh could say would bring him back. When the song finally came to an end Dan turned back to Leigh, but couldn't remember what they had been talking about.

"There's something about this place that really gets to you, isn't there?" she asked.

Dan chose not to answer, but smiled instead and ordered a couple more drinks from the waitress.

Just a few feet away Joe sat in his favorite spot at the end of the bar and knocked back his first beer in one large gulp.

"Hit me again, big guy."

Groucho picked another cold one out of the cooler and placed it on the bar. "The last time I saw you do that you had rejection written all over your face... you got the same look again only this time it's partially hidden by those bags under your eyes and that white powder under your nose."

"You're pretty smart for a fat ugly bastard," cracked Joe as he wiped his hands over his face. "Don't worry man, I got it under control."

Groucho wasn't convinced. In the last few days he'd seen a sharp decline in Joe's mental state. Depression and drug dependency hung over him like a cloud. Before Joe's mother died, Groucho promised her he'd look out for him and it was tearing the big guy up inside to see this happening. But now wasn't the time to get heavy, so he quickly changed the subject.

"You see that guy in the booth with that good looking woman?" asked Groucho as he pointed towards Dan.

"Yeah, what about him?"

"I know him from somewhere... just can't place him."

"He's a cop," replied Joe.

Hearing the word "cop" triggered an avalanche of memories going back at least thirty years. Groucho looked flustered. He didn't know what to do with himself. Quickly grabbing a wet rag from the sink he started wiping down a section of the bar that he'd just finished cleaning.

"What's up man, you look like you've just seen a ghost?" teased Joe.

"It's nothing," answered Groucho. "I think he gave me a ticket a few years back, that's all."

"It must have been one helluva big ticket," laughed Joe.

"You up for a session tonight?" asked Groucho, changing the subject once again.

"Not tonight, I got things to do."

"You said that the other night when that broad tried to take you home. What's with you? Got a woman whose husband works nights?"

"No, I'm just writing. It's easier when things are quiet. You should try going home at night; I hear it does wonders for a marriage."

Out of the corner of his eye, Joe spotted Dan and Leigh leaving the bar. He quickly finished off his drink, waved goodnight and headed to the parking lot. A black sedan reversed in front of his pickup and waited while a white VW Beetle with Leigh at the wheel drove past and onto the street. When both cars hit the main road they split off in opposite directions. Joe followed the Beetle. It was easy. The car was so slow he could have done it on foot. Keeping a safe distance he stayed with her until she arrived at the lot next to Kim's Hardware.

Joe pulled over, turned off his engine and watched as she climbed the wooden stairs and entered her apartment. A single bare light bulb, dangling from the ceiling, suddenly lit up the room.

"You know," mocked Joe, "what that apartment needs is a nice warm fire."

He'd seen enough. It was time to go home, but not time to go to bed. There was still one thing left to do.

CHAPTER FORTY-SIX

"Great minds think alike," shouted Moose as Dan entered the office still wearing the clothes he was in when he left a few hours ago.

"Or is it narrow minds think along the same track?" added Heinz with a pinch of cynicism.

Dan was happy, but not surprised to see the guys in the office at such a crazy hour of the night. The crucifixion had shaken everyone. Murders were common in Hollywood, but this was much more than a bullet in the head or knife in the back. It had taken sadism to a new level.

"What have we got Moose?" asked Dan throwing his jacket over the back of a chair.

"His name is Emmet Van Sykes, originally from Oregon, parents divorced ten years ago, father died last year. We're trying to find his mother."

"She must be blind or living in a goddamn cave," injected Heinz, "her son's face is on the box 24/7. Why hasn't she called?"

"Anything else?" asked Dan, ignoring Heinz's outburst.

"He's got no priors – lost his job in Oregon last year, then came south."

"Any links to religious groups?" asked Dan with a touch of desperation in his voice.

"Nothing yet," replied Moose.

This wasn't going to be easy. Van Sykes was a loner with no fixed abode. Everyone in Hollywood saw him preaching on the sidewalks downtown, but no one knew him.

He was just another weird smelly guy that people cross the street to avoid.

DAY TWELVE

CHAPTER FORTY-SEVEN

The coal-bunker in the basement of Joe's rented house had not been used since the landlord switched to oil many years ago. But after all this time the inside of the tightly sealed wooden box-like structure was still covered in a thin layer of black dust. At the far end of the cellar it was dust free, but still cold and dark. Joe liked going down there when he wanted to get high. Two large speakers had been installed and connected to the living room stereo specifically for this purpose. Sitting on a pile of faded tattered rugs, while surrounded by other people's junk, Joe endured some of his best and worst hallucinogenic experiences. He was down there again, but this time it was to chill. He needed a steady hand and a gentle heartbeat for what he was about to do and a large joint was his medicine of choice.

There were just two hours of daylight remaining when Joe picked up his rifle, BB gun and a soft cushion and drove across town to the luxurious Hillside apartments. The journey was painfully slow. Marijuana has that affect on you when you drive. With Hendrix blasting from his dashboard speakers, Joe realized that this was a special moment. For as long as he could remember he had been singing along with "Hey Joe" and not once did he have a gun in his hand. Now here he was, just like in the song. It was perfect.

The lights on his truck were extinguished as he coasted gently down the sloping service road at the back of the building; the place was surrounded by an eight-foot high wrought iron fence with a coded electric gate guarding the only entrance to the rear parking lot. Joe didn't need to go beyond the fence. He rolled to the end of the road that ran parallel to the six-story building and stopped beneath a large tree.

From here he had a clear view of all six corner apartments, but he was only interested in one. Quietly stepping out of the cab he took the cushion from the passenger seat and placed it on the hood of his truck. He then picked up both guns and laid them gently on the cushion pointing in the direction of the apartment building. They were already loaded. With the barrel of the BB gun resting on the cushion and Joe leaning on the truck, he trained his sights on the balcony window of the top floor apartment and slowly lowered his sights to the fifth floor, then the fourth and finally the third. Two shots were fired and each pellet sailed across the cars in the parking lot and struck the window on the third floor. Nothing happened. He fired again and again until finally the large floor to ceiling window slid open and a dark figure stepped on to the balcony. Joe quickly put the BB gun on the ground and placed the rifle butt plate against his shoulder. His finger slid delicately on to the trigger as the barrel held firm in the cushion. Lining up the sights he moved left a little and then down until he was locked on to the shadowy form leaning on the railing. He was a heartbeat away from squeezing the trigger when he heard a woman's voice call out, "Is anyone out there?"

Joe ducked his head and slid down over the wheel arch on to the ground.

"Shit," he whispered.

The woman stayed on the balcony for a couple of minutes looking up and down the parking lot before going back into the apartment. Joe was hoping she hadn't spotted the cushion resting on the hood.

Where the hell can he be? thought Joe. *It's nearly five in the goddamn morning?*

Gradually he worked his way up the side of the truck and peeped over the hood to the apartment above. The lights were out and there was no sign of movement.

Joe was pissed off. He hated it when things didn't go according to plan. He was running out of time too. In the distance the sun was getting ready to break over the horizon.

He had no option but to pack up and go home. After placing the BB gun through the open window of the cab he bent down and picked up the rifle by the barrel. He was just about to put it next to the BB gun when a light came on in the apartment. Joe froze. He could see two silhouettes behind the see through curtains. They came together for a short moment and then separated and someone moved towards the window. Joe slid into position.

The large pane of glass rolled aside as before, but this time a tall well built black man dressed in a tuxedo stood on the balcony. The man turned and rubbed his hand over the window as if searching for a crack or a hole in the glass then pivoted to look out over the parking lot. A large bead of sweat rolled off Joe's forehead into his right eye. He blinked several times until he could see clearly. Then the ominous sound of gunfire shattered the early morning calm.

Grasping his stomach with both hands the man lurched forward and arched over the balcony. A second shot from the semi automatic split the top of his head, splattering blood everywhere. The woman screamed, "Marty, Marty!" as she ran from the bedroom and pulled his blood-stained body back on to the balcony floor.

Amidst the chaos Joe collected the spent cartridges and crawled on to the seat of his pickup, keeping his head below the dash. Pressing the clutch and releasing the parking brake he moved quietly down the incline and out of sight. When he felt he was far enough away he turned the key, shifted into second and popped the clutch to kick-start the engine. Within seconds he was a mile from the scene. An anonymous call was made to 911, but despite frantic cries from the victim's wife, not one apartment light was lit and not one person came to help.

CHAPTER FORTY-EIGHT

It had been a long boring night at the station. The guys were tired of looking at computer screens and cross checking names with other police jurisdictions. The good news was that a score of potential suspects had been eliminated because they were either dead or in prison. The bad news was that they were no closer to finding the killer of Emmett Van Sykes. A new day meant more interviews and a host of alibis to check out. Dan was hoping to go home, have a shower and put on some clean clothes, but when he got a phone call telling him about the incident at Hillside apartments he knew that wasn't going to happen.

"We got a shooting over at Hillside, who wants to come with me?" asked Dan.

"I'll go," said Heinz. "Who got shot?"

"Marty King."

"Hello, I'm Marty King?" asked Heinz, mimicking the man's TV commercials.

"No shit," said Moose, "was it really the TV guy? Is he dead?"

"Yes and yes," said Dan as he headed out the door.

King was lying on his back on the balcony when Dan and Heinz arrived on the scene. His stomach had a large hole in it and his head looked like it had been chopped with an axe. A female officer was comforting King's wife, Gloria, who was shaking uncontrollably on the bed. At first glance it looked like she had also been hit because her hands, face and nightgown were covered in blood. Dan knelt beside the bed to talk to the victim's wife while Heinz stepped carefully passed the body to the railing.

He had seen it all before. Desert Storm was a sniper's dream. Countless Iraqi soldiers had been taken out during the conflict with head shots from concealed shooters some distance away. A few were eating, having a smoke or having a crap in the sand. One or two were even going about their business as soldiers trying to kill US Marines. It didn't matter. There was only one rule. Get them before they get you. In a war zone you expect to be shot at, but that would have been the last thing on King's mind when he strolled onto the balcony. Heinz knew the big man would have been an easy target. Standing at six foot three inches and weighing around two hundred and fifty pounds, even Stevie Wonder would have stood a good chance of hitting such a massive frame. The shot to the head, however, was a different matter and Heinz acknowledged this one was a beauty.

When King's body was lifted on to a gurney and wheeled out of the apartment forensics found a BB pellet stuck to his jacket. King's wife may have been in shock and unable to talk, but this tiny piece of evidence spoke volumes. It was becoming clear to Dan that the shooting was well planned and executed. It wasn't just a murder; it was an assassination. Dan followed the gurney down in another elevator and then walked out to the service road to have a look around. Standing on the balcony, Heinz motioned to Dan to move along the fence until he reached a spot that was at a ninety-degree angle to where the body had fallen. Dan called in a couple of uniformed cops and together they paced up and down the road and along the fence line, but the area was clean. There were no cigarette butts, no tire marks, no drops of oil, no spent cartridges, nothing. An inch-by-inch search of the parking lot the other side of the road also drew a blank. It was time for old-fashioned police work, knocking on doors.

CHAPTER FORTY-NINE

Weinberg's plane touched down at LAX forty-five minutes late, but he didn't care. He was just happy to be back on the West Coast. New York City was not how he remembered it. The old neighborhood had changed and all but one of his pals had moved on. The contacts he had made over the last few days were just names in his cell phone and no more. At times he felt both lonely and alone in the city where he was born.

After collecting his bag from the carousel he made his way out of the baggage hall into the arrivals area. A text from his office let him know that his car was stuck in traffic and would be at least another fifteen minutes. To kill time he wandered across the concourse and joined a small crowd that had gathered to look at the television set in one of the airport bars. A news flash announcing, *"Marty King shot dead"*, ran across the bottom of the screen.

Standing just outside the bar he hurriedly pulled the script from his briefcase and flipped through the pages.

He mumbled to himself, "The old lady was the first to be killed, then it was the man on the cross and now it's Marty King. Son of a bitch, he really is keeping to the goddamn script."

Suddenly it occurred to Weinberg that if the killer was being true to the script then he knew exactly where he would make his next move. He was excited, so excited that he jumped in a taxi forgetting all about the car that was coming to take him back to the office.

Weinberg may have been pumped and wide-awake, but Joe was so tired he could hardly keep his eyes open, yet he refused to go to bed. From the moment he got home he sat in front of the TV watching the local morning news eating yet another piece of leftover pizza straight out of the fridge. It was like waiting for the reviews to come out following a movie premiere or an opening night on Broadway. It was important for Joe to know what people thought of his "work". He'd already started putting together a scrapbook with articles from the newspapers and those he printed off the Internet. Using a felt tip pen he highlighted his favorite comments such as *"most bizarre killing"* and *"we have not seen anything like this for two thousand years"*.

When the shooting of Marty King, Southern California's most famous used car salesman and master of self-promotion, finally hit the airwaves, Joe was ecstatic. Exhausted but elated, he bounced to his feet and sat on the back of the sofa. The news clip began with one of King's best known TV commercials and his popular catchphrase: "Hi I'm Marty King, king of the road."

Clapping his hands like a child about to receive a birthday present, Joe sniggered and couldn't resist saying, "Oh no you're not."

The newscaster talked about King growing up as the son of a Baptist Minister and his role in the community supporting children's charities despite not having children of his own. He went on to describe the shooting as the work of a marksman, perhaps someone who was ex-military and then finished with a comment from Detective Dan Scott.

Dan looked uneasy standing in front of a camera with a half dozen TV and radio microphones pushed in his face. He clearly wasn't a fan of the press. He glanced around as if seeking support, but none was forthcoming. It was much too early to make any intelligent observations, so when asked to comment on the shooting he paused for a moment, staring directly into the camera and said, "I will get you. Whoever did this, I will get you."

It wasn't your normal politically correct three minutes of

department bullshit, but it was said with feeling and purpose and it hit a raw nerve with at least one viewer.

Joe laughed when he heard Dan's remark. It was a nervous laugh, the inappropriate kind that is normally an expression of anxiety.

CHAPTER FIFTY

The heat was on. Two murders in quick succession had shaken the department at its core. The Mayor's office was putting pressure on Esposito and in true departmental fashion Esposito passed the buck down to Dan. Pressure was fine, but the station's number one cop didn't need to be told the obvious.

Catch these bastards was not constructive. *Here are another couple of detectives to work on these cases,* or *here's the name of the guys who did it* would have been more helpful.

It reminded Dan of when he was a kid and his soccer team was losing three to two with two minutes to go and the coach yelling, "We need a goal!"

At the far end of the office a large white board stretching half the width of the room was covered with gruesome reminders of the hell Van Sykes and King went through during their last moments on earth. Enlarged pictures of Van Sykes' hands and feet pinned down by huge bloodstained spikes and the cavernous hole in the top of King's head were enough to make even the most hardened cop sick to the stomach. In front of this gallery of gore was an oval table and a selection of comfortable chairs, facilities to make coffee and a vending machine for candy to give the guys a sugar lift when required. It all seemed a bit incongruous. The area, known as the "pit", was for brainstorming. Positioned as far away as possible from computers, phones and other distractions, it was a sanctuary set up by Dan to concentrate on the business at hand. The idea was that anyone could speak in the pit and no one would be ridiculed no matter what they said. Sometimes the meetings were heated and lively, but today the atmosphere was subdued. With two high profile murders and no leads there was nothing to get excited about although Heinz tried his best to get things moving.

"Hey guys, I found Van Sykes' mother," shouted the ex-marine as he walked confidently into the pit.

An expectation of something good drifted across the room. Would she be able to provide information linking someone to the death of her son? Perhaps she knew about a jealous work colleague or an ex who had stalked him since high school.

"What can she tell us?" said Moose no longer wishing to play the game.

"Not much. She's sucking her food through a straw in a home for the walking dead in Portland," said Heinz in his usual uncaring manner. "She has Alzheimer's, it's not all bad you know. You can hide your own Easter eggs."

What a dickhead, thought Leigh as she looked on from the other side of the room, itching to get involved and desperately wanting to be part of the team. As a journalist she'd carried out her own investigations and written hundreds of column inches about murder cases and, although she'd never been on the police side of things, she knew she could handle it. She also knew that Dan was the only detective capable of any kind of lateral thinking. Moose was a big soft cuddly bear unable to come up with an original idea on his own while Heinz had too many issues to allow him to think clearly.

She felt so helpless and as her mind wandered for a moment a feeling of sadness came over her when she spotted the empty chair where Mike once sat. He would love to be here now. Determined and clever, he would have provided Dan with that much needed second voice. But as much as she loved and respected her brother, she believed she could fill the void left by his death.

Aware that it was an interesting mix with the squad as diverse as it was similar, Leigh was impressed that everyone was working towards the same goal although each had different motives for going there. Moose was an ardent supporter of the underdog and the vulnerable and saw Van Sykes as an easy target. Physically and mentally weak, he didn't have a snowball's chance in hell of fighting off his attacker while King didn't even get to see his attacker. Heinz, on the other hand, couldn't give a shit for anyone. He was pissed off that the killings took place on "his" streets. For him, that was enough to justify stringing the killer up by the balls.

As for Dan, Leigh could read him like a book. It wasn't personal, it wasn't anything to do with hate or revenge and it wasn't about getting his name in the paper. It was a job; one that he was born to do.

CHAPTER FIFTY-ONE

Weinberg got a kick out of being an "in your face" kind of guy even though at six foot three inches tall he looked down on most people. He loved to intimidate and often joked that he stooped to conquer. Describing himself as larger than life with witch like features, a tooth that lit up the night and Alice Cooper hair, he knew he wasn't a babe magnet. He didn't care. If he wanted a woman, he'd buy one. Money was the answer to everything. So it came as no surprise that the man who had bad taste oozing out of every orifice would have set up his studio in a stylishly refurbished 1950s service station. It looked like nothing you'd imagine a porn studio would be. There was no peep-hole on a hidden doorway down a side alley, no black walls with fluorescent lights and definitely no lewd pictures in sight.

Instead, a pair of fully restored red Texaco gas pumps complete with matching globe on top stood in the middle of the forecourt while a long black air hose with the meter in working order hung proudly off the side of the building. A few feet away the bright white up and over doors leading to the service bays hung motionless as they had done for several decades. The studio where Weinberg produced most of his low budget films was once the service area where oil filters were changed and flat tires repaired. Exhaust fumes and the stench of gasoline had been replaced by the sweet smell of success. Across the hall and through a narrow doorway was Weinberg's office. It was immaculate. The shelves and the wooden topped counter supporting the cash register, cans of oil and antifreeze had long since disappeared, but the old Coca Cola machine serving up bottles of Coke for ten cents was still in working order. A framed antique poster of a fire helmet promoting Texaco Fire Chief Gasoline hung on the wall as a reminder of simpler times.

Weinberg's large glass top desk was piled high with packages stuffed with show reels and begging letters from wannabe actors and actresses desperate to start at the bottom of the barrel. From day one he discovered that some people would do anything to get into show business and laying it bare on DVD was the latest craze. His predecessor, however, had a different approach and couldn't be doing with resumes, photos or strips of celluloid. Every aspiring actor was told the same thing. *"Come in and show me what you got".*

Like most small filmmakers, Weinberg operated as a one-man band with additional crew brought in as and when required. His latest squeeze, Jolanta, a twenty year old stick thin Polish girl with limited English, hung around to answer the phone, make coffee and provide sexual favors during times of stress and boredom. Opening the mail was strictly taboo and not in her job description. Weinberg trusted no-one, especially a girl from Eastern Europe who had entered the US on a two-week holiday visa two years ago. The world wasn't exactly her oyster. Being illegal meant that her options were limited. It was either sleep with him or clean toilets in some downtown office building in the middle of the night with a bunch of wetbacks.

The next hour was spent sifting through every piece of paper he could find, but there was nothing connected to *"Killing the Dead"*. Jolanta remembered a call from a very rude man asking about this script, but she didn't get his name or number. She did have the sense to ask her boss if he recalled leaving his briefcase unattended during the trip to New York.

At first he laughed at the idea, but when he thought back over the past few days it occurred to him that his briefcase had been out of his sight more than he realized. It was left next to his chair in the first class lounge when he got up to get some food, then again when he made himself a drink and finally when he went to the washroom. On the plane, it was in the overhead locker, while he was grabbing forty winks and making trips to the toilet. The briefcase was also in the hands of the hotel porter in New York for about twenty minutes when he checked in and then while waiting for it to be brought to his room. He also remembered that he had left it on the back seat of his car during the meal at Tata's. Any thoughts Weinberg may have had about retracing his steps to locate the author were quickly dismissed. He had a better idea and that was to follow the script. There was going to be another murder. Weinberg knew how it would be done, where it would be done, but not when. It was time for him to get into position and wait.

CHAPTER FIFTY-TWO

The local TV News Channel and Talk Radio struggled to be heard above the sounds of "Hey Joe" blasting from the stereo. It was a disturbing scene. Chest bare and looking through bloodshot eyes, Joe swaggered from room to room singing at the top of his voice. The louder he sang the further his saliva flew into the air. It was Christmas, his birthday and the 4th of July all rolled into one. Joe was finally living the dream and things could only get better because the best was yet to come.

"You're talking about me," he shouted, as he pressed his face against the TV screen where a man in a dark blue suit with a microphone stood frozen like a deer in a car's headlights. Police scurried back and forth behind the presenter while onlookers gathered outside the entrance to King's apartment building hoping for a glimpse of something grisly they could tell their friends about.

"I wrote that and I played the lead," shouted Joe, as his spit washed across the front of the screen.

"What do you think of me now assholes?" he added falling back onto the couch.

There was such a racket in the living room that it was impossible to hear his cell ringing, but a slight vibration on the front right hand side of his jeans caught his attention.

"Yeah," he yelled after wrestling to get his phone out of his pocket.

"Where the fuck are you man?" Gomez's tinny sounding voice echoed back through the phone.

"What?" Joe couldn't hear properly so he kicked the "off" button on the TV with the toe of his boot and hurried across the room to lift the needle off the record. Finally he leaned over and yanked the plug from the wall to silence the radio.

"That's better... who is it?"

"It's me, Gomez, where are you... you should have been here forty-five minutes ago?"

"Holy shit," said Joe suddenly realizing he still had a day job, "Cover for me, I'm coming."

Ten minutes later Joe had showered and changed and was heading off to work. He didn't want to go, but he had no choice. He was two months behind with his rent and, no matter how hard he squeezed the buffalo, he still had to eat and drink. Most important of all he needed money to buy drugs. Weed, pills and powder had been a part of Joe's life for as long as he could remember and he wasn't about to give them up now. And if anyone was to blame for Joe's chemical dependency it was his mother. She always said, *"If they're old enough to ask the question, they're old enough to know the answer"*, and she definitely practiced what she preached. At the tender age of eleven, when Joe saw her smoking a joint in the back room of some hillbilly bar in a one-horse town in Northern California, he'd asked naively, "What's that?"

"Here, stick it in your mouth and breathe in."

After a couple of drags the young boy turned green and began throwing up in the toilet. It should have been enough to put him off smoking for a few years, but it didn't. His mother was his only role model and he wanted to be just like her.

CHAPTER FIFTY-THREE

Leigh took a call from Maurice Delaney. He wanted to speak to Heinz, but the detective refused to pick up the phone. Heinz felt he had bigger fish to fry with the crucifixion and the shooting of Marty King and didn't want to waste time on a suicide.

"I'm sorry, he's in a meeting," said Leigh. "Can I get him to call you back?"

"I've already left three messages."

"He's been very busy lately," she said trying to defend the indefensible.

Delaney broke down and started to speak and cry at the same time, "She didn't kill herself... she wouldn't do that... not now anyway."

"What do you mean by that?" asked Leigh.

Delaney didn't respond. He was inconsolable. She tried to calm him down, but he wouldn't stop crying.

Placing her hand over the mouthpiece of the phone she quietly asked Heinz to take the call, but Heinz's response was to mock. He pretended to break open a couple of pill capsules and drop the powder into an imaginary glass of water on his desk. He then made a stirring motion with his index finger and sucked his finger suggestively before drinking the contents of the glass in one gulp. Finally, he fell dying to the floor with both hands grasping his throat. It was strange, but Leigh wasn't shocked. She knew what Heinz was like and was learning to live with it.

When she returned to the call Delaney had hung up. This whole thing had left a bad taste in her mouth. She felt like she was letting the old man down when she had nothing at all to do with the case. There was a deep desire to help even if it was just to give him a hug. She wondered why she couldn't be like Heinz and just pull the shutters down.

On the opposite side of the room a huge badge with the L.A. Police motto, "To Protect and Serve", hung on the wall over the door. Leigh stared at it for a moment and thought to herself. *If it wasn't suicide then we failed to protect her and by not investigating further we're failing to serve.*

Clutching a piece of paper with Delaney's address on it, she grabbed her bag and shouted across the room that she was going for an early lunch.

CHAPTER FIFTY-FOUR

At least a dozen cars were lined up at valet parking when Joe rushed on to the lot. It was exceptionally busy because of the light drizzle that had just started to fall. He recognized most of the cars as belonging to people in the film business. Film people don't like rain. They don't like anything that makes them look bad.

Savage, his manager, eventually stopped barking out instructions and went back inside the restaurant. Gomez had done a great job of keeping his boss sweet and was anxious to speak to Joe.

"I told him your father had to go to hospital," said Gomez with a childish grin. "You got a father?"

"No," Joe said flatly.

"Then you better get one and while you're at it give him a disease and a hospital to stay in."

"Thanks, you saved my ass."

"No problem, man. Hey you, shoot anyone with that gun yet?"

Joe almost choked. Sometimes he had difficulty working out if Gomez was joking or not and this was one of those times. He studied the Mexican's face for a moment until he was sure he knew nothing about King.

"Yeah, I drove down to the border the other day and took a shot at your sister."

Happy to play the straight man Gomez responded," How did you know it was my sister?"

"Because she had a moustache just like yours."

At that moment Savage called Joe into the restaurant.

"Good luck," said Gomez.

"I don't need luck, I got leverage remember, I saw him

164

dippin' that new waitress."

"You got nothing," yelled Gomez, "he left his wife for her two days ago."

"Oh… shit," blurted Joe as he walked slowly to the entrance.

————————————————————

Savage didn't beat about the bush. He looked Joe straight in the eye and asked him about his father. Although his question implied that he cared, his tone was suspicious. Joe knew that Savage wasn't his biggest fan and he would have to be convincing. Thanks to Gomez he was prepared and gave a performance that would have impressed the most cynical of Hollywood casting directors. It was all there. He didn't miss a trick. The phone call in the early hours of the morning, the rush to his father's hospital bedside, the somber look on the doctor's face and the elation Joe felt upon hearing that his father was going to be OK. Savage ate it up and Joe went back to work knowing that he'd done it again.

"What happened, did he buy it?" asked Gomez.

"Did he? I just sold a fridge to an Eskimo," said Joe, chuckling inanely.

Gomez slapped him on the back, but as they walked away from the restaurant they noticed that Savage's girlfriend had been standing just a few feet away.

CHAPTER FIFTY-FIVE

When Leigh stopped outside 154 Anna Avenue she sensed an eerie silence in the neighborhood. There were no children playing on the lawns and no little old ladies gossiping on the sidewalk. Even the power walkers were nowhere to be seen. Marilyn Delaney had spent most of her adult life on this street and she had helped make it a decent place to live. Perhaps her neighbors were just showing her the respect she deserved or maybe doubts surrounding her death had created fear in the community.

Leigh was nervous. The house, with its curtains closed and black wreath hanging on the door, was not welcoming. It was like the life-blood had been sucked out. Aware that it was illegal to pass herself off as a police officer she decided that when she met Mr Delaney she would be economical with the truth. It was easier than she thought it would be.

"Hi, Mr Delaney, my name is Leigh. We spoke on the phone when you rang the station earlier today," she started confidently, as the old man opened the door to her loud knocking.

Delaney's face lit up despite the pain he must have been suffering. The opportunity to talk to someone who just might listen must have been a real boost to his spirits.

With less than an hour to spend at lunch, Leigh tried to be as direct as possible without appearing insensitive. "You said on the phone that your wife wouldn't kill herself now. What did you mean by that?"

Delaney hesitated and verbally stumbled, "I... I... I have cancer and only a few months to live. She promised to stay with me until... "

"Maybe she just didn't want to be alone?" Leigh suggested.

166

"We talked about that. She said she would give it a while… if things were too unbearable then she would join me."

"Do you realize what you just said?" asked Leigh.

"Yes, I do." Delaney replied.

"This will make it almost impossible for the police to believe it was anything but suicide."

"I know… but it wasn't. We were together for forty-five years and I would have known if she was going to do something like this."

"Do you mind if I look around?" asked Leigh.

"No, go ahead."

Leigh knew that Heinz would have been out of there in a heartbeat. Everything Delaney said supported the suicide premise, so why was she sniffing around the couple's bedroom? She was stalling. She felt sorry for the old man and didn't know how to extract herself from the house or the fact that she was his only glimmer of hope of finding a more agreeable explanation for his wife's death. The longer she delayed things the more she wished she wasn't there. Heinz was an asshole, but he knew what he was doing. She'd learned a lesson today. Go with the facts, not your heart.

Leigh looked at her watch. Time was running out. She had just twenty minutes to get back to work. While Delaney excused himself to answer the phone, her fingers gently turned the fragile pages of the family photo album. She smiled as she glanced at the faded color wedding photos and the press dried gypsophilia stems which had been carefully positioned in the book over forty years ago. The order of service and hymn list had also aged and curled up at the corners, but the wedding invitation, which was folded in half, stood the test of time.

"We cordially invite you to attend the wedding of our daughter Marilyn Elizabeth Monroe to Maurice Delaney on", Leigh stopped and then read the line again, *Marilyn Elizabeth Monroe. Why do parents do that?* she thought.

She already knew the answer, but she felt she had to ask the question.

"Was Monroe your wife's maiden name?"

"Yes and boy was she happy when she changed it to Delaney. Her father was a big fan and thought it would be 'fun' for her to have the same name."

"Was it?"

"No, it was hell. She took a lot of kidding and a few lumps. Sometimes parents can be so stupid," Delaney said.

Leigh had to go. She told Delaney that she would make a few calls and get back to him. In truth, she had no one to call, but she wanted to leave him with something to cling on to. Her heart was in the right place, but it was a dumb move and she was about to get it in the neck from both sides. As far as Delaney was concerned, she was now in charge and Heinz was no longer on the case. What would he do if he discovered she wasn't a cop? What would she do when it came time to tell Delaney his wife took her own life? On balance, Delaney was probably the least of her worries. Heinz was a certified crazy and if he found out about this he would flip. What right did she have to investigate his case? She was in a no win situation. The more she thought about what she'd just done, the more she regretted it.

While Leigh was getting ready to face the music, Weinberg was getting ready to take a giant leap into the unknown. Attaching a writer's contract to the script, he snatched a couple of shirts off the rail in the walk-in closet at the back of his studio and threw them into a brown leather overnight case along with three pairs of underwear and some white socks. An unopened bag of freebies handed out to first class passengers was also tossed into the mix.

Jolanta was down at the local deli collecting a take away box of pastrami on rye sandwiches with pickles and coleslaw on the side. This was an exciting time for Weinberg.

Killing the Dead may be his best shot at serious filmmaking and he didn't want to miss out. He wasn't turning his back on porn. How could he? Life in the "blue" lane had given him everything he ever wanted including his gold tooth, but New York had been a wake up call. Things were changing and he needed to look beyond erotica. It had nothing to do with art or respect from his peers. It was all about making money and hanging on to the good things in life. Weinberg came from nowhere with nothing and he would do anything to keep from going back there.

"Let's go," he shouted to Jolanta.

"Where?" she asked.

"To a motel."

"I don't have clothes."

"You won't need them."

Jolanta giggled and climbed into the Cadillac like an obedient puppy.

CHAPTER FIFTY-SIX

"Like a moth to a bright light" is how Dan once described the effect a murder has on certain members of the public and he wasn't just talking about the weirdos who want to know all the gory details. Some people want to make it part of their lives with a need to confess whether they are guilty or not and a high profile murder attracts even more moths to the light. Perhaps it's just attention seeking or possibly it stems from a troubled past. Maybe the alternative put before them by an aggressive interrogator is just too unpalatable so they take an easier option. No matter how it breaks down it usually ends up wasting valuable department time and resources.

"I've had three confessions in the last hour," said Heinz to Dan who was also working the phones. "The first guy said he killed Van Sykes, but couldn't remember how many nails he'd used or where he'd put them. He then admitted to shooting King with a pistol. The others couldn't even tell me where the killings took place. Where do these sick bastards come from? Is the circus in town?"

Dan smiled. "I can top that. I just had a sixty-eight year old woman tell me that her dead husband killed both Van Sykes and King from beyond the grave. I guess she felt he should suffer some more because being married to her wasn't punishment enough."

At that moment, Leigh entered the office and went quickly to her desk, avoiding eye contact with the others in the room. Keeping her head down, she turned on her computer and started tapping on her keys.

"You got a minute?" asked Dan.

"Sure," she said as she walked over to the pit feeling like

a naughty schoolgirl who, for the second time in a matter of hours, was standing in front of the teacher. Leigh was smart enough to have given Delaney her cell number, but what if he forgot and rang the office? If Dan knew what she'd been up to she'd be in deep shit. Paying a visit to Ramos was bad enough, but she could be forgiven because of her brother. Dropping in to see Delaney was completely unforgivable.

"I made a couple of calls," said Dan. "The first one was to a guy I know working with immigration at the border. He said their records show that the Ramos brothers were not in Mexico at the time your parent's were killed."

Initially, Leigh was relieved that her private meeting with Dan had nothing to do with her lunch hour investigation, but then she was bitterly disappointed to hear that Sergio Ramos had not run down her parents.

"That's impossible, his car was there."

"That was my second call. It's always there, that's where he keeps it," Dan replied.

"Can we have someone check it out?" asked Leigh.

"Too late... Ricardo bought a new one the day you went to see him. His brother's old car has disappeared, probably crushed or sold for scrap."

Leigh stood quietly for a moment as she thought about what Dan had just said. "So, if I had come to you before going to Ramos, we may still have the old car as evidence."

"From what your contact in Mexico told you the old car had been cleaned and then repaired so the chances of finding anything incriminating were slim."

"But there was a chance?"

Dan didn't need to say anymore. Leigh was aware that she'd blown it. If she'd been playing poker she'd be broke. You can't lay your cards on the table at the start of the game and expect to keep the upper hand and that's exactly what she did when she went to Ramos' house. The case was closed and the file was in the bottom of a drawer gathering dust. This is when the guilty relax, take their eye off the ball and become cocky. It would have been a perfect time to carry out an investigation.

There was an ugly silence in the pit as they avoided eye contact. Dan checked his cell and Leigh shuffled pointlessly through a pile of papers that had been left on a chair. The longer they went without speaking the angrier she became. She wasn't annoyed with Dan, she was mad at herself because she was impulsive just like her brother. She was pretty and feminine, but she felt like she'd charged into the arena like a goddamn bull. Finally, Dan broke the silence.

"Look, you screwed up, we all do from time-to-time, but you also did a great job. At least now we know there is a strong possibility that the Ramos family were involved in the death of your parents which also might help to explain why Sergio shot Mike."

Dan was a gentleman. He had a way of telling you what you did wrong without making you feel foolish. There was no need to embarrass or humiliate or grandstand. Leigh liked the way he did things. The more she saw of him the more she wanted to be with him.

CHAPTER FIFTY-SEVEN

As Weinberg pulled off the main highway into a motel parking lot, Jolanta asked innocently, "We are staying in this place?"

There was a sense of disappointment in her voice and it was justifiable. The motel was a dump. A winding gravel drive leading up to reception was filled with potholes and dotted with weeds that stood several inches high. Peeling white paint hung off the wooden slatted walls of the single story building that ran parallel to the busy road while a flickering red neon sign announced to passersby that rooms were still available. If a twenty year old illegal immigrant from Eastern Europe was uneasy about staying in this place how would Mr "First Class" feel? He was about to find out.

Weinberg opened the screen door to the office and a strong smell of body odor savaged his nostrils. He grimaced and swallowed hard as he came face to face with an unshaven overweight man in his mid forties wearing a sweat stained sleeveless T-shirt. Without saying a word, the man raised his arm above his head revealing an armpit so wet that perspiration ran along the side of his body like water gushing from an open faucet. Smashing the palm of his hand on the counter he gloated as he stared at Weinberg before turning his hand over to reveal a flattened fly.

Why bother, thought Weinberg, *just invite the buggers to nest in your armpits and they'll be dead in seconds.*

"You want a room?" asked the man as he flicked the dead insect on to the floor.

"Yeah," Weinberg responded, trying to keep the disgust out of his voice.

The man leaned to the left and looked out at Jolanta sitting in the Cadillac. "You want to pay by the hour or by the night?" he asked with a smutty look on his face.

"By the night and give me a room in the middle."

"That'll be two bucks extra."

"Why?" asked Weinberg.

"Better view."

Weinberg thought for a second about reaching over the counter and grabbing the obnoxious son of a bitch by his elongated chest hairs and slugging him in the face with his free hand, but he couldn't and he wouldn't because he was a coward. Besides he had more important things to do. It was time to settle in and wait and it wasn't going to be fun.

If Jolanta was depressed seeing the motel from the road, the porn master knew she'd be suicidal seeing it from the inside. It was not for the faint hearted. As the door to their room flew open to expose a large deep red discoloration on the carpet, a mouse bolted along the skirting board and took shelter in the closet. Stale air seeped quickly into their lungs and onto their clothing. Weinberg dragged his finger along the bedside table revealing a thick coating of dust before discreetly drawing back the corner of the frayed blanket on the bed and then hurriedly replacing it so that Jolanta wouldn't see the sorry state of the sheets. The room hadn't been cleaned for months, possibly years. Dirt was everywhere, neither one of them wanted to sit down. This was Weinberg's worst nightmare.

"Hey, at least there's a television," he said, trying hard to lighten the mood.

"What's that thing on top?" asked Jolanta.

Weinberg moved to get a closer look, "I don't fucking believe it," he yelled as he banged the top of the TV with his fist. "It takes quarters... you gotta pay to watch the goddamn box."

CHAPTER FIFTY-EIGHT

Gomez lifted a newspaper from the back seat of a white Buick he'd just parked and was reading the front page when he turned to Joe.

"So what do you think about this crazy fuck who nailed that guy to the cross? Is he sick or what?"

"I didn't know you could read," said Joe, grabbing the paper out of his hands.

"It says here he escaped from a nut house," added Gomez pointing half way down the page.

Joe was curious. He spread the paper over the hood of a nearby Chevy and began to read the lead story that suggested the killer was an escaped madman from Napa State Hospital. According to the article, William Bradley, a thirty-eight year old male Caucasian from the Bay area, broke out of the hospital three months ago following his incarceration for killing two migrant workers on a farm just outside of San Francisco. One of his victims was dipped up to his waist in an acid bath and left to die while the second was buried alive. The newspaper journalist compared the inhuman death of Van Sykes to those of the migrant workers and concluded that only someone with a severely diminished mental capacity like Bradley could commit such a crime.

Bradley's photograph was front and center on the page. Joe punched the picture. Being compared to a madman didn't bother him. What really pissed him off was that someone else was getting recognition for his work.

"They know shit," he said aloud before remembering that Gomez was standing next to him.

"What?" replied the startled Mexican.

Joe had to think fast, "How does some asshole sitting at

a computer know who did this? They'll say anything to sell papers."

"Bradley did it before, what's to stop him doing it again?" replied Gomez.

"Read my lips, he didn't do it," said Joe in a loud voice.

Gomez backed off as his car-parking buddy was becoming more and more irate. Joe's chin protruded and his neck muscles tightened. There was evil in his eyes. Gomez always expected the unexpected from Joe, but this was different. For the first time, Gomez was afraid.

It was the end of his shift and, as Joe made his way past the back door of the restaurant, Savage called his name.

"What?" shouted Joe in a voice that was filled with anger.

"You're fired," said Savage, his face split from ear to ear with a wide grin.

Joe stopped in his tracks and turned to face his manager, who was standing in the kitchen doorway. "Stop bustin' my balls," he said.

"I'm not… here's your money, get the fuck off the lot."

An envelope containing cash landed at Joe's feet.

Joe raised his arms in disbelief. "What have I done now?" he asked.

Savage turned his head slightly to the right and beckoned his girlfriend to come forward. He placed his arm around her shoulder and spoke with a smug look on his face, "You sold a fridge to the wrong fucking Eskimo."

Joe knew there was no point in arguing. Savage never liked him and it was only a matter of time before they would part company. As more people came out of the kitchen to see what was going on, Joe shook his head in disbelief, picked up his money and walked across the lot. Once again he felt he was the victim and never considered that this was of his own making. Racing his engine, he popped the clutch and threw up a cloud of dust and small stones. He flew by the back door without even glancing at the small crowd that had gathered there, but stopped when he came alongside Gomez.

"I'm gonna be big, you can tell everyone you knew me!"

Although Bradley's name had just made it into the papers, Dan knew about him long before the press did. In fact he'd been trying to track him down since the Canal Street crucifixion with stakeouts at three addresses in the city where Bradley had previously hung out. The Hollywood cop wasn't happy that things were now out in the open. Putting Bradley's name and picture in the paper was a double edge sword. There was always a slim chance that some good citizen may recognize the killer and do the right thing, but seeing his picture in the paper could drive him underground and force him to change his appearance. Relying on help from the public was not something Dan encouraged. The last thing he wanted was a group of red neck vigilantes patrolling his streets.

It was now eleven p.m. and Joe was on his way to PJ's when he was stopped at a police roadblock. Scenes like this were not uncommon in L.A. whenever something serious was going down. What was unusual was that this was a quiet leafy residential street with not a bank or liquor store in sight. Dan and Heinz were on the scene quickly and had taken up their positions outside the front of the house. They were preparing for a long night.

Joe was unlucky. Had he been two minutes earlier he would have avoided the barricades. Now he was first in line, right behind the barrier with no way out. A uniformed officer didn't want to talk when questioned by a handful of people standing at the barrier, but a local man, who had just been evacuated from his home, was more than happy to hold court.

"I saw a light on next door and called 911… the Klein's are in Europe so I knew something was wrong, thought about goin' over myself and checking things out… used to do a bit of boxing when I was a kid you know, glad I didn't, the crazy bastard started shooting when the cops arrived... just about everybody on the street has been moved out, some were still in their pyjamas."

This had not been a good day for Joe. He lost his job, Bradley was raining on his parade and now some retard burglar was preventing him from having a beer. It had crossed his mind to walk to PJ's, but he quickly dropped the idea when he realized he would have to walk back as well. There was nothing else to do but chill, so Joe returned to his truck and switched on the radio. It wasn't long before the guy who was doing all the talking appeared at his window.

"Wanna know something?" the man asked, looking round to make sure no one else was listening.

"Sure," said Joe.

"My teenage son is still in the house next door," he whispered, pausing and glancing over his shoulder and then, with a touch of arrogance, continuing to talk. "He's filming everything from the attic window with his phone. We already made a deal with Channel 7 News."

"No shit?" said Joe.

"Wanna see what he just sent me?"

Joe could have said no and told the guy to fuck off, but he still would have showed him the images. This was his moment, his fifteen minutes of fame, and nothing would change that. He would talk about this for the rest of his life and each time he did the story would be embellished until one day he'd be the one in the house taking the pictures instead of cowering safely behind police lines.

Opening the passenger door, the man climbed into the cab and pushed the play button on his cell. At first the pictures were grainy, but then when the intruder moved to the upstairs window his face was caught in the moonlight and it was clear that this was no thief, it was Bradley.

An hour ago, Joe had never heard of William Bradley. Now he wanted him dead. If Bradley was captured alive, and was as crazy as everybody said he was, he may just take credit for the crucifixion of Van Sykes. That would ruin everything for Joe just when things were going so well. He needed a plan.

"Do the police know what you're doing?" asked Joe.

The man shook his head. "They will in a minute tho' when the news goes live."

This was Joe's chance. He got out of the truck pretending to go for a piss. When he got far enough away he called directory assistance and asked for the number for Klein on West 4th street.

A minute later the pictures went live on Channel 7 News and a minute after that five cops were seen running into the house where the kid was hiding. Joe called the Klein's number.

"Yeah"

"Are you that retard, Bradley?"

"Who's this?"

"Turn on the TV – Channel 7."

"Fuck you."

"Turn it on and smile numb nuts, you're on Candid Camera."

A moment passed and then Bradley returned to the phone. "Who's doin' this?"

"Look out the window dummy, I'm next door in the attic."

_____

Bradley was fuming. Looking up at the house next door he saw a shadowy figure framed inside the small opening in the attic. He let off a couple of wild shots through a closed bedroom window tossing glass splinters into the air.

This was exactly what Joe was hoping he would do. It was the starting pistol, the green flag and the get set and go all rolled into one. Before anyone had time to draw breath, World War Three was unleashed on the floor where Bradley was hiding. For the next ninety seconds bullets rained down on him from all directions and when the shooting finally stopped and the dust had settled, Bradley was dead.

_____

This was not the outcome Dan wanted. He saw the bigger

picture. Like everyone else, he was happy there was one less sicko in the world and the California taxpayer no longer had to foot the bill for Bradley's detention, but he also wanted to question him about the crucifixion. Standing over his bullet riddled body, he knew this was no longer possible.

"I counted at least twenty slugs in this guy," said Heinz. "I hope they're taking him home by car because he'll never get through the LAX metal detector."

Heinz's remarks drew a few chuckles from nearby cops, but Dan didn't even crack a smile. He had more important things to deal with. A female officer gestured discreetly for him to join her at the doorway. She led him along a corridor and then down a metal spiral staircase into a dimly lit utility room where the Klein's washer and dryer were located. A large chest freezer stood open along the back wall. Blocks of melting ice cream, water filled ice cube trays and steaks dripping with blood littered the terracotta tiled floor. As Dan approached the freezer he knew he wasn't going to like what he was about to see. Two cops, one with a solitary tear running down his cheek, stood with their heads bowed at either end of the seven hundred liter box. Dan was prepared for the worst, but not for this. A pretty young girl with long blond hair and wearing a light blue dress was lying face up in the freezer. She looked like she was asleep, but she wasn't, she was dead.

Heinz now entered the room and stood next to Dan in front of the white enamel coffin.

Without taking his eyes off the girl, Dan whispered, "If you so much as open your mouth, I'll kill you."

––––––––––––––––––––

Joe climbed back into his pickup to find the man with the big mouth curled up in a ball on the floor beneath the dash. Aware it was now safe to come out, the coward slowly unravelled himself and gingerly stepped down on to the road. Most fathers in this situation would have gone crashing through the barrier to find their son, but not this guy. He stayed on the safe side of the cordon talking to anyone who would listen.

"I called 911, I saw the light on next door and knew something wasn't right."

Even though his father wasn't concerned, Joe knew that the kid would be fine. The odds that Bradley would hit anyone while shooting upwards into a small opening were slim and Joe was willing to bet those odds to keep his story alive.

DAY THIRTEEN

CHAPTER FIFTY-NINE

It was extremely uncommon to see Esposito in the office before nine a.m. Some days he would get there just in time to go for lunch and there was nothing anyone could do about it. At sixty-four years of age with forty years service under his belt he knew he was fireproof. With less than six months to retirement he was already winding down and looking forward to the day when the "19th hole" became his new office. On the rare occasion that he did show up for work at the same time as everyone else it usually meant one of two things. Either he had fallen asleep at his desk following an all night office Christmas party or he was getting ready for a photo opportunity. Since the festive season was still months away it had to be the latter. Whereas Dan preferred not to be in the spotlight, Esposito loved it and would do anything to get a mention in the papers or a quote on the news. Deep down inside he was just another politician. When things went well he was in your face 24/7. When things didn't go as they should, he was the invisible man.

After a short briefing Esposito made his way down the stairs to the front door where the press were waiting. Dan was told to be there as well so he tagged along, reluctantly. They couldn't have been more opposite. Up beat and looking like a man safe in his comfort zone, the olive skinned sexagenarian stood tall in a uniform that would have impressed the top brass at West Point. His lead detective, however, looked tired, dishevelled and a little fed up. He didn't want to be there.

After what he saw at the Klein's house, he didn't want to be anywhere.

Photographers, cameramen and journalists jockeyed for position like flies around a cow's asshole as Esposito flashed his million dollar smile and then introduced himself before launching into his account of what happened on West 4th Street a few hours earlier. He spoke like he'd been there from the start, but his squad knew that he didn't arrive at the house until long after it was over.

"On my instructions, the team staked out a house on West 5th Street where Bradley lived with a cousin about six years ago. He was just one street away from being arrested when, we believe, he spotted newspapers scattered over the Kleins' front porch. We checked with the delivery boy who was unaware that the Kleins were on holiday. Bradley got in through a window at the back of the house and it wasn't until three or four hours later that we got a call from a neighbor to say that the place was being burgled. We were hoping to end it peacefully, but were forced to open fire when Bradley began shooting at my officers."

"What about the girl?" a reporter asked.

"Her name is Sissy Holliday... she's nine and lived next door. We think she wandered into the Klein's back yard to get her ball, that's when Bradley grabbed her."

"She was gone for hours; didn't her parents notice she was missing?"

"Her father was on a night shift and her mother was... asleep."

"I heard she was drunk and had passed out," the reporter suggested.

"I can't comment on that," said Esposito.

"Did Bradley kill Van Sykes?" another reporter asked.

Dan knew what was coming next and didn't want to be a part of it. If he spoke to the press he would contradict his boss, so it was best to keep quiet. Looking around he saw Leigh making her way from the car park to the door; he caught her eye and mouthed the word, *help*. She instinctively knew what to do.

Just as Esposito told the gathering that Bradley was most likely responsible for the crucifixion and there were no other suspects, Dan's phone lit up. When a reporter asked the detective if the Van Sykes case was closed, he dodged the question by answering his cell and quietly slipped back into the building.

"I owe you one," said Dan gratefully.

"Tonight then?" smiled Leigh.

"Sure, why not?"

CHAPTER SIXTY

A gentle knock on the door woke Weinberg from the worst night's sleep he ever had. His tall lanky body was slouched painfully into a small wooden chair he had placed next to the window. His neck was stiff and his left foot was asleep. It took a long time for him to stand upright, get the blood flowing through his veins again so he could open the door, but when he did, Jolanta was waiting there with fresh coffee and donuts she bought from the gas station across the street. Despite having spent the night in the car she was smiling.

"Do we check out now?" she asked.

Weinberg couldn't do this to her anymore. He had to be there, she didn't. Twelve hours in that motel room felt like a lifetime and there was no way of knowing how much longer he would have to stay. It was unfair for him to inflict this filth on her just to have sex on tap.

"Come on," he said, "I'll take you home."

Jolanta extended her arms and gave him a huge hug as she giggled and whispered in his ear.

"That's the least I can do for you," said Weinberg, "but let's wait until we get back in the office."

CHAPTER SIXTY-ONE

Opinions at the station couldn't have been more divided. There were those who believed, as Esposito did, that Bradley crucified Van Sykes while others, like Dan, disagreed.

"Bradley's victims were made to suffer," said Dan to a crowded pit, "cruelty was the key. Van Sykes was nailed to a cross, which is pretty goddamn brutal, but the killer then stabbed him to bring about a quick death. This goes against everything Bradley stood for... and besides there seems to be more to the crucifixion than just a cruel way to die, it's like there's some kind of meaning or purpose. I think we should go back to square one. Let's forget about Bradley for a minute."

"Are we looking for one or two killers?" asked Moose.

"I don't know," replied Dan as he approached the giant white board containing the names and photos of the two victims, "I just know we need a break."

Pointing to the first victim he asked, "Emmet Van Sykes, what have we got?"

Heinz responded quickly with information about the victim's past employment and family, but nothing he said gave the team any insight into who may have killed him or why. Moose stepped forward next and provided details of possible suspects and their alibis that had all checked out.

"So, we have nothing," said Dan, "absolutely nothing."

A silence fell over the pit. There was nothing to say. They had no evidence, no witnesses and no suspects. They'd hit a brick wall.

"OK," said Dan enthusiastically. "What about Martin Luther King, what have we got on him?"

Leigh was busy sorting files on the other side of the room

when she heard Dan mention Martin Luther King. She was confused and thought it might be a silly joke to lift everyone's spirits, but nobody laughed. *What has he got to do with anything,* she thought, *he died over forty years ago?* She stopped what she was doing and tried to read what was written on the board, but it was too far away. As she moved closer to the pit Moose stood up and blocked her view. He talked about suspects and the type of rifle used, but again nothing he said was helpful. By this time Leigh had carefully side stepped the big man and was stationary in the middle of the pit. Her mouth was dry and her heart was beating faster. Dan turned to look at Heinz who was waiting to speak next when he saw her reading the section of the board with Marty King's personal details.

"I thought his name was Marty King?" asked Leigh.

"It was," said Moose. "Marty was born just after the real MLK was assassinated. His dad, who was also a Baptist Minister, thought it would be fitting to name his son after the great man, but Marty hated it and changed his name when he started selling cars."

"Martin Luther King," she mumbled to herself, "Martin Luther King... Holy shit!"

"What the fuck is she doing?" shouted Heinz.

Leigh ignored Heinz's remarks and whispered quietly to herself as if she was in some kind of hypnotic trance. "Marilyn Monroe, Jesus and Martin Luther King... Holy shit!" she said again.

"What is this, amateur hour?" quipped Heinz.

Dan stood next to Leigh and grabbed her gently by the arm. He then placed his hands on her shoulders and twisted her slowly so that she was looking into his eyes.

"Leigh," he said sternly, "what's going on?"

"It's the same guy."

"Who's the same guy?" asked Dan.

"The killer... one guy has committed all three murders."

"This is priceless," laughed Heinz, "since when do one and one make three?"

Dan was starting to lose patience. "For Christ sake, what

are you talking about?"

Leigh snapped out of her trance although her heart was still pounding and her breathing was in short bursts. "The same person was responsible for all three murders."

"You said that already," shouted Dan, "but there were only two murders."

Heinz couldn't resist adding, "Maybe that's the way them thar hillbillies do their sums in Montana."

"Marilyn Delaney is the third victim," said Leigh, "well actually she was the first."

"You son of a bitch," screamed Heinz, "I investigated that case and it was clear cut suicide."

"Why would she kill herself when her husband had only six months to live?" replied Leigh.

The room fell silent. Leigh was not just questioning a decision made by an experienced detective; she was standing toe to toe with the biggest chauvinist on the planet.

"And how do you know he had just six months to live? I didn't know that, it's not in my notes."

Leigh looked briefly at Dan and after a long pause the words no one wanted to hear tumbled quietly out of her mouth.

"I went to see Mr Delaney."

Dan flinched.

"Fuck me," shouted Heinz, "she's the goddamn Yoko Ono of Homicide."

Leigh fired back at Heinz. "They made a pact, she would stay with him until he died and then if she couldn't cope she would—"

"She would what, kill herself?" added Heinz quickly. "But then she thought about being in that big house all on her own and said 'fuck it', I'm out of here now."

Tears were streaming down Leigh's face as she stood isolated in the middle of the crowd. Dan held his position in front of the white board, but Heinz was on his feet, moving forward and looking to go in for the kill.

"Her name was Marilyn Monroe," she said, trying desperately to hold back the tears while she made her point.

Heinz was about to jump in again when Dan interrupted, "Shut up, for Christ sake, everybody shut up."

Again the room fell silent.

Looking at Leigh he gestured for her to carry on speaking.

She repeated herself, "Her name was originally Marilyn Monroe."

Heinz couldn't hold back any longer. He threw a handful of papers into the air and shouted, "So what, her husband was dying and her life was so fucking boring that maybe she wanted to do something exciting, something different for a change and what better thing to do than kill yourself just like the dumb blond movie star you were named after?"

"Hang on," shouted Dan.

In no time the situation had gone from a discussion to a disagreement to all out war. The entire office was hooked on every word. Keyboards lay silent and phones were left ringing. It wasn't unusual for cops to shout at each other or even throw the odd punch, but it was strange to see someone cry. Cops don't cry easily. If Leigh was hoping her tears would force Heinz to back off, she was mistaken. He was hard and oblivious to sentiment and had put forward a convincing argument. If she had nothing more to add then her time in the office would be over. She'd have to go and her theory on the killings would probably go with her.

Moose handed her a tissue and she wiped her eyes. It was make or break time. There would be no second chance. Looking directly at Heinz she began slowly taking time to clear her throat.

"I'm sorry I went behind your back, but Delaney sounded so desperate and you wouldn't take his calls. It's no excuse I know and I can understand why you're mad at me. All I ask now is that you listen to what I have to say with no interruptions… and then I'll leave you all alone."

Heinz looked around the room; everyone was staring at him and waiting to see what he would do. Reluctantly he nodded and took a couple of steps back.

After a long pause she continued, "Marilyn Delaney's maiden name was Monroe and she died from an overdose just as Marilyn Monroe did... And she was found lying naked on her bed exactly like the dumb blond movie star."

A knowing smile appeared on Heinz's face.

"The second victim looked like Jesus and acted as if he was Jesus and was killed on the cross just like Jesus. The third victim's real name was Martin Luther King and he was shot by an assassin's bullet while standing on a balcony just like his namesake was in 1968. Three deaths in the last few days and all are in some way connected to famous people who are already dead. It can't be coincidence."

Leigh bowed her head and walked back to her desk. As she sat down one of the secretaries shouted, "Way to go girl!" and started clapping her hands. Then more people joined in and the applause became louder. Suddenly it stopped. Esposito entered the room and wanted to know what was going on.

"Moose's birthday," shouted Dan.

"Have a good one Moose," said Esposito, "see you later."

Dan hated himself. It was unforgivable, but it had to be done. They all knew that Esposito sucked up to the media and would give his right arm to break a story like this one. If Leigh's theory was correct then the last thing Dan wanted was for it to become public. Leigh may have worked out what was happening, but Dan could see the implications this would have if it got out.

"Listen up," shouted Dan as Esposito made his way down the stairs and out of the building, "what goes on in this office stays in this office. Talking about an ongoing investigation to anyone outside the department is a firing offence. Is that clear?"

Trying to drive this key message home was fine, but Dan wasn't born yesterday. If his years as a cop had taught him anything they taught him that most people take care of themselves and if there's a buck to be earned from making a phone call then someone somewhere will drop the dime. Leaks appear everywhere from the highest government office and corporate boardrooms to that most sacred of institutions, marriage. People love to talk especially when they get paid for it. Putting this case to bed before it woke up the entire city was now a priority.

Heinz's behavior in the pit was a concern and, even though there were more important things to do, Dan felt it was the right moment to talk. While the rest of the staff got back to work, Dan confronted the ex-marine head on. He was tired of Heinz's bigoted remarks. They were offensive and upsetting office morale and it was time to sort things out once and for all. The guy had issues and it was easy to spot their origins. The switch from military to civilian life had not been an easy one. The locker room mentality was something Heinz would hopefully shake off, but coming home from Iraq to find his wife in bed with his brother was a killer blow that would not heal overnight. Dan tried to be understanding and let things slide, but he just couldn't do it anymore. The top cop's ultimatum was delivered in a language that Heinz would understand; shape up or ship out. Heinz appeared visibly shaken as he became aware that the job he loved was now on the line. Dan knew that being a cop was all that the ex-marine wanted to do; there was nothing else he could do. It was time to change and there was only one place to start. Dan looked on as Heinz slowly made his way across the office. Every eye was watching him. It must have felt like being in a spotlight and he would have hated it, but he kept going. Finally he stopped, looked down and said, "I'm sorry for being such a jerk."

"And I'm sorry for not doing things properly," replied Leigh graciously.

"Friends," said Heinz as he reached out across her desk with his right hand.

Surprised and delighted, Leigh nodded and shook his hand, but as far as she was concerned the jury was still out. Maybe California men were different, but Montana was littered with guys like Heinz and never before had she seen one change so quickly.

"Come on now, we've got a meeting," said Heinz.

"Why me?"

"Dan will explain."

When Leigh sat down in the pit she noticed that a picture

of Marilyn Delaney aka Marilyn Monroe was now up on the board next to Van Sykes and MLK. She smiled not knowing there were better things still to come.

"You're not a cop, you don't get to carry a gun and you can't arrest anyone, but I want you to be part of the squad as a 'special adviser' on this case. You OK with that?" asked Dan.

What a strange emotional day this had been. It started with a high-spirited flirtatious moment on the steps of the office and then went quickly down hill with news of young Sissy's horrific death and the heated exchange with Heinz. Then, out of the blue, Heinz wants to be her friend and Dan makes her an offer she can't refuse.

"Sure, I'm OK with that," she said still trying to get her head around what was happening. "Is everyone else?"

If she was expecting high fives and huge hugs then she was in the wrong place at the wrong time. Recent events created a somber mood in the office, however, she got the odd smile, thumbs up and a welcome aboard, but that was it. She was now part of the squad.

Dan knew that California was no stranger to serial killers, and if Leigh was right, another one was already making headlines. Zodiac, The Sunset Strip Killers, The Freeway Killer, The Vampire of Sacramento and The Gallego Sex Slave Killers were just a few of the many evil men and women to plague the Golden State over the last fifty years.

"Most of these sick bastards," said Dan, "had a favorite way of squeezing the life out of their victims. The weapon of choice was often a gun, knife, axe, poison, you name it. If there is a new serial killer on the block then he's definitely not a one trick pony. He's already used drugs, crucifixion, and a rifle so keep an open mind. Now let's get to work."

CHAPTER SIXTY-TWO

It was the middle of the day and Joe was stoned out of his mind. It was also his birthday, but there were no cards and no cake. The only visible sign of celebration was a birthday message on his laptop from Hotmail. With head back, body swaying and arms thrashing out of control, he danced like the father of the bride at a wedding while singing "Purple Haze" at the top of his voice. When the song ended he stopped moving, but the room kept spinning. Falling head first over the back of the couch, he conveniently landed face down in a cushion while his right arm smashed on to the floor, "Ouch," he yelled, "that hurt."

Lost in his own little world, Joe was shocked to hear someone calling his name.

"Tubbs."

"Huh?" Joe struggled to lift his head to see what was going on.

"It's rent time."

"Catch you next week," came Joe's muffled reply as he lowered his head back onto the pillow."

"Like fuck you will," said the familiar voice.

"Come on bro', I'm sleeping."

"I'm not your bro' and if you don't get your ass off that couch and get me some money I'll kick your sorry butt out the door."

"You and whose army," slurred Joe.

Joe was feeling brave because his landlord was a puny middle-aged man who probably never worked out or played sport in his life. He wasn't big or physical and Joe could take him if it came to a fight, but who fights with their landlord and still has a roof over their head? He couldn't understand where the bravado was coming from until he rolled over and looked up and saw three black faces staring down at him. Seeing double was a regular occurrence for Joe, but seeing triple was something new. He blinked and then blinked again.

"Meet my boys. This is Jermaine, he's the baby at six foot and two hundred pounds, then there's Washington, he's an inch shorter but about fifty pounds heavier."

"OK, gimme a minute," said Joe as he rolled off the couch on to his hands and knees.

"Take all the time you want."

Joe disappeared into his bedroom and shut the door. Removing an envelope filled with cash from an old pair of socks stuffed in the back of a drawer, he counted slowly and carefully.

"One for him, two for me, one for him, two for me." When he was finished he rolled the bills, fastened them with an elastic band and went back into the living room.

"Paid in full," said Joe as he tossed the money towards his landlord.

If Joe thought he wasn't going to count the money then he was either stupid or more stoned than he thought.

"You're a month short," he said after counting each bill and placing them in a pile on the coffee table.

"Isn't that all I owe you?" asked Joe unconvincingly.

"Nice try asshole, you got two weeks or you're history."

As the landlord made his way to the front door, Washington stood and stared at Joe.

"What?" asked an irritated Joe.

"You look familiar, do you work at that gas station near—"

"I'm an actor," Joe interrupted quickly as he steadied himself and ran his hand through his hair to reveal his face, "I was in—"

Washington interrupted before Joe could finish, "I know, I know," he said excitedly, "you were in that soap… what was it called?"

"*The Club*," said Joe.

"That's it, "*The Club*", it was filmed in a gym wasn't it?"

asked Washington.

"A health spa," Joe corrected him.

"Are you doing anything now?"

"As a matter of fact I'm right in the middle of something that promises to be very big."

"What's it about?"

"Can't say yet, but I'm sure you'll read about it soon."

On his way out of the house, the Landlord turned and threw a five dollar bill back at Joe. "Get yourself a broom, this place is a pig pen."

"Hey, you should be happy I'm here... when I moved in, it was a shit hole."

CHAPTER SIXTY-THREE

Dan paced back and forth in front of the white board while rubbing the back of his neck.

"I heard from Ballistics, the shot was fired from a Remington 740 semi-automatic 308 caliber, there was no match, it was probably stolen from a hunting lodge up north. This guy's either very good or very lucky."

"Are we sure it's a guy" asked Moose?

"If it's a woman then she's not working alone," stated Heinz, "A woman could have overpowered Delaney, but not Van Sykes."

Heinz spotted Leigh peering over the top of her note pad with a look that had sexist pig written all over it.

"Seriously, it took a shit load of strength just to hold him down, never mind hammer nails through his bones. And what about lifting the cross with Van Sykes nailed to it? That couldn't have been easy. And then there's the shot to King's head… I don't know too many women who could do that."

Once again Heinz saw Leigh glance over her note pad, only this time the look said, *I could have done that.*

Dan kept it moving, "OK, it's a man, that's a start, what else?"

"We could make a list of well known persons who had suspicious or violent deaths," suggested Moose.

"Are you shittin' me?" asked Heinz.

"Like Lincoln, Garfield, McKinley and JFK?" said Dan.

"Four assassinated presidents," added Leigh, "I'm impressed, but you forgot Presidents Harding and Taylor."

"You love conspiracies, don't you?" said Dan shaking his head.

"So we make a list a mile long and then what?" asked

Heinz. "There must be thousands of celebs who died in unusual circumstances. How far back do we go?"

"He's already killed Jesus Christ... I guess we start there," concluded Dan.

"You're serious, aren't you?" said a bewildered Heinz.

Suddenly it was like a scene from a school classroom with everyone scrambling to get the teacher's attention. With pen in hand and a notepad on her lap, Leigh hurriedly wrote down names as they were tossed into the air. Some of them brought back memories that made her smile while others sent a cold chill down her spine. Mussolini, John Lennon, Buddy Holly, Glenn Miller, Sharon Tate, Bobby Kennedy, Michael Jackson and Princess Diana were just a few that found their way on to the pages of her pad. Calls from Heinz to include Rasputin and Attila the Hun were ignored.

"What about Lana Clarkson?" shouted Moose.

"Who?" questioned Leigh.

"She's the girl murdered by Phil Spectre," said Dan.

"Who?" asked Leigh.

"Just write it down," said Dan.

The list grew longer as the day dragged on. Deaths from airplane crashes alone filled over three pages while gunshot and drug related fatalities turned the exercise into a joke.

"This is crazy," said Leigh.

"I agree," added Heinz, "there's gotta be another way to do this."

"There is," said Dan.

"Please tell me you just thought of it now," said Leigh.

Dan nodded and smiled. "Van Sykes was easy to find, he lived and preached on the streets so most people knew he existed, but did anyone know Delaney's maiden name was Monroe... or Marty's name was really Martin Luther? Of course not, but the killer did so maybe he knew both victims. I'm not saying King and Delaney hung out together, but—"

Heinz interrupted and quickly finished his sentence with, "Maybe King's mother cleaned house for the Delaney's."

"A sexist AND a racist, why am I not surprised?" Leigh laughed.

"Let's give it a shot," said Dan looking at Heinz and Moose, "check out their friends and their friend's friends and then cross reference them and see what you come up with."

"What should I do?" Leigh asked.

"Stick with the list, right now it's all we got."

"What are you up to?" asked Leigh.

"I'm off to the spa for an hour in the hot tub."

"Huh?"

"I wish," laughed Dan. "I'm going downtown to fight City Hall. I need a replacement for Mike, but I'm not holding my breath. Did you know if we got rid of Esposito and his bloated salary we'd have enough money to hire three more detectives? They do it in baseball, wouldn't it be great if we ran the police force like they run the Dodgers?"

Leigh was hoping this was a rhetorical question. She didn't follow baseball, but she got the drift of what he was saying and didn't want to get involved. Office politics was not her thing. Was it ridiculous to pay Esposito a six-figure salary just to dress up like a war hero every time the cameras come out? Who knows? One thing was for sure; the man was an accident waiting to happen.

CHAPTER SIXTY-FOUR

Joe was lying on his back on the couch smoking a joint while staring at the damp patch on the ceiling. The words, *"you look familiar, are you an actor?"*, played over and over in his mind. He smiled. He loved to be recognized. It didn't happen very often and usually when it did it was followed by some caustic remark about the show or his performance. Things were different now. His storyline was making headlines and his acting was flawless. There was just one thing that was eating him up inside. No one knew that he was the brains behind the biggest thing to hit L.A. in years.

As much as he loved to reminisce, it was time to move on. Pulling his cell out of his pocket, he slowly tapped in Marion's number and was just a moment away from pushing the call button when he stopped and yelled, "You idiot! What are you doing? Why not just send a fucking email to the cops?"

Putting the phone down on the coffee table, Joe went back to staring at the damp spot and mumbled, "It's time to get ready for the next chapter. Will it be puff or blow, blow or puff? Fuck it, I'll do both."

Meanwhile, Weinberg had returned to the motel alone. He had stocked up on coffee and sandwiches and even brought along a bag of quarters for the TV. A large plaid blanket was removed from the back of his Cadillac and draped over the chair he had placed by the window. Lying on the bed was not an option. Even if it was clean and bug free, he couldn't allow himself to fall asleep. To help pass the time he called

New York and got confirmation from Lonnie that he was still happy to part with his money. There was no point in spending another sleepless night in this squalor if his old friend wasn't going to come up with the goods. If Lonnie had any doubts about investing, they quickly evaporated when Weinberg described his stakeout in the world's sleaziest motel. It sounded, *"So Hollywood"*, rejoiced the man from Manhattan. He was hooked. The two Spielberg wannabes talked of rights and royalties and big studio partnerships, but in reality they were just like a couple of kids fumbling in the dark. Weinberg was hoping this would be a life changing experience. He had no idea what lay ahead.

CHAPTER SIXTY-FIVE

A call came in from Tijuana for Dan and was put through to Leigh in his absence.

"My name is Inspector Alonso Cesar from the Tijuana Police Force, who am I speaking to?"

"Leigh Turner, how can I help?"

"Are you working with Dan Scott?" asked the Inspector in a professional tone.

"Yes, I'm part of his team," she replied in a confident voice.

"The other day Dan asked me about the Ramos family and sent me a picture of Mike Turner, the cop who was shot by one of the Ramos boys."

There was a short pause and then the inspector asked, "Turner is a popular name, you weren't related were you?"

"He was my brother," Leigh responded flatly.

Inspector Cesar paused for an even longer period until he eventually asked, "And were you related to Mr and Mrs Turner who were killed by the hit and run driver a while back?"

"They were my parents." Again Leigh kept her response neutral.

"Holy Mother of Mary, I'm sorry for your loss, for all your losses," the Inspector said; his voice sounded a little desperate like he was struggling to find the right words.

Leigh didn't comment. She had nothing to say and for the next thirty seconds the Mexican cop was also speechless.

"Are you OK?" he finally asked in a voice that was no longer official.

"I'm fine," she said.

"I'm so sorry," he repeated.

"Thank you."

"I'll continue. Last night we arrested a guy called Rolando Ruiz following the robbery of a local pawn shop and when we checked his cell phone we found a picture of your brother."

"Did he say why he had his picture?" asked Leigh, who was suddenly short of breath.

"He said he was paid to keep his eyes open for anyone asking about the death of your parents."

"Who paid him?" she gasped, guessing his answer.

"The same guy he sent the picture to, Ricardo Ramos."

Leigh was livid. The fat bastard had lied to her. He said he knew nothing and put the blame squarely on his hapless brother who, according to Ricardo, mixed with the wrong crowd and was destined to die a violent death.

"Son of a bitch," she mumbled.

"Pardon," said the Inspector still hanging on the line.

"Nothing, thanks for that, I'll tell Dan you called."

Five seconds after she hung up the phone, Leigh was heading for the door. She was steely eyed with a face that looked like it had been carved out of stone. As she stomped down the stairway she ran into Moose and Heinz. They knew instantly that something was wrong.

"What's up?" asked Moose.

Leigh tried to ignore them and barge past but the big guy stood in her way.

"At least I know it's not me this time," joked Heinz.

"Let me go," she shouted.

"Not until you tell us what's going on," replied Moose.

Leigh sat down on the stairs and began to cry.

Heinz sat down beside her. "I thought I was the only one who made you cry?"

She smiled, wiped her eyes and, with a little more coaxing, went on to explain where she was going and why.

"And what were you gonna do when you got there?" asked Heinz.

"I hadn't worked that out yet."

"Come on," said Moose.

"Where?"

"To pay Ramos a visit."

"Dan won't be happy," said Leigh.

Heinz stood up and helped Leigh to her feet. "He'll get over it and besides he can't fire us all... well, not in the middle of an investigation anyway."

If Leigh thought that following Ramos to Venice Beach a few days ago was exciting, then driving across town with two cops checking their Glock 22 handguns was close to orgasmic. Weighing in at just twenty two ounces empty, the lightweight pistol looked like a toy in Moose's huge calloused hand. With a magazine capacity of seventeen rounds, and a couple of extra clips stashed in a pocket, this polymer-framed gun was not built to amuse, it was designed to kill over and over again. Leigh had grown up with guns and had spent her life hunting, but this was different, very different. Her heart was racing. She was so nervous she could hardly sit still. When Heinz asked her to describe Ramos' house, she gave out so much detail it was hard to believe she didn't live there.

"The front door is about fifty feet from the sidewalk; you enter into a large living room... two big sofas and lots of Mexican throw rugs... TV on the right and the living room opens on to the kitchen with a back door on the far side of the fridge. There are at least two bedrooms down a short hallway to the right of the kitchen."

Heinz was impressed. "You're good," he said, "for a girl."

Leigh was smiling inside because it meant a lot to her to get a compliment from Heinz even though he took something away in the same breath.

When Heinz pulled up in front of the house Moose reached forward to the front seat and placed his hand on Leigh's shoulder.

"We are just here to talk to Ramos, as far as we know he has done nothing wrong. Remember, it's not a crime to have a picture of someone on your phone... OK?"

She nodded and they made their way up the path to the

front door. Ramos saw them coming. As he walked across the living room floor, Moose opened the screen door and stepped inside the house. Heinz followed closely behind him and broke off in the opposite direction. As Ramos lurched forward to stop them from getting any further, the two detectives reacted instinctively. Jamming their hands under the Mexican's armpits they lifted his massive frame up off the floor and carried him across the room to a waiting sofa. It was a routine they had carefully choreographed over the years.

"What the fuck? Who are you? What do you want?" shouted Ramos as he fell back on to a large pile of cushions.

Heinz showed him his badge and asked, "Where's your cell?"

Before he could answer Leigh picked a black and silver Sony Ericsson up off the coffee table and scrolled through the texts until she came to the one that held a picture of her brother.

"Why do you have a picture of Mike in your phone?" she screamed. "You said you knew nothing about it."

"It's not what you think. Anyway you have no right to come in here."

"That's funny," said Heinz, "I swear I heard you say please come in."

"He's right, maybe we shouldn't be here," said Moose, "maybe we should call the boys from Immigration and have this talk down at his car wash."

"OK, OK," said Ramos, "but you've got it all wrong."

Suddenly a noise from down the hall put the cops on high alert. Heinz pulled his handgun from his shoulder holster and moved slowly along the uneven wooden floor boards that creaked with every step he took. Ramos tried to say something, but his mouth was swiftly covered by Moose's hand. Unable to speak, the Mexican made frantic gestures with his arms until the pressure of a Glock against his temple stopped him in his tracks. There were two rooms on the right side of the hall just like Leigh had said. The door to the first room was closed. With his gun in his right hand, Heinz gradually turned the doorknob with his left and pushed the door wide open. The room was empty. With both hands back on his pistol, Heinz crept along the corridor to the second room where the door was slightly ajar. Every step he took announced his arrival like a train station loud speaker.

Fucking floors, he thought.

Standing with his back to the wall to the right of the door he waited and listened. A rustling sound could be heard from inside the room. Carefully he leaned forward and gently pushed the door open a couple of inches with the barrel of his gun.

"Ricardo, is that you?"

It was the voice of an elderly Mexican woman. Heinz immediately felt more at ease as he hid his gun behind his back and warily stuck his smiling face through the opening while quickly scanning the room. A large woman in a white linen dress was lying on a bed reading a book.

"No, I'm a friend," he said, "just looking for the washroom."

Heinz shut the door, went back to the living room and gave Moose the all clear.

"That's my momma," blasted Ramos as he wiped sweat from the detective's hand off his face, "for Christ sake, she's eighty-three!"

"Give me a minute," said Leigh as she walked towards the bedroom.

Ramos tried to get to his feet, but a straight arm from Moose put him right back on the sofa.

Leigh knocked on the bedroom door and then went inside.

"Hello Mrs Ramos, my name is Leigh."

"Hello, are you my son's new girlfriend? He said he was going out with a pretty American."

"No, we're just friends. Are you staying long in L.A.?"

"I don't know. Ricardo says he wants to look after me for a while."

"That's nice; will you be taking in the sights?"

"I don't think so, I prefer just to sit and read. Anyway, he would never let me drive his car."

Gazing into the old woman's eyes she saw the look of a

child who had done something wrong. She had a gut instinct and decided to go with it.

"Is it because of the accident?" Leigh was trembling as she asked the question.

"Did he tell you about it?" Mrs Ramos asked.

Leigh nodded.

"I shouldn't have been driving my son's car. He told me not to."

Leigh had been praying for this moment since the day her parents died. She recalled telling her brother at their funeral, "If I ever get my hands on the bastard who did this, I'll kill them."

Her prayers had now been answered. She was inches away from the woman who crushed her mother and father, but instead of hate she felt pity. Instead of revenge she just wanted closure.

"Were they killed instantly?"

"Yes," said the old woman, "I wouldn't have driven away if they were still alive."

When Leigh returned to the living room, Ramos could see from the look on her face that she knew everything. All of a sudden he had verbal diarrhea.

"I was just trying to protect her," he said. "I had to know which Tijuana cop was investigating the accident so I could pay him off if he got too close. Unfortunately, Mike started asking questions and his face ended up on my phone. Sergio saw it the morning of the shooting and when Mike stopped him later because of the tail-light, Sergio must have thought he was coming after him to get to momma. It was unlucky."

Leigh shook her head in disbelief, aware that her brother's death had been the result of a series of incredible coincidences.

At the same time, Heinz stepped outside to answer his phone and within a few seconds came rushing back into the house.

"We gotta go," he said hurriedly. "I'll get a patrol car to pick up Mrs. Ramos."

"No," said Leigh.

"What?" asked Heinz.

"It's over, please let it go."

Heinz was shocked. As far as he was concerned it wasn't over. The old lady had committed a crime.

"It's not your call."

He looked at Moose for support, but the big guy was standing firmly behind Leigh.

"It is her call," said Moose.

Realizing he was fighting a lost cause Heinz shrugged his shoulders and headed for the door.

"Some things are not always black and white," said Leigh.

"They are in my world; let's go," Heinz replied.

As they left the house, Ramos got to his feet. "Thank you, Miss Turner... thank you."

Leigh turned to acknowledge Ramos and saw his mother standing next to him. She had only just become aware who the pretty woman really was. With tears streaming down her face she mouthed the words," I'm sorry, so sorry."

"What's the rush?" asked Moose as Heinz sped away from the house with lights flashing and siren wailing.

"Dan called, Esposito just held a press conference."

"So?"

"The whole world now knows that someone in L.A. is killing dead celebrities."

Back at the station the switchboard was lit up like a Christmas tree. Every telephone was ringing and every caller was demanding the same thing... police protection.

'My name is Lennon... my name is Lincoln... my name is Kennedy'.

Suddenly everyone was a target and it was no longer cool to share a name with a famous dead person. Cops and civilians manning the phones tried to instill calm while the media was enjoying a feeding frenzy, with some broadcasters encouraging viewers to stay in their homes and not put themselves in a position where they could be killed like their celebrity namesake. Esposito's moment of glory had created panic in the city.

When Leigh and the boys arrived in the office all hell had broken loose. Esposito and Dan were screaming abuse at each other in the middle of the room. The gloves were off. Esposito accused Dan of withholding details of an ongoing investigation and inviting an untrained "pencil pusher" to be part of the squad. Dan retaliated by saying that his press conference, which was based on a theory put together by the pencil pusher, had spread unnecessary fear throughout the community. When the two cops finally ran out of insults they walked away in opposite directions, but before leaving the room Esposito ordered Dan to take Leigh off the case.

CHAPTER SIXTY-SIX

"I'm so happy, I could shit!" shouted Joe as he bounced up and down on the sofa still holding a joint. "Thank you Channel 7 News, thank you CNN, thank you God and oh yes, thank you Captain Esposito for this fantastic publicity that no amount of money could buy."

Joe was right, it was fantastic and there wasn't a hint of costly paper advertising, expensive TV trailers or flash red carpet premieres in sight. The suits at Disney and Warner would give their right arms for this kind of coverage and he was getting it for free. This was no middle of a football game, sixty-second commercial where everyone gets up for a beer or goes for a piss. This was wall-to-wall, non-stop, milk it dry exposure. The press conference may have lasted less than five minutes, but the ramifications of what was said would run and run while the true meaning of what was said was only just beginning to sink in. Experts from all walks of life were hurriedly placed in front of the world's press. Psychologists, ex-cops and journalists cluttered the airwaves with their theories on who was doing what and why. Security supremos advised on the benefits of window locks, CCTV cameras, outdoor sensor lights and of course that most coveted accessory... the handgun. Finally, a long list of possible targets emerged with one Internet betting firm citing JFK as the next most likely victim with John Lennon running a close second.

"So predictable," sneered Joe, "they call themselves experts... they haven't got a clue."

Once he'd turned off the TV, he quickly pushed the play button on his stereo and jacked up the volume before descending the stairs into the basement. With the music piercing his eardrums and tiny drops of moisture flowing from his nostrils he paced the cold dark room like a boxer waiting to enter the ring. His shirt had been removed and tied around his waist and a thick layer of coal dust sat menacingly beneath his puffy red eyes and around the nipples on his chest. Sandwiched somewhere between euphoria and depression, Joe reached into his boot and grabbed his hunting knife and plunged it deep into the mattress that was upended against the wall.

"They haven't got a fucking clue!"

CHAPTER SIXTY-SEVEN

It was the end of a long day and Leigh was sitting at her desk far away from the buzz and excitement in the pit. She was once again filling in forms and preparing time sheets although her mind was still working on the case. Being away from the action was driving her crazy. The tiniest taste of police work had made her hungry for more.

"You OK?"

Leigh had been daydreaming and didn't notice that Dan was standing beside her.

"I'm good. How's it going?"

"Not very well. The guys did a cross reference on Delaney and King's friends and got nothing. Hey, it was a long shot."

"It was still worth it. What now?"

"We're putting together a short list of names, we don't have the manpower to watch over all of them, but—" Dan stopped suddenly. "I feel so damned helpless. There's no way we can hope to catch this guy by staking out one or two people with dead celebrity names. Shit... I bet we found at least twenty-five guys called John Lennon. What about the 'Sharon Tates', 'Brian Jones' and 'John and Bobby Kennedys' out there?"

Although still feeling pain of her own, Leigh was aware that Dan was also suffering. "I think we both need a drink" she said.

Dan looked at his watch and nodded. "See you at PJ's?"

Leigh made her way down the stairs to her VW that was parked facing the street. She started the engine and reversed out from between two cars and turned left towards the exit. A blue Nissan, which was two spaces away, made the same maneuver so she stopped and waited for the car to move on. While she waited she looked out the window and gazed at the sign on the building next to the police station.

"Bureau of Vital Statistics," she said quietly to herself, "Bureau of Vital Statistics."

The car in front then drove off, but the old VW remained stationary. She continued to stare at the sign until the sound of a car horn caught her attention. Esposito was on her tail motioning for her to get out of the way. With her engine still running, she opened the door and ran back to him.

"I think I know where our killer got his information about Delaney and King," she said excitedly.

"Miss Turner, you're no longer part of the investigating team," replied Esposito in a condescending manner.

"I'm not asking to be put back on the team, I just want to—"

Esposito interrupted, "I hear you're into conspiracies... is this another one of your little creations?"

"Listen—"

"No you listen, the police force is no place for amateurs, now please move your car."

As their discussion became more heated, Dan pulled up to the Captain's bumper and got out of his car. In fact the entire parking lot had come to a complete standstill and other drivers started blowing their horns.

"What's going on?" Dan asked.

"Dan, tell your secretary to move her car or I'll make a call and have someone move it for her."

Leigh persisted. "I think I know where he's getting his information."

"Who's getting what information?" asked Dan

"Last chance or I make the call," shouted Esposito.

"The killer... he's getting everything right here... in this building," said Leigh, pointing to the ugly gray mass of concrete next to the police station.

"That's it I'm making the call," Esposito said angrily.

"Hang on Jerry," said Dan, "let her finish then she'll move."

Reluctantly, Esposito put his phone down.

Leigh crouched next to Esposito's window so that she could make eye contact with him. She knew it would be easier to keep his attention if he was staring at her face rather than her breasts.

"I think the killer is either working in this building or has access to the information stored here. How else could he find out Delaney's maiden name was Monroe and Marty King's name was really Martin Luther King, that's it... that's all I wanted to say."

Esposito stared out the windshield while she went to park her car. He tilted his head to one side and said. "I've got to admit it Dan... she's got great tits."

"Jerry!" yelled Dan angrily.

"OK, only joking, she's good."

"Jerry, it's a no brainer. Put her back on the team and if she gets lucky then you get the credit and those political aspirations of yours may just become a reality. If she falls on her face... no one will ever know she was there."

"But she's not a cop," Esposito pointed out.

"That makes it even better. You recruited her from outside the Department... it was a stroke of genius," Dan said.

"Are you forgetting that I canned her in front of the whole office?"

"No, what you actually did was take her off the case until a special employment contract approved by the Department was drawn up."

"Mmm, I like that. When will that be ready?"

"It'll be on your desk first thing in the morning."

"Great, do you want me to go into the BVS with you?"

"No, I'm fine," Dan said.

"If that's all then... I'm out of here. Oh, by the way; are you sleeping with Hannah Montana?"

With a straight face and a mischievous twinkle in his eye, Dan replied, "Are you sleeping with Walker in Personnel?"

"Why do you ask?"

"Because her purse is on the back seat of your car."

"Oh shit!" shouted Esposito as he looked over his shoulder only to find there was nothing at all on the seat. He glared at Dan who laughed and tapped the side of his nose with his finger.

"That wasn't funny!" shouted Esposito before driving off.

Dan wasn't at all surprised that Esposito was having an affair. It wasn't his first and it sure as hell wouldn't be his last. What he couldn't understand is why his boss hadn't learned a thing from three failed marriages and a fourth teetering on the edge. Once again, he was steaming off to have sex with an unattractive, overweight woman just because she was there. Was he lonely, insecure or did he just want to get laid? His indiscretions were legendary and known by everyone including his latest wife, but like the others before her, she thought she could change him.

With Esposito gone, Leigh turned her attentions to Dan as he moved confidently across the lot. Dressed in a dark blue suit with a pale pink shirt open at the collar, he looked more like a successful businessman than a cop. A five o'clock shadow and a touch of gray around the temples provided a seamless mix of ruggedness and sophistication. Once again Leigh blushed like a teenager.

He's nearly as old as my father, he's set in his ways and he still listens to the Beatles, she thought, *but just being near him gives me goose bumps.*

"OK, why the smug look?" she asked.

"You're back on the squad, well done."

"You're the one who should be congratulated," she said.

"Speaking of congratulations, I heard what happened with Ramos."

"You're not mad?" she asked tentatively.

"Why should I be mad?" asked Dan sarcastically, "you went to see the brother of a cop killer when you told me you wouldn't. Two of my detectives not only entered his house without a search warrant or probable cause, but they manhandled him and put a gun to his head. Would you like me to go on?"

"No," said Leigh lowering her head.

Dan continued, but this time he was serious. "You've got to promise me this will be the last time you act on emotion. I don't want this son of a bitch to 'walk' on a technicality. Anyway, you did the right thing... you just went about it the wrong way... again."

"Do you still want that drink?" she asked, quickly changing the subject.

"No, but I'll take a rain check. I'm going to see what information I can get out of the cleaners in there before we interview the staff in the morning."

"I've got a bottle of red wine and some spaghetti Bolognese at home... would you like to join me later?"

"It could be much later."

"I can wait," Leigh said.

CHAPTER SIXTY-EIGHT

Joe stepped out of the shower, wrapped a towel around his waist and wiped his hand across the mist on the mirror. Gone was the coal dust that blackened his face and chest. As he stared at his reflection he scraped his hair off his forehead with both hands revealing eyes that resembled two piss holes in the snow. He looked pale and gaunt. Substance abuse was taking its toll. Turning towards the shower cubicle he reached out and gently caressed the nylon curtain with the back of his hand. It was a familiar motion that reminded him of when his mother would stroke his cheek with the back of her finger tips just before she was about to leave him. There was never a comforting kiss or an off the ground bone crunching hug like he would see in the movies. It was always controlled, distant and brief.

Dropping the towel on to the bathroom floor, Joe strutted confidently into the bedroom where he was greeted by an unmade bed and a room littered with dirty underwear, T-shirts and socks. Five open drawers in a large oak dresser gave the appearance that the room had just been turned upside down by a burglar. Falling backwards on to his bed, he gradually squeezed into a pair of jeans and then threw on his favorite Grateful Dead T-shirt before pulling on a pair of dusty dark brown cowboy boots. A stainless steel hunting knife slipped easily down the inside of his left boot.

Back in the living room Joe surfed through dozens of cable channels until he found a cooking program. A playful look came over his face. He waited for a few minutes until an effeminate chef, wearing an immaculately clean white apron, placed his newly prepared dish on the top shelf of the oven and removed an identical dish from the bottom shelf.

"Here's one I prepared earlier," shouted Joe as he mimicked the man on the box.

Then as the chef removed the lid on a steaming hot casserole dish filled with bubbling beef bourguignon, Joe lifted his deep blue Dodgers ball cap off the coffee table to reveal two six inch lines of coke.

"I bet mine's better than yours," he said with a laugh as he lowered his head to the table.

A sudden surge of physical strength shot through Joe's body like a lightning bolt while his mind was lit up and refueled. Breathing heavily he grabbed his truck keys and cell phone and headed for the door only to return to pick up the motel key he had stolen several days ago. Slipping it into his back pocket he looked up at the sky and said, "Alfred, I think you're going to like this."

After spending a couple of hours interviewing security guards and cleaners in the BVS Building, Dan and the team drew a blank. The guards were either on duty or had rock solid alibis when Van Sykes and King were murdered and not one of the migrant mop jockeys was capable of turning on a computer let alone hacking into one of the country's most sophisticated and protected systems. It was yet another dead-end and time to call it a day.

It was just after eleven o'clock when Dan pulled up outside Leigh's apartment. He turned off his engine and sat in the dark thinking about what to do next. The first thing you learn in any workplace is that you don't shit on your own doorstep, but an invitation to dinner from a woman as young and beautiful as Leigh doesn't come along every day. It was too good to refuse even if he was her boss and it was way outside his comfort zone.

Is it too late? he thought looking at his watch. *Should I have brought flowers or a bottle of wine?*

When he was younger, *"come in for coffee"*, was a euphemism for *"come in for sex"*. Had the word "dinner" replaced "coffee" over the years or did she really intend to give him something to eat? He was confused. Before she appeared on the scene things were simple and predictable, with divorcees and widows fighting to sit next to him at dinner parties thrown by friends eager to set him up. He was aware that women of a certain age know what they want and how to get it without strings attached. He liked that. Tonight, however, was a whole new ball game.

"Are you going to come in or would you prefer to eat in the car?" said Leigh with a big grin.

Dan was caught off guard. He didn't see her standing next to him. It was one of those moments when he wished he hadn't said or done anything, but instead he mumbled unconvincingly about making a phone call and then pretended to shuffle some papers around on the passenger seat before getting out of the car and following her up the stairs.

When he last saw the place on the day of the funeral it was a mess, but a woman's touch had turned what once resembled a frat house into a home. Most of the gaps in the floor were covered and every last piece of electrical wiring had been tucked away out of sight. Flowers, plants, a mirror and a couple of large posters were strategically positioned around the room to hide gaping holes in the walls while multi colored cushions did their best to give a lift to an otherwise depressing space.

There were two places set at the table in the left hand corner of the kitchen. In the center of the table a single white candle had been burning for some time, dripping pools of wax on top of the symmetric creases of a newly opened dark blue table cloth. Red wine from a half empty bottle was poured into Dan's glass before a handful of spaghetti was lowered slowly into a pot of boiling water.

Dan removed his jacket and laid it across the arm of the

sofa. After unfastening the Velcro straps, he slipped out of his lightweight shoulder holster and carefully placed it under his jacket. This was the first time that she had seen him without a revolver nestled under his left armpit. He was always fairly chilled, but without a Glock strapped to his body he was positively horizontal. Being "off duty" suited him. He looked relaxed as he walked over to a poster partially covering a large hole in the wall. While he was there, a gentle breeze blew through the opening forcing the poster to puff out into the room.

"I like what you've done to the place," he said, "but don't you miss the basics like walls, floors, and a ceiling?"

Taking a long look at Dan from the far side of the room, Leigh realized that there's nothing sexier than a man with a sense of humor, unless of course he also has good looks and a great body. She could feel herself tingling. Her cheeks grew warm.

"Be careful where you step," she said, "I haven't nailed down the floorboards yet. By the way, did you get another detective for the squad?"

"Yeah, they gave us Waggoner from Vice, but he's away on vacation for ten days. How about you, did you ever find an electrician?"

"A friend of Mr Kim's keeps promising to have a look, but hey, come on let's eat."

Leigh was calm and back in control of her feelings, but before Dan arrived she was in a state of panic for different reasons. Hell bent on making her apartment more welcoming, she raced from store to store before returning home to complete a manic sixty-minute makeover. It was unnecessary and she knew it. She also knew that she had lit the candle much too early, drunk most of the wine before her guest arrived and left price tags on the mirror and table cloth.

As for Dan, he was in heaven and why shouldn't he be? A beautiful woman and a home cooked meal were a far cry from eating fast food for one in front of the television.

When the power failed and the lights went out half way

through dinner it could have been the end of a wonderful evening, but instead it was just the beginning.

"What should we do now?" asked Dan.

"I usually wait a couple of minutes and if the lights don't come back on, I go to bed."

Dan immediately asked, "Has it been two minutes yet?"

Leigh's face went warm when she'd taken in what she said. She didn't mean to invite Dan to bed, but she certainly wasn't about to turn him away. Instead she smiled, reached across the table and touched his hand.

"Follow me," she whispered as she blew out the candle and led him to the bedroom.

CHAPTER SIXTY-NINE

Joe pulled off the road when he spotted a pay phone on a grass verge next to a bus stop. It had been years since he last made a call from a phone booth, but as soon as he opened the glass door he understood why the cell phone was invented. A strong smell of piss permeated the cubicle and obscene graffiti messages covered every available inch of space. The phone book that had been secured by a small metal chain had been ripped from the wall and left shredded on the floor along with splinters of glass from the shattered overhead light. Joe fumbled in his pocket for some change then quickly dropped a coin into the slot while holding the door ajar with his left foot. Scrolling through the names in his list of cell contacts, he stopped when he came to Marion. He read her number aloud as he pressed the corresponding chrome buttons next to the hand set. As soon as he heard the ring tone he put his phone back in his pocket and pushed open the door with his free hand.

"Hello," shouted Marion trying desperately to raise her voice above the background noise.

"It's Joe."

"Who?"

"Joe... you know, the writer who parks cars." Joe said, trying to sound casual.

"You mean Joe the writer who parks cars and who looks a gift horse in the mouth?" she asked.

"Sorry about that, can I make it up to you?"

"When?" she asked.

"Now," said Joe.

"OK," she replied.

"Where are you?"

"At PJ's where else?" she answered.

That wasn't good, thought Joe. Everybody knew him there.

"Are you alone?" he asked.

"I will be in a minute... my friend is leaving, why?"

"I'll meet you in the parking lot in about ten minutes," said Joe.

"Why don't you come in?"

"It's a long story, I'll tell you later."

"You're strange... See you in ten," she said.

Joe let the phone drop and quickly retreated from the booth, clearing his throat and spitting out foul tasting saliva as he went. It was like someone had emptied their bladder in his mouth. At the side of the road he bent over and took several long deep breaths before he was able to get rid of the horrible odor that had crept through his nostrils and seeped into his lungs.

As he was about to drive off, he looked in his mirror and saw the phone booth arrogantly waiting for its next victim. Conscious there was no traffic, he slipped the gear stick into reverse and revved the engine before popping the clutch and crashing his tailgate into the glass structure. It fell like a house of cards.

Ten minutes later Joe backed uneventfully into a parking space behind PJ's. Marion was still inside the bar so he waited nervously fiddling with motel key number seventeen which he had taken from his back pocket. The longer he waited the more restless he became. Questions he didn't want to answer filled his head. Finally after about half an hour she appeared around the corner and Joe flashed his lights. As she made her way to the truck she stumbled, but recovered before falling. She was drunk. Her entrance into the cab was even clumsier, but again she made it without tipping over.

"Sorry," she said with a slurred voice and a silly grin, "it's hard to leave when you can't find the door... Let's go for a drink."

"I think you've had enough, how about somewhere quiet?" he said as he reached over and pulled the seat belt across her lap and locked it before lowering the window to give her some fresh air.

"Your place or mine?" she chuckled.

As the pickup moved slowly out of the parking lot and headed in the direction of motel alley Marion stuck her head out of the window and threw up.

"Sorry not a good first impression is it?" she said wiping her mouth with her sleeve.

"It doesn't matter," said Joe.

"You're a nice guy, you know that?"

Joe didn't answer because hearing that he was a nice guy made him feel uncomfortable. She wanted to talk, get to know him, but that was the last thing he wanted so he kept his mouth shut and his eyes on the road. Then suddenly, as if to tease or announce his intentions, he pushed his Hendrix cassette into the machine and started to sing.

"Hey Joe, where you going with that knife in your hand?"

Marion may have been totally out of it, but she momentarily came to her senses when she heard him singing the wrong words.

"It's 'gun', silly... where you going with that 'gun' in your hand?"

Once again Joe let her words wash over him. He just smiled, reached down to his boot and gradually pulled up his knife until it fit firmly in the palm of his hand. A moment later Marion rested her head on his shoulder and fell asleep.

When Joe approached the entrance to the motel he turned off his lights, pressed down the clutch and coasted quietly past the office and a lone black Cadillac Escalade parked outside room ten. To avoid being seen, he glided to the end of the motel and made a sharp left turn before stopping behind the building out of sight of the office. Once he had unlocked Marion's seat belt he gently moved her head off his shoulder and scurried around the truck to open her door. Carrying her into the room was not something he had planned to do, but it was better than waking her up. This was their first night together and Joe had no idea how she'd react. Maybe she'd be a harmless quiet drunk or one that liked to giggle to herself. On the other hand she could be aggressive or insist on singing at the top of her voice. He couldn't take the chance so he cradled her in his arms, opened the door and gently lowered her onto the bed. It was only a matter of seconds before she woke up.

"Where am I?" she said with eyes half open.

"You were asleep," Joe said quietly.

"Is this a motel?" she asked.

"I didn't know where you lived and my place is being decorated so… "

"So you rented a motel room. You're a nice guy. What's that smell?"

Joe walked around the room like an expectant father. Sensing he was nervous, Marion grabbed his hand as he passed the bed and pulled him down on top of her.

"You feel good," she whispered seductively.

Joe didn't know whether to shit or go blind. This wasn't supposed to happen, it wasn't in the script and for a moment he was tongue tied, but then he uttered, "Let's take a shower."

"That's kinky," laughed Marion, "come on then."

Rolling out from under Joe, she moved to the edge of the bed and started to unbutton her blouse.

"You too," she said to Joe who was still lying on the bed.

"I gotta get something, you jump in the shower… I'll be right there."

Joe pretended to be searching for his keys then walked casually to the door before turning to see Marion stepping naked into the shower. Without looking back she shouted, "Get lots of them, it's gonna be a long night."

But Joe didn't leave the room. He didn't have to. He had everything he needed. Standing at the edge of the bathroom he watched and listened as water crashed down on the metal shower tray and steam billowed into his face. Marion giggled to herself as she sang Joe's line about the knife while the nylon shower curtain, streaked with yellow stains from years of use and abuse, clung to her legs like a magnet to a fridge door. Without taking his eyes off the silhouette of her small but shapely body he bent over and removed the six-inch stainless steel blade from his boot. Holding the knife in his right hand he edged forward gradually until he was a heartbeat from the cubicle. Slowly he reached out with his left hand and calmly pulled back the curtain. A huge smile turned to a look of disbelief and fear when Marion saw the knife coming towards her. There was nothing she could do but watch helplessly as the razor sharp blade tore open her stomach only to be withdrawn and thrust into her neck. A projectile of blood splattered across Joe's body as she clutched her throat in vain. Another blow to the chest followed by countless stab wounds to her arms and legs sent her crashing to the floor where blood was flowing faster than the shower could wash it away.

It wasn't long before it was over. With his chest pounding, head bowed and arms hanging by his side, Joe stood motionless and exhausted.

Unable to speak or move and partially covered by the curtain, Marion opened her eyes and looked up at him.

He knew the look. It was the same look that Delaney and Van Sykes gave him before they died. It was a look of desperation, helplessness and wanting to know why. Why me?

Drenched in a cocktail of blood, sweat and skin fragments and speaking without an ounce of passion in his voice, Joe said that it was her parents who were to blame.

"They gave you that name," he said coldly, "it's their fault."

A small white towel was removed from the rail to wipe his face, arms and the blade of his knife before the towel was tossed on to the floor. Almost immediately he picked it up again and used it to scrub his boot prints off the faded white tiles beneath his feet. This time he hung on to the towel.

"Why should I make it easy for them?" he questioned as he walked around the room wiping away his prints.

The sound of a muffled cell phone ringing diverted Joe's attention to a black leather purse lying on the floor next to the bed. Unzipping the bag, he lifted the phone and saw the word "Mom" on the screen.

"It didn't have to be like this," he said talking at the screen. "If only they'd been nice, it could have been so different."

Eventually the ringing stopped and "mom" faded to black. Joe's moment of reflection was short lived.

As water continued to rain down on Marion's lifeless body, he rubbed his prints off the phone, chucked it into the shower and made his way out of the room to the truck, where he climbed on top of the cab. From there he lifted himself on to the roof of the motel and walked quietly towards the motel sign illuminated with red light bulbs. Using the towel to protect his hand, he unscrewed several of the bulbs before returning to the end of the building and lowering his body down onto the truck.

Seven rooms away, Weinberg had fallen asleep in the chair, but woke in a panic when he heard footsteps on the roof.

If only Lonnie could see me now, he thought as he put on his shoes, gathered up his blanket and waited in the dark next to the partially opened door.

If this doesn't make a great movie then I don't know what will.

The sound of ticking tappets and the crunching of loose gravel beneath Joe's tires as he drove across the parking lot sent a shiver down Weinberg's spine. The Porn King waited until the Chevy was past his room then crept to his car and threw the blanket on to the back seat. Still keeping his eye on the truck he ran along the front of the motel to room seventeen. He had to be sure. He had to see for himself. When he got there the door was wide open and the sound of running water could be heard from the parking lot. Trails of blood streamed from the bathroom to the doorstep. He didn't need to go any further. From the step he could see the mutilated naked body of a young woman lying in a heap in the shower. There was no movement, no cry for help.

"This fucking guy's for real!" he said aloud as he hurried back to his Cadillac.

The pickup had about a minute head start, but with empty roads and a powerful V8 engine it wasn't long before the

Escalade closed the gap. Joe drove straight home and parked his truck in the drive beside his house. Fifty yards away Weinberg, still visibly shaking, sat watching his every move.

CHAPTER SEVENTY

Leigh had been awake for hours replaying the events of the evening in her mind. It was a magical night that gave her hope of more to come, but now in the cold light of day she was frightened that her heart would be broken. Never before had she thought "long term", but last night had changed everything. She wasn't desperate. She was happy being single and was not affected by the "ticking clock" syndrome perpetuated by mothers and grandmothers everywhere. She was in love. He was available, attractive and a good man and appeared to enjoy her company but there was a problem and it was the same old problem that haunted so many couples. No, it wasn't about money, sex or trust. It was about work and being married to his job. Like the chicken or egg who knows which came first? Did his marriage fall apart because he couldn't leave his work at the office or did he bring his work home because his marriage was falling apart? It was never going to be easy and she knew it.

Lying on her side with her head resting on her hand she smiled as she ran her fingers playfully across Dan's bare shoulder and down his arm. He twitched slightly and rolled over on to his stomach exposing his back and a circular scar at the top of his shoulder. She knew instinctively that he had been shot. If growing up in small town Montana had taught her anything it taught her to recognize a gunshot wound. Every year at the end of the hunting season and after a session of heavy duty eating and drinking, the local gun club held a contest and only those with bullet wounds from hunting accidents could compete. Acting as judge for the competition and reporter for the town newspaper, Leigh was given the opportunity to see up close what a tiny piece of metal could do to human flesh. Contestants were awarded points for having the most wounds, the largest wound and the one nearest to a vital organ. It was a light-hearted event that really opened her eyes, because despite their injuries, some of which were life threatening, none of the injured wounded men or women quit hunting. Every single one of them told her, *"It comes with the territory"*, and she knew that's exactly what Dan would say. It was just one more thing she'd have to come to terms with if their relationship got serious.

When Dan's cell phone rang his body jerked violently out of a sound sleep into an upright sitting position. Half dead and temporarily blinded by the early morning sunlight crashing through the unobstructed window, he jumped out of bed and stepped on a loose floor board, instantly falling on his ass. Leigh wanted to laugh, but wasn't too sure if the top cop could laugh at himself. She didn't have to worry; his sense of humor was still intact.

"Can you get my cell please; I'm kinda busy picking slivers out of my ass."

Leigh giggled, "I said to be careful where you step."

Wrapped in her brother's bathrobe, she moved quickly into the living room and found Dan's phone in his jacket pocket. Moose's name was flashing on the screen.

"What's up?" asked Dan, still sitting naked on the floor.

"A woman's been murdered at The Baytrees Motel."

"Was it our man?"

"No… there's no sign of a dead celebrity, but it's a bad one."

"Rope it off… I'm on my way."

Dan hung up the phone and put his backside on the edge of the bed while Leigh draped a blanket over his shoulders. Moose wasn't prone to exaggeration and didn't have the vocabulary to embellish, so when he said it was bad, Dan was expecting the worst.

Rubbing his hands over his face to wipe the sleep from his eyes he turned to Leigh and said, "It's a shame; I was really looking forward to a big old fashioned Montana breakfast."

Food was the last thing on Leigh's mind. She just wanted to spend the day wrapped in Dan's arms, but she knew that wasn't going to happen.

Dan quickly picked up his clothes that lay scattered around the bedroom. Once dressed, he was in police mode. Strapping his shoulder holster in place and wearing a serious face, he asked, "You're welcome to come along, but it's gonna be grisly."

After years of being on the wrong side of the tape, there was no way that Leigh was going to pass up an opportunity to step inside a crime scene. It was a dream come true. As a reporter she was told what the police wanted her to hear with the information restricted and sanitized to protect the victim's family, the public and any ongoing investigation. When her brother Mike was alive he often teased her about the newspaper articles she wrote knowing she only had half the story. She found it frustrating and, despite being good at what she did, it was not always easy getting to the truth.

"Wait for me," said Leigh running down the stairs with her shoes in her hand. "There's no way I'm going to miss this."

Moose wasn't the sharpest tool in the box, but even he could tell that something was going on when Dan and Leigh arrived at the motel in the same car, drinking coffee from Starbucks and looking like they had been dragged through a hedge backwards. What made it even more interesting was that they didn't seem to care if anyone knew. The big guy wasn't bothered, that's for sure; in fact he was happy for them. Dan had been alone for a long time and was in danger of turning into a grumpy old man and Leigh needed someone nice after the nightmare of losing her family. His only concern was that office romances last about as long as holiday romances and inevitably end in tears. The last thing he wanted was to see them get hurt.

"What have we got Moose?" asked Dan.

"Female, Caucasian, late twenties... with multiple stab wounds... the guys from The Print Unit are in there now, but don't get your hopes up too high, the room's flooded."

"What about the manager, did he see anything?"

"No, he said he hasn't had a customer for weeks."

"Maybe he should put in a pool?"

"Don't know if I believe him... there's no damage to the door," said Moose.

"Let's check it out." Dan said.

As they walked towards room seventeen Leigh took a long hard look at the building. Dusty windows, broken screen doors covered in cobwebs, peeling paint and a feeling of utter isolation gave it the appearance of a set from a horror movie.

What a dump, she thought, *why would anyone come here?*

As Dan and Moose ducked under the tape she stopped and looked back at the sign on the motel roof. Something was bugging her. Something wasn't right.

"You coming?" asked Dan while holding the tape above his head.

"What does that sign say?"

The guys gave her a puzzled look and then glanced up at the sign.

"The Baytrees Motel," replied Moose moving towards the room.

"Look again please," she said apologizing for the abruptness in her tone.

"The Baytrees Motel," Moose repeated.

"Yeah The Baytrees Motel," added Dan.

"That's what it should say, but if you look closely, and I know it's hard to see in the sunlight, you'll notice that the light bulbs illuminating the 'y', 'r' and 'e' are not lit."

"What's strange about that, the whole place is falling apart?" added Moose.

"Shit," said Dan, "I don't believe it."

"What... what don't you believe?" said Moose.

"This guy's got balls." said Dan, a grudging admiration creeping into his voice.

"Dan... Leigh! Will someone please tell me what's going on?" Moose asked.

"The sign says... The Bates Motel."

"Oh my God," said Moose, like in that movie?"

"*Psycho*," said Dan.

"Alfred Hitchcock," added Leigh, "and I'll bet you breakfast that the dead girl is called Marion, and if he's real good it'll be Marion Crane."

Just as they arrived at the door to room seventeen, two men in white hooded coveralls with elasticized slipper covers over their shoes came out carrying a body in a bag. The bag was lowered gently to the ground and the zip was opened to reveal the girl's face and chest. Most of her blood had been washed away in the shower leaving the body relatively clean, but a gaping hole in her neck together with countless slices to her torso left everyone in no doubt that this was a merciless frenzied attack. Leigh put her hand to her mouth and turned her head. For once she was glad she'd come to work on an empty stomach.

"We found the room key on the bed," said one of the Forensics guys.

"Any ID?" asked Dan as Moose searched her bag.

"She's got an ID from FedEx and a California Drivers License, you ready for this? Her name is Marion, Marion Bergdorf... Nice one," he said glancing at Leigh, "I guess we owe you breakfast."

"I'll take a rain check on that if you don't mind," she said still trying to compose herself. "You know in the movie, Marion was killed, wrapped in the shower curtain, and then put in the trunk of her car, which was driven into a nearby swamp."

"No swamps around here," said Dan. "Look, our killer found the perfect venue with a name he could easily change and a girl with a name that he didn't need to change. He did what he came here to do and his MO is still the same! He's done it again... I just hope someone saw something."

"You know, I read somewhere that Hitchcock used hot chocolate to simulate blood in that film," said Moose.

"You gotta get out more," replied Dan.

A few feet away the owner of the motel, Jack Michalec, looked on impassively as he waited by his office door to be interviewed. Despite knowing that the place would be crawling with cops and press, he apparently didn't feel the need to change the clothes he wore to bed the night before. Wearing just a pair of flip flops, pee stained boxer shorts and a dirty white cut off T-shirt, he cut a comical figure with the veins on his over stretched stomach resembling a school map of the Mississippi Delta.

"He's not the killer," mumbled Dan but still he had to go through the motions.

"Were you here all night?" Dan asked.

"Yup," came Michalec's lazy response.

"Did you hear or see anything?"

"Nope."

"Were you alone?"

At this point Michalec hollered, "Honey," and a young scantily clad black girl came out from a room adjacent to the office.

"She works for me as a chambermaid," he said adopting a pompous tone.

"If she's underage... " Dan threatened.

"She's fine," Michalec said quickly, interrupting Dan in mid sentence. "I'm not as dumb as I look."

Dan rolled his eyes then continued, "We found the key in the room."

"I don't know how it got there, honest; I guess someone coulda stole it when I was in town and Honey was out cleaning. Beats me how it got there, I haven't rented a room in weeks."

"Why am I not surprised?" mumbled Dan as he flipped through the blank yellowed, dog-eared pages of the motel log book.

"Kids try to break into the rooms to party so I go out before bedtime and then check again first thing in the morning. That's when I saw the girl... I didn't touch anything... called 911 right away. You should be thanking me for being a responsible citizen."

A moment ago Dan would have been happy to pack up and call it a day, but Michalec's verbal diarrhoea suddenly raised alarm bells. Honey also looked uneasy and nervous, scratching and rocking from side to side. Dan knew they were hiding something.

"Honey, can you remember the last room you cleaned?" asked the detective.

"Sure, it was room four."

"Why did you clean that room?"

Honey looked embarrassed, but after a little coaxing, replied, "Coz we had sex in there."

"And which room are you going to clean today?" asked Dan quickly.

Michalec opened his mouth to interrupt, but Dan raised his finger in a gesture to remain silent.

"Room ten," revealed the girl without hesitation.

"Why room ten?" Dan pressed.

Honey froze. Realizing what she had done she looked to her fat friend for support, but got only a scowl in return.

"Why room ten?" repeated Dan.

Once again the girl looked across the room for help and this time Michalec came to her rescue. "OK, I rented the room to a tall Jewish guy and a skinny blonde girl, could have been a hooker, but definitely not the girl in the shower."

Dan had heard enough and asked Moose to fill in the blanks. Fat, ugly and stupid was no way to go through life, but it wasn't against the law. The fat man didn't kill anyone and didn't lie about the key. Why would he? There was nothing to gain. If he lied about anything he lied about renting out his rooms. He took cash and no records were kept. Everybody in a cash generating business does it. This was not something for homicide. It was a matter for the tax man.

As Dan walked towards his car Michalec shouted, "Who's gonna clean up the mess in seventeen?"

Glancing at the young black girl now nestled comfortably into the owner's side, Dan replied in a mocking pompous tone, "Your chambermaid, of course."

CHAPTER SEVENTY-ONE

Weinberg turned on the radio as he sat in his car just down the street from Joe's house. A news flash cut short The Beach Boys' falsetto harmonies to announce that *"Psycho does Psycho"*. The chilling report, spelled out the grim details of "The Bates Motel" slaughter by the man the press dubbed the Celebrity Killer.

"Tension was growing in the city," said the newscaster in a melancholy voice. "If a young girl can be mutilated for just having the same name as a fictional character in a movie, no one was safe."

Weinberg was confused. He was still doing nothing, but he felt he had suddenly gone from standing on the side lines to playing a part in this death script and it was scaring the hell out of him. By not reporting Joe to the police he was complicit in the crime.

Was he doing the right thing? he thought.

Making porno films was a far cry from joining forces with a serial killer. It all seemed like a good idea when he had his old friend and three thousand miles as a safety net. Talk was cheap in New York, but here in L.A. it was a different story. Sitting a few yards from the man who less than two hours ago brutally killed a beautiful young woman for no other reason than to act out a work of fiction, was a reality check.

It was still early in the morning in New York, but Weinberg didn't care. He had to talk to Lonnie. He was in a bad place and needed reassurance they were doing the right thing and Lonnie was the best person to put his mind at ease. The diminutive New Yorker was a hustler and a born bull-shitter and Weinberg knew this. Respectability, opportunity of a lifetime and a chance to mix with Hollywood's elite flowed effortlessly from Lonnie's mouth and was music to Weinberg's ears. Lonnie told him exactly what he wanted to hear, but the kicker came when he said the money was in a suitcase under his bed. Lonnie certainly knew which buttons to push. The conversation was a shot in the arm, a boost of confidence for the lanky Weinberg and when he hung up the phone he was back on track and ready to meet with Joe.

"When is the best time to talk to a serial killer?" he joked "Is it immediately after he's sliced and diced his victim in the shower or is it best to wait until he's cleaned up and had breakfast?"

Weinberg decided it was best to wait.

Covered in blood from head to toe, Joe walked quickly down the hall to the bathroom and stepped fully clothed into the shower. This wasn't a new experience, but it was the first time he had done it sober. With the temperature dial hovering on "hot", he soaked himself for ten minutes before scrubbing his Levis and T-shirt with a bar of soap and a shrivelled up sponge he'd found under the sink. Marion's blood gradually trickled down his legs and under his boots to the drain, but it was nothing compared to the flood he had witnessed at the motel. The sight of her blood gushing from her wounds, like a river breaking its banks, made him feel nauseous and faint. He tried not to think about it.

"It's done," he said, "it's time to turn the page."

Finally, when the water disappearing down the hole was no longer red, he turned off the tap, got out of the shower, removed his clothes and hung them over a broken plastic chair positioned in the sunshine in the back yard. He was exhausted and desperate to get some sleep, but his heart was still thumping like he'd overdosed on double espressos.

"Fuck it," he said, "if you can't beat 'em, join 'em."

Fifteen minutes later he pulled into an underground car park beneath the local Galleria. The elevator took him to the second floor where he strolled confidently into the TV and stereo section of a large department store and manually adjusted the volume and station controls so that each TV set showed a different news program. It was chaotic. Surrounded by flashing images, ear piercing news bulletins and mindless commercial jingles, he rotated slowly with his eyes closed and his arms stretched out like the wings of a giant bird.

"They're talking about me," he said in a voice that no one could hear. "I wrote that... I did it."

Staff and customers stared in amazement as Joe performed a celebratory ritual until one by one the TV sets were turned off and he was face to face with two very large security guards.

"Are you OK?" asked one of the guards.

For a moment, Joe looked startled and unsure where he was. He stood stiff as a board while his eyes darted around the room.

"Have I done something wrong?" he said softly.

"No, not wrong, just a bit weird. We don't get many people dancing to the news up here."

"Do you know who I am?" asked Joe.

"No."

"You will," he replied with a touch of arrogance as he turned and headed for the stairs to the parking lot.

CHAPTER SEVENTY-TWO

Entering through the security door from the Homicide office, Heinz flashed his badge as he introduced himself to a startled BVS employee. Normal procedure was to give advance warning and arrive at the front door, but the ex-marine loved the element of surprise.

"Screw protocol," he would say to the rookies on the beat, "catch 'em with their pants down and you've got them by the balls."

Within minutes a flustered supervisor came running down the hall.

"Hi, I'm Mary Lou Judd, how can I help?"

"Show me how your system works," Heinz ordered.

"Why, what's happened?" she laughed. "Has someone stolen your identity?"

Heinz didn't react and knew instantly she didn't like him. *Big deal*, he thought

"What do you want to know," she asked coldly.

"If you type in someone's name and open their file, can you tell if the file has been accessed?"

"Sure, it leaves an electronic marker."

"Let's use this computer," he said pointing to a desk where no one was sitting.

Mary Lou nodded, sat down and tapped in her password to get into the system.

"Fire away," she said, smiling.

"Marilyn Monroe."

Mary Lou looked frightened and looked up to ask, "You don't think someone got the information here do you?"

"Just type," said Heinz wearing his police face.

As the thirteen letters were punched into the system a

list of fourteen possible match ups appeared at the top of the screen and a cursory check revealed that six had been accessed. One by one she went through the half dozen files until Marilyn Delaney's name and address appeared.

"Bull's eye," said Heinz.

"Thousands of files are accessed every day," she said with astonishment, "it doesn't mean her file was opened by the person who killed her."

"OK, let's try Martin Luther King," Heinz replied arrogantly.

This time there were more than two-dozen match ups with eleven files accessed, but it didn't take long for the address and personal details of the man known as Marty King to pop up.

"Double bull's eye," said an over-excited Heinz much to the obvious annoyance of the supervisor.

She'd had enough. It wasn't just one thing she disliked about the man standing next to her: it was everything from his childish behavior and his silly "high and tight" haircut to his sexist attitude.

"It could still be coincidence," she uttered with a hint of desperation in her voice.

The detective looked at her and grinned condescendingly. "I'll take it from here," he said pulling back her chair.

"Coincidence, what a dumb thing to say," she mumbled as she walked away from the desk.

As much as she hated to admit it, Heinz was probably right. Two of the victim's names had been accessed and a few days later they were both dead. That was one helluva coincidence. *How could this happen,* she thought, *surely no one here would do that?*

Mary Lou returned to her work-station and rang Prakash, the department's IT guru. Without explaining in detail what was going on, she asked him if he could find the computer that was used to open the files.

"No problem," he said, "I'll check the IP address and get back to you."

Within minutes Prakash was on the phone. "Was that a test?" he asked.

"What do you mean?"

"The files were accessed from your computer... two nights running."

Mary Lou was stunned.

"Anything else?" asked Prakash.

"No, no.... thanks for that," she stuttered.

"You OK?"

Mary Lou put down the phone and rested her head in her hands. "You son of a bitch ,Joe," she said angrily, "how could you do this... I trusted you?"

––––––––––––––––––––

Down the hall, Heinz was making notes on which of his top ten celebrity names had been accessed.

"Jesus Christ," he said looking at the list. "John Lennon, Bobby Kennedy, John F Kennedy... he's done them all."

With more than a hundred opened files to view, Heinz knew it was going to be a long day, but he also knew that he might be able to cut short this investigation if he found the computer used by the killer. Who knows, he might even find the killer.

––––––––––––––––––––

A call came through on Mary Lou's extension. It was Heinz.

"This pretty little thing sitting next to me says I can find out which computer was used by tracking the IP address. I haven't got a clue what that is, but I need you to get it for me now."

"It'll take a few minutes," said a tearful Mary Lou.

"I'm not going anywhere and hey... don't tell anybody what we're doin', I want this to be a surprise."

Mary Lou sat at her desk for a moment thinking about what to do next. It didn't take her long to make up her mind. She wiped her eyes, turned off her computer and tidied her desk before walking to the elevator. Holding back her tears, she avoided eye contact and remained stone faced as she stared at her pallid reflection in the stainless steel doors. The elevator was packed and dead silent. Once inside, she edged her body into the corner, lowered her head and tried hard to be invisible as she quietly counted the passing floors. Despite having made this journey a thousand times, she still looked up to see which number was illuminated when the doors eventually opened for the last time. Crossing the threshold into the hallway was like passing the point of no return. She knew she could never go back. At the end of the corridor she pushed down hard on the fire exit handle bar and stepped into the bright morning sunshine. With tears now streaming down her cheeks and a nervous shiver racing through her body, she moved away from the reinforced door and then stopped. Her job was her life and her life was her job. There was nothing else and there was no one else. Rolling her head back, she closed her eyes, breathed in and forced herself to take that final step that took her off the top of the building and sent her crashing to the sidewalk below.

CHAPTER SEVENTY-THREE

Freaking out at the Galleria was a stupid thing to do and Joe knew it. Had the police been called, he'd be in deep shit right now instead of enjoying a leisurely walk in the fresh air. Feeling like he was about to snap and desperate for some peace and quiet, he came to the only place where he could silence the voices in his head: his mother's graveside. This was where he found sanctuary after running away from his foster home. Daylight hours were spent on the streets with other runaways ducking and diving to avoid the Department of Social Services while at night he left them to their own devices, climbing the wrought iron gates and curling up next to his mom. After all those years there was still something unnaturally comforting about being surrounded by death.

Approaching his mother's grave, he passed a new burial plot covered in flowers and a wreath made from white carnations spelling the word "MOM". He picked up the wreath and carefully placed it against his mother's headstone. "Look what I got you," said Joe adjusting the position of the wreath to stop it from sliding. "How's life in rock'n' roll heaven? You met Michael Jackson yet? I'm doing fine... wrote some good stuff that everybody's talking about... got a starring role too. Not too happy about the ending, but that's the way it goes, I guess... By the way, I popped into the BVS... couldn't find my birth certificate. Don't need it... just wanted to know... anyway, gotta go, take care... See ya."

The parking lot at the police station was heaving with silent onlookers when Dan and Leigh returned from the motel.

"What's up?" asked Dan to a uniformed officer as he drove slowly through the police cordon.

"A woman from BVS did a high dive off the roof followed by a face plant on the sidewalk," said the officer matter-of-factly.

Leigh shook her head in disgust at his remark

"Word is that Heinz was on her case about something," he added.

Dan got out of the car, slammed the door and ran up the stairs to the office where Heinz was waiting. "Before you say anything, let me explain," he pleaded.

"It better be good," said Dan.

"I spoke with the Supervisor... Er eh," he stammered.

"Mary Lou Judd," said Dan angrily.

"Yeah, that's right, Mary Lou...We discovered that the files for Delaney and King had been opened on the same evening. When I asked her to find out which computer was used, she went up to the roof and jumped."

"And why would she do that?" shouted Dan in disbelief.

"It was her computer."

The room fell silent as everyone waited for Dan to say something. But instead of the top cop taking the floor it was Moose who spoke from his desk a few feet away.

"Did you know that someone commits suicide in the US approximately every seventeen minutes?"

Even if it wasn't a rhetorical question no one responded, but every head in the office turned in his direction.

What's he on? Leigh wondered.

"Look, I talked to that woman and I can tell you the only person she killed was herself," said Heinz, returning to more important matters. He continued, "It may sound crazy, but I think she either got the information for our man or she let him use her computer."

"Why do you say that?" asked Dan.

"Files with names similar to dead celebrities were accessed on two separate evenings between 6 p.m., when everyone had gone home, and 6:30 p.m. when the cleaners entered the building. She worked late on both nights."

"Rip Mary Lou's computer apart and check out her cell," shouted Dan to his team, "there must be a clue in there somewhere, and check out the cameras too."

"Her phone smashed into a million pieces," said Moose, "and there's only one camera and its inside the entrance."

"What?" shouted Dan.

"Cut backs," replied Moose as if reading from a prepared text. "Did you know that California, the world's eighth largest economy if it was a country, faces insolvency?"

Leigh looked at the big guy in disbelief as Dan made his way to the whiteboard where he stuck up pictures of Marion Bergdorf, the fourth victim. Gathering the troops around him and pointing to each of the victim's photos, he painted a grim picture of events so far.

"We have nothing on Delaney, nothing on Van Sykes and nothing on King. They found a hair on the bed at the motel, so we're waiting for test results. If there's no match… then we're back to square one."

Dan knew that with bodies piling up and people afraid to leave their homes, he had to take drastic action. In the back of his mind he knew too that Esposito could take him off the case any day just to get the media off his ass and to prove to the Mayor that he was doing something to help get the "Celebrity Killer" off the streets. He was running out of time.

"I hate to make things sound worse than they are," said Heinz, "but the re-enactment of a murder from a goddamn movie opens up a whole new can of worms. There must be thousands of memorable death scenes he could do. Shit… what about the girls who were barbecued on the tanning beds in *Final Destination* or the girl in *Saw III* who was hung up in the walk in freezer and— "

"OK, we get the point," said Dan stopping Heinz in his tracks. "We can't cover every potential victim, so we're gonna go after just one, the most high profile killing in our life time… John F Kennedy."

This came as no surprise. The squad had sensed that this was going to happen after hearing from Heinz that the name Kennedy was accessed more than the others on the BVS computer. Dan believed that putting all his eggs in one basket was not the most intelligent way of cracking the case: it was the only way. It was risky, but without suspects or evidence there was no alternative.

CHAPTER SEVENTY-FOUR

It was late afternoon when Weinberg returned to the street where Joe lived. Nervous and alone, he sat in his Cadillac thinking about what to say. Although he felt comfortable promoting his films to heavyweights in the business, he had never tried making a pitch to a serial killer. After a couple of false starts, he found himself walking up the drive to Joe's dark and unwelcoming bungalow. A series of timid taps on the rotting wooden door-frame and then on the middle of the door brought no response. Finally, Weinberg planted his fist heavily onto the woodwork.

"Yeah," said a voice from behind a locked door.

"My name is Philip Weinberg."

"So," said the voice.

"I'd like to speak to the person who left a script with me... is that you?"

"What script?"

"Killing the Dead."

Not enough sleep and one too many pills had left Joe with a brain that wasn't working to full capacity. He had difficulty making sense out of what was going on until he poked his head through the curtains and saw the long scraggy gray hair, stooped shoulders and gold tooth.

"Fuck me; it's that porno guy from Tata's."

Wiping his hair away from his face, he opened the door and stared intently at the tall Jewish man on his doorstep.

"Can I come in?" asked Weinberg.

"Sure," Joe said while at the same time thinking, *he looks like he's going to shit himself.*

As the door slammed behind him, Weinberg turned and saw a rifle leaning against the wall.

Joe also looked at the gun and reacted nervously. "I've been burgled twice," he said unconvincingly.

There was an awkward silence as the two men stood face to face just a few feet apart. Weinberg was dying to check out the room, but was reluctant to take his eyes off the man, who looked nothing like he thought he would. In his mind, he pictured an older man hiding behind facial scars, a crooked mouth and dodgy teeth. It was a silly assumption that probably came from watching too many TV thrillers. Apart from having some seriously dark circles around his bloodshot eyes, he appeared quite normal until a casual glance at his bloodstained boots reminded Weinberg that this was not your average guy. Standing so close to the killer of four innocent people was a surreal situation that left him feeling uneasy and anxious to get things moving. They quickly exchanged names, but not pleasantries.

"I've read your script and I like it... it's got strong characters, a clever plot, but it needs more."

Joe looked stunned. He obviously wasn't used to hearing compliments. His jaw dropped and his face came alive, but then his demeanor changed and he looked deep into Weinberg's eyes, suspicion in his every move.

Suddenly he snapped, "Don't fuck with me."

Weinberg took a step back. "I didn't come here to fuck with you; I came here to offer you a deal."

Only a few words had passed between them, but it was enough to give Weinberg concerns about the young man's state of mind. In a split second, and for no apparent reason, Joe had gone from jubilation to rage. His face became contorted and his fists clenched. Realizing that he shouldn't have come to the house in the first place, Weinberg now needed to get out in one piece and move to somewhere more public.

"I got an idea," he said thinking quickly, "why don't we talk over dinner... my treat?"

————————————

For a moment Joe didn't say a word. Everything was happening so fast that he wasn't sure what to do. After being the butt of countless jokes, caustic comments and rejections, it wasn't easy for him to get his head around flattery. Finally he agreed.

"Sounds good," said Joe, "give me an hour."

But Joe knew he didn't need an hour; he was ready to go now.

————————————

When Weinberg got back to the car his heart was pounding and sweat was dripping from his forehead. As he gradually lowered his body on to the black leather seat his underwear slid unhindered between his cheeks.

"Shit," he shouted as he slammed his fist on the steering wheel.

CHAPTER SEVENTY-FIVE

The squad was split into three groups. Heinz was in charge of interviewing BVS staff and checking alibis while Moose went back over the first four murders to see if anything had been missed. Finding the right Kennedy was down to Dan and Leigh and it proved to be a much more onerous task than originally thought. Eighteen files were opened at BVS with thirteen of the Kennedys scattered across California and only five living in the Los Angeles area. Not one of the Kennedy files logged Fitzgerald as a middle name and none of them was married to a Jackie or Jacqueline. To make things worse, there wasn't a convertible owner in sight.

"Why did I think this was going to be easy?" asked Leigh.

"Yeah it's not like in Montana where you track the killer by following his footprints in the snow," joked Dan, "but, if it's any consolation he must have had the same problem. Forget about the Kennedys living outside the city… he's local, I'd bet my badge on it"

"You already have," she said with a grimace.

Ploughing through the white pages, yellow pages, online directories, unlisted numbers, and anything even remotely linked to JFK, such as chat rooms, conspiracy groups, charities and fan clubs, proved tedious and time consuming and in the end produced nothing to help the investigation. Bleary eyed and exhausted, Dan was now having second thoughts about which dead celebrity he should back. He poured himself another black coffee not because he wanted one, but just because he needed to stretch his legs and break the monotony of staring at his computer screen.

"Lennon had the second highest number of hits," said Leigh. "Sorry, no pun intended."

"Let's give it a bit longer," said Dan as he spat a mouthful of cold coffee back into his mug. "And let's get a beer… I need a break."

Earlier the same afternoon, Weinberg returned to Joe's house after changing his sweat-stained shirt and putting on a fresh pair of underwear. This time he stayed in the car. Despite having sixty minutes to get ready, Joe still kept him waiting. When he eventually appeared he looked flustered and his hands displayed traces of black dust.

"Where would you like to eat?" asked Weinberg.

"Tata's," replied Joe without hesitation.

"Tata's it is then."

As the Cadillac crept along at a snail's pace through heavy traffic, Weinberg tried unsuccessfully to engage his passenger in conversation. At best, Joe was monosyllabic, but for most of the journey he said nothing at all, preferring to stare blankly at the red taillights on the car in front of him. It was a long boring ride until five hundred yards from the restaurant Joe told Weinberg to stop the car.

"I wanna drive," said Joe forcefully.

"OK," said Weinberg a little bemused, but eager to please.

The two men got out of the car and passed each other between the headlights. Once sitting comfortably in the driver's seat, Joe reached for the keys in the ignition, but they weren't there.

"Force of habit," said Weinberg dangling the keys between his fingers.

It was like old times when Joe joined the line alongside the decorative red and gold valet parking sign outside Tata's main entrance. Fat balding men with slim young female wannabes glided through the front door while Gomez raced like a blue ass fly from car to car park and back to car again. Joe never thought of parking cars as a real job, but there were things about it that he missed. This "special zone" with "first class" service for the privileged and their expensive cars

250

was a great place to rub shoulders with the rich and famous, drive the best automobiles in town and pick up loose women. But that was yesterday and Joe knew things would never be the same again.

When Weinberg's black Cadillac finally reached the drop off point, both men stayed inside the car to listen to a brief news bulletin announcing that a man claiming to be the Celebrity Killer was in police custody in San Francisco. The report described how forty-nine-year-old Dwayne Hardman was arrested after trying to drown his neighbor, Dennis Wilson, while swimming at Ocean Beach. His attempt to mimic the drowning of the Beach Boys' drummer at Marina Del Ray in 1983 was prevented when Wilson's wife answered her husband's cries for help. A cynical smile came over Joe's face as he shook his head and turned off the engine.

Even with heavily tinted windows, Weinberg could never remain anonymous with "Porn 1" on his license plate. Expecting the loathsome Sultan of Sleaze to step out of the Cadillac at any moment, Gomez almost fell over backwards when his old buddy got out of the car.

"Hey Joe," hollered the Mexican, "where you been, I missed you man?"

Remaining cool and straight faced, Joe tossed the keys in the direction of Gomez and said, "Park this for me, boy."

There was an awkward silence followed by stunned looks all around until Joe smiled and said, "I've always wanted to do that."

Being back on familiar territory had a relaxing effect on Joe. The tension in his face had disappeared and he even managed to give Gomez a hug.

"Savage wants you back, man."

"No shit?"

"The kid who took your place was here for about an hour before driving off in some big shot's Bugatti Veyron. He just kept on going. Fucking hilarious! Probably in Alaska by now... Savage said you were a fuck up, but at least he could trust you."

"More compliments," said Joe sarcastically, "this is my

lucky day."

Once inside, it was easy to see why Tata's was so popular. It was chic, but not stuffy. There was a constant buzz, but it was still possible to hear and be heard. With one of the finest chefs and largest wine cellars in California it appealed to serious foodies, as well as those just wishing to be seen. Ivory colored walls with large black and white pictures of Hollywood greats like Bogart and Bacall stretched around three sides of the cavernous room while a two-story wall of glass completed the structure.

Even though Weinberg was a regular and well known at the restaurant, he had no problem letting Joe take over. After all, this was his moment, his first taste of living the dream. Demanding the best table by the window and a bottle of vintage champagne was predictable and self indulgent, but Weinberg let it go. Insisting on being served by Mario was childish and didn't go down well with management, but Weinberg used his influence to help Joe get what he wanted. It was a strange and uncomfortable beginning and only Joe knew how it would end.

"Why the waiter?" asked Weinberg.

"He pissed me off a while back... I wanted to get even but you know just having him wait on me is sweet enough."

"I think I know how your script ended up in my case," said Weinberg.

"What took you so long to contact me?"

"You didn't leave a number."

"Yes I did," growled Joe.

Weinberg pulled the rolled up script out of his inner pocket and laid it out on the table in front of Joe. The cover sheet was missing.

"Shit," he muttered as he suddenly remembered the page falling under his truck. "How did you find me?"

"I followed the script."

Joe looked surprised and Weinberg looked worried.

"Please tell me there aren't any more of these floating around the city," he said lifting the script in the air.

"That's the only one."

"I hope it is... if not, you're fucked." Weinberg said. He glanced at the couple sitting at the next table, then leaned across his plate and whispered, "I'm not gonna turn you in... in fact I wanna do just the opposite."

"What do you mean?" Joe asked.

"We want you to finish what you're doing then give us the full script so we can turn it round quickly."

"We?"

"I have a backer in New York," Weinberg said conspiratorially.

"What happens to me?" Joe asked.

"You get your ass outta here! We'll help with a new identity... and you spend the rest of your days on a beach somewhere."

"Will I get credit for writing the script?" Joe asked.

"Joe Tubbs will, but you won't coz you'll be someone else."

"So, no one will know it's my work."

"That's right."

"I can't tell anyone... ever?"

"Not unless you want to face the death penalty," Weinberg said.

"Death penalty," said Joe, loud enough for nearby diners to hear.

Weinberg gritted his teeth knowing he should have kept his mouth shut.

Strange as it may seem, it never occurred to Joe that he might be executed. He knew there was a chance he could be shot by the cops, but not strapped to a table inside San Quentin's Octagonal execution room and administered a lethal cocktail of sodium pentothal, pancuronium bromide and potassium chloride.

"Why do you need me... why not just get someone else to finish it off?"

"We don't want it to look like every other goddamn glossy candy coated Hollywood movie. We want it to be raw, first hand, a journey through your dark side. What you're doing is unique and people will flock to see something written by the guy who was there and actually did the... "

Weinberg stopped short of using the word "killing". Joe was upset enough and he didn't want to piss him off even more.

"It'll be exactly as it happened," continued Weinberg, "With every rejection, we'll feel your pain, with every—"

"OK, OK I get it, but I think you're wrong... Hollywood only does gloss and that's what people pay to see," said Joe before knocking back his third large glass of champagne, "Let me think about it."

A couple of miles away at PJ's, Dan and Leigh grabbed the last two seats at the bar. The place was packed out with college kids on one side of the room while an out of control bachelorette party took over the other side. Dan tapped Leigh's beer with his bottle and gestured towards a very small bald man heading in the direction of the girl's table.

"Is that Danny DeVito?" she asked.

Groucho, who was wiping glasses a few feet away overheard the conversation and laughed.

"I wish it was, unfortunately this place doesn't attract people like DeVito. The closest we get are celeb impersonators. You'll probably see a couple more before the night's over."

He was right. Trailing a few feet behind DeVito was a dead ringer for Brad Pitt and a moment later Owen Wilson joined the party. Dan smiled as the crowd of screaming women quickly swallowed up the three lookalikes.

"Are you thinking what I'm thinking?" asked Leigh.

"What's that... I could go there and pretend to be Tom Cruise?"

"In your dreams," laughed Leigh as she got off her stool and walked over to the party.

"Where you going?"

"Police business," she replied in a joking self-assured tone.

"I gotta see this," Dan said. He stayed at the bar and watched as she glided across the floor. He knew that she knew he was watching so with her tight skirt accentuating her narrow hips she swayed from side to side like a boat on the water. She looked good, no matter which way she was facing.

Dan ordered another beer and offered to buy Groucho one as well.

"I'll have a Coke if that's OK?"

"Whatever," said Dan, "rough night?"

"Heartburn."

Leigh made her way into the middle of the pack and grabbed the nearest impersonator, who just happened to be Brad Pitt. Pulling him to one side, she wrapped her arm around his shoulder and put her mouth next to his ear. For young Brad, this was just another day at the office. He was apparently used to women of all ages, shapes and sizes coming on to him, so he relaxed into it, smiled and threw both his arms around her neck. A minute later his smile was gone, his arms were back by his sides and he was digging deep into his pockets.

"When you're young, dumb and full of cum, there's nothing like a little police business to bring you back to earth with a bump," said Dan keeping a protective eye on Leigh.

"I know you," said Groucho taking Dan's money off the bar. "Aren't you that cop that went out with Alice?"

"How do you know that?" asked Dan still watching Leigh.

"I was eighteen. This was my first job; I didn't have much to say so I listened... when she played here she talked about you a lot. You're the one who parked his black and white around back so it wouldn't scare people away."

"Boy, that was thirty years ago, you got a good memory."

"What happened to you guys?"

"We wanted different things."

"Did she ever contact you?" Groucho asked.

"No, the day we split she said she was going to Nashville and that's the last time I saw her."

"She told me she went to New York... Anyway, she came

back and did some gigs here. You know she died here?"

"Yeah, I read about it," Dan replied.

"I think we should talk," said Groucho.

The conversation stopped suddenly when Leigh returned to the bar. She was smiling and anxious to get Dan alone. Grabbing his arm, she twirled him around and headed for the door.

"What are you doing, I've still got a full beer?" said Dan.

Groucho walked along the bar trying to get Dan's attention, but it was too late. He'd already left the building.

CHAPTER SEVENTY-SIX

Even though Weinberg said he would pay, Joe made sure that he was in the washroom when Mario brought the bill to the table. While he was gone, Weinberg began talking to two young Canadian girls who were on their first visit to Hollywood. They giggled nervously when he told them what he did for a living and then looked more at ease when he mentioned he was working on a feature about a serial killer. He could never understand why some people were more comfortable with death than with sex. It wasn't long before he had them hanging on to every word he said and drooling over every name he dropped. During Joe's absence, Weinberg took the opportunity to "big him up" so by the time he returned to the table they were waiting with pen and paper in hand. Joe didn't even think to ask why they wanted his signature and to be honest he didn't care. He was in heaven, enjoying every second of it and taking nothing for granted. To be signing his name for someone to keep and treasure was serious shit. It was a mark of recognition and acceptance so an illegible scribble was unacceptable. Writing a personal note with each autograph was also important to Joe, but even more important was standing tall in the middle of the restaurant. With Savage, Mario and several diners looking on, he milked it for all it was worth, even giving an over the top film star wave as he walked across the room. On his way to the exit, Joe passed an instantly recognizable Hollywood legend sitting with a large group of friends in the middle of the room.

"Hi, I'm Joe Tubbs," he said in a loud voice, "didn't you use to be Warren Beatty?" Joe turned on his heels, laughed arrogantly and pushed through the large glass door.

"You looked like a real star in there," said Gomez with a hint of sarcasm and a lot of laughter in his voice. "The autograph and the wave were great, but the icing on the cake was that white shit under your nose."

Joe smiled, wiped his top lip with his finger and headed for the driver's door of the Cadillac. He kept his back straight and his chin up. There was no way that a ball busting car jockey was going to ruin this moment.

Sensing he had Joe right where he wanted him, Weinberg continued to play second fiddle. Slipping ten dollars into the Mexican's hand, he quickly made his way to the passenger side of the car.

"You coming back?" Gomez shouted through the heavily tinted glass window.

"Not in this lifetime," mumbled Joe as he peeled out of the lot and on to the road.

After being hustled out of PJ's, Dan plopped himself behind the wheel of his unmarked cop car and asked, "What kind of woman takes a guy away from a full bottle of beer?"

"What if he's a celeb impersonator?" asked Leigh ignoring Dan's question about the beer.

"Who?"

"The next victim, think about it, we already agreed that none of the opened JFK files were suitable… and that young hunk… you know the one who couldn't take his hands off me?" Her attempt to tease fell on deaf ears.

"He told me that his agency, Familiar Faces, had a JFK double on their books." Leigh handed over the business card she got from Brad Pitt, a grin lit up Dan's face.

"Did I say something funny?" she asked coyly.

Dan didn't answer, but he couldn't help thinking… *young, smart and beautiful, now I know how Michael Douglas feels.*

CHAPTER SEVENTY-SEVEN

There was no match for the single strand of hair found on the bed in room seventeen, but the boys back at the station had other reasons to be excited. Marion's cell phone had coughed up an incoming number from a call made less than an hour before her death and a gas station attendant, about a hundred yards from The Bay Trees Motel, told them about a tall man with bad hair and a gold tooth who bought a can of bug spray because he was staying in a flea pit down the road. His description matched the one given by Jack Michalec only the guy at the gas station went one step better. He remembered the license plate number.

"Philip Weinberg is the name of the guy who stayed at the motel," announced Heinz while standing on a chair in the middle of the room, "let's go get him."

––––––––––––––––––––

Twenty minutes later a team of armed police officers were knocking at the front door of Weinberg's luxury penthouse apartment. His wife, a large heavily made up woman with shoulder length bleached blond hair, answered the door. Dressed in a white satin Japanese kimono that barely covered her massive breasts, she wasted no time telling Heinz how she felt about her husband while a man half her age waited patiently in the background.

"I kicked that womanizing son of a bitch out months ago," she told Heinz. "He was supposed to work behind the camera, not in front of it. You'll probably find him at his office with some short ass slant or East European slut."

Heinz was a soldier and felt at ease dealing with difficult situations, but he never liked being in the middle of a domestic row. There was something uncomfortably scary about a woman scorned so he was happy to get the hell out of there.

The call to Marion's cell was traced to a phone booth next to a bus stop on Walker Road. Moose went there alone and twice drove by a pile of rubble before realizing it once had a more important function in the community. Digging through the heap of shattered glass and bent pieces of metal, he discovered that the vultures had already taken the coin box and handset.

Jolanta figured the game was up when she looked through the window and saw a police officer's blue and gold badge. Momentarily resting her head against the door, she pictured herself back home in Gdansk, sharing a bedroom with her sister in her family's small apartment not far from the noise and clutter of the local shipyard. Cold, damp and depressing, the stark Baltic seaport was a far cry from the life she had become accustomed to in sunny California. She was devastated. The road to America was not an easy one.

To obtain a US visa, the most sought after passport endorsement on the planet, she had needed to produce a return airline ticket to Poland and have enough money to support herself whilst Stateside. More importantly, she had to convince the US authorities she was a solid citizen with a good job and the intention to return home after her visit was finished. Unemployed, with no immediate prospects, she faced an impossible challenge. Her friends laughed at her and dismissed her plan as a waste of time and energy, but she was determined to do it. She worked twelve hours a day, seven days a week, saving every penny she earned. Her nights were spent waiting on tables and washing dishes while during the day she worked as a receptionist at the American Corner, a US information outpost in her hometown. With aspirations limited to shipyard employment, her parents couldn't understand how their baby girl landed such a plum job with the Americans. But Jolanta knew what she wanted and she knew who to sleep with to get it. Hating every minute of the nine to five life, she stayed with it for the money and to build up contacts within the American government community. The fun loving late night party girl became the conscientious, reliable and sometimes boring employee. When it came time to ask for a visa, she called on her work mates for support. It was a walk in the park.

Now resigned to an imminent arrest, she opened the front door as a tear ran down her cheek.

"My name is Heinz, LAPD, where's Weinberg?" shouted the detective as he stormed into the room.

"What?"

"Where's Weinberg?" he repeated as he and three uniformed officers searched the studio.

"He's not here," replied Jolanta somewhat confused. "Why do you want him?"

"What were you doing at the Bay Trees Motel?"

"B... Bay Trees Motel," stuttered Jolanta. "What's that got to do with me?"

"A girl was murdered there last night."

Jolanta shuddered, but it wasn't out of fear of what happened or sympathy for the dead girl. It was a sigh of relief. She was like a balloon about to burst when Heinz unknowingly let the air out. Now, surrounded by cops asking questions about a murder, she felt safe.

CHAPTER SEVENTY-EIGHT

It wasn't the alcohol or the powder rammed up his nose that gave Joe such a euphoric feeling; he was high on self-esteem. Weinberg had worked him well and it seemed to be paying off. During the drive home Joe didn't stop talking. He talked about the girls from Canada and the looks of admiration he got from his old colleagues and customers in the restaurant. The script and his plans for the next one to be written under his new name and identity were also hot topics. For the first time since they met, Weinberg felt at ease. He relaxed and let his body slump into the soft leather seat. For a second or two he even managed to close his eyes. Then in a moment of silence, Joe reached into his pocket and blurted, "This thing got a cassette player?"

Weinberg froze and his heart started to pound. Having read the script, he knew that a cassette of "Hey Joe" was played before every killing. Something bad was going down and it was time to get out of the car. Clenching his butt cheeks and pressing his legs firmly against the floor, he edged his body gradually up the back of the seat and reached for the door handle.

"Aw shit," laughed Joe. "I thought that would get you goin', but you didn't even flinch."

Weinberg held his breath and turned his head slightly in Joe's direction. There was no cassette in his hand, just a pack of cigarettes.

He made a joke, thought Weinberg. *I'm sitting next to a fucking serial killer with a sense of humor.*

He tried to laugh but couldn't. His mouth was too dry. A silly grimace appeared on his face and an uncomfortable dampness oozed from his backside.

Not again, he thought. Weinberg had some bad-ass friends and moved in dark and dangerous circles, but it was obvious he didn't have the stomach to go it alone. When he was sure Joe wasn't watching he discreetly wiped the tiny beads of sweat that were trickling down his forehead and then balanced on his left butt cheek to separate the seat of his trousers from his underwear.

Re-engaging Joe in conversation, he asked, "So what do ya think, do we have a deal?"

"Sure, why not?" said Joe.

"Do you want to talk money?"

"No, I trust you."

Weinberg had been in the business for years and had never met anyone who said they trusted him or didn't want to talk money.

Christ, he thought, *this guy's either very naïve or very stupid. People in this town don't even get out of bed without getting something up front.*

But Joe didn't want to talk about it. He was happy just to relive his five minutes of glory at the restaurant until he finally pulled the Cadillac into a gas station.

"What are you doin'… we still got a quarter tank of gas?" asked Weinberg.

"I'll pump… you pay," laughed Joe, ignoring Weinberg's question.

Weinberg stepped out of the car, looked at Joe who was already filling up the tank and then glanced back at his precious Escalade.

"You don't trust me, do you?" asked Joe tossing the keys to him over the roof of the car.

Weinberg didn't trust him, but he said he did. In fact, he didn't know what to make of him.

It was a ten-minute drive from the gas station to Joe's place and when the Escalade eventually stopped behind the rusty red pickup, Weinberg got out of the car and quickly ran around to the driver's seat.

"I need a piss, come in for a beer," shouted Joe as he disappeared into the house.

"No thanks, I gotta go… call you tomorrow."

Weinberg climbed into the car, locked the door and took a deep breath. It was like a weight had been lifted off his shoulders. Adjusting his seat to accommodate his long skinny legs, he fastened his seat belt and reached down to start the engine, but the key wasn't in the ignition.

"Shit," he screamed as he searched frantically down both sides of his seat and on the floor. "Shit, shit, shit," he shouted as he pounded the dashboard.

With pulse racing and moisture seeping from his armpits, he sat hunched over the steering wheel and gazed at the open front door. Two, three, four minutes passed, but there was no sign of Joe. Weinberg had to make a decision; he couldn't sit there all night. After waiting for another couple of minutes, he took his cell out of his pocket and pressed the numbers 911 and then walked towards the front door with his right thumb hovering above the call button. Standing with one foot inside the house and the other on the doorstep, he arched his body and stretched his neck to look behind the door. The rifle wasn't there. A shiver ran down his body as he called Joe's name

"I'm in the cellar," replied Joe. "Grab the beer on the counter and come on down."

Leaving the front door wide open, Weinberg tip-toed into the dimly lit room where an open bottle of beer was waiting as promised. Reaching for the bottle, he narrowly missed the tip of a needle that was lying just a few inches away.

"And don't touch my shit," shouted Joe, "it's a special one for later."

Weinberg glared at the syringe filled with a white liquid and shook his head in disgust and then made his way to the stairs at the back of the house, circling slowly as he went.

"I didn't know that houses in California had cellars," hollered Weinberg, desperate to maintain voice contact with Joe.

"There aren't many, that's for sure."

Looking down from the top of the stairs, he counted six narrow steps leading to a concrete floor. The opening was dark and narrow and definitely not inviting. A strong damp musty odor seeped from the darkness below. Placing his foot on the top step he leaned slightly forward and shouted, "You got my keys?"

"Yeah, sorry about that, force of habit I guess. Come here, I want to show you something I think you'll identify with."

To say that Weinberg was nervous was an understatement. Shit scared would have been more like it because he knew how quickly Joe could flip. To gain some sort of advantage without seeing Joe's face, he tried concentrating on the sound of his voice and listening for any signs of stress or agitation. But Joe was fine, pleasant and warm and the more he spoke the happier Weinberg felt about lowering himself into the unknown.

"Keep your head down," said Joe with a chuckle.

"This better be good," replied Weinberg as he side-stepped his way down to the cold concrete floor. "Where are you?"

"Over here," said Joe from the far corner of the room.

Stooping to avoid hitting the overhead beams, he inched slowly towards the sound of Joe's voice. As he got closer and the light improved he saw something that sent a violent shudder through his body, forcing his beer to fall crashing to the floor. At the same time, the ominous sound of Jimi Hendrix's "Hey Joe" blasted through the speakers and appeared to shake the foundations of the house.

Weinberg looked down at his thumb as it descended towards the call button on his cell.

"I wouldn't do that," shouted Joe as he appeared out of the darkness with his semi-automatic now pressing against the back of Weinberg's head.

"What do you think of the set I built? It's pure Hollywood, isn't it?" Joe asked.

"You can't do this... what about our deal?" pleaded Weinberg.

"Did you really think I was going to change my face, my name and live like a hermit on some fucking beach somewhere? You don't know me, do you? I want everyone to see that I'm the one who wrote this... I'm the one who played this role... Remember, it's guys like you who made me do this. If I had been shown some respect, this never would have happened."

"Please... please don't," cried Weinberg as Joe looked on impassively.

Desperate to get inside Joe's head and aware that begging wasn't going to work, Weinberg tried to appeal to his writing and acting instincts.

"It's not in the script, you can't do it, it's not in the script," he shouted.

Joe stared at Weinberg's long lanky trembling limbs and watched without emotion as urine ran down his leg to form a pool around his shoe.

"That's true," said Joe. "I'm impressed, but you're too late. I just did a rewrite."

CHAPTER SEVENTY-NINE

Jolanta didn't get to America by being stupid. She was manipulative and flirtatious and would do anything to save her own ass. Wearing just a short denim skirt and a low cut T-shirt, she sat down in front of LA's finest and slowly opened her legs. Heinz quickly grabbed a coat and threw it over her lap.

"Sweetheart," he said, "I'm not particularly interested in what you had for lunch. I just want to know what went on at the motel. Now we can do this here without the bullshit or we can do it downtown."

Jolanta got the message. This wasn't Poland and Heinz wasn't Weinberg. She sat up straight, pressed her knees together and for the next few minutes told the cops everything she knew, which wasn't much, because Weinberg didn't tell her a lot. She talked about the disgusting motel and how she slept in the car while he sat up all night in a chair by the window. In the morning, she said he drove her back to the studio where they had sex and then he returned to the motel. The last time she saw him was the next day when he came home just long enough to change his clothes and take a shower.

"He looked pale, mentioned something about buying a film script," she said.

"You said he changed his clothes… where are they?"

"They're still on the bathroom floor where he left them. I didn't want to touch them."

"Why?" asked Heinz.

"Because he shit his pants."

Heinz took a moment to reflect on what she had just said. What would make a grown man crap in his pants? It could have been something he ate or maybe he had too much to drink, or did someone or something literally scare the shit out of him?

The ex-marine had no reason to doubt her, but he still waited until a rookie cop had a look at Weinberg's things and gave him the thumbs up. A cursory examination of the clothes revealed no traces of blood; nevertheless, Heinz had everything bagged and tagged for a more detailed inspection back at the lab.

Sifting through papers on Weinberg's desk, Heinz picked up an airline ticket, put it in his pocket and immediately got on the phone to Dan. "He's not our man... he was in New York when all of this shit was going down. I've put out a call tho', coz I'm sure he knows something."

Heinz was aware that Jolanta was concerned; after all, Weinberg was her meal ticket. "What's going on Officer Heinz?" she asked. "And why won't he answer his phone?"

"I don't know," said the cop, "but I've got every officer in the city looking for him."

The young Polish girl eased herself off the bright red leather sofa and glanced towards the door.

"Can I go now?"

"Sure," said Heinz, "but first, that lady over there wants to ask you a couple of questions."

"Who is she?"

"She's from Immigration," replied Heinz with a grin. "Got a passport?

Back at the station the phones were red hot and extra employees were drafted in to help with the huge number of calls. It was utter chaos with some callers claiming they'd just seen the "Celebrity Killer", while others were confident they knew him. Most, however, just wanted protection. A woman, who said her name, was Diana, asked for a police escort through Sepulveda Tunnel while a man, identified only as Mr Presley, said he wanted someone to stand guard while he went to the toilet.

"This is crazy," said Moose, "these people don't need protection, they need counselling."

At that moment Esposito appeared at the doorway, but was unwilling to step into the room. He used to be one of the guys, happy to get his hands dirty. When things got busy he rolled up his sleeves and worked his ass off alongside cops and administrators alike, but not anymore. His days were numbered and he was coasting to the finish line. Despite this, everyone knew that he was looking for the headline grabber that would catapult him upwards and onwards and he didn't care whose toes he stepped on to get it.

"What have you got for me Dan?" he shouted.

Esposito was the senior officer and Dan was obliged to give him an update on the case, so he did just that.

"We're looking for a guy called Weinberg," he yelled from the far side of the room.

"He's a big gun in the porn business. We know he was at the Bay Trees Motel the night Marion was killed."

"Good work," said Esposito. "Let's see if we can wrap this up in the next twenty-four hours."

It was only a brief conversation, but it sent shivers around the office. What the hell was Dan doing? Esposito may still be the guy in charge, but he couldn't run a bath let alone a criminal investigation. He was a loudmouth and now it was only a matter of time before Weinberg the witness became Weinberg the suspect.

While others in the office looked on in dismay, Leigh saw things differently. "You're not just a pretty face are you?" she laughed. Dan just pretended to shuffle through a pile of papers on his desk.

"Did you know there's a guy in Austria called Adolf Hittler?" said Moose to no one in particular. "He spells his name with two t's, but still, I bet he's glad he doesn't live in L.A. right now."

The big guy's throw-away piece of trivia was not only amusing but relevant and immediately added yet another name to the long list of likely targets written on the end of the white board. JFK was still the front-runner, but Hitler was a possibility even though they didn't expect to find his name in the phone book and getting rid of the nasty Nazi wouldn't be easy. The killer would have to locate a suitable victim, poison him with cyanide and then shoot him in the temple with a handgun. The more the idea was kicked around the crazier it became. Heinz wanted to know if the killer would go the whole nine yards and take out Eva Braun as well. Even though it was messy and complicated, it had to be considered. After all, nailing someone to a cross in the middle of the city was hardly the cleanest of hits.

While the debate continued around him, Dan took a call on his cell. When he hung up he shouted to Leigh, "I just got hold of the guy who owns Familiar Faces and he's agreed to see us now, let's go."

It was late at night and the ride across town was relatively traffic free. Leigh opened her window and let the cool evening air caress her face while Dan talked non-stop about getting that *"son of a bitch"* before he killed again. Leigh wasn't interested; she had other things on her mind. Twenty-four hours ago they were making love and she had been looking for some kind of sign or acknowledgement from Dan ever since. She really didn't know what she wanted… a kiss would have been nice or maybe just a warm smile or even a goddamn wink. This was the first time they had been alone and she thought he might say something, but he didn't.

Familiar Faces, a large commercial operation set up to provide walking talking doubles of the rich and famous, was located in an old refurbished furniture warehouse just a stone's throw from Sunset Blvd. It was an easy place to find because it was the only building on the block with its fascia covered in Banksy style graffiti portraits of Elvis, Marilyn and countless other super celebrities. The business, a magnet for those short on talent but big on looking like movie stars, rock legends and ex-presidents was run by Nigel Tweedy, an Englishman in his mid thirties. Dressed in a striped multi-colored Paul Smith shirt, silver gray Armani trousers, black and white spats and lime green socks, the eccentric Londoner greeted Dan with a head to toe once over that lasted much too long and a hand shake so limp that Dan thought he was shaking the Englishman's sleeve. He wasn't just light on his loafers; he was positively floating on air. A bow from the waist, a wave of the right arm across his body and a tender kiss to the back of Leigh's hand reminded Dan of when he was a kid watching Aramis in *The Three Musketeers*. To say their host was theatrical was an understatement, but he was only just an appetizer for what was to follow.

Inside the lobby, high above the white marble floor, a replica of that famous chandelier from *The Phantom of the Opera* lit up the entrance like a runway while posters and paintings documenting one hundred years in the entertainment industry lined the hallway leading to Tweedy's office where a twelve foot cardboard cut out of King Kong stood guard at his door. As his guests lowered themselves on to a large sofa draped in a huge Union Jack, Tweedy left the room and returned several moments later with some tea and shortbread biscuits.

"Cheers," he said delicately raising his cup in the air. "Now, what can I do for you?"

"You have a JFK lookalike?" asked Dan.

"I do, would you like to book him for the next LAPD Ball?"

"No, but I'd like to stop him from getting killed," Dan snapped.

Tweedy looked confused and it was understandable. When they spoke on the phone earlier, Dan didn't tell him why he wanted to see him right away. If the detective couldn't trust his own captain to keep his mouth shut, there was no way that he was going to let a member of the public know what was going on. But now it was decision time. To get the information he wanted, Tweedy would have to know. Dan leaned across an outline of the Queen tastefully etched into a glass coffee table and glared into the Englishman's eyes. There were no threats and no macho gestures... just a simple question, "Can I trust you to keep schtum?"

Tweedy nodded as he smiled at Dan's use of East London slang.

"We think your JFK double may be the Celebrity Killer's next victim."

Tweedy almost choked on his Earl Grey, "Bloody hell," he blurted before quickly apologizing to Leigh.

"Are you sure?" he asked after a long pause.

"No, it's just a hunch, but we have nothing else at this time," Dan replied.

"I don't understand," said Tweedy, "on the way over here I heard some guy on the radio say you knew who the killer was and it was just a matter of time before he would be behind bars."

Leigh caught Dan's eye. She could tell that he was annoyed yet at the same time, relieved.

"That's not true," said Dan, "he's still out there and we think that sooner or later he's going to go after the big one... JFK."

"He's a big earner," said Tweedy, "I don't want to lose him." And then he added, "Sorry, that sounds rather callous and corporate America doesn't it?

"Can you show me what you got on this guy?" asked Dan.

"Sure." Tweedy logged on to his PC and brought up JFK's details and reeled them off to Dan. "His real name is Stan Gardner... left school at 16... unemployed construction worker... now earns $75,000 a year... I guess you could say his face is his fortune. He's the real deal... even drives a black '61 Lincoln Continental convertible."

"Boy, that's tempting fate," said Leigh.

"Did you know that he was the first guy in our agency to be a celebrity lookalike sperm donor? Now even ugly parents can have good-looking kids. Isn't American wonderful?"

Dan bit his tongue, pointed to the PC and said, "Can we?"

Tweedy got the message and continued to read from the screen, "His next booking is on Thursday at 3 o'clock... Hang on, there's a client link to another one of my doubles. Mmm... it looks like the same person has booked John Lennon as well, only two hours earlier."

A couple more clicks of the mouse and yet a third booking appeared, "You're not going to believe this," Tweedy said excitedly.

"What?" Dan asked anxiously.

"Buddy Holly is number three... again, same client, same day and two hours before the Lennon gig."

Suddenly the flamboyant Londoner became serious. "If this wanker is trying to put me out of business, he's messing with the wrong guy."

Leigh looked inquisitively at Dan.

"Any more names on the list?" Dan asked.

"No, that appears to be it... for now anyway."

Dan paused for a moment and thought about the conversation back at the office before asking reluctantly, "Have you got a Hitler?"

"We had one, but he kept getting the crap beat out of him, so we let him go. It wasn't worth the hassle."

"Who made the bookings?" asked Dan.

"Anonymous, I'm afraid. An envelope with instructions and cash were left at reception. It's not how we like to do it, but if the client pays up front and doesn't want to be identified then we normally respect their wishes."

Seeing Leigh and Dan's look of disapproval Tweedy quickly added that his female doubles were always chaperoned to and from their performances and that every precaution was taken to protect his artists.

"Is there any chance someone will remember who dropped this off?" Leigh asked.

"Doubt it... we get hundreds of deliveries every day but I'll ask in the morning."

With the envelope and instructions placed in a clear plastic bag, Dan headed for the door.

"We'll get back to you," said Dan. "In the meantime," he

added pointing to the letter inside the bag, "make sure they stay off the streets."

Tweedy didn't look happy.

The Englishman's head was spinning as he made some quick calculations. Keeping his guys off the streets indefinitely was going to cost him big time. If Familiar Faces couldn't come up with the goods, one of his competitors would and that's the last thing he wanted.

Screw that, he thought, *it's only a bloody hunch.*

As Dan sat behind the wheel of his car he let go a huge sigh and then glanced down at his watch. In less than forty-eight hours Buddy Holly was due to appear at Long Beach Airport. Two hours later, John Lennon was pencilled in to arrive at the Dakota Chop House and then JFK was scheduled to drive his '61 Lincoln Continental convertible to PJ's via Santa Monica Blvd where the possibilities for an elevated rifle shot were endless.

"If this is our man then he's playing with me," mumbled Dan. "The son of a bitch is trying to run my ass all over this city."

Leigh could see that Dan was worried. He looked tired and deflated. It had been a long shitty day and there was no end in sight. With nothing concrete to go on, she knew that he was about to put everything on a Hail Mary pass. It was scary. There were so many unanswered questions like what if the next victim wasn't JFK or what if the killer had used a different agency or what if he didn't use an agency at all? Just because three impersonators were booked on the same day by someone wishing to keep his identity a secret didn't mean people were about to die, or did it?

Being a detective was more stressful than she had ever

imagined. No wonder they drink and their marriages fall apart, she thought. Not only do they face life and death situations but they have to make life and death decisions as well. If Dan goes with his gut feeling and ignores the other lookalikes, their pictures could also end up on the white board. If he tries to protect everyone then he runs the risk of spreading himself too thin and no one gets covered.

But sympathizing with Dan's dilemma didn't prevent her from having feelings of her own. She was torn. Her head was saying he was preoccupied and to back off, but her heart was telling her something completely different. It was love and the more she saw of Dan the more she wanted to shake him and tell him to *"stop and smell the roses"*. She knew what he was like before she slept with him, but he was easy to love, too damn easy.

When Dan dropped her off at her apartment she thought about asking him to come up for a drink. She didn't, she knew he would say no. Right now he was a man on a mission focusing on one thing only, the capture of the Celebrity Killer. Nevertheless she had to say something.

"What happens now?"

"I'm going back to the station and—"

"No, I mean what happens with us?"

"What do you mean?" Dan asked.

"Was the other night just a one off?"

"Of course not, I already told you that."

"Don't just tell me, show me... Dan you haven't even looked at me since you crawled out of my bed this morning."

"I've got a lot on my mind right now, but don't worry everything is under control... see you in the morning."

As Dan pulled away and Leigh climbed the stairs to her apartment, a man standing in the shadows on the far side of the street lit a cigarette, turned his back and slowly disappeared into the night.

CHAPTER EIGHTY

Groucho was leaning against the cooler while wiping a bead of sweat from his forehead when Joe tapped on PJ's front door.

We're closed," he shouted in a voice struggling for breath.

"It's me, Joe."

A nod from the large bartender sent a young waitress scurrying to unlock the door.

"Hi stranger," said Groucho.

"Hey what's up, can I get a beer?"

"Sure."

The big guy bent down to grab a bottle from the fridge and suddenly pressed both hands against his chest. He grimaced and slouched over the sink for a few seconds before slowly propping himself up against the bar.

"Jesus man, what the fuck's wrong with you?"

"It's just heartburn, it comes and goes."

"Heartburn my ass, you should see a doctor."

Groucho wrapped his massive hands around the neck of an opened bottle of Coke and lifted it to his lips.

"I'm OK. Look, a couple of sips, a bit of gas and hey presto, I'm good."

Joe wasn't totally convinced even though the color was returning to his old friend's face. Most people in this situation would have bundled their buddy into the car and taken him straight to hospital, but this was a strange relationship. They'd known each other since Joe was a baby, but they weren't close. Joe had never met Groucho's children and had met his wife only once when he bumped into her in the parking lot. Maybe it was a guy thing, but personal matters were personal and neither wanted to cross the line. Joe's suggestion to see a doctor was a deviation from the usual cars, girls, sports and music, but it was as far as he was going to go.

"Did you hear about, Marion?" asked Groucho quickly changing the subject.

"Huh?" said Joe as he looked away awkwardly.

"You know, the one you met here a few days ago, medium height with dark hair and a fit body"

"Oh yeah I remember, what about her?" replied Joe still acting as if he knew nothing.

"Shit man, where have you been… have you had your head up your ass all day? They found her in some sleazy motel ripped to pieces by that crazy fucker they call the Celebrity Killer."

Groucho's remark really hurt. Joe wasn't surprised when the press and some online blogs suggested he should be hung, drawn and quartered, but this came from the guy he'd known all his life, his mother's best friend and his late night drinking buddy.

"That's too bad," said Joe putting on a sad face. "I didn't know… I've been writing all day."

"If you want to write about something, write about what this sick bastard is doing… boy that would make a great script for a movie. By the way, what are you working on?"

Joe chugged down the rest of his beer, placed it on the bar and wiped his mouth with the back of his sleeve. "I can't say right now, but all will be revealed in a couple of days."

"Is it any good?"

"I think so. I'm getting lots of feedback and I know a guy who's dying to get hold of it."

DAY FOURTEEN

CHAPTER EIGHTY-ONE

It was three o'clock in the morning and the telephone lines at the station were still in meltdown. The place was manic. Not one person from the day shift had left the office, leaving the squad on the skeleton night shift struggling to find places to sit down. Everyone wanted to get involved and despite the lack of witnesses or forensic evidence, spirits were relatively high. A delivery from an all night pizza company four blocks away brought a large cheer and helped to lighten the mood, but it was going to take more than a slice of dough, a layer of tomato sauce and a sprinkling of salami to make everyone feel good again. They needed something, anything... no matter how small or insignificant. So when Heinz returned with the Weinberg lab report every eye was watching him.

"The only thing they found on Weinberg's clothes was shit," he said. "The girl was clean; well her clothes were clean anyway. Immigration is holding her and we're still looking for him. We think he saw what went on at The Bates er... Bay Trees Motel. He's tall with bad hair, a gold tooth and drives a huge black Caddy with 'Porn 1' on the license plate. Come on everybody, it's not like he's a polar bear in a snowstorm."

At that moment Leigh walked into the office and across the floor, placing a couple of large plastic bags filled with assorted donuts next to the coffee machine. A loud cheer erupted once again.

"I couldn't sleep," she said looking at Dan, "and besides I've something to ask you that's been bugging me all night."

Dan pointed and then moved towards the hallway where it was less chaotic, but Leigh stayed where she was. A teasing look appeared on her face. With Moose, Heinz and several others within earshot he was reluctant to take this any further. Earlier in the evening he'd driven away knowing she wasn't happy and now she was back. It could only be about one thing. Like most men, he would rather stick needles in his eyes than talk about his private life, but discussing these things in public was unimaginable. However, Leigh gave him no alternative. She was going nowhere and neither was her enthusiasm for an answer. Prepared for the worst, he took a deep breath and asked, "OK, what's your question?"

"What's a wanker?"

As Leigh started laughing Dan smiled and shook his head. It was a big time wind up and she knew that he knew what this was all about.

"A wanker is an offensive term they use in England for someone who is not very nice," he said looking directly into her eyes.

Watching this little piece of theater unfold, Moose commented."Am I the only one who doesn't know what's going on here?"

"No, not this time," replied Heinz.

"I've also been thinking about something else," said Leigh.

"Will we understand it?" interrupted Moose.

Standing next to the white board, she pointed to the gruesome pictures of Van Sykes.

"Look at the cross," she said. "How big do you think it is?"

"Its about eight feet high and six feet wide," said Dan.

"Do you think the posts were nailed together before they were taken to the murder site?"

"Definitely, he wouldn't have been able to build a cross and hold Van Sykes down at the same time and besides, there's no way he'd want to spend any more time there than he had to. Why?"

"I think we're looking for a guy who drives a truck or a large van. Even if the boards weren't fastened before he got there... you couldn't get something that big in a car."

Heinz chuckled, "Nice one, but we've got that already."

Leigh sat down. She felt stupid.

"I don't know if this helps or not," shouted Heinz," but Weinberg's girlfriend said something about him buying a script. Maybe our guy's a writer."

"Nice one," said Leigh quietly.

"Just trying to keep up," replied Heinz sarcastically.

"OK, OK," shouted Dan as he began writing on the white board, he drives a truck; could be a writer… anything else?"

"He's strong," yelled Moose.

A long pause followed until Moose eventually explained that a certain amount of strength was needed to nail Van Sykes to the cross and then place it upright.

"I said that on the day he was killed," said Heinz in a patronizing tone.

Moose raised his middle finger on his right hand and stuck it in front of Heinz's face.

"I've got something," said Dan, "it's a long shot, but I think our killer could hang out at PJ's. Marion was last seen alive there, Familiar Faces regularly sends impersonators there and JFK is booked to go there tomorrow."

At this point everyone in the pit joined in with a loud chorus of "nice one". It was a frivolous reaction and not in keeping with the seriousness of the situation, but it showed unity and for that, Dan was happy.

"One more thing," said Leigh almost too embarrassed to speak, "I think he's white."

Another roar of laughter followed when two black girls working the phones nearby repeated the well-worn phrase, "nice one".

The room quickly fell silent as Leigh continued, "I know this will sound racist and I apologize, but in Montana there's no way a little old white lady like Mrs Delaney would open her door to a black man if she was home alone. And as there were no signs of forced entry, we can only assume she let him in. I don't think she would have done that if he was black."

Leigh backed away awkwardly while a couple of nervous coughs echoed around the room.

"Nice one," whispered Heinz sarcastically. "I'm so glad I didn't say that."

The uncomfortable silence in the pit was short lived as Dan took control and swiftly dealt with the matter.

"Leigh's probably right, but let's keep an open mind. Come on now, we've got work to do."

As the pit emptied out, Dan signalled for Leigh, Heinz and Moose to stick around. He'd made a decision about the three impersonators booked for Thursday and wanted to run it by them.

"I'm still going with JFK tomorrow," he said confidently. "Buddy Holly and John Lennon are decoys to waste our time and resources."

"Are you sure?" asked Leigh.

"What's he going to do with Holly, charter a small plane and then crash it into an empty field somewhere? It's bullshit, it's not gonna happen."

Moose jumped in without thinking, "What if the guy's a pilot… takes Holly up in his plane and then bails out with the only parachute?"

Dan wasn't sure what to make of that remark so he paid no attention to it.

"Like I said, it's not gonna happen. And Lennon is another red herring. He's scheduled to be outside the Dakota Chop House at one o'clock; the busiest time of day… the street will be crawling with witnesses. He'd have to be crazy or suicidal to shoot him there."

"Does this mean that Holly and Lennon will show up without cover?" asked Heinz.

"No, they won't be going at all. I'm gonna call Tweedy and tell him to keep both of them at home just in case."

"What about JFK?" asked Heinz.

"That one will go ahead only I'm gonna take his place in the car," Dan said.

"What?" shouted Leigh, "Have you gone crazy? What about—?"

The muffled sound of a ringing cell phone interrupted her in mid sentence and had everyone reaching into their pockets. Dan raised his hand indicating it was his phone.

"Yes sir... yes... yes... anytime...OK I'll see you in ten."

"I have an audience with the Commissioner, downtown."

"At this time of night?" questioned Heinz.

"Yeah, he heard Esposito's latest press conference and thinks we're winding this one up, he wants to thank me personally... Shit, he's *not* going to be happy."

CHAPTER EIGHTY-TWO

Weinberg's Cadillac was barely visible from the road. Joe took away a section of the rotting wooden picket fence that stretched from the back corner of the house to a small shed and was able to hide most of the car in the yard. Chunks of the fence were strategically placed to cover the rear end of the vehicle and the license plate. Joe was lucky. There were no screaming kids, no husband's borrowing lawn mowers and no nosey old ladies within a hundred yards of his house. In fact there were no neighbors at all. The economic climate had clearly worked in Joe's favor. The bungalow was situated at the end of the street on a large plot of land earmarked for development, but the current recession had put the brakes on most construction projects and this was one of them. If he wanted to, he could literally get away with murder there and no one would know it. But with Weinberg's face and car details plastered all over the news, he wasn't about to take any unnecessary risks. Things were going according to plan and would continue to do so as long as he kept to the script.

Hiding the Cadillac was just one of many things on Joe's "to do" list. A visit to the mall was on the cards as was a call to Gary, an actor he worked with a couple of years ago. His watch told him it was still too early to do either so he rolled a "J", turned on the television and made himself a cup of coffee. As he sat at the kitchen table scribbling notes on a scrap of paper, the morning sun was coming up over the horizon and settling comfortably into a cloudless blue sky. It was another beautiful day in paradise, the kind of day that makes you feel glad to be alive. Maybe it had something to do with paranoia or growing up in bars and clubs across the state, but Joe wasn't big on letting in the outside world. With curtains drawn and lights on 24/7 he chose isolation over inclusion. Inside there was no concept of time, like a Vegas casino, it was impossible to tell night from day.

Joe hardly ever watched TV but when he did, it was usually to catch one of his own rare performances. He considered it money well spent when he subscribed to a channel featuring re runs where even the most ghastly programs were aired. Things were different now. He was live and on every channel. Gone were the days when he scoured TV guide listings and waited until some ungodly hour of the day or night to catch an out of focus glimpse of the back of his own head. Every news item and bulletin said something about Joe, the "Celebrity Killer" or the "Hollywood Hitman" as some journalists were now calling him. This was his time and his story and although most news items, no matter how sensational, grow tired after a few days and begin to lose their importance and ranking in the program, this one was destined to run and run. California has had more than its share of serial killers so why was this one still hogging the headlines? It was simple. It stayed at the top, because so many people could be victims. Members of the public were scared and the media knew it and milked it for all it was worth. A recent TV phone-in that included a panel made up of a social worker, teacher, police officer and psychologist heard one caller say that every postman had access to names and addresses and should be questioned about the killings. The caller's comments were immediately dismissed as ridiculous and irrational by the panel, but a recording of the forty-five second conversation bounced from channel to channel eventually giving this man's piece of illogical thinking credibility. Attacks on postmen doubled within hours of the broadcast.

During the night, Captain Esposito, dressed to impress in a full military style uniform, declared on live television that there was only one man in the frame and his name was Weinberg, a sleazy purveyor of porn. The cop's message, which was replayed throughout the night, sent an uneasy calm over the city while the conversation in every home, bar and work place was the same. If the Celebrity Killer's face was on every TV set in the state he would have to lie low and it would only be a matter of time before he was caught. Citizens of L.A. weren't about to celebrate in the streets, but there was a sense that the worst of the storm had passed.

Dan watched as Esposito slowly dug his own grave. The detective knew that we trust cops as we trust our teachers, family doctor and priest and when they let us down the collateral damage hurts and is extensive. It was painful to see his captain's love of the limelight take precedence over the job and as a result, push confidence in the Force to an all time low. But he knew that when people put two and two together, Esposito wouldn't stand a chance. The media would tear him apart and they did. This was the second time in a matter of days Esposito cried wolf. Neither William Bradley's death nor Weinberg's capture would bring an end of this sordid affair.

Now it was the commissioner, with Dan alongside, who was facing the cameras with the unenviable task of telling the city and the world that this evil man was still at large and Weinberg was just a possible witness, not a suspect.

––––––––––––––––––––

Joe thought he'd died and gone to Hollywood heaven. Not in his wildest dreams could he have imagined his writing and acting would have such a profound impact on both this great city and its magnificent police force. As he watched the farce unfold on the screen in front of him he looked up at the ceiling and screamed. "Mom, you watching this… your boy done good, didn't he?"

CHAPTER EIGHTY-THREE

When Dan arrived back at the station he unexpectedly came face to face with Esposito at the top of the stairs. Holding a small cardboard box filled with his personal possessions he looked into Dan's eyes and said sternly, "You hung me out to dry."

"You hung yourself Jerry; I just gave you the rope."

Esposito may have been looking for someone to blame, but he wasn't stupid. He'd been around the block more times than most and knew deep inside he'd played a dangerous game with his career. Shrugging his shoulders and looking almost relieved to be going, he muttered, "Sometimes you get the bear... sometimes the bear gets you."

Although Dan didn't say anything, he was surprised at his couldn't-care-less attitude about leaving the job until it all became clear.

"I wasn't fired, you know," he said proudly. "We made a deal... I go now and it's medical... I still get the pension, the retirement party and even the goddamn mantel clock."

As he turned towards the stairs a young shapely woman with long blond hair flashed him a good morning smile. He smiled back at her and commented, "I'm going to miss this place."

Tucking the box under his left arm, Esposito reached out with his free hand. "No hard feelings?"

"Take care," said Dan, shaking his hand firmly before they headed off in opposite directions.

"Hey," Esposito turned around and shouted, "you sure Weinberg isn't your killer?"

There was no reply, just a loud cheer as Dan pushed open the door to his office.

"Dan's the man," yelled someone from deep inside the room.

"Three cheers for Dan," screamed another.

A few feet down the hall, Esposito cut a sad and lonely figure as he stood on the deserted stairway clutching his things.

"I was the man once," he whispered. "I was the man."

CHAPTER EIGHTY-FOUR

Joe had punched Gary's number into his cell earlier that morning and now he was impatient, waiting until he felt it was the right time to call.

"Screw him," he said pushing the call button, "if he isn't awake now then he will be."

"Is that Gary?"

"Yeah, who's that?"

"It's Joe Tubbs."

"Who?"

"Joe Tubbs, we did a commercial together a couple of years ago."

"What commercial?"

"The one about hemorrhoids... remember, you were the guy with the bad ass buying cream in the drug store and I played the customer in front of you."

"Thanks, I've been trying to forget that one. Got my balls busted big time for doin' it... made some good bucks on repeats though, did you?"

"No, they don't pay much when it's just the back of your head in the shot."

"OK, now I remember you. You're the guy who told the director to stick his camera where the sun don't shine when he tried to cut off your pony tail," Gary said.

Joe was embarrassed; he'd forgotten that he'd stormed off the set and someone else had taken his place.

"Whatever," he said desperately trying to move on. "A new production company has just taken on one of my scripts and we need someone to play a hitman."

"Why me?"

Joe lowered the phone to his waist and muffled it against

his T-shirt. Throwing his head back in dismay he whispered, "What the fuck is wrong with this asshole, he's a waiter in a shit restaurant... just take the goddamn part."

"Because I like your name," replied Joe calmly after putting the phone back to his mouth. "Look man, I was an out of work actor once—"

Gary interrupted, "Hey, I got a couple things bubbling."

"OK, then do it as a favor for me... I'm stuck and need someone tomorrow to check out a location and run through some timings before we shoot next week. If you like what you're doing then the part is yours."

"Let me check my diary."

Rolling his eyes, Joe lowered the phone and quietly mimicked, "Let me check my diary... Let's see, if I move the appointment with Spielberg, bump the audition at Disney... "

Suddenly Gary came back on the phone. "I'm good."

"That's great; thanks man, here's what you have to do."

There was a definite change in mood after the morning press conference. Fear had been put on hold. Phone calls coming into the station were no longer about sightings or protection. They were ugly and hateful as the public vented their anger and frustrations on the police. Dan's team was tired, heads were down and spirits were low as body blows came from all directions. With no leads and no suspects it was easy to criticize, so everyone did. The Mayor promised that heads would roll while the media took a lighter approach, comparing the incompetence of Dan's squad to the screw ups in the *Police Academy* films, but without the humor. Stealing the tag line from the motion picture, they wrote, 'Be a cop, join the farce'. It was hurtful and unfair.

"Don't they know that this has nothing to do with us?" shouted Moose.

"They don't care," said Heinz.

"In Montana, when the weather closes in," said Leigh with a teasing grin, "we don't pull down the shutters... we put on a sweater and go out and face the storm."

A puzzled look came over the big man's face as he turned to Heinz for clarification.

"That was really profound for a… " said Heinz stopping in midsentence when he saw the fire in her eyes.

"In California," said Dan, joining the conversation, "we don't even bother to put on a sweater."

Moose was now totally confused, but kept his head down hoping that someone would say something he understood.

"So we're all agreed then?" asked Dan.

Everyone nodded including Moose who discreetly pulled Heinz aside. "What's going on, what's wrong?" the big man asked.

Nothing was wrong; in fact things were better than ever. Ironically, the pressure from irate calls, City Hall and the media had brought the squad even closer together. They were focused and determined to get through the crap left by Esposito. It was like they had been on a team-building exercise without even leaving the office. With Dan in charge there was a new confidence and a sense that things were going in the right direction. Convincing the commissioner earlier that morning to delay appointing a new captain and put him in control of the investigation was not easy, but Dan did it. Now it was up to him. Getting it wrong was not an option.

CHAPTER EIGHTY-FIVE

Joe hated shopping. He had no time for the brain dead assistants who were all over him like a rash as soon as he walked through the door and he loathed standing in long tedious lines for the privilege of giving some monosyllabic check out girl his money. But there was no one else to do it for him. Besides, how could he ask someone to buy him a toy gun and a balaclava without arousing suspicion? He had to be careful. Individually, none of the items on his list would ring alarm bells, but purchased together, who knows? Maybe he was just being paranoid or over cautious; nevertheless, he was so close and didn't want to blow it now.

By lunchtime, every single item on Joe's little scrap of paper had been ticked and he still had more than four hours to kill. With a dozen bars within spitting distance and PJ's a good fifteen minute drive away it would have been easier to grab a cold beer nearby. But Joe didn't even think twice about traveling across town to his favorite watering hole even though the place would be empty. Few people go to PJ's before dark because there's something very unnatural about natural light shining on a beer stained floor. Without the cover of night, mystery and atmosphere disappear, leaving the room's blemishes for everyone to see. Even the smell of stale beer seems stronger and harder to take in daytime. And being with friends in safe surroundings was a priority right now. The last thing he needed was a crowd of new faces asking questions he couldn't or didn't want to answer. More importantly, he was worried about Groucho. The big guy was like most men when it came to health problems. Do nothing, tell no one and hope it goes away. Joe would have bet his truck that Grouch's wife knew nothing about his chest pains.

"Heartburn my ass," he said.

As Joe's rusty red pickup moved gradually along with the bumper-to-bumper traffic, a black and white sat menacingly on his tail when he stopped at an intersection a hundred yards from PJ's. With eyes fixed on his rear view mirror, Joe didn't see the light turn green and it took a short blast from the cop's siren to get him to move. He was startled and panicked. Slamming his foot down on the accelerator, he popped the clutch and shot off down the road, missing the entrance to the bar. At the time he was annoyed with himself and thumped his fist down on the steering wheel, but when he looked back down the road he smiled. His erratic driving may have just saved his ass because it prevented him from coming face to face with the boys in blue. While Joe was busy doing his impersonation of a drag racer, the cop car swung into PJ's lot and pulled up next to the front door. Joe immediately swerved into a gas station on the opposite side of the road and parked facing the bar. Carefully he lowered his shopping bag off the seat and on to the floor and draped an old rag over the top. With the ignition turned off and the radio on, he rested his head against the window and stretched his legs the entire length of the front seat. Joe was anticipating a long wait. No matter what the cops wanted, Groucho would make sure they had a drink and something to eat while they were there.

'It made sense', the big guy would say when talking about the police. 'Take care of them and they'll look after you'.

Barely ten minutes had passed when a short slim man wearing gas station overalls tapped on Joe's window. Speaking English with a heavy accent, that sounded Indian or Pakistani, he told Joe that he was on private property and if he wanted to watch cars go by he must do it somewhere else. Joe was tempted to pull out his Toys R Us water pistol and ram it into the man's face just to see if he could make him piss his pants like Weinberg, but common sense prevailed.

Lifting a large bottle of water off the floor instead, Joe explained, "My engine's overheated, five more minutes and I'll be out of here."

As the man nodded and walked back to the station, Joe smirked and said arrogantly, "Gullible bastard."

It was another ten minutes before the police left PJ's and Joe made his way across the street. Not knowing what had happened, he expected the worst and wasn't disappointed. Groucho was alone in the bar, which was bad news for Joe. Having others around may have helped take the sting out of his attack, but it wasn't to be and Groucho went straight for the jugular as soon as he walked through the door.

"What have you been up to?"

"The usual," said Joe trying to stay cool.

"What does that mean?" said Groucho sternly.

"You know, working, writing, drinking… why what's up?"

"The cops were just here."

"So?"

"They think the Celebrity Killer hangs out here."

"And?"

"They also think he owns a truck and could be a writer or in show business."

"Why would they tell you that?" Joe asked, trying to keep his cool.

"One of the cops is an old friend of mine… we went to school together. He's not gonna make it up."

Joe was shocked; he could feel the color draining from his face whereas Groucho was bright red with anger. Underestimating the police was careless and could bring everything to a screeching halt unless he could convince Groucho that he wasn't involved. He had to stay calm, but go on the attack. His old high school football coach once told him that the best form of defense was offense and that's what he was about to do.

"So did you give them my name?" he asked.

"Of course not, I wanted to talk to you first," Groucho said indignantly.

"But you think I'm the one killing these people, don't you?"

"You certainly tick all the boxes."

"I don't believe you're saying this. You've known me all my life."

Leaning against the bar with his eyes trained on Joe's face, Groucho looked tired. There was a shortage of breath as he tried to speak, "Tell me I'm wrong then."

Joe thought for a moment then went into performance mode. He knew he was going to get one shot at this so it had to be good. Groucho was straight and would turn his own mother in if he thought she was guilty, so he had no chance of slipping away quietly if there were any doubts.

"You told me that the cops 'think' he owns a truck and 'think' he's a writer and 'think' he drinks in PJ's. What do they actually know – zip, zero, nada. There are over twenty million cars and trucks in this state alone and there's probably the same number of writers... and how many thousands of male drinkers pass through this place each month? Jesus, there must be a shitload of guys like me who tick all the boxes."

Looking at Groucho's expression, Joe could tell he wasn't totally convinced so it was time to play his ace.

"If you think I'm the Celebrity Killer then you must be in on it too."

A look of disbelief came over Groucho's face as Joe continued.

"The night the guy was crucified you and I were drinking right here, don't you remember... we talked about it the next day?"

This was exactly what Groucho was hoping to hear. He didn't want Joe to be a murderer. With a history of violent threats and psychiatric counselling, Groucho knew Joe's life wasn't amounting to much, but at least he wasn't a killer. There was a problem though. He wanted to believe him but couldn't actually remember what happened that night because it was like most every other night; they drank too much and had little or no sleep. It was a routine that went on for years and was now beginning to take its toll on the big man. Not only was his body turning to shit, but his mind was not far behind. He remembered talking about the killing the next day, and who wouldn't, it was the weirdest thing to happen in L.A. in a long time. As far as the late night drinking was concerned, he wasn't sure when it happened or if it happened at all.

"I'm sorry, I just can't remember," mumbled Groucho with a hint of embarrassment in his voice.

This was great news for Joe. If Groucho had remembered he would have realized that Joe arrived at PJ's just after closing time, thirty minutes after Van Sykes' official time of death. Joe continued to pour on the pressure feeling that he had the big guy on the ropes. He was fighting for his life and was prepared to do whatever it took to win, including punching below the belt.

"Great, fucking great. So what you're saying is that because you have Alzheimer's light, I get to die of lethal injection."

Joe's remarks were painful and brought tears to Groucho's eyes and despite his size, he appeared beaten and frail. In a voice that had been reduced to a whisper, he tried one last time to convince Joe to do the right thing and go to the police if only to clear his name, but Joe responded sarcastically.

"Oh that's a fantastic idea. I can see it now. Hi Officer, I'm Joe... I drive a pickup, I'm a writer and I drink at PJ's, but I'm not the Celebrity Killer and my friend here, who can't remember what he did yesterday, will vouch for me."

With head bowed and body slouching against the bar, Groucho stared impassively at a tray of dirty glasses and empty beer bottles. This was the worst day of his life and if he could turn the clock back he'd do it in a heartbeat. The hurt inside was even more painful than when Joe's mother died. Losing her was tragic, but was not entirely unexpected because of her lifestyle. This was different. It was like being hit by a lightning bolt on a sunny day; he just didn't see it coming. The meeting with the police left him in no doubt that the guy standing just a few feet away was their man and nothing he said had changed his mind.

A long period of silence was suddenly broken when Joe muttered, "I have nothing else to say. I'm going, do what you have to do."

Dragging himself slowly along the bar, Groucho reached out to grab Joe's arm.

"Please don't go son… let's talk some more."

Joe whipped his arm away and stared coldly into Groucho's eyes and said, "I'm not your son."

Then, as he turned his back on his oldest friend and walked towards the exit, an uneasy feeling ran through his body. It was a strange mixture of emotions filling him up inside. He felt bad and yet, at the same time he felt good. Leaving Groucho this way was the pits and never should have happened. It tore him to pieces. Putting in the performance of a lifetime was awesome and quickly erased any feelings he had of sadness or remorse. Joe had been here before and his priorities were still the same.

_____

Alone and exhausted with sweat pouring down his face, Groucho shuffled his feet across the floor like a man twice his age before finally collapsing face down into a booth. Stabbing pains shot along his arm as he tried desperately to dig his cell phone out of his pocket. Suddenly his temperature fell through the floor and he began to shiver violently, making the phone's journey along his body even more difficult. Blurred vision prevented him from reaching the outside world and no matter how many times he blinked he still couldn't see the keypad. Then his luck changed, the moisture in his right eye cleared long enough for him to press his quivering index finger down firmly on the numbers 9-1-1.

CHAPTER EIGHTY-SIX

Being told to keep Holly, Lennon and JFK off the streets until further notice did not go down well with Tweedy. The client paid in advance and left specific instructions for each impersonator to follow and the Englishman didn't want to let him down. Besides, he saw no evidence of any kind that his look-a-likes would be targeted; it was purely a hunch.

Less than twenty-four hours after their meeting, Dan called Tweedy to let him know his plans. Although he thought the chances of something happening to Holly and Lennon were extremely slim, he still couldn't rule anything out and didn't want them going to their gigs. Undercover police with cameras would be at Long Beach Airport and The Dakota Chop House just in case the same face showed up in both places. JFK was still their priority and all of the Department's resources would be thrown into this stakeout. Dan was adamant that JFK should stay away from PJ's.

Tweedy was livid, arguing if the risk was negligible and the police presence was virtually non-existent, why couldn't it be business as usual. As far as he was concerned all three assignments were legitimate.

Holly was contracted to go to the airport and surprise lifelong fans, Mr and Mrs Hank Levine, before they took off in a private jet to Lubbock Preston Smith International, a stone's throw from where Charles Hardin Holley aka Buddy Holly was born. Lennon was to appear unannounced at The Dakota Chop House for Beatles addict, Sally Ann Crowley's sixty-fifth birthday bash. And JFK was signed up to go to a bachelorette party at PJ's although details of his assignment were much more complex than the others. Not only was he told what to wear, when to start his journey and which route to take, the client also insisted he keep the Continental's top down, rain or shine.

Tweedy was first to admit that the unknown client was a pretty sick bastard with a macabre sense of occasion. It didn't mean he was a serial killer though. Like every business, it was all about satisfying a need and Familiar Faces certainly did that. It just turns out that some people's needs are stranger than others.

Following his conversation with Dan, Tweedy did a little detective work of his own. After all, he had nothing to lose. If the gigs turned out to be a hoax then he pulled his guys and still pocketed the money. But when he rang Long Beach Airport and tried to obtain confidential information about passengers and flight plans, the voice at the other end of the phone threatened to call the police. The Manager at The Dakota had no such security issues, but could only advise that they regularly catered for birthday parties and that star impersonators were always welcome as long as the content of their act was suitable for families. Tweedy made two calls to PJ's, where JFK was to perform and both went unanswered. In the end, what did he achieve? Absolutely nothing. But with nothing to support Dan's theory either, the boss of Familiar Faces decided to ignore his advice and go ahead with all three bookings.

Dan wasn't upset by Tweedy's dissent; in fact he couldn't give a shit. Maybe if he'd told him how many times the killer accessed JFK and Lennon's files on the BVS computer things would be different, but why should he? He felt he'd said enough to the Englishman and was fed up with him second-guessing every move he made. He was a cop investigating a series of murders for Christ sake and all he was trying to do was convince him that saving lives should come before making money. Maybe he was naïve about these things. Being a public servant can do that to you. One thing for sure, he knew how to get what he wanted and he wasn't about to let some money-grabbing Limey get in the way.

It was the end of the working day and plans were being made for the next twenty-four hours. Dan's gut feeling had suddenly become a little more tangible following the booking of three look-a-likes by an anonymous client. Not much to go on, he thought, but still a whole lot better than what he had yesterday.

Forming a small circle around a table in the pit, the squad listened as he handed out assignments to the video surveillance team and seven of L.A.'s best marksmen. With blown up photographs of all of the locations, positions were marked and timings calculated. Nothing was left to chance as they so often say, although ironically, the whole thing was about as certain as a throw of the dice.

As the team dispersed, Leigh, Moose and Heinz cornered Dan and sat him down.

"What's with you driving JFK's car tomorrow? You got a death wish?" asked Heinz.

"Someone's gotta do it and it may as well be me. Besides, there's gonna be a mess load of guys with guns ready to blow his head off the minute he shows his face," Dan replied.

"What if he gets a shot off first?" queried Moose.

Looking very serious and staring directly at both men, Dan replied, "You guys are too good to let that happen."

A few feet away, Leigh stood alone, dying to say something, but there was nothing she could say that wouldn't embarrass him in front of his team. Her stomach began to churn and her mouth went dry. Turning away quietly, she crept down the hall to the washroom where she stood looking at herself in the mirror.

"What the hell is wrong with you?" she whispered. "Their wives and girlfriends go through this every day. You're not a wife and you're not a girlfriend... so what's the problem?

Get it together!"

Her head was talking but her heart wasn't listening so to get through this she would have to fake it. Being selfish and revealing her feelings was out of the question; Dan didn't need any unnecessary distractions. A light splash of water on her face followed by a gentle pat dry with a paper towel didn't help and all attempts at an insincere Hollywood smile fell flat as well. After running a brush through her hair she returned to the pit to find most of the squad had left to get some sleep. They knew they had to be sharp. Dan was counting on them.

"I'm heading off too," said Leigh to Dan who was gently running his index finger over a large wall map of the city.

"See you in the morning," said Dan without taking his eye off the map.

"Yeah, see you in the morning."

———————————————

Twenty minutes after she'd left the station Leigh had traveled just a few hundred yards down the road. She'd had enough. Even the sound of her own heartbeat was driving her crazy. She desperately needed some music and didn't care what it was. Anything would do as long as it took her mind off Dan and what he was about to put himself through in the next twenty-four hours.

"This must be the only car in America without a radio," she said in a loud angry voice as she drove her brother's Beetle through the painfully slow evening traffic.

"And this must be the only city in the world where you can use up a gallon of gas and go nowhere. Rush hour… that's a joke. Damn, I hate this place and I hate this car, and Mike, I hate you for getting killed."

Resting her forehead on the steering wheel, Leigh broke down and cried. Grief wasn't allowed in California though and a barrage of beeping car horns forced her to sit up and drive.

"Wankers!" she yelled at the top of her voice. It was

therapeutic and immediately brought a smile to her face, but it didn't stop the pain in her heart.

The L.A. sun had already settled when Leigh pulled into her parking space and began climbing the stairs to her apartment. She wasn't looking forward to the evening ahead. With no television, nothing in the fridge and more power outages than Baghdad, it was going to be a long lonely night. Turning the key in the lock, she pushed open the door, stepped inside and flicked on the light switch as she closed the door behind her.

"Damn," she whispered when the lights failed to come on. "Double damn," she said even louder, when she couldn't find the flashlight she'd left by the door for moments just like this. Unable to see anything ahead of her, she moved cautiously into the room with outstretched arms. Like a toddler learning to walk she took tiny purposeful steps; a box of candles was just a few paces away. Then, as if someone had taken the floor from beneath her, she collapsed when her right foot disappeared into a gaping hole. A pain shot up her leg and slivers sliced into her hands as she instinctively tried to protect herself. Lying face down, she knew that something wasn't right. When she last left the apartment every board was in place and her flashlight was next to the door. She lay still and listened as her fingertips fumbled over what seemed to be pieces of wood. Holding her breath, she waited. Suddenly, a beam of light lit up a narrow path across the room in front of her. Arching her back and lifting her chin she saw a large mound of broken floor boards at the base of the wooden support pole that stretched from floor to ceiling. Quickly she flipped over on to her back and was temporarily blinded by a powerful light. Sensing that someone was standing over her, she kicked out wildly with her left foot and caught the attacker right between the legs. A loud groaning sound confirmed a direct hit. Turning back on her hands and knees she scrambled just a couple of feet across the floor before the attacker grabbed a fist full of her hair and reined her in like a wild horse. A roundhouse swing with the side of her right arm caught the assailant on the bridge of his nose, forcing him to loosen his grip, but a follow through blow to the top of Leigh's head sent her crashing to the floor for the last time.

The next few minutes were spent drifting in and out of consciousness as blood from her head wound streamed over her eyes and down the front of her face. The power clicked in and every light in the room came to life. It was an ominous sight. Duct tape covered her mouth and both hands were tied around a pole behind her back. Her shoeless feet were buried deep in newspaper and floorboards, while a strong smell of kerosene filled the room.

————————————————

"Hi," said Joe, playfully lifting one of her closed eyelids, "I hear you're looking for me."

Leigh mumbled incoherently as words continued to pour out of his mouth. "Sorry about hitting your head with the flashlight, that shouldn't have happened... it's not in the script you know but you forced me to improvise when you started all that kung fu shit."

There was no response. With head hanging and knees bent, her lifeless body had already surrendered.

"They all want to know why," said Joe as he placed his mouth next to Leigh's ear.

"Why me, they ask? Blame your parents... it's their fault."

Reaching into the front pocket of his jeans he pulled out a pack of matches and in the same motion flipped up the front cover with his thumb. He began to sing, "Hey Joe where you goin' with those matches in your hand?"

Chuckling like a little kid who just said something clever for the first time, he lit the match and was just about to drop it when he heard a loud cough. He immediately blew out the small flame and stood motionless in the center of the room. Staring at a hole in the floor, he gradually turned his head and lowered his body until his ear hovered above the opening.

"There's someone downstairs," he said quietly. "What the hell are they doing in the hardware store, it's supposed to be closed?"

Joe stood up in a panic, grabbed his victim by the shoulders and shook her violently. "Wake up, wake up," he shouted angrily. "What the hell is going on?"

There was no response, but Joe refused to give up. His finger pressed against the side of her neck revealed a faint pulse so he continued shaking and slapping her until his arms grew tired. He was running out of time and running out of ideas and then he saw a plastic bottle of water on the kitchen table. Clutching the container in both hands he squeezed hard and flushed the entire contents into her face. Slowly her head lifted and one eye opened.

"Why are people downstairs?" repeated Joe as he removed the duct tape from one side of her mouth.

"What day is it?" mumbled Leigh in a barely audible voice.

"It's Wednesday, but what the fuck has that got to do with anything?"

"Open late on Wednesdays."

"Shit," said Joe, "that changes everything. I can't do this. It's not in the script."

As Joe paced back and forth looking for inspiration Leigh tried to get his attention.

"What?" said Joe impatiently.

"Can we do this tomorrow?" she said in a slurred voice.

"Cute," said Joe.

"I know why you chose me, but how did you find out?" she said seeming anxious to engage him in conversation.

"Because I'm good at what I do… and if those idiots in Hollywood had recognized my talents, I'd be making movies and you wouldn't be here. Now shut up, I'm trying to think."

"You're going to die, asshole," Leigh hissed.

"It doesn't matter what happens to me. It's what I'm doing that's important and what I'm doing is death proof."

The last thing Joe wanted to do was hang around, but causing the death of some random person not connected to the story was also out of the question. He had to keep to the script, if not, what was the point?

There was only one real option and that was to wait until the Koreans had closed up and gone home for the night.

With time on his hands, Joe took his cell out of his pocket and plopped his weary body down on the sofa. There were three missed calls and then a text from the same phone. It was Groucho's wife. She had been trying desperately to get in touch with him to let him know that her husband was in hospital after suffering a heart attack.

All of a sudden, Joe was caught between a rock and a hard place. He had to go, but if he set the fire now, there was a chance others might die. If he just walked away, then everything he had done would be wasted. It didn't take him long to work out that the fire would have to start as soon as the hardware was empty and the tools he needed to make this happen were in the store below.

Joe flew out of the apartment and within a couple of minutes he was back. A white plastic bag with *"Kim's Hardware"* emblazoned on each side was turned upside down on the floor to reveal a digital timer, duct tape and an electric paint stripper. Before the device was placed on a bed of kerosene soaked rags, duct tape was wrapped around the trigger of the stripper to keep it locked in the "on" position. The clock on the timer was set for twenty minutes, five minutes after the store would close. Joe plugged the paint stripper into the timer and then plugged the timer into the socket on wall and the seconds began ticking down.

———————————————————

Dazed and barely able to see, Leigh listened as her attacker slammed the front door and pounded down the outside stairs to the parking lot. She was alone and grateful to be alive, but aware that time was not on her side. Her muffled cries for help went unnoticed and razor sharp splinters sliced into her feet as she attempted to attract attention by stomping on the woodpile beneath her. With head hanging and just about every ounce of strength in her body gone, she breathed a sigh of relief when the power failed and the room was plunged into darkness.

To the electrician, who didn't show up yesterday, thank you – thank you – thank you, she thought.

A moment later she passed out, but was instantly revived by a room full of bright lights and the whirring sound of her fridge coming back to life.

"Shit," she murmured.

Over the next few minutes the power flicked off and on several times and each time the lights went out she thanked God for keeping her alive a little bit longer. Visions of her parents and her brother sat comfortably in her mind as she prepared herself for the inevitable, because no matter how many stoppages there were, eventually the fire would start.

CHAPTER EIGHTY-SEVEN

With so much going on around him, Dan was reluctant to go home and get some sleep. Weinberg was still missing, Tweedy was threatening to sue, the Commissioner wanted hourly updates and the press were hounding him for anything they could get. Being a "hands-on" guy, he found it difficult to delegate. Control is what he wanted and what he got, so he wasn't about to pass the buck or complain. What he needed more than anything right now was to clean up and just splashing cold water in his face wouldn't cut it. Something more drastic was required to wash away the odor from his pits and the uncomfortable squishy feeling in his groin. Taking Heinz with him, he marched quickly to the basement and stripped off inside an empty cell.

"Go for it," shouted Dan.

"Are you sure?" queried Heinz with a sadistic grin.

Dan nodded and turned his back as Heinz pulled down the lever and blasted his boss with the full force of the station's fire hose.

Heinz laughed, "Hey, it's like being back in Iraq, talk you raghead, talk."

It didn't take long for the thunderous roar of ice-cold water echoing off concrete to attract a crowd. Fortunately for Dan, Heinz was enjoying this more than he could have imagined and without even blinking his eye turned the hose on his colleagues, sending them scurrying back to the office.

Once the whistling had stopped and jokes about his manhood had run dry, things got back to normal. With a fresh cup of coffee, a clean shirt and a long night ahead, Dan was ready to revisit every file connected to the "Celebrity Killer". As he leafed through the stack of red plastic folders filled with personal as well as gruesome details, one folder was missing.

"Anybody seen the Delaney file?" asked Dan.

"Try Leigh's desk," said Moose.

"No, there's nothing on top," said Dan looking from across the room.

"It could be in a drawer, that's where she hid it from me last time," said Heinz with a touch of bitchiness in his voice.

"Whoa, someone's still got the hump," laughed Moose.

Dan went over to the desk and started opening drawers. The first two were empty, but the third had a picture frame lying face down. He picked it up, turned it over and saw a cut out of a newspaper clipping with a photo of Leigh.

"Hey guys, look at this," he said with a huge smile, "our girl from Montana is famous."

As Moose and Heinz made their way slowly over to the desk, Dan read the headline printed above her picture. His light-hearted expression changed dramatically. He now looked like he was staring death in the face.

"Oh no," cried Dan putting the picture frame down and reaching for his cell.

Heinz picked up the frame and read the headline out loud.

"Joan of Ark wins Miss Homecoming Queen Contest." He continued, "Eighteen-year-old Joan Leigh Turner of Ark Montana beat three other contestants to win…" Heinz stopped and looked at Dan trying to get through to Leigh.

"Pick up… pick up!" Dan yelled, becoming increasingly agitated.

There was no answer.

"She could be asleep," suggested Heinz.

"Come on… pick up."

"Look Dan, we didn't know about this so how could anyone else know?" said Moose with a hint of desperation in his voice.

But Moose had worked with Dan for years and had never before seen him like this. False alarm or not, there was only one thing to do. "I'll get the car," he shouted as he grabbed his shoulder holster off the back of his chair.

The clock on the kitchen wall was definitely not Leigh's friend.
It told her what she didn't want to know. And what she didn't
want to know was that this battery operated cheap piece of
plastic from Korea was just thirty seconds away from striking
quarter after ten. She hated the fact that it was immune from
power cuts and was telling her she was ten minutes past her
live by time. With one eye swollen and covered in congealed
blood, she squinted with the other and watched as the red
second hand jerked along like a man walking down the
street in a diving suit. Slowly and deliberately it plodded
forward, never varying pace or direction. Sensing her time
was running out, she changed her gaze to the paint stripper
and waited. She didn't have long to wait. The ticking of the
timer suddenly went silent as electricity escaped from the
wall socket and raced along the chord to the paint stripper.
Flames shot out of the barrel and quickly lit the rags and
newspaper beneath her feet. Never before had she felt so
helpless or so afraid. As the fire grew and smoke formed a
cloud around her head, she held her breath and tried to bury
her face in her armpit. It was pointless and she knew it.

The sound of squealing tires and wailing sirens could be
heard across the city as police and fire department vehicles
headed in the direction of her apartment. Dan's hunch had
become his worst nightmare and he blamed himself for
letting it happen. As with all his relationships, he wasn't
there when it counted. Maybe, he thought, if I'd spent more
time with her this could have been prevented.

When Moose finally brought the car to a screeching halt
in front of the burning building Dan jumped out first and
ran up the stairs. Heinz drew his gun and followed close
behind. Just as the two men reached the top of the stairs, a
huge figure of a man cradling Leigh in his arms appeared
from out of the smoke filled room.

"Ramos!" shouted Dan.

"Freeze greaseball," added Heinz with his handgun pointing at Ramos' face.

"It's not what you think," said Ramos gasping for air.

Dan lifted Leigh out of the big man's arms and took her to a waiting ambulance while Heinz casually rested the barrel of his gun on Ramos' forehead until Moose put the cuffs on him.

"You guys gonna carry me or can I walk by myself?" asked Ramos, referring to the time they roughed him up at his place.

"Get moving," snapped Heinz, "I'd rather have sex with your mother than touch you again."

With Leigh on her way to the hospital, Dan moved quickly into the back seat of a black and white and sat next to Ramos. The Mexican, still struggling to clear his throat and blink the smoke out of his eyes, looked reasonably relaxed considering what he'd just been through.

"It's not what you think," he repeated calmly.

"If you knew what I was thinking you'd be praying for mercy," replied Dan with fists clenched.

"Look, I didn't try to kill her, I was watching out for her."

"And why would you do that?"

"Momma made me," mumbled Ramos.

"What did you say?" questioned Dan.

"Momma was so ashamed of what we did to Miss Turner's family… she made me promise to take care of her while that crazy bastard is still walking the streets."

"Are you shittin' me?" asked Dan.

"I swear on Momma's life it's true. I've been here every night since."

"I don't believe you."

"Two nights ago you showed up around eleven, sat in your car for a few minutes and then Miss Turner came down to see you and as they say, the rest is history."

"OK, OK, but what happened tonight?" asked Dan sheepishly.

"I planned to be here, but my car wouldn't start. When I

arrived, I saw smoke; kicked down the door, and there she was, gagged and tied to a pole."

"I know what you found," Dan said.

"How do you know?"

"It's a long story. Turn around."

Dan unlocked the handcuffs and let Ramos out of the car. The Mexican rubbed his wrists and started walking away.

"Ramos," shouted Dan.

"Yeah."

"Thank you."

Ramos replied with a brief wave and in doing so, accidentally bumped into Heinz still holding a gun.

"Do you ever think there will be a time when we meet and you don't stick a gun in my face?"

Heinz thought for a moment then shook his head, "I doubt it."

CHAPTER EIGHTY-EIGHT

Joe stopped and turned off his engine two blocks from the Hollywood Community Hospital when he could have parked in the lot right next to the building. He sneaked in through the back entrance sign posted, "Employees only", when the front door was wide open, and he climbed four flights of stairs when he could have taken the elevator. Up until now, things had gone as scripted. Everyone who was supposed to die did die. There were no loose ends, but things had suddenly changed. Not knowing if Groucho called the police or if "Joan of Ark" was dead left him feeling uneasy, and not knowing that Kim's Hardware was open late was stupid and made him feel like an amateur. He was both angry and afraid.

As he quietly opened the heavy steel plated fire door the familiar smell of disinfectants, drugs and hospital food attacked his nostrils. A deathly hush, broken by sporadic moaning, cast an eerie veil along the cold empty corridor. It was late, patients were asleep and the only nurse on duty was watching *The Tonight Show* in a small room behind her work-station. Finding Groucho was easy; his wife's text had taken care of that.

At first, Joe thought he'd walked into the wrong room because the guy in bed looked nothing like his upbeat friend of three decades. It was hard to believe that underneath the plastic tubing, synthetic patches and face mask, was the joker and the rock that made PJ's such a great bar. It was scary. He should have been serving beer, making wisecracks and tossing red-necks out on the street, but instead he was relying on a machine to keep him alive.

It came as a surprise that Groucho's wife wasn't there, yet

Joe was happy. He hated small talk almost as much as he hated hospitals. With no movement from the big guy, Joe was itching to leave until he spotted the TV remote on the table next to the bed. A moments channel surfing lead him to a special news report on the fire.

"Celebrity Killer strikes again – Joan of Ark burned at the stake." read the banner running across the bottom of the screen. Joe punched the air in a silent celebration. But when it was revealed that the woman who suffered this ordeal survived despite concussion, smoke inhalation and minor burns, he smashed the remote on the floor and left the room.

_____

After spending a couple of hours at Leigh's hospital bedside, it was time for Dan to get back to the station. Although still unconscious, Leigh's move to a single room was a clear indication from her doctor that she was going to be fine. An around the clock police guard was under instructions to call Dan the moment she woke up. Meanwhile, across the hall, Groucho was still fighting for his life.

_____

One guy who had no problem communicating was Esposito. Moments after hearing about the fire the disgraced ex-cop was back in front of the nation's TV cameras telling the world that he never wanted Miss Turner to work as a special consultant on this case.

"It happened just after I left the force," he said staring directly into the lens.

"Lying bastard, he has no shame," said Dan as he turned off the television. "I've got his signature on her contract."

"You gonna say something?" asked Moose.

Dan shrugged. "What's the point."

There was no way he was going to win a pissing contest with a guy who had more medals than socks. Anyway, he had other things to worry about. The press were banging at his door and the city wanted to know, *if you can't protect one of your own, how are you going to protect us?* If Dan didn't think the pressure could get any worse, he was wrong because it just had.

Focusing on the day ahead wasn't easy. Every time he turned around some one else was throwing stones.

In the next life I'm going to be a journalist, he thought. *Why be the dartboard, when you can be the dart?*

CHAPTER EIGHTY-NINE

At exactly ten minutes to eleven, Chip Alexander, aka Buddy Holly, parked his car in the Long Beach Airport parking lot, put on his black rimmed glasses, slung his guitar over his shoulder and strolled casually along the tree lined path leading to the main door. Two minutes later when he stepped on to the departure concourse he was surrounded by security staff and detained incommunicado for the rest of the day. Intending to perform without a license was the reason given for his detention. He would finally be released without charge at four o'clock.

At about 12:45 p.m., John Lennon, born J.J. Horn, was two blocks from The Dakota Chop House when he entered a convenience store to buy a pack of gum. As he exited the premises, a man going in the opposite direction bumped into him. Out on the sidewalk in front of the shop, Lennon was arrested for shoplifting by an off-duty cop who claimed he saw the impersonator steal a pack of cigarettes. Lennon, who didn't smoke, protested his innocence, but was detained and refused permission to make a call. He was eventually released without charge at four o'clock.

It was now two-thirty p.m. and Leigh was still unconscious. With nothing more to go on, Dan had to make a decision with what he had.

"How are we doing Moose?"

"Everything has been taken care of."

"You realize that Tweedy's going to sue us big time unless he decides to have the SAS kill us first."

Moose laughed. "We've stopped two of his guys... if we make it three out of three then you can forget about being sued."

"Let's go for it." Dan said confidently.

This was it, thought Moose, as he put a call through to Heinz who was waiting on the other side of town.

"It's on," said Moose, "see you on Highland."

For some unknown reason those two little words made the ex-marine tingle. He'd been in much more dangerous situations, many of which were life threatening, but this was different. There was so much at stake. Everything depended on him getting it right. Maybe he should have told Dan that he hadn't done this kind of thing in a long time, but it was too late to go back now. With hands shaking and sweat beading on his forehead, Heinz drew a long thin wire from his inside pocket and lowered it quietly into position.

Five minutes later Stan Gardner, stage name JFK, ran a comb through his hair, checked his teeth in the mirror and then rode the elevator to the parking garage beneath his apartment. A cry of disbelief could be heard three floors up as the tanned good looking young man stood staring at an empty space where his prized Continental should have been parked.

Heinz had a grin that stretched from ear to ear when he pulled up behind Dan on Highland.

"Nice one," said Dan as he looked down at the black 1961 Lincoln Continental convertible. "How did it go?"

"Piece of cake," answered Heinz, carefully placing his left hand over scratches on the paintwork above the door handle.

A nervous smile came over Dan's face as he lowered himself behind the wheel of the massive fifty-year-old beauty. Looking around, he suddenly became aware that the huge expanse gave him nowhere to hide. He was like a duck in a shooting gallery.

"This is goddamn crazy," Moose blurted out, "you sure you wanna do it?"

It was a weird situation. Moose and Heinz stared at Dan knowing he may not make it. They wanted to catch the killer, but secretly they were both hoping he wouldn't show. Nevertheless, the time for talk was over. At least that's what they thought until a police car with two uniformed officers came up from behind and made a sharp maneuver to cut in front of the Lincoln.

"Please stay where you are and keep your hands where we can see them," said a serious sounding voice from inside the car.

"I don't fucking believe this," said Heinz.

As the two cops stepped onto the street they instantly recognized Dan and his team.

"What are you doing… this car has been reported stolen?"

"We know, that's why we're here," Dan told them.

"So, three guys from Homicide are out picking up stolen cars today?"

"Yep."

"Things must be slow."

"I can explain," said Dan.

"Please don't… we weren't here and we didn't see you. I just hope the next guy who pulls you over doesn't shoot first and then ask questions."

The detectives were shocked. It never occurred to them that Dan could be taken out by a cop. The odds of being shot in this car had just doubled.

CHAPTER NINETY

One of the last things Leigh remembered before passing out was the combined sulfurous and acrid smell of burning hair and flesh. It came as a pleasant surprise then to wake up with the sweet scent of flowers wafting under her nose. With bandages on most parts of her body, a throat that felt like she'd gargled slivers of glass and a headache that seemed to start at her feet, she opened her eyes and focused on a stunning bouquet of white roses and freesias.

"They're beautiful," she muttered softly.

"From your guardian angel," said a large female police officer standing against the door.

"Who?"

"The guy who pulled you out of the fire, Ramon or Rambo or something like that... anyway, his name and number are on the table next to you."

Leigh looked at the card that was leaning against the vase. It was signed Ricardo Ramos. She was confused.

"What was he doing at my place?"

"You can call him in a minute, but first you've gotta speak to your boss."

Leigh took the phone from the officer.

"Hey boss," she said wearily.

"It's good to have you back... how are you feeling?"

"I've been better."

"Stay in bed and get some rest, that's an order."

"I will," she promised.

"We were lucky we found the newspaper article in your desk, but how do you think he knew about the 'Joan of Ark' thing?"

"I don't know... I haven't been called Joan in years... I've never liked the name; it's so old fashioned... I hated it even more when we moved to Ark... I started using Leigh when I became a journalist."

"I wish I'd known." Dan said.

"Sorry, I didn't think it was important. There is something you should know about the killer though, he's a writer just like Heinz said... and it appears that he's following a script. He doesn't want collateral damage."

Leigh waited, but there was no response, just static.

"Did you hear me?" she said anxiously.

Finally after a long nerve-racking pause, Dan's voice could be heard in the background speaking over the police radio, "Just passing the first optimal shooting point."

Leigh almost dropped the phone. Her mouth went dry and her heartbeat flew right off the chart... she'd completely forgotten what day it was. The "suicide run", as some guys at the station were calling it, was taking place now.

The night before she had things to say and didn't say them and almost died. *How stupid was that?* she thought. He would never have known how she felt about him. Now the same thing was happening all over again only this time there was a chance he could die. Leigh couldn't wait any longer.

"I love you," she said.

There was a long period before Dan spoke, "I guess I better not die then."

"I'll kill you if you do," she said before realizing how corny that sounded.

"Just passed optimal point two," said Dan over his radio, "one more to go."

For the next thirty seconds nothing was said. Only the purring sound of the big Lincoln engine and the noise of traffic in the background broke the self imposed silence.

Then in a quiet expectant tone Dan announced, "One hundred yards... get ready."

Leigh held her breath and jammed the phone tight to her ear. If the guy was going to take a shot it was going to be now. Afraid to move, she waited for what seemed an eternity. Then with a mixture of relief and disappointment in his voice, Dan shouted, "Sorry everybody, I got it wrong. Let's pack it up."

It was a devastating blow that would affect not only the investigation, but also Dan's future in the force. He bet the farm on this one and came up empty.

Leigh wasn't convinced it was over though. Putting her personal feelings aside, she was sure he was on the right track. There had to be something more. Then it hit her.

"Are there any bushes or trees up ahead of you?" screamed Leigh over the crackling background noise of Dan's radio.

"Why?" yelled Dan.

"Kennedy was shot from a grassy knoll on the right side of the road."

"He was killed by Lee Harvey Oswald from the Book Depository... didn't you read the Warren Report?"

"No, but I watched Kevin Costner in *JFK*." Leigh replied.

As the Lincoln crept along the route laid out by the unknown client, Dan spotted a large bush and a couple of trees in front of a cement wall off to his right. The closer he got the more apparent it became that someone was there. Fifty feet from the bush, Dan shouted into his radio.

"There's a guy wearing a balaclava running towards the wall two hundred and fifty yards down the road from point three. Looks like he's armed. I'm in pursuit."

The Lincoln crashed the curb and came to a stop up on the grass. Dan flew out of the convertible without opening the door and headed for the wall. Once on the other side, he chased the man, dressed entirely in black, down a narrow alley, across a parking lot, over an iron gate and into a small vacant lot. He was running straight at Dan's team of sharpshooters. It was almost as if it was intentional. When the man finally made it to the far side of the lot he stopped abruptly and stared directly into the faces of four heavily armed police officers. With legs apart and a handgun down by his side, he ignored their calls to give himself up. Instead, he raised his right arm slowly as if to put himself in a shooting position, giving the police no option but to defend themselves. On Dan's orders they opened fire and the man fell to the ground like a stone.

Throughout the chase Dan's phone had been left open and when Leigh heard gunfire in the background she flinched and let loose one hell of a scream. By the time things returned to normal and he had taken his cell out of his pocket, she was shaking with fear, not knowing what had happened.

"We got him," Dan said excitedly. "Thanks to you and Kevin."

Burying her head in the pillow, Leigh said a silent prayer before getting back on the phone, "Is he the same guy?"

"You tell me... he's white, six feet, about thirty, average build, long dark hair... does that sound like the guy who attacked you?"

"Yeah, that sounds like him."

Dan then pulled a wallet containing a driver's license from the man's blood soaked pocket.

"Our Celebrity Killer is called Gary Gilmore... the name means nothing, but we'll run a check on him."

"What did you say his name is?" Leigh asked, concern in her voice.

"Gary Gilmore, why is he a friend of yours?" said Dan light heartedly.

Leigh didn't answer; she needed more time to think. But when she did come back to him she rained all over his parade.

"He's not the Celebrity Killer."

"Why, just because he's called Gary Gilmore?" Dan was confused.

"Exactly! Gilmore murdered two people in Utah in 1976 and gained celebrity status after he was executed. A British punk band even wrote a song about him."

"Gilmore is a common name," said Dan thinking this was just another one of her conspiracy theories.

"OK, how did your man die?" Leigh asked.

"We shot him, you know that."

"I mean describe what actually happened."

Dan rolled his eyes; he'd heard that question before. "He stood in front of four cops, raised his gun and they blew him away."

"Do you want to know how Gary Gilmore was executed?"

"No, but I think you're gonna tell me anyway," Dan said.

"He died by firing squad, just like your guy did. Same name, same death, it's too much of a coincidence."

"How do you know this stuff?" asked Dan slightly exasperated.

The implications of what she was saying just didn't bear thinking about. If she was right, the police not only shot an innocent man, they also did the Celebrity Killer's work for him.

Celebrations were put on hold while Dan tried to think of a way out of this, but every road he went down was a dead end. He was in denial, unwilling to accept that this entire operation was a set up. Yesterday it was Leigh who was targeted; today it was the whole goddamn force. That's impossible, he thought, no one could do that. He wanted proof, something in black and white; something he could see and touch. He wanted more than just a guy's name and a similar death experience. He wanted something that would jump up and bite him on the ass and shake him until he believed. He wanted, he wanted, he wanted and eventually he got it when Moose handed him Gilmore's firearm, a child's water pistol covered in black tape.

This changed everything because Gilmore had no intention of shooting anyone. A moment later things took an even more bizarre twist when a listening device was pulled out of the dead man's ear.

"Gilmore wasn't alone," said Dan turning around, "someone else was pulling the strings."

Tucking the water pistol in his belt, Dan raced across the stone covered lot to an apartment building, pulled down the sliding fire escape ladder and climbed about twenty feet. As he scanned the area, a rusty red pickup truck moved slowly away from the scene. Dan's mind flashed back to the time he questioned a man just outside Homicide who claimed to be a computer technician. The guy was somewhere he shouldn't have been and he drove a pickup just like this one.

"Smart ass," he shouted, "it's you isn't it?"

The long run back to the Lincoln nearly killed him. He was exhausted and gasping for air.

Why couldn't I be twenty years younger and still have that membership to the gym, he thought.

In the distance stood the last remaining hurdle between him and the car, the cement wall. Using every ounce of energy he had left, Dan increased his speed and at the precise moment, leaped forward throwing his aching limbs towards the wall. With fingers clinging on precariously, he gradually pulled himself up and over to the other side. To his surprise the car was right where he left it. The police radio was missing, but he didn't care, he had wheels. Then like something out of a scene from *Gone in Sixty Seconds*, the detective lowered his hands beneath the dash, grabbed two exposed wires and put them together sending the fan belt spinning and the pistons pumping. It was time to catch up and it wasn't going to be easy. Without a siren or a flashing light no one was going to move over for one of the oldest cars on the road. The best he could hope to do was keep the truck in sight and call for back up. As he bounced over the curb and rolled back on to the road, he plucked his phone out of his pocket and without even looking called 911. Something wasn't right. There was no clicking sound from the keyboard and when he glanced down at the screen it was black.

"Shit."

Back at the hospital, Leigh was trying everything to get out of her room, but the cop wouldn't budge.

"Sorry," she said standing in front of the door. "Dan's orders, he wants you to stay here."

"Let's go together then, that way, I'll still have a body guard."

The cop just shook her head.

Leigh felt so helpless. The last thing she heard before Dan's cell died was the sound of a car engine starting. He was on the move and she wanted to help, but first she had to get by the Rottweiler on the far side of the room. It was pointless calling Moose or Heinz. They wouldn't do it. They were loyal to Dan. She needed someone who wasn't a cop and his telephone number was right next to her bed. Picking up the card that lay against the vase, Leigh excused herself and disappeared into the en suite washroom. It was an easy call to make. Despite the hard feelings she had for the Ramos family, Ricardo saved her life and she wanted to thank him. She also wanted his help.

Any doubts Leigh may have had about Ramos were quickly brushed aside when the big guy told her to look out her window. There he was standing on the street, waving like a child to his mother.

He really is a guardian angel, she thought. After a brief conversation, the Mexican took hold of the situation and ran with it. Within a few minutes a woman carrying a clipboard and wearing a doctor's white coat, complete with stethoscope tumbling out of the pocket, entered the room and asked the cop to leave so she could examine her patient. Once the officer was out of the room, the woman gave Leigh her clothes and her wig and disappeared under the bed covers.

"Be careful," she said, "the man across the hall just died and there are lots of people out there."

A minute later, Leigh walked out of the room with her head down and her face partially hidden behind the clipboard. In her rush to get away, she accidentally collided with a priest who was making his way towards the dead man's room. When Leigh finally got to the street, the car door was open and the engine was running. Ramos was ready to go.

"I owe you for this," she said gratefully.

"You owe me nothing," said Ramos politely, "but if you want, you can thank my cousin Maria next time you're at the hospital. She works as a cleaner up on the fourth floor."

Leigh was thankful for his help and didn't want to appear

pushy, but when Ramos put his foot down and set off confidently in a westerly direction, she just had to ask, "How do you know where to go?"

"I got eyes everywhere, I put a call out to my cousin to look out for the Lincoln with the pig... er, cop behind the wheel. He tells his cousin, who tells his friend, who tells his sister and before you know it the whole Mexican community is on the street looking. It's like smoke signals only more environmentally friendly. We do it all the time, especially when we're tracking black and whites."

A couple of miles up ahead, Dan was still following the pickup. Traffic was heavy and neither vehicle was going anywhere in a hurry. He wanted to get closer, but he couldn't afford to take the chance, the Lincoln was easy to spot. Under normal conditions, two or three bland colored vehicles would be called in to trail a suspect, but with his radio gone and his cell phone dead, he was on his own. About a half a mile along the road, the pickup finally turned off the main drag and headed in the direction of the suburbs. Dan tried to keep up, but he couldn't. The light changed when he got to the intersection leaving him stuck behind a couple of cars. It seemed like he was there forever. He became irritated and pressed on his horn knowing the light was still against him. Then as the signal turned green and Dan bolted around the corner he saw the brake lights on the truck illuminate, yet there was no reason to stop or even slow down.

"He waited for me," said Dan. "He wants me to follow him."

He was right. Every time it looked like the truck was getting too far ahead he would take his foot off the gas.

This is it, he thought, *smart ass wants a showdown.*

The longer Dan stayed behind the wheel the further he got from familiar territory. Most of his life had been spent in L.A. yet he'd never seen this part of the city. The streets were quiet, the houses more remote.

As the Lincoln turned yet another corner and went along yet another desolate street the game of cat and mouse finally came to an end. The tarmac had run out of places to go and there were no more houses to pass. Fifty yards away, Dan sat and studied the wooden clad bungalow where the pickup had stopped. There was no sign of life.

With his pistol held firmly in his right hand he climbed out of the car and sprinted to the front door. It was locked. Crouching low to keep beneath the window, he side-stepped quietly to the corner of the house and then crept towards the rear of the property until his foot touched on a pair of wooden exterior doors that appeared to lead to the cellar. A garden hose wedged through a small gap between the doors traveled along the ground to the back yard. A closer inspection revealed that one end of the hose was plugged into an exhaust pipe. This was an ominous sight. If Dan had listened to his head and stuck to the basics of training he would have run to the nearest house and called for back up. But right now his heart was in control and he couldn't give a shit about what the manual said he should do. As he slowly lifted the right hand cellar door he winced when a loud squeaking sound from the rust caked hinges shattered the afternoon calm and a small cloud of black smoke blanketed his face. Fresh scratch marks were clearly visible on the inside of the door. Squeezing his body through the narrow opening, Dan lowered his feet gently on to the first step and finally to the cold concrete floor where he found the source of the scratches, the lifeless body of a cat. He sensed that this was just the beginning; it would only get worse. Moving forward with one arm stretched out in front of his face, and no longer able to rely on the thin stream of outside light, he followed the garden hose running along the floor. The basement was cold and damp, but Dan was sweating. If asked, he would be the first to admit he was shit scared and it was fear of the unknown that was getting to him. As his eyes desperately tried to scan the basement and his feet walked along the hose, he arrived at a thick wooden door. Fumbling to find the handle he jumped when the lights came on and the sound of Hendrix blasted through a set of speakers just a few feet from his head. Dan knew what was going on.

"He led me here and now he wants to show what he's done," he mumbled, "but why me?"

Taking a step back and staring at the door of what looked like a coal bunker, Dan suddenly felt a chill run right through his body, a large white Swastika left him in no doubt what was coming.

As he pulled the door open he saw a man lying on the floor with a crudely made yellow star stuck to his lapel. His hands and feet were bound and the garden hose had been rammed into his mouth, held securely by duct tape. Hair from his shaven head had been placed in a bowl on the floor. In a small glass jar next to the bowl was his gold tooth. Dan searched desperately for signs of life, but he was too late.

Weinberg, thought Dan.

"Get rid of the anger, stay calm, but keep the fear," he said quietly as he sneaked across the floor and started climbing the stairs into the house. Silence and darkness returned.

This is it, he thought.

With both hands on his weapon, he glided down the hall and into the living room. "Clear," he whispered.

Creeping along the corridor leading to the back of the house, he quietly opened the bathroom door and looked inside. "Clear," he said again as if to comfort himself.

Further down the hall he opened the bedroom door. The curtains were closed and the room was dark, but a small penlight had been deliberately propped up at an angle on a chest of drawers so it would shine on a framed photograph. Checking the closet first, then under the bed, Dan finally went to the photo. It was a picture of Alice, his old girlfriend, holding a baby. Lying next to it was the script, *"Killing the Dead".*

While trying to piece things together, Dan took his eye off the ball allowing someone to sneak up behind him and knock the gun out of his hand. The cop retaliated by throwing the script at his assailant's head and then followed through with a blow to his chin. Cursing and spitting blood, the attacker lowered his body and charged like a raging bull into Dan's stomach, knocking him back into the chest of drawers and spilling the photo of Alice out into the hall. Back on his feet, Dan delivered a succession of left jabs before landing a roundhouse right that sent his attacker crashing through the open door. Another punch from Dan hit him so hard he was forced to retreat into the living room. Sensing he had momentum on his side, Dan lunged forward, but stopped abruptly when the man pulled a knife out of his boot. The two men stood motionless in the center of the room. Both were breathing heavily.

"What's with the picture of Alice?" asked Dan as he pushed the broken frame to one side with his foot.

"She's my mother."

Dan seemed shocked, but didn't say anything.

"You dated her?" continued the man.

"I did… and if she was alive today, she'd be ashamed to call you her son."

"Maybe she'd still be alive if the father of her child had stuck around. She was weak and vulnerable and a good strong man could have made a difference."

The man took a moment to catch his breath and wipe his forehead. "Why did you leave her?"

"I didn't leave her," said Dan, "we… we just chose to follow different paths."

"Oh yeah, that's right… she was a druggy and you were a law abiding citizen."

Stepping over the water pistol that had fallen during the fight, Dan started circling to his left, looking to gain some sort of advantage while his attacker kept talking.

"Ted Bundy was spot on when he said, 'we serial killers are your sons'. How does that make you feel?"

"Are you saying what I think you're saying?"

"You work it out, you're the detective."

"Oh I get it. That's why you made it so easy for me to follow you here. You want to get even. Well I'm sorry, I can't help you, I'm not your father."

"Mom said she didn't know who my father was, but Groucho said... "

Dan interrupted, "What did Groucho say?"

"When you guys split up, she left L.A. and then came back a few months later with me."

"That proves nothing! Grouch put two and two together and got five. He's wrong; I'm not your father, I don't even know your name!"

The man looked startled at that. "I'm Joe, Joe Tubbs," he said. "You knew she was pregnant and that's why you deserted her." Joe had tears in his eyes by the time he'd finished talking.

"That's not true... I loved her, but we couldn't stay together."

"Come on admit it, Mr Big Shot Cop you're my father, the father of a serial killer."

With his heart racing and head bowed, Dan couldn't take anymore. He didn't want to do this but he had no choice.

"I first met Alice when I was just out of the Academy. I was working West Hollywood and got a call that a woman had passed out in a store nearby. She looked in bad shape so I put her in the patrol car and took her to County Hospital... they found a tumor and the next day she had a hysterectomy."

"What's that?" asked Joe.

"They removed her womb."

Joe still looked puzzled.

"She couldn't have children," Dan explained.

"I don't believe you... you're making it up," screamed Joe.

"County has the records. Check 'em out for yourself... Look, I loved your mother and was with her every day for two years after she had the operation, but I'm not your father."

For a moment both men stood silent and still until Joe said casually, "Fuck me; it was bad enough not knowing who my father was... now you're telling me I didn't have a mother either."

"Alice raised you, she was your mother."

"But where did I come from. I don't even have a birth certificate... Was I adopted or stolen or what?"

Dan looked away because he didn't have an answer. Another long pause followed.

"When I wrote this script it didn't have a happy ending, but boy this is the pits."

"Maybe you should have left it on the page," Dan suggested.

"I tried, but they wouldn't let me."

"You should have tried harder."

"That sounds like something a father would say," said Joe with a mischievous look in his eye.

Joe barely had time to finish what he was saying when he was spooked by a noise coming from the rear of the house. Taking a step back, he looked through the kitchen window and spotted Leigh and Ramos trying to break down the door as the sounds of police sirens wailed in the distance.

"Why don't you give me the knife? There's been enough killing," said Dan, reaching out his hand.

"And do what? Die of a lethal injection or if I'm lucky rot in prison with a bunch of perverts chasing my ass all day."

"Come on give me the knife, there's no way out of this," Dan pleaded.

"You're wrong, there is a way out of this," said Joe thrusting his knife towards Dan's face and forcing the cop to take evasive action. With Dan now a couple of steps further away, Joe reached down and picked up the water pistol.

"What are you going to do with that, squirt me in the face?" asked Dan sarcastically.

Joe smiled. "It's a shame you guys didn't stay together, I think you would have made a great dad... See you on the other side."

"I doubt it," replied Dan.

The nearby sound of shattering glass and splintering wood left Joe unmoved. He stood still with eyes fixed on Dan and, as the footsteps from the back of the house grew louder, he braced himself. When Leigh entered the dimly lit room Joe was threatening Dan with a knife in one hand and a gun in the other. Racing through the kitchen she grabbed the loaded syringe off the counter, leaped into the air and slammed the needle into the side of Joe's neck.

"No!" Dan shouted at the top of his voice, but it was too late. Clutching his neck, Joe dropped to his knees then tumbled forward on to his chest. At first he lay still and appeared to be dead. Then with gritted teeth and eyes rocking into the back of his head, he began crawling to the bedroom. Ramos headed towards the dying man, but Dan raised his arm to stop him. Joe was no longer a threat.

Pale, exhausted and shaking uncontrollably, Joe crawled to within inches of the bedroom door before collapsing with his hand on the picture of his mother. A soft groan followed by a long slow exhalation of air signalled the end.

A moment of calm returned to the room as Leigh and Dan, with backs to the wall, slid gradually to the floor while Ramos turned on the lights and called an ambulance.

Staring at the water pistol lying just inches from her foot, Leigh knew exactly what she'd done.

"He wasn't going to kill you, was he?" she said.

Dan shook his head. "Don't feel bad, he tricked me into killing for him too."

"I hate to say it, but he was good at what he did," said Leigh picking up a page from the script that lay scattered around the room. "Do you think anyone will ever make his movie?"

"I don't know, but I can guarantee one thing."

"What's that?"

"There'll be no shortage of copycats."

Leigh closed her eyes, placed her hand on Dan's arm and gently lowered her head on to his shoulder and whispered, "Well, if there are, we'll be ready for them."

"You said 'we', does that mean you're gonna stick around?"

"Would you like me to?"

"Yes."

"And if I don't?" Leigh smiled.

"I guess I could live in Montana."

The End

About the Author

Paul Ferguson was born in England, spent his childhood in Ottawa Canada and obtained a BA degree in History from The State University of New York in Oswego.

His writing career began in the 70s when he wrote lyrics for pop songs, radio commercials and the film score for the movie *Assassin*. Paul also wrote lyrics for winning entries at the Japanese, Spanish and Irish song festivals.

After playing professional ice hockey in Europe, Paul spent over twenty years as an ice hockey commentator working with the BBC, ITV, Sky and Eurosport. In the mid eighties he wrote a book on how to play ice hockey (published by David and Charles).

Short film script writing earned Paul a BAFTA nomination for *My Darling Wife* in 2008 and since then several of his scripts have been made into short films.

Lightning Source UK Ltd.
Milton Keynes UK
UKOW040633110712

195754UK00003B/1/P